The *Spicy* Secrets of a Jet-$et Temptress

PART 1: LEARNING THE LIFE

LANTANA BLEU

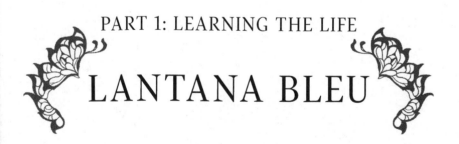

PART 1 OF
THE SPICY SECRETS

All rights reserved.

No part of this book may be reproduced in any form or by any electronic or mechanical means, including information storage and retrieval systems, without written permission from the author, except for brief quotations in a book review.

This is a work of fiction. Names, characters, places, and incidents either are the product of the author's imagination or are used fictitiously, and any resemblance to actual persons, living or dead, business establishments, events or locales is entirely coincidental.

Copyright Lantana Bleu 2015
Illustrations by Spahic Danira, spahic_danira@hotmail.com
Book cover design and interior by Scarlett Rugers Design
ISBN: 978-0-9970958-0-7
Imprint is: Lionesse Books

For Manny

"Every man who knocks on the door of a brothel is knocking for God."
—G. K. Chesterton

"Ten men waiting for me at the door? Send one of them home, I'm tired."
—Mae West

"The prostitute is not, as feminists claim, the victim of men but rather their conqueror, an outlaw who controls the sexual channel between nature and culture."
—Camille Paglia

"I believe that sex is one of the most beautiful, natural, wholesome things that money can buy."
—Steve Martin

PREFACE

This is a highly-embellished story based on the real-life experiences, loves, lusts, and intimate musings of a modern-day (and literary) courtesan. The "Spicy Secrets" contained within, although entertaining, are intended as tiny lessons or reminders, should you wish to come under the tutelage of a jet-set temptress.

Perhaps you wish to become a consummate professional companion yourself. Or, much more likely, you simply wish to enhance and spice up your life with the unique knowledge and techniques of temptresses. Whatever your intention, I hope that while being entertained with Melisse's story, you will also turn her sweet, funny, and wise teachings to your advantage.

Please allow me to take your hand now and lead you on the wild journey of Miss Melisse, a woman who may sell her time, charms and sensuality for a high price, but whose heart is decidedly *not for sale*.

Lantana Bleu
- Author

AUTHOR NOTE FOR READERS:

For entertainment purposes (so as not to interrupt the flow of action) the use of condoms in certain erotic scenes is not explicitly stated. Please assume that in each and every instance of sexual contact, the proper precautions were indeed taken.

PROLOGUE

A Conversation Between Sugar and Spice

The two women sat together in a small, cozy living room on the top floor of a brownstone on Manhattan's Upper East Side. The room was warm and welcoming, its walls covered in old landscape paintings, the furniture draped in plush fabrics, with black-and-white framed photos of earlier days sitting on every surface.

The older, elegant woman, known as GG in "the business," gracefully poured them tea from the silver Moroccan teapot, as her young companion, Melisse, wearing racy red lingerie under a long, see-through red lace robe, watched.

The tea was delivered into two delicate porcelain cups. After taking a long, refreshing sip of fine Noblesse tea, GG (whose "real" name was Gillian Gladly) began.

"I've been feeling a bit…shall we say…concerned about you, Melisse. The clients say you're a shy one. Now don't get me wrong—they think it's charming *now*, but still, my dear, you can't go on like this. You're going to need what I call 'an opener,' especially as you get more involved in The Life, with dinners, the overnights, the traveling, and all the rest."

"An opener?" Melisse wasn't sure she'd heard correctly. "I don't understand…"

"Yes, a conversational opener. Something to help you break the ice, or to use when things get boring, or if the client is shy, or when you have no idea what the hell to say to each other."

"I see. Hmm...I suppose I *do* need something like that. Any ideas?"

"Well," GG replied hesitantly, "I'm actually a bit reluctant to share mine with you. You see, it was *my* conversational opener, one I used all my professional life. It was my anchor whenever I wasn't sure what to say or do, and let me tell you," she smiled, remembering, "it always got things going in the right direction."

"Do you have a copyright on it, GG?" Melisse teased as she sipped her tea, eyeing the other woman over her cup. She had never tasted such delicious tea!

"Not exactly." GG smiled. "It's like chicken—you can cook it up in many different ways."

"And are you sure you want to give it up?" Melisse asked innocently.

"Do I look like I still need it? The last time I turned a trick was thirty years ago!" The older woman was clearly fishing for a compliment.

"You *do* look like you still need it, and I know you're still seeing clients up here when nobody's looking! But I'd love to have it now. I think I need it more than you do, GG! You can talk to anybody."

"Oh, thank you, darling. Yes. It's..." GG hesitated. It was a game of hers, stopping midsentence so people would listen to her with their complete attention.

"Yes?"

"All you do is say to your client, 'Tell me one of your spicy secrets.'"

"'Tell me one of your spicy secrets'? That's *it*?"

"Yes, dear, but you need the variations. Like, 'Tell me *all* your spicy secrets...' or, 'I know you've got some spicy secrets and I want to know all about them,' or, 'You look like you have a spicy secret! What is it?' Melisse, I could go on forever...because *everyone* has a spicy secret or two!"

"It's genius!" Melisse breathed in appreciation.

"Isn't it?" GG agreed, taking a long, sensuous sip of the Noblesse tea.

"Can I have it?"

"I confer it to you, but you must..."

"What?"

"Keep it a secret!" GG giggled, as her nearly empty teacup almost fell off its saucer.

> **Spicy Secret: Create your own distinctive and sexy "opener."** Use it to quickly plumb the depths of your client/conversation partner's psyche. It allows you to quickly bypass small talk (which bores him *and* you) and engage him at a level that reveals his sensual tastes, preferences, and longings.

CHAPTER 1

The Present:
Introducing "Miss Melisse"

When Miss Melisse emerges from the passport control area and into the terminal at JFK airport in New York City, a casual observer would never guess that she's a jet-setting, modern-day courtesan, or, as they say these days, "a VIP companion."

In other words: she is a high-priced hooker who discreetly turns expensive tricks for the horny movers and shakers of the world who put a high value on her charms.

> **Spicy Secret: If you don't place a high value on your own time, body, mind, and charms, nobody else will, either.**

Here's how Melisse was once described by a client, who was extremely impressed with her ability to please him:

"She was blonde, cool, and gracious, I'd guess in her late twenties, a petite version of Grace Kelly. But she was definitely lustier, with sparkling eyes, pouty lips, rosy cheeks, and outrageous curves all packed into a slender, but stacked, body. And, my God, she was a sexual athlete, which I hadn't expected! I guess if I'd seen her in a bikini, I might have suspected it… She reminded me of a modern pinup girl, with plump thighs, a small waist, and a flat stomach sloping way out to a very round bum. She covered it beautifully with expensive, elegant clothes… And just thinking about her and the way she talks, with that high, breathy voice, and the way she walks, with those twitchy hips, really gets me going."

> **Spicy Secret:** In the seduction business, it is not necessary to be drop-dead gorgeous or to have a beautiful face or body in order to succeed. While men may think they're seeking beauty (and women buy into that idea, too), what men actually fall in love with, treasure, and want is your femininity.
>
> Guard the femininity, enhance it, gilt it, show it off, perfume it, and publicize it. The closer you are to being his direct opposite, and the more he perceives you as a woman (by looking feminine, doing womanly things, using feminine gestures, speaking in a feminine way, and living in a womanly space), the more he'll want you, pay you, and go out of his way to be around your deliciously *feminine* self.

It's almost impossible to read her from her body language alone. While she might be having tea and dessert at a European café or restaurant (she speaks fluent French and Italian, by the way), she could easily be perceived as the pampered, untouchable fiancée or wife of a powerful, wealthy man.

> **Spicy Secret:** "A woman can look both moral and exciting—if she looks as if it was quite a struggle." — Edna Ferber

But *this* petite gal isn't dependent upon just one man (to her mind, that would be kind of stupid—like an investor having an undiversified portfolio!) so she's taking care of herself via "friendships" with many.

She appears to be behaving herself with her genteel, to-the-manner-born bearing as she delicately savors her tea and nibbles on a dessert, never letting her fork scrape the plate.

> **Spicy Secret:** "One of the marks of a feminine woman is refinement, which implies good social breeding. This means to be tactful, courteous, diplomatic, considerate, sensitive to the feelings of others, and the picture of propriety, good taste, and graciousness. A refined person is careful to not offend anyone, is never rude, impolite, inconsiderate, crude, coarse, or vulgar." —Helen B. Andelin, *Fascinating Womanhood*

In reality, she's probably fantasizing about the adorable waiter who just served her dinner. She can visualize inviting him upstairs to the hotel room for some funny chatting, giggles and a good shagging.

Of course, it's impossible when she's sharing that hotel room with a flabby, pale boor who ejaculates in thirty seconds, and then spends the rest of the time he paid for her lying there, fast asleep. But that's his prerogative—to use his costly time with her any way he likes.

Snore.

> **Spicy Secret:** Let boors be boors and let sleeping men rest.

And anyway, she knows her fantasy about the waiter must remain just that—she would never think of cheating on a client while she's still on his clock (unless she was 1,000% sure she could get away with it)! Ethics, professionalism, and discretion are the pillars upon which she's built her life as a modern-day courtesan.

> **Spicy Secret:** A long-standing code of ethics and standards of behavior for *professional temptresses* (and many other professions) has existed since the

> beginning of time. Don't try to rewrite the rules. Instead, work with them and respect them. They are there for a reason, and ultimately your friend.

No, indeed, you'd never guess to look at this stunning blonde that soon she'll be propping her stomach up on a big, soft pillow, pushing her bottom up in the air, and breathlessly demanding, "Just do it. Doggy! Now!"

> **Spicy Secret:** This doesn't apply to all cases, but in general the more powerful the man is outside the bedroom, the more he likes to be told what to do in bed. And the more powerless he feels outside the bedroom, the more he'll want to tell you what to do in bed.
>
> Likewise, a more relaxed man craves intensity in the bedroom, while the more intense man craves relaxation. Whatever he needs or wants, you're the shimmering chameleon who can provide it.

She's learned that the world's richest and most powerful men (and even the occasional politician, lawyer, or doctor) love to hear that "Do it now, doggy!" command, and they comply every time. Her clients also wait for her to give them a loving hug good-bye after a passionate interlude, never imagining that, as a part of her respect for their privacy, she's trained her brain to forget about them completely until they contact her again.

Forgetting is easier now than it was in the beginning. It took years to learn that most men she met for business didn't give a damn about her—not really, not deep down. So she'd learned to feel comfortable swimming in the shallow pool of their short-term needs and fantasies. Long ago, she'd stopped trying to share any part of her real self, or to establish friendships with guys who turned out to be unworthy shitheads who could care less about her as a person. This wasn't everyone, of course, for there were some truly special, precious people in her life, and she had the hard-earned discernment to know exactly who was who and to treat them accordingly.

> **Spicy Secret: Know your proper place in his life and happily stay there until he shows you with his actions (and/or his money) that he's willing to treat you otherwise. Talk is cheap. So ignore the words and read only his actions.**

She knows that most of the clients who pass through her life for a time will probably end up dumping her at the earliest sign of a maturing face or a sagging body, so Melisse beats them at their own game by a) being obsessed with anything and everything "anti-aging" to keep herself in play, b) making sure most of the guys are just "mental history" even before they're out the door, and c) accepting the aging/maturing process is actually a gift that *lifts* her market value—like the ascension of fine wines into ultra-desirable status as they age.

> **Spicy Secret: The mature escort (even one with a few well-earned laugh lines) is actually in high demand as long as she's super-fit, has a fresh, rested face and an even fresher attitude, and treats her older patrons like kings. Her look, style, experience, and sophistication can be highly desirable to certain men who don't want to play around with kids. A wonderful, beautiful woman can literally "work it" at *any* age, as long as she's honest in her promotions that she's mature, with all the wonderful things that go along with it.**

As Melisse emerges into the bustling terminal, she gratefully sniffs the sooty spring air wafting in through the revolving doors and knows, once again, that she's exactly where she belongs. Manhattan is her home, and she's now just a short ride away.

"Need a ride?" someone beckons, one of the usual drivers illegally hawking rides into the city.

She shakes her head no. *I don't take rides with strangers…hmmm… well, that's not true…I take other kinds of rides.* She giggles to herself as her eyes scan the horizon for a suited man who should be holding a sign with her name on it.

> **Spicy Secret: You are precious cargo. Treat yourself accordingly and handle your life, business dealings, and relationships with this in mind.**

This time, she's just returned from London, sitting in coach instead of first class, as she often did when clients invited her on a trip across the Atlantic. They'd often assumed she'd settle for nothing less (which wasn't true).

> **Spicy Secret: Where you sit on a plane for eight hours of your life (or what kind of car you drive, etc.) does not define your worth as a person. Get over pretentious temporary displays of wealth to impress people you don't really give a rat's ass about.**
>
> **Save that money and go for the *true* signs of wealth that come from investing wisely: your financial, emotional, and personal freedom, a.k.a., true prosperity.**
>
> **Spicy Secret: What is one way to define prosperity? "Prosperity is the ability to do what you want to do at the instant you want to do it." — Raymond Charles Barker, 1954, in *Treat Yourself to Life***

Malcolm, her London client (and one of those who'd revealed himself to be a true friend as well as client) loved to indulge her. This time, when she requested that he book her for a return seat in coach instead of first, he had chuckled with delight, at first believing she was just being coy.

"Really?" he asked. "Why?"

Melisse had pressed a hand gently over his and asked lightly, "Malky, I *know* you want to spoil me with a comfortable flight home and that is soooo lovely of you…but do you think it would be OK if I just flew economy and kept the difference in the cost of the first-class ticket in, ummmm…you know…?"

> **Spicy Secret: With paying gentlemen friends, always evade the subject of actual cash whenever possible. Refer to it as anything but "money" or "cash."**

"*In cash?*" Malcolm asked, pretending to be shocked.

"Yes, in, uh…you know…*that pretty green stuff…*"

"Pretty green stuff? You mean, *money?*" he laughed.

"Malcolm! I don't know what you're talking about. I've never heard that word before… *Money?* But I like the sound of it! Hmmmm…" Melisse smiled gently, rubbing his shoulders as he reached for the phone to call the concierge who would charge his mysterious black card and then have an envelope of cash delivered up.

"You know how I am…I'm always on a budget."

> **Spicy Secret: You are always "on a budget" when you're with a benefactor. Never let him see you blowing his (now your) money on frivolous things—that is, if you want to receive more of it later.**

Though he didn't refer to it again, when it was time for her to leave he'd handed her an envelope filled with thousands of dollars, along with a handwritten note that said, "Fly with the masses and live with the classes! I like your sense of economy. Have a safe trip, little Lisse. I loved seeing you, as always!"

Cash was always nice, of course, but the handwritten notes from clients to say "thank you" always touched her. It was almost as good as winning a million bucks. Well, almost. And the thousands in her plane fare envelope would combine with the "entertainment fee" she'd been wired by Malcolm for her to come for four days, to be wined, dined, shopped, and spa'd in London. And, of course, the fee was compensation for the completely unrushed time she'd spent expertly indulging him in acting out his very favorite fantasy sequence.

Melisse would put it in a special savings account, with a 10 percent "tithe" back to wherever Melisse was receiving spiritual support at the time (or her favorite charities or people in need, like a foundation for eradicating the sexual enslavement of women, or to support a no-kill shelter for homeless cats, and so on).

GG, her beloved mentor, had taught her well. Tithing, she had explained early on, provided divine protection that kept her girls safe and out of trouble. And Melisse had GG to thank for introducing her, five years earlier, to sweet Malcolm: rich, well connected, and missing a woman who could accept and work with his kinks. And when you were in The Life, every lucrative introduction counted.

> **Spicy Secret: Your endgame as a high-class professional is to have a large stable of "regulars." The "regular" client is a recurring source of income and (usually) provides a more anxiety-free experience (compared to meeting new people). Treasure, cultivate, pamper, and spoil your "bread and butters," but treat each new contact as if he, too, will one day join that category.**

Today, in the terminal, Melisse is greeted by a well-dressed chauffer from an elite car service, holding a little sign with her name on it. He actually seems to light up when he sees her coming through the main door of Arrivals as she gives him a knowing wink and a slight nod. It says, "You're mine. You're the one for me (at least the one who will be driving me home)."

> **Spicy Secret: Men the world over, from every walk of life and in even the most casual circumstances (from the grocery bagger to the banker signing your home loan) all love receiving the little smile/nod/wink combo. Even though it may feel strange and outrageous to do it, it's harmless and reads as fun/flirtatious to most men on the receiving end. What they do next with it is entirely up to them. Try it some day!**

Apparently of Middle Eastern descent (her personal favorite among the varieties of men populating the earth), the chauffeur reaches out to help her with her cart. It's heavy, filled with her suitcases containing her "working wardrobe for London" —and a few choice new dresses and hats Melisse picked up shopping in Knightsbridge with Malcolm.

As she gratefully ducks into the black car (another perk of traveling on Malcolm's tab) and eases into the soft leather seat, she sees the driver's eyes watch her settle in. She feels a slight pulse inside her silky Sabbia Rosa panties after looking up at his dark eyebrows and the midday stubble shadowing deep dimples.

The thought of the two of them in bed together flashes across her mind. At the same time, she definitely needs some sleep as jet lag begins to set in.

"Miss Melisse? Are you comfortable back there?" the driver asks her.

"Oh, yes, just fine. What is your name?" she asks conversationally.

"Hakim, Miss. I have some cold water for you in the little case back there."

"Ah, I see. Thank you, Hakim."

The water tastes very refreshing, and again she breathes a sigh of relief. *Home at last.* But tomorrow evening she'll be on the road again, stopping just long enough to pack before turning around and getting on yet another flight. This time, it will be a private jet out of a small airport in New Jersey. It will make a couple of stops and then land in Dubai.

Damn, I could have just left directly from London for Dubai! But if I did, then Sheik Jazzy would know I was probably with another man in London, and I'd risk hurting or offending him and possibly losing him as my best client. So I'm crossing an ocean just to avoid offending someone... Oh, well, we do what we have to do...

God, another week of Jazzy, she groans inwardly. But Melisse turns her thoughts away from the approaching demands of Sheik Jazzy and tries to stay "in the moment." She ponders who among her "Category B" friends she might invite over for some personal relaxation. Breakfast in bed tomorrow morning is probably a good place to start!

Melisse defines "Category B" as her small collection of casual boyfriends. Well, let's be honest, *lovers.* They're the furthest type she can find from her usual genre of privileged, spoiled clients, and Hakim is a prime example of a potential Category B candidate: he's cute, looks great in his suit, he's short, solicitous, swarthy, and from a different culture. He also works hard in a service profession, just like she does.

As they get closer to Manhattan, Hakim looks in the mirror and asks her, "Do you have a preference for how I should get in?"

Melisse stifles a smile as she considers images of him "getting in," then says, "Ummmmm...I'll let you choose. Whatever you think is best today. Maybe the tunnel..." she offers, giving him a quick wink.

Spicy Secret: "She gave me a smile I could feel in my hip pocket." —Raymond Chandler

Melisse's clients are usually much older than she is, and most of them lack real skill and physical prowess as lovers. Many don't even engage in full-on sexual intercourse, opting rather for other activities. Some are afflicted with odd fetishes, addictions, cluttered minds, messed-up marriages, and—not surprisingly, given the era in which they were raised—many have had little variety in sexual experience, (given that they married their high school or college sweethearts), apart from their sexual experiences with hookers (and hookers don't count).

All this has created in Melisse a keen craving for simple, long-lasting, lustful, joyful sex. As far as she's concerned, pure sex without love is just fine! (*But wouldn't it be amazing to have both?* she often sighs to herself.) She always welcomes opportunities with friendly, healthy, normal, fit, unspoiled men who won't complicate her life—just like Hakim.

> **Spicy Secret: Collect some yummy "Category B's."** Most single men are tickled pink to be compartmentalized—if you let them know exactly where they stand, *don't* lead them on, and take good care of them sexually. Their special presence in your life keeps you juicy. And your obvious satisfaction actually has the power to magnetize and attract other great men to you!
>
> You've heard of the principles in the book, *The Secret*? Well, there's a Spicy Secret or two out there, too, and these are the sexy "Laws of Attraction" that can manifest some real *pleasure* in your personal life. Who needs a new car to magically appear when you can conjure up a hot guy to drive you in his!

But often enough, she wonders—with all this compartmentalizing of men into categories—whether she has also locked her heart in one of the boxes somewhere, and forgotten where she put it.

CHAPTER 2

In London with Malcolm

As Melisse and Hakim make their way home in traffic, Melisse thinks of her time in London seeing Malcolm.

Malcolm is in another special category: he's a "Near and Dear" (her term for longtime clients she is so comfortable with, she can actually allow her real self to show through once in a while). But even though they have a beautiful rapport, Malcolm is still a handful—literally!

The first time Melisse ever met Malcolm was at the Four Seasons Hotel in Manhattan, where he often arrived from London to do business as a "consultant" to "people who had been taken advantage of, or compromised, financially," as he put it. Her first visit to him had taken place when she was just starting out in The Life and was being trained by GG, probably the world's nicest madam and now an old friend.

GG's luxurious, discreet bordello was on a quiet, leafy street on the Upper East Side. It was an entire town house unto itself, with suites on every floor, each featuring a beautifully decorated bedroom and en suite bathroom, real wood-burning fireplaces, a full-time housekeeper tidying up after the girls, and a plush parlor where the gentlemen made their selections before heading upstairs with their "dates."

Melisse had met Malcolm when she was 26, just when GG's place was beginning to feel very limiting. GG had sensed that Melisse was getting restless and might be preparing to go out on her own, or "go independent." That meant Melisse would get her own apartment and begin screening and seeing her own clients, which GG preferred not to happen. She'd come to love Melisse almost like a daughter, and felt that going independent carried risks Melisse might not be ready for or trained properly to handle. But because she knew going independent was probably inevitable for Melisse, she decided to begin preparing, or "polishing," Melisse by sending her out to "minister" to a very special client, a substantial man, a VIP staying at the luxurious Four Seasons Hotel (whose posh rooms could tell many a story).

When Melisse arrived at Malcolm's room, she realized why GG had referred to her visit as a "ministry." Malcolm was enormous, and wasn't about to walk into a bordello's living room to face a couch full of beautiful women—most whom would find his near-freakish weight disgusting! And he was certainly not capable of huffing and puffing up three long flights of stairs for a quick lay.

No, Malcolm required someone "just right," "totally sweet," and "a little spinner"(all his own words) who could stay up all night and talk if he wanted, and who would do exactly what he needed, to the letter.

Melisse had arrived that first night knowing what to expect, having been prepared by GG, and had fortified herself for the task ahead by drinking five cups of strong green tea, followed by several swallows of a caffeine drink strong enough to keep dozy truck drivers awake all night.

When he opened the door, Malcolm had smiled devilishly, his dimples disappearing into his fleshy jowls. He wore beautifully detailed pants in a gigantic size and a dress shirt of fine cloth stretching like a sail across his massive body.

Spicy Secret: True professionals look into the eyes of their clients and seemingly give no mind to their bodies (except to comment on something nice about them, which they'll gleefully discover when he undresses—i.e., his hairy chest, his big balls, a strong back, or the perfectly shaped head of his cock).

"Hello, there!" Malcolm welcomed Melisse as she stepped into his suite, and she found herself liking him almost instantly. Over champagne and small talk, he outlined just how he wanted his favorite fantasy scenario to play out.

Melisse was to play his wife. They would be traveling together in New York, and she had just come in from shopping to find him in bed with a woman he'd picked up at the bar downstairs. She would be furious—jealous to the point of insanity, and proceed to shove the blonde out the door!

Then, Melisse—as "wife"—would go after Malcolm with a belt she'd conveniently pull out of her shopping bag, supposedly a gift she had bought for him but would now use to punish him. In their struggle, she'd push Malcolm to the floor and begin whipping his balls with the belt. After that, she would grab his balls, pull down as far as she could, and then twist them with one hand as hard as possible.

Hmmmm...

"You are to alternate between twisting my balls," he explained, "and then whipping them, spanking them, hitting them or flogging them with the belt, your hands, or whatever else you can get your hands on. I will not fight back."

Melisse absorbed all this without comment, implying this was not at all unusual. But it was—for her.

"When I finally crawl up to the bed, beat up but horny as hell, you're to jump atop me and ride me as hard as you can. And I like nasty names thrown at me while you're doing it, until I come."

Hmmmmm... At this juncture, Melisse had wiggled her nose ever so slightly. "Don't worry, Melisse," Malcolm said. "There's nothing you can do that will hurt me. I love it all. Now's your chance to vent any frustrations of your own, and the harder you hit, *the bigger I'll tip!*"

Despite the lure of more money, deep inside Melisse was not happy with the scenario he'd just described. It just wasn't in her nature to treat someone so badly. But this was what he wanted, and as a budding professional she knew she had to listen and then provide exactly what was requested.

Spicy Secret: Like an actress, draw on past experiences of lust, love, anger, or otherwise in order to enhance your performance. Then, let them "have it!"

Melisse had had no idea how exhausting S and M could be, but she was beginning to learn that people who were supposedly masochistic were actually very controlling when it came to organizing their sex play. This was blatantly obvious when Malcolm gave her such intricate details about how he wanted to be dominated.

During their first meeting, after the hard part was over (the furious screaming, the belt beating and ball twisting), Melisse had indeed jumped on top of Malcolm. She'd propped his vast butt up on some pillows, and once she lifted away his disgusting "panis" (the veil of fat hanging down over an obese man's penis), she put on his condom and sat down to pound on his hard cock. She'd half expected him not to be hard at all, but his cock had somehow responded to the excitement of his being "caught in the act," complete with a punishment. She looked into a mirror beside them and saw herself resembling a tiny bird sitting on a huge sculpture.

"Sorry, I'm a bit of trouble..." he said as he grabbed her hips.

"No, not at all," Melisse said, and then, back in character, "You're a world-class asshole! How dare you talk to me like that! I can't believe I caught you fucking around with another woman up here, you little slut monger!"

"That I am," he whimpered eagerly.

"What an asshole you are! I think I should beat the living shit out of you again with my belt!" Melisse growled convincingly, with the desired results.

"Oh, slap me, honey, slap my face! I deserve it."

Melisse hesitated. Should she?

"Go ahead," Malcolm encouraged her, out of character for a brief moment. "You can do it."

SLAP! "You sure do deserve it, assfucker."

"That's the way! Ohhhhh!" He turned the other cheek for more.

SLAP! "Take that, Motherfucker!"

They were now rocking together and Melisse felt an enjoyable hardness rising up inside her. She rather liked Malcolm's lively personality and he seemed incredibly gentle and kind. The man was a Casanova trapped in the body of a whale.

What would she say if she really *were* his wife?

"You choose the trashiest, sluttiest, easiest little cunts you can find and fuck them because you have a *real* woman for a wife, and you can't handle it. You know you don't deserve a goddess like me, so you have to go out and get trash! Is that it?"

Malcolm was straining, working for his orgasm, sweating buckets.

"Yes! You are my goddess! I'm sorry, and I will never see her again. How glad I am that I get to finish up with you, lovey, instead of that little piece of ass, although I *was* enjoying fucking her..." he chuckled.

SLAP! Melisse reached back and slammed her right hand back and down on his balls and gave them a twist.

"Yowwww!" The slap caused Malcolm to buck up his hips, which drove his cock deeper into Melisse, and together with the friction of his stomach rubbing against her, she came...and he came from the excitement of seeing *her* come...

"Ohhhhhh..." they sighed together.

He collapsed and struggled for air. "My God, that was nice!"

She couldn't believe she'd just come from a little bit of friction with a fat man's belly! Oh well, that was Melisse. *So I like sex—I like what I do for a living. That's a good thing!*

Spicy Secret: Sometimes having an orgasm while working is inevitable (And that's OK!)! Have YOU ever had an orgasm you didn't like (even just a little)?

Melisse delicately extricated herself from Malcolm while letting the condom stay on, grabbed it away expertly with a tissue, and brought him a warm, wet towel.

> **Spicy Secret:** After sex, make a habit of bringing your man a warm, soapy towel and spoil his cock with a mini sauna (but not too hot, eh)? He'll think he's died and gone to geisha girl heaven.

After a few moments of calm, Malcolm said, "Now, let's get to the food!"

Melisse was glad she could finally stop for the evening. Up until now, she'd rarely been required to use such cruel, filthy language in her newfound profession. But it wasn't so bad because she really liked Malcolm and realized it was all part of the theater the two of them were putting on. Her cheerful nature restored, she realized she was starved, and put on one of the hotel's posh robes and slippers before indulging in a gluttonous meal with her huge new friend.

They ordered delivery from a famous steakhouse nearby, a rare treat for Melisse. She carefully perused the menu and chose some delicacies she'd never make at home.

They dined on a huge feast of crab legs, petit filet mignon, mashed potatoes, and creamed spinach, followed by molten chocolate cake. As they ate, Melisse and Malcolm talked about many subjects that interested them both, but nothing from the heart—not yet, anyway. That would come later, after years of knowing each other, when Melisse would learn that Malcolm had married one of GG's ex-girls, but that it had deteriorated into an exercise in romantic futility on his part, and a money grab on the part of his wife.

> **Spicy Secret:** For high-strung working girls and those with tummy troubles, here's a tip: steer your regular clients to eating *after* your sex date, not before. It's just better for your digestion and you can "pig out" more when you're not worried about performing later.

Sated with sex and food, Malcolm sipped from a flute of champagne and sucked the last bit of the delicious crab out of a crab leg. Then he asked, "Melisse, we're friends now. If you don't mind my asking, how ever did you get to working with GG?"

"It's a long story," she replied, stalling. She'd been warned that he would want to stay up all night talking, and she wasn't sure how much of their relationship should be fantasy. She could also see that her new client was trying to go "behind the fourth wall," as they say in the theatre, and usually she preferred keeping her fourth wall up. And yet, Malcolm, with his exotic history of travel and secret missions, seemed capable of respecting her personal revelations.

"First, please tell me your real name," he asked.

"It's Melissa. But please continue to call me Melisse."

Most of the self-absorbed men she had met passing through the bordello didn't even know her real name, but she liked the French sound of "Melisse" and had made it her "working" name.

Also, she had reasoned, if she was ever recognized by a client outside of work who called her by the name "Melisse," it wouldn't sound too different from "Melissa," and therefore it would be less of a giveaway to whomever she might be with.

"Start at the beginning, Melisse," Malcolm said. "When you really started thinking about this as a career option. You know, if *I* were a thin, beautiful woman, it's what I would be doing. So please, allow me to live vicariously through you…"

"Oh, Malcolm…I don't think…"

> **Spicy Secret: Appointments with clients are not therapy or "spill" sessions. No matter how much clients may probe to know more, the inner workings of your heart, mind, private life, and childhood are not to be fodder for their entertainment or curiosity.**

"No, tell it. I want to hear every detail. You know, I believe we'll be good friends, and I want to understand you, just as you're beginning to understand me."

And hearing those words, Melisse tried to find a way to skip to the good parts, the light and spicy parts that a client would like, and not the sad parts that would only drag the evening down.

"Well…" Melisse began… "I was barely eighteen years old…"

"First, had you been abused as a child?" he interjected, a bit too much like a talk-show host looking for a juicy tidbit. But she let it go. He meant well. He was just repeating that old familiar assumption that many people made: that every call girl had been abused in one way or another as a child.

But how to not answer without appearing rude?

She looked away and flashed back to her childhood for a few seconds. It was very simple: Everything that troubled her about her home life as a girl had bred in Melisse a deep thirst to escape to beautiful places with lots of creature comforts. Best of all, she'd wanted—and now had—the security of earning her own money, however it was earned.

She was a butterfly who'd managed to fly away with some magical dust still left on her wings. And if the wings had been dusted off initially, they were now double-coated with magical sugar from her sugar daddies. Lifting off was an easy pleasure and she even had enough sweet stuff to now sprinkle around on others.

And it felt so delicious to have so much control over the men in her life—or at least how much time she had to spend with them.

And she would never turn back, or go back—mentally, at least. She'd been to plenty of expensive psychoanalysts. She likened the process to scratching at sores so they never healed. She'd moved on. So instead of handing over her hard-earned dollars to a shrink every week, she'd treated herself instead to lunches out, facials, and new dresses. Her idea of "transference" had become transferring her cash in exchange for some girlish fun.

"No. I wasn't abused. I just wasn't exactly a 'daddy's little girl.'"

"Better off for it. At least you're not a spoiled brat."

"Yes, at least I'm not a spoiled brat." Melisse smiled, but knew she'd way overcompensated by spoiling herself and letting the portfolio of men in her life spoil her.

Spicy Secret: Clients aren't paying to be burdened with your baggage, but they *are* paying you to burden you with *theirs*. Keep yours hidden, and open and close theirs with care. And the same rules apply to those

non-client, attention-challenged men in your life: serve up your pain in mysterious, manageable sound bites or not at all (except to your therapist, whom you're paying to listen) lest they get overwhelmed by your confessions.

Melisse artfully turned the conversation back to Malcolm for the rest of the night. Malcolm shared stories from his "thin" days, when he was a brilliant young academic with both a law and accounting degree, rising quickly in a Swiss bank, but seeking more excitement and greater financial rewards. After being contacted privately by a client of the bank to help with some special projects, he turned soldier of fortune, acting as a bounty hunter for the world's rich and famous.

He chose to work with those who had been embezzled, defrauded, or otherwise screwed out of their money. With cunning and zest, he tracked down the criminals through clever investigations, forensic accounting, and hacking and bribing insiders. He then retrieved his clients' stolen money through threatened or real violence, all without the expense and red tape of his clients having to take the criminal slime balls to court. Sometimes it was criminals going after criminals, and that's when things got messy.

This had been during Malcolm's youthful career. He called them "structured settlements," and his crisp British accent lent a gentlemanly veneer to it all.

"Sir, if you could kindly make my client whole again, I won't have to torture you or dismember certain members of your family," he had said more than once. He'd been based in Monaco, where most of the top financial criminals of the world lived, banked, or eventually passed through.

"Ah, Melisse, those were the days. I had a permanent tan and I was getting laid a lot back then," he mused. "Now I just find my salvation in a good filet and a fine claret. And hopefully, in someone like you."

Melisse had not yet visited Monaco in this early stage of her career as a jet-set temptress, but later she would be invited there to "minister" to the same financial criminal types he was describing.

That night before going to sleep, Malcolm embraced Melisse and said simply, "Thank you, dear. You don't know what a comfort you are to me. I've been looking for you for a long time."

> **Spicy Secret: The wealthy, lonely man is often acutely aware of the inestimable value of that rare woman who can provide emotional comfort, physical satisfaction, and discretion in one beautiful package.**
>
> **The expense of your time is of little consequence to a man aligned with these priorities.**

They fell asleep dreaming of the smoked salmon, Eggs Benedict, and banana pancakes that room service would bring around the next morning before Malcolm took off for his flight home.

When he came back through New York from the UK, he immediately requested that GG send him Melisse for the whole night. GG was pleased and so was Melisse.

GG said, "My dear, you've obviously got a knack for taking care of these VIPs, the needy ones. I've never seen Malcolm ask for the same girl twice. This is a miracle!"

Melisse shrugged, but was secretly pleased. "He likes my stories… and we both love to eat!"

GG added, "I'm told it's more than food and stories that he likes when you're around!"

"What can I tell you, GG? I have a lot of pent-up anger and I'm good with his belt. Call it therapy."

And thus began a tradition of Melisse's visits to see Malcolm in New York, and eventually in London. Their visits never deviated from the "getting caught *in flagrante delicto*" fantasy complete with the ball-twisting and slapping, the cursing sex with her on top, excellent and copious "destination" meals, and all-night true confessions.

In London, her visit always included half-day spa treatments at the Barclay Gardens Hotel in Belgravia, where Malcolm liked to stay with Melisse, just down the road from Harrods, the incredible department store.

Melisse loved the Barclay for its gorgeously decorated hotel bar. She usually discovered someone famous, or at least notable, hiding out there in the evenings, and she and Malcolm would often have fun over their nightly port and hot cocoa as they watched everyone, making up stories about the well-heeled denizens of the bar.

> **Spicy Secret: A great bar or café game to play with clients (when and if things get dull) is: "What Are They Saying?" In this game, you watch two people from some distance away and take turns putting sexy words into their mouths, giving them a dialogue based on their gestures and reactions. It's always good to get men laughing—and if you play it right, a bit turned on.**

One winter night, Malcolm and Melisse watched a famous willowy blonde actress having a quiet drink with friends. Melisse was fascinated by the actress and tried to covertly watch her to learn even more about femininity from her movements and gestures.

Malcolm asked her, "So, Miss M, do you fancy yourself more of a healer or an entertainer?"

She sipped her delicious, aged port and handed her glass over to Malcolm for a taste. "I am...merely a purveyor...or a sharer...of an elixir in life that can only be experienced à deux. I need you—as much as you need me—to enjoy it, Malky."

> **Spicy Secret: At every moment, he must feel appreciated and needed as an essential part of the experience you're both having.**

CHAPTER 3

In Good Hands

Melisse's thoughts return to the present as her elegant black car gets closer to Manhattan. She considers Hakim, the driver, whose presence up front makes her slightly nervous, but in a good way. It's been only a day or two since a hunky guy had put his hands on her, and she's already thinking about finding someone here and now for a follow-up shagging.

On her latest trip to London, while Malcolm did his consulting work from the comfort of their suite, Melisse had enjoyed several treatments in the rooftop spa at the Barclay Gardens after a dip in the pool and a long stint in the sweltering steam room. And on that occasion, she was lucky enough to encounter a rare, elusive creature: a "straight" male masseur.

She'd been feeling quite juicy that morning, just lying in bed thinking back on some of her lusty encounters with her "Category B's." So when Sam, her new masseur, greeted her in the massage room, he seemed too good to be true.

A formidable, dark mahogany man of Caribbean origin with a charming French accent, big hands, big biceps, and a solid body, Sam was the silent type. He greeted her politely and then left the room. She knew he was giving her time to crawl naked under the light blanket on the heated massage table and lie on her stomach, awaiting his Swedish massage.

After a half hour of his hands pressing down on the curves of her silky body, heated by his fingers and warmed oil, she felt all resolve to behave herself dissolving with every stroke, especially when he ran his fingers up and down her neck and scalp. She could feel the heat emanating from his crotch as it brushed lightly against her arms while he moved against the table, massaging from her shoulders down the middle of her back to just above her butt.

As her body melted (and her pussy overheated!) she forced herself not to cry out for him to come closer—much closer. She breathed deeply, trying to hide her arousal in this professional setting at a very posh hotel. They both knew he could lose his job if she reported him.

But he seemed to read her body, as well as her mind. While she was still on her stomach, he gently spread her legs apart and rubbed up the backs of her thighs with both hands firmly, for a seeming eternity. It had her squirming. There was no hiding her arousal now.

She spread her legs a little wider than normally acceptable when he reached the very top of her thighs. She felt something warm, like a hot breeze blowing on her pussy, and then she felt the most wonderful sensation of a big, juicy, hot tongue parting her butt cheeks and circling her asshole gently.

"Please be silent," he leaned up and whispered in her ear.

Both surprised and excited, Melisse moaned in pleasure into her face pillow as his tongue kept circling her bottom, like a spiral going deeper inside her moist asshole.

God, this feels fantastic! And then the tongue roved lower, circling around her labia, finding her clit and sucking at it gently. Just as she was about to burst, his tongue roved back down to the entrance to her pussy.

It was on one of these trips of his tongue and lips back to her pussy that she felt a most delicious orgasm coming on. She let it take her, stifling her moans in the face pillow. Her legs went limp and she spread them further. Even while she was coming, it was just a tease: his tongue made her yearn to have something bigger inside her. *Please, stick it in!*

As she turned over onto her back and slid down toward the edge of the table, she reached out with one hand, motioning him to lower his pants. Wordlessly, and almost painfully slowly, he unzipped them and pulled them down to reveal a dark, meaty cock of impressive size, standing straight up, glistening in the candlelit massage room.

He took her legs—now hanging loosely off the table—and pulled her flush against his crotch. Holding his hard cock, he rubbed it over her pussy like a giant vibrator, giving them both delicious pleasure as he moved it slowly up and down over the length of her, from her asshole all the way up to the top of her clit. In delighted agony, she turned her head to one side and bit into the sheet that had come loose from the table.

In one long, delicious moment he pushed the fat head of his cock inside her and slowly let it enter, little by little, deeper and deeper. Once she felt him all the way in, she wrapped her legs even more tightly around him. He leaned down and silently wrapped his arms around her back, quietly lifting her up so he was standing with her arms wrapped around his neck and her legs wrapped around his waist, his cock deep inside her.

Soundlessly, he rocked back and forth inside her as she moved her hips to match the rhythm, burying her face in his neck. He hadn't even stepped out of his white pants and shoes, which were down around his legs. They were both breathing heavily as she felt his cock stiffen and swell inside her as she rocked her hips and slid her pussy lips up and down on his big tool. Their movements became faster and faster as they both neared an explosive climax and she grabbed around his back tighter, digging her lips into his shoulder so nobody would hear her screaming in pleasure.

As she came hard with her lips pressed to his body, she felt his big cock exploding deep inside her, and he shuddered again and again, savoring the small shudders afterward. Then he gently laid her back down on the table.

But Melisse was not about to let this cocksman get away—not just yet. He was still hard, so she grabbed his cock and pulled him to her.

"I want to come again," she whispered, grinning. "Can you…?"

"I can do that," he whispered. "It will be my pleasure, miss."

He lay down heavily on top of her as she spread her legs and he bucked his hips as quietly as he could while she strained upward, feeling the pleasure of his hot cock ramming deep inside her, not quite as hard as before but deliciously pliable as it pressed on her clit. Another wave of pleasure came over her as she felt the lips of her soaking pussy collapse around him in another pulsating orgasm.

"Jesus fucking Christ," she sighed. "That was sooooo good...Sam, you are amazing..."

Spicy Secret: When thrilled with a man's lovemaking skills, it doesn't hurt to state the obvious.

"Me, too," he whispered in her ear, finally going soft and pulling out of her, then reaching back to grab some towels.

"Now slide back where you were," he said. "I need to finish your massage. I still have your feet to do."

"Yes, sir," Melisse sighed breathlessly, turning back on her stomach, where it had all begun. She felt a wave of bliss come over her again as he took her small feet into his hands and rubbed them firmly with hot oil. Ah, this was heaven!

Yet, Melisse had to think straight. *I mustn't tip Sam beyond the norm, otherwise Malcolm might suspect exactly what happened in here when it shows up on his bill! I'll just give Sam some extra cash on the side.*

Spicy Secret: *Discretion* is your middle name. And your first name.

Melisse snaps out of her memory of Sam, the London masseur, as she and her driver, Hakim, reach the familiar landmarks of her neighborhood on the Upper East Side. Oh, how she loves these tree-lined streets.

"Ah, here we are, Miss!" Hakim announces when they reach the front of her building. He double-parks, jumps out, and opens her car door, then helps her inside her building with her luggage, where she hands him a nice cash tip.

Spicy Secret: Tipping well is a spiritual practice and just makes good sense. It makes the world go round in all kinds of places and all kinds of circumstances.

Gratefully, he places his hand to his heart and lightly taps, this being one of her favorite gestures by a Middle Eastern man. That, and the kisses on the forehead. Those always make her melt. "Thank you!" he gushes.

"Are you by any chance free tomorrow morning?" she smiles.

"Oh. Do you need a ride? You'll have to call the company and ask…"

"No…I mean…*another kind* of ride…"

He looks momentarily confused. Then he understands. A sheepish grin covers his face. "Ohhhhh!" He nods. "It is my day off, actually. What time should I…?"

"I'll be ready at 8:30 a.m. And don't eat. I'd love to serve you breakfast. What do you like?"

"*Anything!*"

Melisse loves the "*anything*" types. They're so easy to please—and so easy to be pleased by…

Spicy Secret: "It is not sex that gives the pleasure, but the lover." —Marge Piercy

CHAPTER 4

Return to the Lair

Melisse's apartment—or her "lair," as she calls it—is in a small, slightly shabby brownstone building on the Upper East Side of Manhattan. It's in a highly desirable location: a quiet, tree-lined street between Madison and Park Avenues. Around the corner are fancy bakeries and delis where a girl with a small kitchen can get a delicious lunch. And of course, she enjoys being near one of the world's greatest art museums, where she often goes to enjoy looking at world-class works of beauty, form, and symmetry. It's a counterbalance to the organized chaos of her lifestyle.

She also enjoys the vicinity of all the designer consignment boutiques, where she takes small excursions between appointments to browse through the cast-off clothing of rich women.

And she can't help thinking, *I screw their husbands and then I buy the wives' used clothes! How should I feel about that?*

One time, she'd been invited to a bachelorette party as a guest entertainer/educator to train some rich wives in giving "mind-blowing" blowjobs. It was being hosted by a musically talented woman famous for being married to a billionaire husband often called out in the *Daily News* for some naughty financial shenanigans.

At the party in the woman's massive penthouse, her friends gathered for the show and looked at Melisse incredulously as she cheerfully gave her "blowjob on a dildo" demonstration to the increasingly inebriated women, amid giggles and lusty calls for "more!"

It all stopped when one woman said, looking around at the others, "Wait. Why do we need to do *that* when we've already bagged the whale? We're all set now, so who cares!"

They'd all laughed hysterically and then ignored Melisse, gurgling down their champagne and turning the conversation to their offspring, possessions, and vacations. Melisse had stood there awkwardly with the dildo in her hand, feeling like quite the amateur in the company of all these calculating women. In some ways, they were the true pros, she the innocent.

What whores, she thought as she gathered her things and left, but not before sticking the "demonstration dildo" straight up in the big bowl of guacamole on the buffet table when nobody was looking.

As she exited the penthouse and the maid shut the door behind her, she giggled as she heard a woman shrieking, "There's a cock in the guac!"

Spicy Secret: "Pros" come in all shapes and disguises.

As she follows Hakim inside her building, she lets him take her in-flight bag and wheel her suitcases over the carpeted hallway back to the small elevator where they squeeze inside together. She wonders if the enterprising women from that party (who had whined, screwed, or connived their way to lifelong financial comfort) were getting the same pleasure she expected to get from this humble immigrant.

Melisse's instincts tell her that she's chosen a man who will pleasure her in a way that the rich women's money can't buy. She can smell Hakim's manly scent tinged with a nice cologne, and she is eager to get inside to unpack, relax, and sleep well in preparation for their next encounter.

She smiles at him after he deposits her bags at her door. "See you tomorrow morning," she calls out as he turns to leave.

He gives her a knowing look and goes back inside the elevator. "Tomorrow," he says with a sweet wave.

I'm finally home, she breathes in relief. She thanks her lucky stars whenever she steps over the threshold of her darling apartment. It's the only one on the top floor, with vintage details like high ceilings, perfect wood floors, sliding French doors, and a big bedroom in the back with a vintage marble mantel fireplace overlooking a garden. It's spacious enough for one delighted, grateful woman and the revolving door of guests she selects to entertain in her home.

An apartment like this is every New York call girl's dream, thanks to the privacy, the posh address, and the retreat-like setting that clients fantasize about revisiting.

Melisse guards this place with her life and avidly screens every new client to make sure nothing might occur which could lead to her losing her precious apartment. And oh, what she's done with this place since she acquired it five years ago! It is a soft, serene, antique, almost Parisian retreat bathed in creams, pale blues, gold, pale rose, and white. Mirrored dressers, chandeliers, light marble-topped tables, and velvety fabrics recall the Belle Époque. Fluffy art deco wool rugs, poufy chairs, and old gilded mirrors complete the effect.

Her enormous white iron king bed takes center stage in the spacious back bedroom, draped in gauzy curtains. Fine linens and a floral duvet invite one to snuggle into its perfect cloud-like softness. Fresh flowers in vases adorn most surfaces, sitting on perfectly polished vintage silver platters. Everything in her home is in its place, and even the men who visit are very clear about their place there.

They know they are special friends, kept always at a respectful distance, and invited here for a time of pleasures with Melisse that exists mainly in their dreams and fantasies… But once in a while—when they choose to indulge—it is a place they can slip away to and actually visit before returning to their lives.

And now her heart melts, just as it does whenever she sees him—her Butterball. A spicy orange tabby, Butterball is fat, fluffy, and loving. Now he's swishing around her legs in greeting. She can hear the hum of his deep purr, and she falls into the couch for a long meet-and-greet where he alternately curls in her lap and then gets up to touch her face with his nose.

Butterball has brought her the most natural, unconditional love she has ever known. Stroking her cat's soft fur is the most relaxing activity she can imagine, apart from what it might be like to make love with her one true love—whenever he appears sometime in the future.

But for now, Butterball *is* her one true love, and she can't wait to curl up with him in her big bed and feel his weight when he sleeps above the covers between her legs.

I wish I had The One and Butterball here together, she often thinks when she's stretched out alone in her huge bed. *Is it possible?*

**Spicy Secret: "What greater gift than the love of a cat?"
—Charles Dickens**

A wave of exhaustion hits Melisse as she begins to undress. First to go: the ugly, high-pressure support hose she wears on every flight to protect her legs from varicose veins. She's had both the reticular and varicose veins removed by a cosmetic surgeon and is determined never to have more of them. She glances behind at her legs to make sure her investment is still intact: yes, all looks fine.

Pulling out the flat stacks of cash—Malcolm's flight money—from her money belt, she locks them in the small safe in her closet. Melisse's First Rule of Money is: *Show respect and protect your money, and it will respect and protect you in return.*

She goes over to her small Hollywood Regency style desk and unlocks a drawer, taking out a beautiful, fabric-covered scrapbook with the words in a beautiful calligraphy on the cover:

"La Fantasia—My Secret Fantasy Spa for Women"

In this book are her clippings, photos, and notes for the business project that holds the highest place in her heart. She opens to a page in the back and writes down a number, then smiles with satisfaction at the total and opens to a section with pockets, the repository of all her hopes, dreams, and solid plans for La Fantasia.

She removes some swatches of beautiful, shimmering fabrics from her purse, carefully chosen while visiting a decor shop in Notting Hill during her trip to London. She tucks them into the notebook, imagining them as the future curtains for one particular guest suite at La Fantasia.

She closes the book and rubs her hand lovingly over the pale pink linen cover. She sighs a little. *It will all come together. Someday.*

> **Spicy Secret: "We act as though comfort and luxury are the chief requirements in life, when all we need to make us really happy is something to be enthusiastic about." —Charles Kingsley**

Reaching for the old-fashioned phone and answering machine on her desk, Melisse pushes the Play button to hear her messages. Although cell phones are now the norm, and Melisse certainly has the latest model (with an encryption feature installed by Malcolm for her protection), she still prefers using a landline for her calls, and for the machine to catch the calls she misses.

There's also a sentimental attachment: GG had passed these on to her, and GG was about as "connected" as one could be in this business. Melisse never knows which interesting client or lucrative opportunity might be awaiting her on GG's old line. Wisely, she never talks about money and sex in the same conversation, so she never worries about being listened to. She's trained herself and her clients never to say anything incriminating during a call, and to keep any financial discussions to a terse email or two.

> **Spicy Secret: An old dramatist's adage that works wonders for "ladies of the evening," as well as women on the dating scene: "Show, don't tell." Your goodies are meant to be enjoyed up close and personal, so don't give your sweet stuff away online or over the phone (by engaging in cyber sex, "sexting," and the like). Unless you're doing professional "camming" or phone sex (and that's your job!) keep your mouth closed (and camera off) except to arrange your professional rendezvous (or make your "live and in person" date).**

As she plays through her messages, she yawns. So far, there's nothing pressing that she wants to respond to tonight. Overall, it's an uninspiring lot...

Message One: "Melisse, it's Harry Quint. I want to make sure you're going to come back from Dubai with your virginity still intact—ha-ha! Don't let that sheik you down—Ha, get it? Sheik you down—I know, not funny. Ha, you know I love you, kid...I'll be keeping you in my thoughts, prayers, and fantasies. Give me a call when you get back, OK?"

Message Two: "Melisse, it's Mr. Funsaki. Me come to New York Hotel St. Regis in two weeks. Want to have you for sushi again. Karaoke fun time. I call you with my info when I get landing."

Message Three: "Melisse! It's Brad, from L.A. Remember me? We met before you left! I had a great time and I want to see you again when I'm in town next week. This time I want to do the Devilish Dinner package. Let me know when you're back so we can hook up er uh, cook up, buh bye..."

Message Four: "Hey, Melisse, it's Kin. Welcome back. I fed Butterball double today. I wasn't exactly sure what time you'd get back; you didn't leave your flight number. Hope I did the flowers right—they had some good lilies at the market. Talk to you later! Oh, I emailed you the flight and hotel details for your photo shoot in Miami later in the month and I sent a memo about where you need to call in your card in order to hold the booking... Thanks, bye!"

Message Five (heavy French accent): "Ms. Melisse? Bonjour. This is Josiane from L'Immobilier in Cannes. Please call me when you have a moment. I think we have located *zumthing* that might be perfect for your *projet*. It's very secluded, a villa outside Mougins. It needs some improvements, some cosmetics, but I think it is good...call me! Au revoir!"

Message Six: "Hiiiiiii, huuuuney...it's your Jazzy! I am so hotty thinking about your body. I am still hot like hot fire coals after a long fire. I am feeling your sexy breasties so big in my hands this morning when I was dreaming of your visit. See you in Dubeeya in a couple of days. I call you again, huuuuneeey...big smoochies..."

Melisse rolls her eyes. Jazzy is nuts and can be annoying and even embarrassing, but he has a huge fortune at his disposal and right now

Melisse is at the top of his pyramid of favorites, and has been for quite some time. If La Fantasia is ever to become a reality, his business could be a game changer.

Write him back now or make him wait?

Hmmm....The biggies have to wait. Never seem too eager. Leave them hungry for a little bit more.

She scans her emails and sees a note from someone named "Mike," who doesn't even use her working name, "Miss Melisse," in his salutation. She would immediately trash it for that sin alone, but before she does, she reads his pathetic request and formulates her response.

> Hi, Dear,
>
> This is Mike visiting New York and staying near JFK Airport at the Marriott. I am white, 38 years old and in good shape, 5'5". I like your website and you seem like a nice all-around lady. Would you be available tonight? Would you accept 150 USD? Sorry but I am short on cash... Thanks. Please let me know as soon as you can, please.
>
> Thank you,
>
> Mike

Spicy Secret: A sense of humor is essential in life—especially in The Life!

Hmmmm... She thinks for a moment, grins, then taps onto the keyboard:

> Dear Mike,
>
> Thank you so much for your enticing offer to spend several hours making the long journey to and from JFK to serve and pleasure you for a ridiculously low fee. Maybe I can offer you an even cheaper alternative? At JFK near Terminal 3, lower level by

the baggage storage area, there is a buffer brush machine for shining shoes. For about $1.25 in quarters you could also run that machine on your weenie. Unfortunately, if you do not climax before the machine stops, you will have to insert more coins to keep the machine going.

Safe travels, happy buffing, and thank you for thinking of me!

Kind regards,

Miss Melisse

Melisse giggles to herself. But she doesn't hit the "Send" button. Telling off clients in writing or even in person might be momentarily satisfying, but it's not the best business move if you want to preserve your reputation. A true courtesan is committed to giving pleasure and seducing slowly over time, not gaining short-term satisfaction and pissing off men by saying things like, "Hey, save a hooker and go fuck yourself!"

> **Spicy Secret: Never hit "Send" unless your message contains something sweet. And if it's a sour, slightly sarcastic, or even threatening message (even when well deserved) DO NOT hit Send. Wait a day. See if you still feel the same way about the offending idiot tomorrow, and if his faux pas is worth possibly losing your temper/reputation/income.**

Next, she dials from her landline to a local voice mail number dedicated solely to the "straight" men in her life (*straight* meaning not paying clients). As usual, there are no messages for her from any of her guys in "Category B." That's because her unofficial rule is that she calls them when she needs them, not the other way around. Still, it would have been nice if one of them had at least left a message that he missed her, asking if he could come over and make love with her as soon as she got home!

It's OK, I've got Hakim tomorrow, she thinks, anticipating how his stubbly chin will feel pressing into her face or the back of her neck as he caresses her…and then gives her the good, hard pounding she expects from him in the morning.

Suddenly, the phone starts ringing. Startled, Melisse picks up. "Hello?"

"Melisse? It's Jan from Hospice Cares." There's a certain respect in Jan's voice, as if she is fascinated by Melisse, yet afraid of her at the same time.

"Hi, Jan, how have you been?"

"Good, good! I think you just got back?"

"Yes…but it's OK. I can talk…"

"I know this is so last minute, but the family says it's urgent."

"Sure. I need to stay up so that I'll sleep all night…it's perfect timing. Can you give me the details?"

CHAPTER 5

A Special Kind of "Happy Ending"

The hospice families who call Melisse when someone is nearing the end always seem to live in nice, middle-class homes and tend to be very open-minded. Otherwise, her form of therapy would have been out of the question!

This time, she goes to a rambling apartment in a building near the United Nations. Even before she reaches the front door, Melisse picks up the scent of the man's impending transition to the Other Side. When people have been sick in their homes for a long time, the clean smells of hospice nursing aren't strong enough to mask the scent of a long illness, with Death just around the corner.

Hospice also reminds Melisse of her own mother, Pearl, buried now in California, who died of colon cancer under hospice care not long ago.

When Pearl's cancer had advanced to the point where they sent her home to die, Melisse took time off from work and came home to northern California to care for her. Ironically, being a freelance call girl afforded her the luxury of spending time with family without worrying about any major financial downside or getting back to a structured job.

The hospital had pulled the plug on her mother's intravenous meals and sent Pearl home to slowly fade, passing away in an ether of opiates.

Melisse had to give her mother anti-nausea suppositories, and when her mother apologized for needing her help, Melisse replied, "It's OK, Mom. I'm used to sticking things up people's butts!"

Her mother, always her daughter's biggest fan, had winced as she chuckled. She had been supportive from the beginning when Melisse had told her she was going to become a "modern" courtesan. When Pearl saw that Melisse's mind was made up, she had told Melisse that if she planned to go that route, "Then just be the best damn hooker you can be!"

Melisse would never forget that, as her mother left this world, her last words were: "You're my beautiful daughter." Growing up, Melisse had yearned to hear her father tell her that she was pretty, but the words had never come. At least her father was honest. She was really not so "pretty" as a child, but that had all changed with her "extreme makeover" many years later, and now it was a whole different game.

Now, she could never get enough compliments.

She suspected that this need to be "validated" as attractive was one main reason (apart from the cash) she had turned to men who would pay for her attentions. After all, if they paid you—and paid well and often—it must really mean you were a beautiful woman worth possessing. But "the business" had taught her otherwise: that it was *really* all about the character and personality.

> **Spicy Secret: "When a woman is tender, soft, fun-loving, lovable…who stops to inquire if she has beauty in the classical sense? Regardless of her features or form, to most men she seems a paragon of femininity. To them, she is beautiful!…The presence or the absence of beauty is of minor consequence in the attainment of true femininity."** —Helen Andelin, *Fascinating Womanhood*

But no matter how much men paid and how often they praised her, Melisse never really believed them. It was her mother's last compliment that she trusted most.

Now, Mr. and Mrs. Levy, the son and daughter-in-law of the dying man, open the door while a nurse in uniform stands respectfully behind them. They welcome her with awkward smiles, and Melisse feels Mr. Levy sizing her up even as he continues to smile graciously at her.

"It's so good of you to come," Mrs. Levy says. "Can we give you something for the visit?"

Melisse is slightly taken aback at the reminder that she normally does sexual things for money. In this case, that's not going to happen.

"No, no, not at all. This is just something special I do, and I'm happy to help."

Her husband looks shaky; he's beginning to realize that there's not much more time left for his father, and his face is pale, his mouth drooping. "This is my father's last request, you know, since they took him off the food tube. He wants to spend one last time with a… beautiful woman," Mr. Levy says as he gives Melisse a once-over. "I couldn't deny my dad his last wish."

Melisse nods but doesn't smile. She looks toward Mrs. Levy and lightly taps her arm. "I'm so sorry for what you've been through."

Spicy Secret: When "off-duty," just "turn it off" and play it straight when men's wives are around. Nothing is crueler than flirting with another woman's man right in front of her.

Mrs. Levy looks uncomfortable, and asks, "Can we get you something to drink, Melisse?"

"No, no, I'm fine. Just let us have our privacy and I promise to take good care of him."

Mrs. Levy opens the door to the bedroom, and the nurse goes inside to make sure all is in order. She shows Melisse a bell she can use to call, then closes the door behind her as she leaves.

Melisse hears Mr. Levy say outside the door, "I wish *I* were terminal…" before getting shushed away down the hall by Mrs. Levy.

Melisse clicks the door shut behind her and sees a small man lying in a hospital bed; he turns his head toward her and looks over at her. Then a smile touches his lips.

"Hi, there! How are you doing today?" she asks cheerfully.

"I'm one big tumor," the elder Mr. Levy replies, struggling to get the words out with a touch of humor.

"You don't look like a tumor to me," Melisse says cheerily. "You look pretty darn handsome. *Very relaxed*."

Spicy Secret: "Angels fly because they take themselves lightly." —Jean Cocteau

The room is somewhat dim and has been lit thoughtfully with scented candles placed between clusters of bouquets. Melisse reaches for a lamp and puts the light up a notch. She imagines he won't want to miss what she is about to do.

"My name is Melisse, Mr. Levy."

"Hi, Melisse. Thanks for coming. Call me Sy."

"Sy…would it be okay if I get more comfortable?" she asks, coming closer, slowly easing off her trench coat.

Spicy Secret: "Remember that a person's name is to that person the sweetest and most important sound in any language." —Dale Carnegie

Under her trench, she's wearing nothing but a beautiful short silk slip in a bright pink shade. She gives Sy a few seconds to admire this vision, then slides it over the top of her head and stands before him completely nude.

Spicy Secret: Never deprive your date or loved one the exciting vision of you slowly undressing for him (and possibly asking for his help). But leave the re-dressing part for the privacy of the restroom (unless he expressly offers to help with that because he enjoys it, as well).

Then, Melisse slides off her kitten heels and sees Sy come alive a little bit more as he realizes what is going on. His eyes widening, he says, "Ohhh!"

"I'd love a hug," Melisse tells him. "Can I get into bed with you?" At his nod, she gently folds the sheets back and gets in the bed next to him. Then she puts her arms around him, cradling his head against her breasts. He wraps his arms around her waist and sighs as she kisses him on the forehead.

She is suddenly aware that this is all he really wants—just to be held. His face crinkles with a big smile, and Melisse hugs him closer and places his hands on her breasts. And there, in a dying man's arms, she finally succumbs to her jet lag and sleeps the sleep of the dead.

As she snores like a small lion, Sy hugs her closer and listens to the sweet sound of a warm, beautiful woman lying peacefully in his arms.

"I've finally died and gone to heaven," he whispers.

Spicy Secret: Hugs and cuddling are the little-known "secret sauce" of the world's most successful courtesans.

Coco Chanel once said, "As long as you know *men are like children***, you know everything!" And children love to be cuddled.**

CHAPTER 6

Hakim's Breakfast

The next morning, Melisse wakes up in her bed with Butterball, her constant companion. He nudges her awake with his wet nose on her face and the kneading of his paws on her chest.

"Ohhhhh…my little boody cat," Melisse coos. "Just you and me together in our *purrever* home." Often when she wakes up, she feels grateful for the beautiful apartment and the luxurious surroundings (and the gifts of her health, intelligence, and beauty, which help her maintain it all). Yet she is beginning to increasingly feel the absence of a special man, someone who would suit her perfectly, forever.

But a big part of her often wonders if forever is a little too long to expect of a relationship with another flawed human being, particularly when most men she's met are clearly not hard-coded for "forever" (or *purrever*) monogamy.

And neither am I, frankly.

Yet she often yearns for a man who will sleep with her and wake up beside her, who will light up her life with a broad smile or a hearty laugh. Like the beautiful spring sun streaming into her bedroom, her true lover would warm her with his companionship and make her feel that all was well in her world.

Yeah, right. She's also acutely aware of that old saying: "Familiarity breeds contempt." So maybe she doesn't want to become so damned familiar with a man and see him every single day (and his dirty socks and underwear lying around) (and a bathroom that looks like a walrus was just splashing around in there) AND maybe she didn't want to let him see her (the passing storms of moods, the shocking amount of personal maintenance, the insecurities, the lack of trust in men, the neuroses...) every day!

Ah, but that could all be overcome... And she could be the light in his life, transferring to him freely all that is special about her that she normally puts a price tag on.

You mean, close this candy store? Are you crazy?

But it's another morning like many others. There are so many things to do: pack and tie up loose ends before leaving for a whole week. There is a long flight to the Middle East again this evening. So she now has one full afternoon to totally enjoy being alone before the almost constant performance she will give for Sheik Jazzy, who hardly lets her leave his side once he is with her.

Ah, Jazzy: overbearing, needy, whacked-out, weird, oversexed, eccentric, dissolute, embarrassing, and, fortunately, filthy, filthy rich— and generous.

But first, breakfast for that sweet chauffeur, Hakim, who will be here in a couple of hours. For Melisse, there is always a special sensuality when preparing breakfast for her morning lovers. The fruit juice is always squeezed by hand, and the man's favorite food is lovingly prepared (barring Eggs Benedict, which she can never get right).

So this morning, Melisse drags out the Belgian waffle maker, an artisanal bottle of maple syrup, and some slices of turkey bacon, intuiting that Hakim will like something on the sweeter side, accompanied by a breakfast meat but no pork, as he might be Muslim. She stirs the batter for the waffles and puts it aside, to be used after they are both sated and starving.

> **Spicy Secret: If there's one meal to learn to cook and excel at preparing for men, make it a varied, hearty breakfast. Reservations can be made for all the other meals. And in a pinch, toss him a tube steak.**

The other sensual joy in Melisse's life is the ritual of preparing herself for men, whether clients or "Category B's." From the bubble bath, to rolling her hair in a 1940s style à la Veronica Lake, to the final hint of mascara on her lashes, the whole process can take up to two hours. Her favorite part is a long bath with a delicately scented oatmeal/vanilla bubble bath as she rubs her entire body with a "black soap" bought in Marrakech, lightly scented with jasmine. This stays on a few minutes to help aid an intense exfoliation, and then it is rubbed off vigorously with the *kessa* glove, also from Morocco, and akin to thick sandpaper.

Next, a good scrub with a long back brush.

> **Spicy Secret: Don't neglect to thoroughly clean and/or defuzz those hidden and "harder to reach" places on your body. Just because *you* can't see them doesn't mean your man won't notice. A high-quality back brush is a great investment, as is a bit of so-called painless laser hair removal for those nether regions. A copious dusting of powder in areas prone to sweat gives an extra layer of softness, and some powders even come in a "tasty" variety—lickable!**

Melisse brutalizes her skin for several minutes, but in doing so arrives at a body so silky that she often feels like she might slide off her sheets if the person she's fucking doesn't catch her first.

> **Spicy Secret: Starting early in life, a rigorous daily brushing with a dry brush on the thighs and butt (in addition to the exfoliation glove) has the potential to help stave off cellulite forever. You can also use the handle to spank your clients if you accidentally break your paddle.**

To further enhance the silky softness, she rubs a large glob of African shea butter in a mint tea scent in the palms of her hands, warms it to an oily consistency, then rubs it deeply into her skin from neck to toe. That's a secret that GG taught her to help her skin remain eternally moist and youthful.

Once again, she wishes there were a darling guy she could truly love and live with to join her on this part of her ritual.

Spicy Secret: The best commandment of all—pamper thyself!

When "Category B" lovers come to visit, Melisse prefers not to talk much, instead enjoying the experience of mutual abandon. It's different with her clients, who seem to need almost as much conversation as they do sex. Clients sometimes use her to share aspects of their lives they might not even share with their therapists, with sex as an afterthought. Their biggest need might be for a good listener, someone without a hidden agenda.

In fact, Melisse finds herself having many dinners where she functions as simply a gorgeous therapist, quietly listening to whatever they wish to talk about, and in some cases gently prodding them with questions to go deeper or in other directions.

Sometimes, a client will confess to being new to the business of engaging a prostitute, and will say he is "newly married but out exploring" (because he realizes he now misses the variety of his single life and he can't possibly adjust). Or he'll admit to being a "first-timer after many years of marriage" (because "Everything is great" but after thirty years of marriage we "Don't have sex anymore!" or "She's gotten fat and let herself go…sadly (sigh)…" (And often enough he has, too, if he'd only take a closer look or step on a scale)!

When, from his conversation, a man seems clearly still in love with his wife, it hurts Melisse to think of him "cheating" and subconsciously messing up a good thing with lies and omissions (on top of the lies he's telling himself about how it won't affect the way he treats her).

But who is she to judge?

So often she wishes she could just send him back home to communicate and try to make things better *without* his getting laid (but that would mean her not getting paid), but that's not good for business, and it's not her role.

Her time, insights, and charms are not a charity operation.

> **Spicy Secret: Don't judge, attempt to fix, or feel sorry for the men who visit you; just take care of them and give them what they want in terms of sex or companionship. They're big boys and can figure out the rest of their lives for themselves.**

Turning him away would be a futile gesture anyway, and he would only be out searching again soon, she tells herself. Because by the time a seriously coupled man has made it into the arms and bed of an escort, he is often at the last stop of a long and tortured mental journey that led him to what he sees as a "reasonable solution" to his domestic satisfaction problem.

> **Spicy Secret: Long-married but sexually lonely men are stoic and thoughtful warriors: they'll do almost anything to preserve a good thing and avoid hurting their negligent wives and/or families. Discreet meetings with escorts—*not* couples therapy—are often their final polite answer to the very private, painful love and sex problems that have slowly become unbearable in their lives.**

Right now, however, Melisse is not thinking of how she will satisfy her lonely clients.

She is thinking of how she will greet this new man who will enjoy her bed this morning! Hakim—the chauffeur—arrives, looking shy. He is wearing dark jeans and a nice dress shirt, and is carrying a small bouquet of flowers he must have picked up at the corner grocery store, given the plastic wrapping.

"Oh là là…such beautiful flowers, thank you! I love tulips!" she says, giving him a kiss on the cheek.

Spicy Secret: Whatever flowers (or candies/gifts/tokens of appreciation) he brings are the most beautiful you've ever seen or received. Gush over them for a while.

Melisse is pleased. It's the thought that counts. Actually, it's the *effort* that counts. Instinctively, Hakim removes his shoes at the door and she reaches out to take the flowers, kissing him on the cheek. "Come, join me on the couch," she urges to help break the ice. He takes a seat, and she brings him a large glass of chilled orange juice. Gratefully, he clutches the glass and sips the drink, petting Butterball as Melisse arranges the tulips in a vase she has brought and set before them.

It seems that he, too, doesn't need much conversation. Melisse doesn't mind at all; who knows what it might reveal. For a moment, she wonders if she misjudged him. He seems tentative, like someone on a blind date who might be having second thoughts.

And so she's surprised when she sits down beside Hakim in her silky robe (with nothing on beneath), and he suddenly grabs her and begins kissing her—gently, not with a thick tongue ramming down her throat (which she hates) but with a delicacy and reserve. Often everything about a relationship can be told in a kiss, and this one tells her he will respect her boundaries, and that someone before her taught him to be an appreciative lover.

She moves back and allows him to reach inside her gown, where he puts one hand around her waist to pull her closer while gently massaging her breasts with the other.

"Mmmmm...you smell so good...Melisse..." he says. His hand leaves her breasts and reaches down as his fingers gently massage her increasingly wet flower.

The couch starts to feel too limiting. She slowly undresses him, running her hands over his chest, his perfectly defined abs, and in between his thighs. She sits down as he steps out of his pants, and when he is totally naked, she then leads him gently by his cock, over to her bed.

> **Spicy Secret: Lead a man you like by his hard cock to wherever you'll be making love. Don't worry, this is nothing new—it's been leading him all his life anyway.**

Once she's sitting on the bed with him standing in front of her, she grabs his hips and slides his perfectly proportioned cock inside her mouth.

Melisse feels him getting harder and harder as she moves his hips back and forth with her hands, and she guides his cock deeper and faster inside her mouth as her tongue works exclusively on the head. She then holds her breath, but breathes out slowly through her mouth and lets his cock slide all the way to the back of her throat as far as it can go.

> **Spicy Secret: A calm and well-practiced "deep throat" (without gagging) is well worth mastering as a great pleasurable treat to give your man. If you really want to take it over the top, learn to love licking his balls, which might be considered the seat (more of a beanbag, actually) of his emotions.**

He moans. "Ohhhhh, Melisse, you are too good!"

Just when she thinks he is about to blow from the excitement of being together for the first time, he pushes her away and makes her stop.

"I am not here for this. I come to take care of you," he says in his charming imperfect English spoken with a Jordanian accent. "I can control myself. I will not come until you tell me you are ready."

Melisse smiles. *Perfect.* She lies back and spreads her legs and looks at him invitingly. Hakim's eyes widen at the inviting sight of her.

> **Spicy Secret: Forget a viewing of the *Mona Lisa*! No more beautiful picture exists for most men than an attractive woman beckoning him with her legs spread wide apart.**

"Hakim, I'm feeling totally lazy today, really. I'm just going to lie here on my back and let you fuck me."

"And I will do this," he says, lying down on top of her, his hard cock pressed against the lips of her pussy, pressing for entry. "I will do this and I am not going to stop. You can use me as you wish, and come as much as you want."

"I think I can do that." Melisse smiles contentedly, thinking, *Oh, yes! Full permission granted to enjoy myself any way I want—woo-hoo! My instincts were right, after all!*

And without fail, Hakim begins an unforgettable session of relentless fucking, with few breaks in between for her to compose herself before the next vigorous ramming. Under business circumstances, Melisse might find this annoying (and worthy of a supplemental charge), but his soul is so sweet and giving that it's a delicious privilege to give up control to one so eager (and good) at pleasing.

All the while, Hakim holds her tight and she enjoys the feeling of being contained in his arms as he moves her first this way and then that, into many different positions, like a rag doll. *Mmmm…the ultimate relaxation.*

But she is no doll, and she's enjoying every minute of passive pleasure as he varies the movements of his perfectly hard cock diving deep and fast into her.

After the first orgasm (which crept up on her as he was slamming away on top of her) he no longer gives her a break, and she begins coming easily many times over, relaxing her body and feeling only the pleasure pounding around inside her pussy, knowing that she has his permission to use his cock any way she pleases and that he will last until she achieves all the satisfaction she can handle.

Finally, when she's reached a point of exhaustion and her pussy is almost numb from all the activity, he turns her over, squirts a bit more lube on her for their next round, and puts a pillow under her stomach.

"I'm going to fuck you now," he says. "For me!"

"Isn't that what you've been doing?" she laughs, breathless, her damp hair matting on her forehead.

"No. That was just to warm you up, but I may not last much longer," he says, sliding into her from behind.

With one slow stroke, he begins pounding her vigorously from behind as she presses her soaking-wet pussy up against his right hand, which is now beneath her and working a quick circle over her clit. The sensation is too direct on her clit and she squirms in discomfort, but he keeps at it, fucking her from behind and working her clit without letting up. Then her discomfort turns into pleasure as her clit gets accustomed to his rough touch and his dreamy cock as it rams into her pussy.

She feels another wave of pleasure coming over her as he pounds at her with a steady rhythm and she squeals, "Ohhh, God…you're going to make me come again! Ohhhhhh!"

"Come! Me, too!" he moans. "Aaaaaaarrrrrggghhhh…" And for a moment he sounds like a lion biting into his delicious prey.

Exhausted, Melisse collapses onto her back as Hakim dives down next to her. "Where. Did. You. Learn. To. Do. That?" she gasps.

He chuckles, trying to catch his breath. "I had a girlfriend once and she could never, ever come. I tried everything—for years! Nothing worked. But I learned how to stay hard and give a woman pleasure. Not that girlfriend, but after her, others. And those—they came."

"There's a silver lining in every cloud," Melisse says, smiling.

"You are the wet part of my cloud and I am very glad we met," he says, putting an arm around her.

"Mmmmm, me, too. But now…I'm making you breakfast."

"Oh, yes." He smiles. "And then we start again. I have all day."

"Ha!" she laughs, thinking how nice it would be, but she does have the usual preparations to make before Jazzy and Dubai…

"I'll give you a 'rain check' on that," she says, laughing. "My cloud needs to re-moisturize after a storm like that, Mr. Hakim. 'Cause… you're a rainmaker!" she laughs, getting up to make a breakfast fit for a king.

Spicy Secret: Know when it's time to call it a day (or night). It never hurts to leave a little something for next time.

CHAPTER 7

A Call from the Wild

After Hakim leaves, having subjected her to an exuberant farewell hugfest, Melisse stands at her kitchen sink washing her dildo collection. She'll have to bring a few with her for the trip to Dubai, just in case Jazzy decides to ask her for one to enhance their playtime.

She personally hates dildos and vibrating toys, finding that they just add another element of "plastic" and "impersonal" to her already-plastic interactions with men she might not ever see again. But when it comes to Sheik Jazzy, she welcomes any and every stage prop that will get her through the week.

She also loathes flying commercial to certain stricter countries when she has to travel with dildos or vibrators. If your bags get searched at customs, the agents can have a field day holding up the offending toys, asking, "And what is this, miss?"

"Ohhhh...that? That is a clearly a *dog toy*. See the teeth marks from Gus, my dog...?" (Meaning Gus, her client in DC who runs a special division of the CIA, who takes a suite at the Mayflower once a month and flies her in to "party." Gus, who likes to be tied up, treated like a dog, and impaled after playing "fetch" by grabbing her rubbery pink dildo with his teeth.)

So it's always such a relief to fly by private plane when visiting Jazzy.

When her landline rings, Melisse unfurls a long phone cord so she can keep working at the sink while talking to whomever it might be.

"Helllooooo, huuuuuney, it's meeeeeee..."

Sheik Jazzy. He tells her he's standing in one of the huge courtyards of his decadent palace (the green spaces inspired by the Alhambra in Granada, Spain, and the architecture and jewel-toned decor resembling The Palace of Versailles meets a Bollywood wedding).

He can't wait to see her, he says, although he's trying to enjoy the company of his "visiting entertainers."

"They sent me crap for entertainers this time," he complains. She then hears a parrot's voice repeating, "Crap entertainers!" It can be none other than Pasquale, Jazzy's pet parrot, who lives in the garden where Jazzy "houses" his visiting entertainers.

"Ohhhh, Jazzy, you poor thing! The entertainers aren't good? That is *awful*."

"They're sucking," he whines.

> **Spicy Secret: When a client or the man in your life is complaining about petty or inconsequential things, let him exhaust (and embarrass) himself by expressing it. Then give him a very sweet, but very short line of babying, like "Oh, you poor guy. I'm so sorry that (xyz) is so bad…blah…blah…" Then quickly change the subject. Treat him like a man. It's time for him to either man up or shut up. If you baby too much, he'll feel like you're his mother. And that's not good for your sex life. Or business, if he's a client.**

Melisse can see it all now. His "girls" are enjoying the pleasures of his many swimming pools, perfumed gardens, and numerous pagodas and sunken gazebos with comfy couches while they wait impatiently to be squired away for their "night with Jazzy," which sometimes never happens. But Jazzy always makes sure that even if they don't get the big "jackpot"—a night in his chambers—they get their contracted fee and won't go back to their countries empty-handed. Jewels, substantial leather goods from Hermès and Ferragamo, and envelopes stuffed with US dollars are the little bonuses his "entertainers" will receive after leaving the palace and returning to their home countries, where they work as models, strippers, actresses, and beauty contestants.

The women who stay in the palace must abide by Jazzy's strict guidelines: they're not allowed to leave until they are escorted by his "courtesy van," which will deliver them to the vast hangar in Wadijazzizi where he keeps several planes fired up. The jets return the girls to Dubai after about a month of "work," where they'll find their own routes home to every corner of the world using pre-funded debit cards found in their "travel allowance" envelopes.

Melisse has never visited Jazzy's palace because based on the intimacy she's established with him (and given her full knowledge of his crazy ways), she has some concerns about becoming his "esteemed guest" in Wadijazzizi. His three wives also live in the palace, and seeing a client in his home with a wife (even one of several) is something she finds distasteful (even if it's a huge palace where she will most likely never see them)! And strangely enough, Jazzy has never asked her to visit him there…though he hints at it often enough, saying, "We should have a sleepover in my palace, honey." Of course, the answer is always, "No."

Melisse knows all about Jazzy's parrot, Pasquale, a huge bird of brilliant colors standing on Jazzy's shoulder, cackling, as Jazzy talks to her.

Meanwhile, Jazzy is observing several long-term resident monkeys playing around the palms where he's standing, while a long string of "women of the harem" snake around the garden path, waiting to be chosen as his "treat" for later that evening. Jazzy, though, is more interested in talking to Melisse.

He waves away one beautiful woman after another, and after each rejection, Pasquale cackles, "Get outta here!"

Jazzy looks up at his feathered pal, who appears poised to ram his beak into Jazzy's forehead for a quick kill. "You dirty bird, *you* get outta here!"

The bird repeats back, "Get outta here!"

Jazzy chuckles, "Motherfucker."

"Motherfucker."

Melisse, hearing all this on the line, giggles. "Pasquale?" she squeals, trying to talk in parrot talk, hoping he'll hear her. "Pasquale?"

The bird tilts his head for a moment and caws quietly and contentedly near the phone, as if asking, "Who is it?"

"Who do you love, Pasquale?" Melisse caws. Pasquale caws happily.

"He loves you, Melisse. This piece of shit bird has fallen in love with your voice. I swear, every time we talk…"

As Jazzy stands talking to Melisse, a tall, beautiful woman walks up and stands smiling before Jazzy, anticipating her acceptance as if she were Miss Brazil. (Maybe she is?)

Jazzy looks her up and down, then nods her away. She doesn't look slutty enough for Jazzy's tastes tonight. He's in the mood for more of a "hoochy mama." Jazzy gives the bird a secret sign.

"Get outta here!" the bird cackles. "Motherfucker."

The woman extends her middle finger and turns around to walk away.

"Did you just flip the bird, young lady?" Jazzy asks, laughing. She keeps walking.

"Shit for brains!" Pasquale cackles. "Shit for brains!"

Melisse, overhearing all this, just shakes her head. "Oh, boy," Jazzy reports. "The monkeys are at it again, slinging their shit around."

It seems the word, *shit,* has incited one of the monkeys to pick up a freshly produced piece of poop from his bottom and throw it at the rejected woman as she walks away. It hits her squarely on the back and runs down her beautiful caftan. Jazzy gives the monkey a covert thumbs-up.

"Ewwwwww!" Miss Brazil screams. She flies into a fit of rage and comes after Jazzy and his bird. Jazzy finds it very exciting to watch her temper flare.

"Hey, hey, here she comes at me. Oh, Melisse, she is very pissed!"

Jazzy's security man intervenes and hauls her away. He rubs his crotch. Miss Brazil has been there three fucking weeks already and has never been "chosen" (which will get her more tips and jewels she can resell back in Rio). As much as he likes a beauty queen in a rage, Jazzy wants someone with more meat on her bones tonight.

Also, the beauty queens always seem like they're trying to come up with the "right" and most polite answer to everything, and this is extremely boring to a man like Jazzy.

Jazzy asks Melisse, "Are you still there, honey bunny?"

"Yes, Jazz, I'm here."

Jazzy waves away the remaining women. They frown and shuffle back into the palace and leave him alone for his call. "Sorry, cuddlebug. I was fighting with Pasquale again. Sometimes I want to shoot him. Or serve him to my tigers. His mouth is so dirty I can't give him to the zoo, as it would embarrass me."

"You know you love that bird, Jazzy," Melisse teases.

She's now washing a small black butt plug in her kitchen sink. This is the "warm-up call" she has to endure to spice things up for him. Jazzy will be waiting eagerly for her at the Burj Al Arab hotel in a few short hours. After all, the "spice up" is part of her service.

Spicy Secret: As part of your "service package," get him warmed up with a spicy call before "the big event."

"So how are you, Jazzy! I can hardly wait to see you!"

"I know, little miss cum bubbles. Do you miss me as much as I miss you?"

"Ohhhh, yes, my Masterprick. My luuuuv juices are…uh…" she squirts some dish soap onto the dildo *"squirting* from my…?"

She grabs a brush scrubber from a clay Buddha sponge holder.

"…big, swollen Buddha clit! I'm trembling with how much I miss you, Big Clitmaster Daddy." She rolls her eyes.

Jazzy asks, "Do you miss Big Daddy's Love Dong Dong?"

Melisse dries the dildo with a dish towel. "Ohhh, Big Daddy King Kong Ding Dong. I wanna swing from your big swinging dick tree." She can hear Jazzy swooning in anticipation of his trip over to Dubai to meet her for a week of "Funfest." *As if having fifty international beauty queens at his beck and call isn't enough.*

"And I am missing your little tight hubbly bubbly pipe. But Big Daddy Ding Dong will be sucking from it and getting high from licking off your love juices soon enough."

"Ohhh, yes! My love juices are boiling for you."

"Be careful on the flight, Lisse," he tells her, laughing. "I am sending my special new lady pilot on this one, and the steward is also new. I just released him from my small prison here for writing some bad checks, so I am rewarding him for his good behavior in jail with a new job as a steward on my planes. But I am going to unleash him on you first."

"*Unleash* him on me? You make him sound like a dog!"

"He *is*. He's a horny, horny dog, just like his master. Watch out, my princess, and if he doesn't make you happy in some way, you can give him a little smack. Or a bigger one! You do that so well! He needs to learn how to handle himself with my guests, and this will be his first big trip out of Wadijazzizi."

"Hmmmm…" Melisse hears Jazzy's diabolical laughter echoing through his courtyard. She already has an idea of what he's planning for her, and hopes the steward will at least be cute.

"Well, see you tomorrow, little Melisse. Tally-ho! And I mean 'ho' in the nicest way."

Silence on Melisse's end.

"Melisse? Are you still there?"

"Oh yes. Well, uh…tally-ho, Big Daddy! I must run now! I can't wait to see you. Ciao ciao!"

> **Spicy Secret: When foolish buffoon patrons make an insulting remark about your chosen profession, a long moment of silence and a quick conversational segue should be enough for them to "get the hint" and not do it again.**

CHAPTER 8

The (Very) Friendly Skies

Melisse chooses her in-flight wardrobe carefully, selecting a medium-length white cotton jersey dress. It features a fitted bustier bodice and flutters with a full skirt. Over this, she wears a light turquoise overcoat. Her aquamarine pendant necklace and matching earrings sparkle, discreetly nestled in her breasts and earlobes. A pair of turquoise-blue Manolo Blahnik kitten heels, decorated with leather florets, enhance her feet, now perfectly presentable after a last-minute pedicure.

In New Jersey, she boards the stunning, compact, perfectly outfitted private jet that will whisk her away like a magic carpet ride to Dubai. The gorgeous pilot comes back to her seat to greet her.

"Welcome, Miss! I am Halima, your pilot, at your service."

Halima's long, dark curly hair is contained under a stylish cap, and her skin is dewy, with an all-over tan and exquisitely done makeup, dark kohl outlining her large brown eyes feathered by long eyelashes. Her white uniform is crisp and beautifully tailored, Armani perhaps, and her very expensive gold watch with a diamond bezel has all the signs of having been a gift from Jazzy.

A moment later, Halima is joined by her copilot, Jalil, a powerful-looking, tight-bodied guy who politely introduces himself and then quietly returns to the cockpit. Melisse wonders if Halima has ever spent any private time with Jazzy (or Jalil), but thinks the answer is probably no. Jazzy is very particular about separating his activities, and given the rarity of a beautiful and capable female pilot, would probably prefer to keep himself in her good graces by not exposing her to all his bad behavior.

"Jazzy said you would be a woman, but I didn't believe him!" Melisse laughs. "This is great!"

Halima sits down in the seat across from Melisse, to be on her level. "I know! It's a dream come true for me, to fly a plane like this and be able to boss around a guy like Jalil," she laughs, turning to look back at her copilot. "I hope you will enjoy the flight. If we have any turbulence coming, the alert lights will go on and I'll ask that you put on your seat belt for us, but I hope to just let you sleep all the way there. We will be stopping in Casablanca for a little break, and we've got a beautiful breakfast planned for us at the terminal—a real Moroccan breakfast. I'm so excited!"

"Ah! I love Moroccan breakfasts!" Melisse says, thinking of the sweetest of fresh green tea boiled with fragrant fresh mint, breakfast crepes, *amalou* (which tastes like a sweet peanut butter), eggs scrambled with air-dried beef, and a handful of yummy olives. If it's not too foggy in Casa, it's always such fun to eat a Moroccan breakfast while sitting on a blanket under a shady tree in the little courtyard outside the private plane terminal.

And sometimes, if there's a longer stopover, there will be a private driver/guide arranged to take her into Casa to the old *souk* for shopping, or to have lunch. Sometimes, depending on the schedule, it's sexy sunset drinks overlooking the ocean at Cabestan, one of Melisse's favorite restaurants in the world—if only for what might be the world's sexiest restaurant bathrooms. The private rooms are equipped with individual sinks and cushy chairs to make for a potentially long and sexy visit (should you invite your dining companion to sneak in).

Melisse's thoughts turn to one particularly hot escape into a "restroom" with a particularly cute driver/guide named Abdoo, who'd once been assigned to her for the evening stopover. He'd sat on the velour chair while she'd straddled him as they fucked deliciously between the main course and dessert.

"Melisse? Are you with me?" Halima enquires.

"Oh! I hope you'll be joining me for breakfast!" Melisse suggests, tearing her thoughts away from her ride on Abdoo's cock. She'd actually like to know more about this beautiful young pilot and how she achieved the nearly impossible—getting a fabulous job with Jazzy!

Halima then gives Melisse a significant look. "Melisse, did you know that Sheik Jazzy has installed cameras on the plane now? He can watch everything we do from his home."

"No, I didn't know that, but I kind of suspected it would happen sooner or later," Melisse says, giving her a knowing look back. She senses someone coming up from behind her, and Halima quickly collects herself and stands up.

"I think you know the plane already; the bedroom is all ready for you back there and… Ah! Here is Ahmed; he is still in training…I will let him take it from here. Let me know if you need anything. I'll be coming back later to check on you personally."

Melisse watches as Halima returns to the cockpit, but not without noticing her shapely hips and confident walk. *Beauty and brains*, she thinks, a bit enviously.

Spicy Secret: Be gracious to trainees; remember the first time that YOU had to perform or give a service?

Ahmed, the steward, approaches awkwardly from behind her with a glass of Perrier and a slice of lemon, balancing it precariously on a tray.

"Hello, Miss Melisse. I am Ahmed, your steward for the flight." He doesn't seem like an ex-convict who's been jailed for writing bad checks. He looks more like a handsome construction worker who's surprised to find himself in this sleek private jet. Melisse notes his muscles bursting out of his new uniform and gives him a sweet smile, taking the drink he's offering.

"How are you tonight, Ahmed?"

"I'm well!" he says, sounding relieved and deliriously happy to be free. A dreamy expression crosses his face for a moment as his eyes flash ever so briefly on Melisse's décolletage. *His hunger for a woman must be unbearable*, Melisse thinks. After all, he's just been sprung from lockup and immediately promoted to steward on Jazzy's private plane.

"Are you hungry?" Ahmed asks suddenly, as if remembering that he's here to serve Melisse. "I mean, may I offer you a little preflight snack? A few chips or a fruit and cheese plate? Or caviar and a glass of champagne?"

Melisse knows from Jazzy's description of Ahmed that he's allowing her to seduce Ahmed on the flight if she wishes. Of course, his motives aren't exactly unselfish—he expects to hear all about it. He may even watch it on the plane's new camera (hidden, of course).

Since the days of their first meeting at the George V Hotel in Paris, Jazzy has always been the ultimate voyeur, one of those secret swingers who prefers to see, rather than be seen. Rare in a man, sexual jealousy is refreshingly *not* one of Jazzy's defining qualities, and in this regard he's quite a generous lover.

Melisse gazes at Ahmed's sturdy legs and the lines of his lean body and his endearingly anxious expression. He must have had lots of time to work out in Jazzy's private jail because he's practically bursting through his uniform like the "Incredible Hulk" from that old TV show.

Here is a man ready to serve her, and she's already enjoying a fantasy or two about them in the big, soft bed she'll be sleeping in.

Melisse sips at her water, curious about how all this will play out, especially since Ahmed seems ready to pounce on her as soon as they hit ten thousand feet.

"Caviar and champagne." She smiles. "That sounds absolutely delicious right now."

Spicy Secret: Your perpetually strict diet is a constant triumph over temptation: But it's OK to cheat on it once in a while if it makes you smile!

"It will be out in a moment," he says worshipfully, and disappears.

Once airborne, Melisse eases her seat back after a big gulp of lemon-infused water and a good misting of Evian with orange blossom and grapefruit essences. She places a lavender-scented silky eye mask over her eyes, and contemplates going back to the little bedroom for a snooze.

Later, she thinks. *Right now…just calm down…you're in the right place at the right time, right where you need to be…don't question this…just live it…just breathe…you are on your way to see a client…a client whose patronage is jetting you to where you really want to be…La Fantasia…just be patient…this is just a step on your journey…*

Sometimes, when Melisse has a moment like this, when nobody can reach her, nobody can call or make a demand, when perfection is not expected…she sits in a seat hidden away where she can quietly be Melisse, and she thinks back over how she ever got to this place.

What led her to be sitting inside a slick private jet hurtling through the air between countries, the reluctant courtesan to a wily sheik? Will the path ever lead to her being the future owner of the world's most secret, sexy, and exclusive getaway for women: La Fantasia?

Her crazy choices as a younger woman turned out to lead to a life of privilege, certainly, but at a price. Sometimes it feels like a very high price when she lies alone at night, without a true love to cuddle her or talk with her. It especially feels like a high price on Saturday nights when joyful couples are out enjoying themselves in Manhattan, Rome, Paris, or South Beach, and she's either home alone, walking by herself in the streets of Manhattan (or Rome, Paris, or South Beach), turning a trick with someone she doesn't love, or being a "friend with benefits (and limits)" to one of her "Category B's."

Still, she wouldn't have chosen differently. Her spiritual teachings have taught her well, and she knows she is (probably) at the right place at the right time.

That reminds her. Time to talk to the Universe before jetting off again.

Universe, guide and protect and direct me on this trip. I trust you to keep me safe and send me everything I need and want, in the perfect moment I should have it.

And please, I affirm that you are sending me a perfect love, a perfect someone just for me, someday. Some way. You choose for me.

Spicy Secret: Live in the present, but take time to reflect on how you got there (and where you want to be in the coming years). But don't regret the past or worry too much about the future—the past no longer exists and the future is happy to take care of itself. Often in ways you'd never be able to predict.

Melisse closes her eyes behind her scented eye mask, breathes deep, and reflects on her journey.

How did a homely little girl from the countryside ever get on *this* particular wild magic carpet ride?

THE BEGINNING

CHAPTER 9

Stripping Scholarship

At eighteen years old, Melisse—suddenly "on her own" and living alone in New York City (and looking like a thirteen-year-old)—stood on a subway platform before her very first audition at a strip bar in Manhattan's financial district, where she assumed the tips would be more plentiful given the vicinity to the stock market.

She waited for the train, wearing a pair of white satin high-heeled lace-up granny boots, a short navy wool skirt with kick pleats like a schoolgirl's, and a matching checkered halter top with a plunging neckline. The getup created quite a stir, and men glanced furtively at her. It hadn't occurred to Melisse that it might be better to change from street clothes into her dancing clothes after she arrived at the club.

She emerged near Wall Street and walked along the street, letting the bright glints of sun settle around her shoulders, filling her lungs with the brackish air of the harbor to calm her nerves.

When she saw The Pussycat Lounge, she took a deep breath. There it stood on the corner, its darkened windows and flashing lights competing with the exaggerated shapes of buxom women silhouetted in its garish sign.

She opened the door and felt the energy drain out of her as she was overwhelmed by the scent of male sweat and stale cigarette smoke mingling with women's hairspray. Then it hit her—the vibration of lust, need, and loneliness—and for a moment she couldn't breathe.

But she stepped inside and entered the secret world of men who desperately need to worship at the altar of topless dancers.

Two nights later, she was pasting a dollar bill to her tummy with her own saliva, leaning back and shimmying her tiny breasts at a man who had asked her to play the "two for one" game with him. She said no and blew him a kiss, considering the game "beneath her."

"Prude," he said, scowling, waving her away. Another girl eagerly took her place and Melisse watched her put his offered dollar inside her Day-Glo G-string, rub it against her pussy, take it out, and give it back to him in exchange for two new dollars as he sniffed his scented money.

That same night, Melisse met Nathanial, Nate for short. He was a big, round, African-American bouncer at The Pussycat, a typical guard/pimp/dealer loaded down with chunky gold jewelry. He told Melisse to take off her police officer costume cap, and she did while continuing to tongue the golden whistle hanging around her neck. She'd purchased the costume the day before, feeling sure that she would end up using it after succeeding at her first audition.

When a customer looked up at her onstage and asked if her badge was real, she went down on her knees where he could see it better, displayed on the one covered triangle on her body that reflected mirrors and lights and turned each man's face into a star. She put her cap on him and slipped his tip into her fake meter maid notebook.

"May your time never expire," he toasted her as she moved down the stage to make another "arrest."

"You show promise. I'd like to introduce you around," Nate said at the end of her first shift. "Girl, when you walked in here I could see your tits were small, but your ass is as fine a specimen as I'll ever find. And I said, 'Here's a girl I can train and take under my wing.' It's a rare stripper who ain't got one or the other. And you sure do dance fine. And this is your first night? You got some costumes like I never seen! You're cool, little lady!"

Nate's white Cadillac had dark tinted windows, an electronic speedometer, and a stereo stacked like the "featured" dancer, Miss Cali Alps, 42DD-24-36, who'd be appearing at The Doll Spot that night. This was where Nate would take Melisse to audition. He opened the trunk to show Melisse that she would be riding along with several kilos of the finest, purest cocaine one could buy in Manhattan.

He also had a few guns in the back. Melisse had grown up with guns. She figured that if he had a few in the back, he probably had one hidden up front, too. *And on him.* Gun people were like that.

When Melisse got into the Caddy, Nate slipped his little pinkie under her nose. It held a small mound of the white stuff.

It would be a first, and her young life at this moment was filled with firsts.

"Sniff up—it's good stuff," he said.

She did as she was told, and it was indeed good, something she'd never tried before, and she liked it. She also felt totally normal and in control.

After they arrived at The Doll Spot, Melisse went downstairs to the dressing room to fix her makeup. Some of The Doll Spot girls were talking about the Cali Alps poster in the dressing room, Cali being a "featured" dancer with gargantuan boobs. Cali and her boobs traveled from city to city, dancing.

"Cali Alps. What's so special about some dumb blonde from California?" said Raven, a dark-haired, heroin-skinny dancer standing in the dressing room looking at the poster, putting Dermablend makeup over her raven tattoo. Big tattoos weren't allowed at The Doll Spot.

Melisse giggled, put her makeup kit on the counter, and sat down in a director's chair. "Yeah," a curvaceous woman agreed from the end of the counter as she applied mascara. "They should keep all the silicone in Silicon Valley where it belongs!"

Someone laughed from behind a locker. Raven was standing there, watching Melisse as Melisse made sure the seams in the back of her stockings were straight.

"Do you work here?" she asked. "Because you're either very early or very late for your shift."

"No," Melisse sighed. "I already did mine over at The Pussycat. I'm just visiting. I'm with someone."

"You mean someone brought you here *on a date?*"

"No!" Melisse cried. "Are you kidding?"

"Candy," Raven said to the girl hidden behind the lockers, "come over here. Get a load of this girl." Candy emerged and the two women stood evaluating Melisse from head to toe, not in a threatening way, but rather fondly.

"How old are you?" Raven asked.

"Eighteen."

"I don't believe it," her friend said. "My God, she looks like she's thirteen years old."

"Believe it," Melisse said. "They all think I'm a runaway." She nodded out toward the customers.

"*Are* you?"

"Well…in a way, I guess I am…I don't want to go home again."

"Why? Were your parents torturing you? Burning you with cigarettes? Or are you pouting because they didn't buy you a BMW for your sixteenth?" Candy asked.

"No, no. It's just…it's better if I make my own way in the world… now."

"Uh-huh."

"I think she needs therapy, don't you?" Candy said to Raven, in a sadly mocking voice.

"Does this look like a doctor's office to you?" Raven guffawed.

"Yeah!" Melisse joined in, giggling. "You two look like you could really teach me something!"

A few minutes later, the two women took the liberty of giving Melisse a full, unsolicited analysis of her professional potential as a stripper, starting with aesthetics:

"First, honey, I'm sorry, but you definitely need a boob job. Not too big, but just…a lot more than what you got. You need two big handfuls, so go for a 34B. And a chin implant wouldn't hurt—you look like a bird! And you need your eyes done, too, 'cause you look like you're half-asleep."

Candy added, "Yeah, like she's Japanese. Maybe she's on something."

"Yeah. NO. This girl? On something? Look at those dilated pupils. And…oh, how's the teeth?"

Melisse smiled big.

"Ohhhh, yeah," Raven laughed. "Get your teeth done. That's, like, the cost of a car but it's worth it. And some plumper lips. Get lipo around your tummy, too. You're a pudge."

"And your ass. It's your best feature," Candy piped in, "but get it higher up. Asses have nowhere to go but down. What goes up must come down!" she cackled.

"That's *it*?" Melisse asked sarcastically.

"Yeah, hon. THEN you can start making bank as a stripper around here!"

Candy whispered to Raven, "She seems more like someone who should be working, you know, in private. Doesn't she? Kinda quiet-like, and classy."

Melisse heard it and listened attentively.

Raven nodded. "Yeah, she strikes me more like one of those high-priced call girls—educated, maybe a little snobby. She doesn't belong here. You know, *those* girls wouldn't be caught dead in a place like *this*."

And *that,* indeed, seemed like a place Melisse wanted to be.

Melisse turned around and looked in the mirror. Maybe they were right. She sighed. But turning tricks was still solely in the realm of fantasy. And high-priced ones? What was *that* all about? She'd read plenty, as much as she could research about it, but still, crossing over from fiction to fact was not yet a possibility.

Spicy Secret: "Whatever the mind can conceive and believe, it can achieve." —Napoleon Hill

"What about hair extensions?" Melisse asked suddenly.

"Yeah," Candy said. "You could go blonde and get extensions. You'll be like a million bucks then. The light-brown thing? It's cute, but you know, you gotta be a *woman*. Like a little Marilyn Monroe. Not saying you need to look like a porn star. I'm not talking down to your ass. But just…"

"Anything else?" Melisse laughed, enjoying all the attention.

Spicy Secret: Even the most successful people are flattered to share their secrets for success. Don't be afraid—or too proud—to ask for their help and advice.

Candy tilted her head. "Yeah. I'm sorry to tell you this, but your nose really needs some refinement. It needs to get smoothed out and moved over to be more centered on your face. They'll probably have to break it, and it won't look pretty at first, but then you'll see…"

"But other than that, you're beautiful, kid," Raven said, slapping Melisse's ass.

Melisse laughed again, loving being innocent enough to slip through the cracks, loving being able to converse with these interesting "women of the night." She loved the pumping music as it permeated her psyche and compelled her to twirl around poles and dangle her spread legs off a stage, to hear the beat and lop off all the old parts, to dance and strip for men who offered up their American presidents' faces, especially the occasional hundred-dollar bill.

A man yelled down the stairs, "Hey, you girls get the fuck back up here and sell some drinks!" It was the harshest, ugliest command she'd ever heard, and she dreaded hearing it again.

"You look like a smart girl," Raven said on her way out. "You should go to college."

"*Back* to college," Melisse corrected.

Raven called behind her, "Yeah, back to Harvard, or wherever you dropped out of." Candy gave her a slap on the ass. "Bye, sweetie! See you around…"

As the girls ran upstairs, Melisse looked at herself in the mirror, remaining stoic. *So I got thrown to the wolves. So what. Now I'll be running with them.*

The proverbial rug had been pulled out from under her, and at a most inconvenient time in her young life. Here she was, still standing (and still shocked) in the dressing room of some strip joint in downtown NYC. It was an interesting turn of events after having just graduated from an elite boarding high school the summer before.

How could you do that to me?

She just took a deep breath instead. *Others have it worse—much worse. Suck it up.*

When she finished combing out her hair, Melisse found Nate back at the bar. He ordered her an introductory Pink Lady and she sipped at it, enjoying its sweetness as she watched Raven and Candy work the stage.

**Spicy Secret: "You can observe a lot by just watching."
—Yogi Berra**

"So why you wanna do this?" Nate asked curiously, taking Melisse a bit by surprise. Between the drinking and the coke, Melisse was becoming bolder than usual in her speech.

"Um, someone once told me when I was little, 'Hey! You know what a shopkeeper once said about strippers and hookers? It's a great business, this selling of your body—you got it, you sell it, you still got it!'" She laughed a hollow laugh.

"That's some fucked-up shit to be saying to a girl," Nate protested. It always amazed Melisse when scruffy guys showed their soft sides.

Nate sighed, his big stomach heaving. Melisse looked away and sighed, too. Her alter ego was back up in her cheap hotel room, staying up this late writing a literary analysis or some such. Now, here she was actually deep in life, and *living* the story of the slow descent (ascent?) of a young woman into the "demimonde," à la Émile Zola.

Back in the Cadillac, sliding toward the South Bronx, Nate talked nonstop.

"Melisse. I could get another dancer in this car who wouldn't be so shy. You don't have to be such a tightass! Here," he said, offering some white powder on the tip of his finger. "Sniff up all you want. This time my stuff is free, and if you want to buy more later, I'll set you up, all right? There's plenty more where that came from. Use my pinkie. There. This stuff ain't gonna hurt you. I'll hold your head steady on these New York potholes. I only use it myself every few weeks, like on nights like this. Hey, I've got a friend having a bachelor party in three weeks. For a couple of hours, there's major money in it for you, but it's full nude. Don't worry, I'll be there. Sound OK?"

Melisse sniffed, knowing this would be one of the first—and last—sniffs in her life. It was okay to try it, but she never wanted to be a slave to anyone or *anything*, and coke was well known to be one of the worst masters. She vowed to herself never to buy coke from this "kind man" with the money she earned by stripping.

"Yeah, sounds OK."

"Good. Remember, the entire time, I'm there and I'll take you on breaks. When Nate says it's time to go out and eat after, then we go out and eat. I've taken my dancing girls to City Island for the best lobster, the best of everything. Do you like lobster?"

> **Spicy Secret: In the dark and hidden corners of young female lives exist certain people, substances, and ideas that would seek to enslave, take advantage of, and exploit their trust and innocence.**
>
> **In an ideal world, their innocence would be protected and prolonged for as long as possible and at any cost. (And some young women need to be saved from themselves before it's too late). "Cheaping out" on our young women (by withdrawing love, emotional and financial support for their studies or ambitions, money for safe housing, etc.) is simply not an option.**

CHAPTER 10

Air on a G-String

Later that night, Melisse stood braless before Tony, of Tony's Wedge, a small "nightclub" in Hunts Point, the Bronx, where during the day, large warehouses took in fruit from around the world and processed it for delivery to the city.

At night, the club's blinking lights were the brightest thing next to the bonfires of the homeless and the lit eyes of crack-house denizens hidden away in the abandoned buildings.

"We want the gig pay, plus cab fare," Nate said to Tony, negotiating Melisse's fee for dancing gigs at Tony's Wedge.

"Done." Tony smiled at her, a handsome devil in his fifties and a former police chief. He handed Melisse a sleep shirt with his logo on it and a logo purse calendar. She was afraid to come up out of his basement office because she'd been told that shoot-outs were often heard in the parking lot.

"Melisse," Nate said, taking her aside in the stairwell outside Tony's office, "Tony would like to spend a little alone time with you, just getting to know you. Don't worry, nothing bad's gonna happen, he just likes to spend a little private time. Is that OK with you? You know, it's part of getting the job."

Under normal circumstances, Melisse might mind, but Tony was a darling, short, charismatic Italian guy with nice clothes, a nice smell, and a super smile.

"It's OK." She smiled. "You sure he won't hurt me?"

"Naaaa…the girls love him. They *fight* over him. You'll see."

When Melisse entered his office, Tony had a boom box turned on, playing Tina Turner's "Private Dancer." He approached her and sat down on the couch.

"Could I have a little lap dance, Melisse?" he asked with a smile. "We don't even need any music, just the rhythm of our beating hearts," he added with a wink.

Melisse walked toward him. "OK…" she said, and began slowly moving her hips, dancing, taking off one piece of clothing after another until she was wearing only her G-string.

Tony unbuttoned his shirt and unzipped his pants. She saw that he was wearing very thin, silky underwear, and the fabric was bulging with a short, meaty-looking cock. He motioned for her to come and sit on his lap facing him, which she did, placing her swelling clit, also covered by a patch of silky fabric, directly over the bulge in his underwear. The pleasure of his cock touching her clit through the fabric of her panties was instant, like a shot of heroin.

She gyrated her hips over his rod as he caressed her breasts, and he moved his hips just a little as she rubbed over and over on his cock, her clit swelling more with every turn. She felt his cock pressing inside her, but not going the distance, given the silken barriers between them.

Then, Tony took his hands and rubbed his fingers up through the nape of her neck and into her hair as they moaned together. The silky fabrics barely protected them from the powerful entry of his cock inside her wet, slick pussy.

"Ohhhhh, Melisse…"

"God…Tony, it's just…"

They both moaned together as their pleasure built. He held and guided her hips so they moved together in unison over his cock. Just the thought of being in this secret basement, sitting on the lap of this handsome older man, who was barely ramming his silk-covered cock inside her, but just rubbing it up and down on her, over her clit…ooh! He made her come so deliciously she moaned, just as he exploded with pleasure, too…

As Melisse collapsed on him, with her hands wrapped around his neck, she knew she would always remember Tony's wonderful spicy scent. This was a real milestone for her as she entered The Life, and she was grateful that she had been treated so well—in every way possible.

"Mmmmmm…that was…mmmmmm…" Melisse said, getting up. "I'm so wet. You're too much for me. I can feel everything through your shorts! But you knew that!"

"Me, too," he laughed, walking awkwardly to the bathroom with his pants halfway around his thighs. "That one made me feel like a teenager again. By the way, you're hired! But you knew that already."

Melisse went upstairs and was blinded for a moment by the bright, blinking lights around a stage. A girl, her skin taut over a smooth layer of baby fat, was climbing a pole, and winked at Melisse when she sat down. Melisse warmed to this new camaraderie, that of girls who actually wore stiletto heels for their intended purposes. These were girls who seldom made reference to Ivy League schools, or took low-paying first jobs in publishing, or talked about their futures with sickening assurance.

In fact, their lack of pretense was a comfort to Melisse, who had quickly learned to curb talking about school or accomplishments, and simply direct her attention to matters at hand, like getting her body sparkled up or de-slicking the bottoms of her high heels for safety on the sometimes wet bar tops.

"Did you enjoy your 'interview' with Tony?" the girl asked.

"Um, a little too much, I think." Melisse smiled shyly.

"How old are you?"

"Eighteen. And you?"

"I'm fifteen," the girl said. "I know I'm too young to be here, but I know I look older. Tony used to run the vice squad, so we do whatever we want up here. Just take good care of him and he'll take good care of you. You can make lots of money here on the weekends. You can work on the side downstairs, too, if you want, or meet people off-premises and send 'em to your place, or go to theirs. I'm going to buy a house soon. Cash, all clear. I do that five or six times over with some rentals and I'm set before I'm twenty. I get checks in the mail and then I can sit on my behind instead of showing it off. That's the name of the game."

Melisse marveled at the teenager's practical approach to surviving and thriving. For a fifteen-year-old, she was one smart cookie!

Eventually, Nate came back up and they hit a few more clubs in the Bronx and the edge of Queens for less spicy introductions. By 4:00 a.m., Melisse had some more bookings on her calendar, a nice beginning to her new career as an adult entertainer.

Nate drove Melisse toward Manhattan and her closet-size room at the Hotel Sixteen, a well-run "single room only" residential hotel where she shared a hall bathroom with ten other residents on her floor. And a few harmless roaches.

She became nervous. Maybe this wasn't the end of the ride. After all, the warehouses of the South Bronx could hide a multitude of threats to a young girl. She imagined herself crawling behind a dumpster to bleed to death in shame if her driver decided to rape and kill her in one of the abandoned warehouses.

Suddenly, she remembered Nate telling her that he had a son. "Hey," she offered, "as a thank-you for tonight, I'd like to take your boy to the park or the zoo sometime, if you ever need a babysitter."

> **Spicy Secret: Disarm and deflect potentially scary situations (and people) by openly showing your caring side or offering up a personalized favor to someone you fear may harm you. If it's a scary stranger approaching, and you're on a street where someone might hear you, just scream, "Get the hell away from me!" at the top of your lungs, over and over again. It may be embarrassing if the person isn't actually dangerous, but it may also save your life if they are.**

To her stunned surprise, the floodgates opened and an avalanche of secrets and anxieties spilled out of Nate. Sweat beaded on his forehead as he recalled that he might not see her tomorrow at the club because he had a shipment to pick up in another town.

"A shipment of what?" Melisse asked innocently.

"Guns," he said, "and other stuff."

"Oh, guns," she said casually. "My father taught me to shoot when I was six. I was on a .44 Magnum by the time I was twelve. That's when I got in an ummmm…let's call it a dispute…and almost accidentally killed my…"

"What the…? Girl, *do not* tell me about this. You are unbelievable. Some of the stuff that comes out of your mouth! It ain't true. Tell me that ain't true."

"It's all true…" But she trailed off without confessing and looked outside the window, turning her thoughts from the guns and instead remembering how, as a country girl, she'd been allowed to freely roam the acres of beautiful green hillsides surrounding her family's property. The two things she'd been given plenty of as a child and now held dear were freedom and independence.

And now, her parents had given her the gift of both, again, in the form of a "fiscal estrangement." Now she only had to turn it to her advantage.

It only took one season in the topless dancing world for Melisse to become disenchanted. Dancing for a living made her feel like a robot, doing the same hip-swaying motions over and over again in front of the same men, but in different clubs, the men all slack-jawed and staring.

Then, there was the same revolving series of strip clubs that had booked her through her new "dancing agent," each dressing room and stage more and more disgusting in its own distinctive way.

As to having a real conversation with the customers? Forget it. She learned to be pleasant, but mostly silent with the customers, knowing better than to clue them in to who she really was. That would only diminish their fantasies of her as a vapid, insatiable, energetic, sexually provocative stripper eager to do just about anything for money, with the stage dancing just a prelude of other options available.

In reality, she was an introverted intellectual and barely out of virginity, having had sex for the first time only a few months before she'd started dancing! She'd found it to be much more pleasant and addictive than all the coke she was being offered.

She was so "green," in fact, that on one of her first nights dancing alone without the benefit of Nate, two men in Staten Island at the aptly named "Ziggy's Clam Bar" invited her out back to do some "Eight Ball." She concluded that they merely wanted to show her a cute device sold at toy shops, and known as a Magic 8 Ball, which would predict her future. Little did she know that when she judiciously rejected the offer of the "psychic ball," she was rejecting yet another offer of drugs that they hoped would lure her into a compromising position.

She didn't want to know her future, if it was just going to be more of this depressing grind.

During her days off, her limbs throbbed with pain, even though she was as strong and flexible as she ever could be. She got so she couldn't work two nights in a row, the cigarette smoke and late hours draining her more and more of her exuberance and innocence, her two biggest selling points (besides her strawberry-like nipples).

"Let's call you Strawberry Shortcake, like the doll," Nate had said once, while offering her another ride in his Caddy (and a pack of sniffs).

"Yes, OK," Melisse sighed.

"Yes to what? Wanna ride along?"

"Yes to the name, only," she said, hailing a cab from her afternoon gig at The Pussycat, which would whisk her away to Queens for a night of dancing at some equally repugnant strip joint.

> **Spicy Secret:** Make up a distinctive, darling nickname or persona for yourself as an erotic entertainer. Personas are wonderful shields for the "real you" to hide behind and help your patrons remember you.

CHAPTER 11

Strawberry Shortcake with Brown Sugar

A few weeks later, Nate picked up Strawberry Shortcake/Melisse in his Cadillac and handed her an envelope containing several large bills. "You keep what tips you earn, too," he said.

"I thought it was supposed to be more," she replied as she counted the money.

He gave her a look. "Hon, I don't set these things up out of the goodness of my heart. This is business."

"Oh."

"Wanna sniff up?" he asked Melisse. She shook her head. One night of sniffing up was enough. She possessed exceptional powers of discipline when it came to drugs and alcohol. Melisse knew if she sniffed again, the sniffing would never end.

"That's good. You know how to say no."

They drove out into Queens and picked up a girl Nate called "Brown Sugar," who got into the front seat with them. Nate handed her a fat envelope with a lot more cash than Melisse had in hers. The girl wore a tight red leather skirt, a matching bandeau top, and red leather over-the-knee boots. It was some getup, and she wore it with confidence, like a costume that she'd worn a thousand times when playing a certain role.

Melisse had made the mistake of wearing her white satin high-heeled granny boots and a tight stretchy white lace minidress. She'd pictured a private room in a steakhouse somewhere.

She didn't sense that anything was amiss with the car when they stopped in front of an auto repair garage somewhere on the industrial edges of Queens near JFK airport. "*This* is where we're dancing?"

"Hmmmm, mmmm…looks to be it." Brown Sugar nodded, sighing. "Nate baby, you have really outdone yourself this time."

"Sugar, don't start. You two girls get down off your high horses. OK, Melisse," Nate prepped her. "You be the warm-up and the backup, the touch and fluff. Sugah here does the main stuff, the fuck and suck, okay, girls?"

Melisse nodded and looked nervously at Sugar, who said nothing.

"Last chance to sniff up," Nate said. Sugar nodded and took in a little coke from Nate's tiny spoon. It seemed to help her "get into character" to go into the garage and rock the guys' world.

Melisse would just do it cold turkey.

"These boys paid premium for our entertainment instead of forking over for food and location, so if you girls can work around the oil spots and the tarps, these boys can have themselves a nice party."

Run! Run now! Melisse thought. *But where?* Melisse looked at her boots and her outfit: it was the white someone would wear if she were a bride. Melisse's thoughts turned for a moment to the naive fiancé of this greasy garage groom. She'd bet she was in this very moment fussing over her oh-so-white dress, with no real idea what all 'da boys' (including hers) were getting up to.

Pull it together.

The guys in the garage were almost bursting to its rafters with anticipation. Twelve or so men—clearly not educated, worldly, sensitive types—stood around listening to a radio blasting out of a car parked inside the garage. They drank from beer cans and threw the empties into a corner. Melisse tried to vibe out who was the nicest-looking guy (the kindest, actually) so she could have a "friend" among the men in the bunch.

Seeing two young women walking into the garage perked them up right away, and they stood a little taller, cutting out the swearing and grumbling for a few minutes. They'd gotten tired of looking at each other, smelling each other, and making lewd remarks about the photos of calendar babes posted on the walls.

They quickly formed a circle around Sugar and Melisse. Nate stepped aside. It wasn't his job to be an MC; he was there to bring in and protect the girls, so he held his fists and his gun inside his jacket and watched through his dark tinted sunglasses as the events unfolded.

Sugar had done this all before, so she said, "Hey, boys. I'm Sugar and this here is Melisse, and we're here to dance and party with you! So who's the groom and who's the best man?"

The men hooted and pointed to a shy bear of a guy fiddling with the music player in the car, getting one of Sugar's music collections going. He was the groom. The man making the most noise was, naturally, the best man.

Soon, some decent music came on and Sugar said into Melisse's ear, "We'll act like lesbians for a while and then we'll go down the row. You tease 'em while they're waiting and then I'll do my thing. If we're lucky, we'll get out in under an hour. They'll touch you, so get them going and make it easy for me. I don't wanna be here screwing these assholes forever."

It was news to Melisse that they had permission to touch her. She had rarely, if ever, let a customer get too intimate without her agreement. Lap dances quickly became "slap dances" when a customer went too far, and many of the better clubs didn't allow it, either.

She looked over at Nate, who nodded. Sugar had her arms around Melisse's neck, and Melisse put hers around Sugar's waist. They looked into each other's eyes as the music began and the garage spun around, rubbing each other through their clothes. Dancing around, they snapped their garters hoping for tips, but nobody contributed. At this point, Sugar intensified the action as she slid Melisse's dress up and over her head while Melisse wiggled Sugar's skirt down off her hips and unlaced her leather halter. Eventually, the girls were wearing nothing but their G-strings.

The men came alive, hooting with enthusiasm as Melisse put her face between Sugar's breasts. She tried to hold her breath, but she could smell the residue of her red leather and eventually the powdery smell of the baby wipes she must have used to keep herself and her kids clean.

Melisse ran her tongue up and down the inside of Sugar's thighs. Sugar turned Melisse around, bent her over, and pulled at her G-string with her bared teeth, then eased it down her legs as Melisse stepped out. Here she was, totally nude in a greasy garage in Queens, filled with men clapping and going wild.

Melisse and Sugar wiggled and rubbed their bodies together and Sugar pulled the best man over to get sandwiched in between them. His callused hands cupped Melisse's breasts from behind, and she gasped as he pinched and pulled hard on her nipples. Was he trying to pull them off the top of her breasts and take them home with him? Melisse reached her hands up and dug her fingernails into his knuckles.

"Ow! Stop that!" Melisse screamed, but he couldn't have heard her over the music and nobody seemed to care. Finally, he let go.

Sugar's body was moving frantically in a way that said, *Let's hurry, let's get this over with*, and Melisse felt his hands reach down, grab her bottom, and spread her cheeks apart. She winced, wondering, *Does he think I get any pleasure out of this?* How could he derive any satisfaction from hurting her? She wondered if men like him waited for occasions like this so they could treat a woman harshly. They probably figured that women for hire were wired differently than regular women, and being "slutty" made it okay to be rough.

Sugar and Melisse sent the best man back into the small crowd and invited the shy groom into their sandwich. Their friends pushed the groom forward because he was shy, and when the girls danced with him they turned inward to "smother him" with four breasts and their hips. Melisse liked him much better than the others. She grabbed around his big belly and rubbed it while he buried his face in the nape of Sugar's neck, probably out of embarrassment.

Here she was, having gone from scholarship ceremonies and academic prizes to dancing nude for hooting men in a greasy garage, all in the space of one short year. Suddenly, Melisse was fighting off an instinct to cry. *I wish this were different. I wish I were different. If only I knew what to do. I'm lost.*

She came back to the present as Sugar led the first man off to a dark corner. Melisse still has indelible images of Sugar kneeling before the man, blowing him, and realizing, *Thank God she wore those thigh-high boots because the leather will protect her knees. She knows what she's doing!*

Sugar indeed moved like a dancer, easing down on one guy after another, tearing condom wrappers apart with her bare teeth. Fucking behind cars, fucking in the garage office, fucking inside broken cars, her hips gyrating in circles, their jeans and underwear pulled down around their ankles.

The images continued. Melisse saw Sugar bent over a car saying, "Come on, baby, come for me, baby" while someone nailed her on the hood of a Toyota, the flesh of her bottom rippling. Melisse saw Sugar on her knees, her mouth in an *O* wrapped around a guy's cock. Melisse saw *him*, the groom, seemingly so shy and gentle, grab Sugar's ponytail while she blew him as he sat in the front seat of one of the repair cars. His teeth were clenched, his face set in a grimace, and he guided her to suck him up and down at the exact slow pace he wanted her to go. When he finally came in one long groan, it was all over.

When the groom walked away, Melisse ran to Sugar with a bottle of water and a Handi Wipe from her purse. Sugar sat down on the car seat, like a spent athlete who'd just finished a race.

The party was over, and where was Melisse? Melisse was right there with Sugar, getting them ready as they lined up for their turn to fuck Sugar. Melisse watched her because she couldn't bear to watch herself in this place.

Instead, Melisse went somewhere else mentally while they relentlessly pinched her nipples and manhandled her breasts until they were bruised like thin-skinned fruits. Her ass was aflame, marked from their grabs to make her come to them, and their slaps to make her go away. Their rough whiskers burned into her neck where they had attempted to sloppily kiss her before she pushed them away in mock coyness. All of this, of course, she provided with a smile as Nate watched it all from afar. She tricked herself into not crying, telling herself she was taking control, for the first time in her life, taking control…

Spicy Secret: "We are all in the gutter, but some of us are looking at the stars." —Oscar Wilde, *Lady Windermere's Fan*

Becoming a stripper had actually given Melisse control over her emotions, but not her circumstances. As a teenager, she had obsessed over boys who didn't want her, and had written tearful love letters that later made her the object of derision.

And now, she was learning how to control her emotions, even under the harshest of circumstances. This control applied to herself, her emotions, and men.

But while she received a lot of attention that night in the garage, it wasn't the kind she really needed. She yearned for the kind that had come earlier from tutors and teachers who had coddled her at boarding school, and the professors from her short-lived time in college. *How can I go back to that?*

Nate drove the girls home in silence. Sugar sat up front, counting her money and thanking Nate as she slammed the car door on her way out. Melisse lay in the backseat with her trench coat wrapped around her. She took off her white satin boots for the ride. She was too ashamed to wear the soiled things back to her room at the Hotel Sixteen in the East Village. She'd rented a closet-size room there with peeling floral wallpaper and paid for it by the week, but oddly enough, she found it quite charming and beautiful, and endeavored to always carry herself in there as if it were the Ritz-Carlton. Given her soiled boots, she preferred to go past the "doorman" barefoot.

"Melisse, you with me?" she heard Nate ask from the front as they went through the Midtown Tunnel.

"Yeah?"

"Listen, hon. I want to tell you about someone. I help take care of some private business for a lady named GG, uptown. You know what she runs? She runs an old-fashioned BOR-dello—a real swanky house of pleasure—right up in the middle of the Plush Side. I'm talkin' the Upper East Side. Girl, these honeys make bank! If I was a woman, I'd sign up with her myself!"

Something sparked inside Melisse. Here was an "inside invitation" to her curiosity about a career as a high-priced call girl.

"Really?"

"Girl, would you like to meet GG? 'Cause I have a feeling she'd *love* to meet *you*."

"Ummmmmm…"

"Ah. OK. I gotcha. It's a little bit intense for you to think about right now."

"Well," she began. Actually, the idea intrigued her. "I'm thinking about it. A lot."

"OK, just let me know when you're ready. But we gotta talk soon, 'cause I see this stripping stuff is like, eating you up alive. You're not like when you first started out. I can't take a girl on gigs when she's like this."

To her surprise, Nate launched into a long, coked-up monologue as Melisse sat up and listened in the back. It was all about what she should and should not do if she started working in GG's uptown bordello.

Apparently, it was a completely different world and way of life than stripping. He made it sound as if she were going away to *marry* this lifestyle. Little did she know that everything he said was true, as she would find out. And some did…marry the lifestyle…forever.

He'd said, "Keep control, keep quiet, keep love, keep faith." She would be OK if she could remember all his advice, but how quickly time and the distractions of The Life had faded her recollection of Nate's instructions.

When she climbed out of Nate's Cadillac that night and walked up the stairs of the Hotel Sixteen, she had a feeling she had turned a corner in her life, and as Nate drove away, his car seemed to dissolve into a million little white pieces, blowing away like snowflakes of cocaine.

Spicy Secret: "When it becomes more difficult to suffer than to change…you will change." —Robert Anthony

Spicy Secret: "Leap and the net will appear." —Unknown

CHAPTER 12

GG's House of Pleasure

One afternoon shortly after the bachelor party in the greasy garage, Melisse stood before the beautiful, gray stone building that housed Gillian Gladly's posh brothel. There were flowers in every flower box and the tall windows were veiled by cream-colored taffeta curtains that both hid and hinted at the luxury inside.

Melisse was nervous, but she had been graciously encouraged by GG, over the phone, to come in for an interview. She tugged at the pretty but ill-fitting floral dress she'd bought at a thrift shop. She looked like she was going to church.

Once she keyed in the correct "intro code" Nate had secured for her, the door was released and Melisse entered a small entry hall with another door to the inside. She noted the camera lens in the corner and nodded. It was a reassuring sign that GG took her security seriously.

After a few minutes, a housekeeper wearing an all-black outfit ushered her further inside, where she was offered a variety of drinks. "Thanks, I'm fine," she said, but she was extremely nervous.

Soon, Melisse was led through a long hallway that appeared to have sliding doors on the right. She was deposited in an enclosed, cozy space in the back of the home. She loved the brilliant navy wainscoting—she'd never seen anything like it.

The room appeared to be a waiting area for the girls, decked out with a huge water dispenser, comfortable couches and chairs, and closets, bookshelves, and mirrors lining the walls. Melisse felt as if she were no longer in America, but possibly in Europe as she'd imagined it. She hadn't traveled outside the USA yet, but she loved the continental feeling she got in this beautiful place.

She stood waiting by the glass door leading to a set of stairs that went down into a lush back garden. There, on the patio beneath colorful lanterns strung up from end to end, stood four of the most uniquely beautiful and international women she'd ever seen. Sexy, yes, but effortlessly so.

These are prostitutes? she wondered. They were fresh-faced and innocent-looking, just relaxing barefoot and laughing, dipping their knives into a big cheese wheel set out on an iron table patterned with mosaic tiles.

You'd never guess.

The women wore loose, silky gowns that shimmered colorfully, like exquisite koi fish reflecting in a green pond. Melisse realized that she was staring, so she stepped back from the glass door, embarrassed.

Spicy Secret: Keep an open mind when encountering a safe but unfamiliar situation. You may be pleasantly surprised by what—or who—comes next.

At the same time, on the top floor in the bedroom of her town house, Gillian Gladly sat at her lighted boudoir mirror, rubbing rose-scented African shea butter into her hands. She credited that daily ritual (among many others!) with having preserved her youthful appearance. Now, in her early sixties, she could, when made up properly, pass for twenty years younger. Or so the girls told her.

GG, as she was known to her girls and friends, wore a silky housedress printed with large pink cabbage roses and satiny slippers. She was slender but sturdy, with a childlike giggle that only added to her charm.

She was so perfectly well preserved, with such a pert body, that it wouldn't have surprised Melisse to learn that GG still took care of some of her original clients who were now friends and came for a weekly card game in her apartment on the top floor.

Her blonde hair was cut into an impeccable, long pageboy, and her blue eyes were often dreamy. Her easy smile was painted on delicately with tiny brushstrokes of a subdued coral lipstick.

And she was a consummate businesswoman. *Pleasure* was her business, make no mistake about that!

Now she was preparing to meet Melisse, a new girl waiting downstairs who had been recommended by Nate, her combination "fixer" (of any security issues or problems) and "transporter" (of cash payments to law enforcement and the Mafia, when requested.) Lately, he had also become a "liaison" (an introducer of any upscale, new members who came in through the world of the strip clubs Nate frequented). Occasionally, he would introduce dancers to GG if he thought they could become assets for her thriving business.

GG looked at herself in the mirror and—as always happened when meeting a new girl—felt small darts of guilt flash around in her mind. There was still something wrong with sending out women in the erotic servicing of men, yet what could she do when she herself was no longer able to service them?

She'd felt the same pangs of guilt when she'd first started thirty years ago. When she began getting requests from her clients for introductions to other women, she reluctantly made the introductions. Little by little, new clients and new women came along whom she could add to her list, all willing to offer erotic services in discreet settings, first in Paris where she'd started, then New York, then in other big American cities, then more internationally.

GG never had to advertise, as "word of mouth" was enough in those very early days. But GG had eventually conceded to a media-driven world and set up a discreet campaign in a worldwide newspaper. And while it cost a small fortune to dominate its classifieds and create a monopoly for herself, the men her ads attracted into her web were fat and juicy spiders, indeed.

And she made sure they were wrapped in silk threads.

As far as she was concerned, she provided a valuable service to her girls: carefully screening, classily marketing, and setting up appointments for women who absolutely knew they wanted to be courtesans, call girls, escorts, or *companions*.

Her cut of 30 percent was modest by modern standards, yet her worldwide volume more than made up for it. She felt that 30 percent was all she deserved for setting women up in a lifestyle that had the potential—for many—to bring loneliness, isolation, depression, and shame. That was the high price of living The Life.

But for those who were willing to pay the price, The Life could also offer incomparable opportunities, freedom, surprising adventures, and—for some—romance.

Spicy Secret: High stakes can bring matching highs—and lows.

GG's biggest source of pride were the marriages that she had brought together over the years by engineering "matches made in heaven" between some of her more open-minded clients and some of her more marriage-minded girls.

If she could have done anything in life besides being a madam, she would have become a very private, exclusive, and international matchmaker working on behalf of love, instead of lust. She'd never bought into the idea of it being "too late" to do something you wanted in life, regardless of one's age. *It's still not too late to become the world's most exclusive matchmaker*, she thought to herself as she powdered her nose. *What about it?*

She sighed. It might not be too late, but she was tired. The phones were ringing. They could go to voice mail, they could put their cocks on ice, and she would call them back after her interview with the potential new girl, Melisse.

Cocks on ice can always get heated back to life.

She chuckled to herself. Cock was so predictable.

Cock paid. And well.

And cock always came back for more. The world over.

And for centuries past it was that way, and it would be for centuries to come.

God love cock.

Now, she sat down for a moment on her tufted red velour couch, where her big orange tabby lay sleeping in a perfect crescent.

She stroked his fur. "I love you so much. Do you love Mama?" He stretched a little and purred. She smiled and felt a warm glow inside, then arose to go downstairs to meet Melisse.

CHAPTER 13

A House for All Seasons and Reasons

"You must be Melisse!" a friendly voice said behind a nervous Melisse, who stood in the dressing/waiting room of the house, looking out onto the back garden.

GG smiled. This was a pretty, small young thing who obviously needed a *lot* of help in the style and beauty department, but her "vibration" felt right. The girl gave off nothing but a sweet, smart energy. In courtesan circles, sweet and smart were the only "natural" ingredients a lady really needed. Everything else was icing on the cake.

"I'm GG. It's lovely to meet you, Melisse," she went on encouragingly. "Would you like to take a tour of the place?" she asked, opening the sliding wood parlor door and revealing a room of such generous proportions that Melisse faltered a bit before walking in.

"Don't worry. It's always a bit slow this time of day. There's only one bedroom occupied right now."

The ceiling of what GG and the girls referred to as "The Living Room" seemed to soar, the room glowing in a warm lamplight. The tall windows faced the street, flanked by sheer gathered curtains that rustled out gently and fell back to the floor.

The largest rug decorating the floor was a subtle Tabriz featuring images of hunters and their prey—lean white gazelles and men with arches. Thoughtful bouquets of flowers were set atop the antique tables and up on a rosewood *étagère*.

Later, Melisse would learn that one of GG's greatest joys was arranging the flowers. They were there to remind everyone that there was a grand mistress running the house!

Melisse clearly admired the arrangement of the furnishings, the materials, and the color palette. GG used a term Melisse had never heard before: "*feng shui.*"

"I tried to give this room a good *feng shui* that makes men want to make love with my girls!" and then she giggled to herself in a delightful tittle. "See? We even have small bamboo plants. These welcome money into our space."

Melisse detected a slight French accent in GG's manner of speaking, but chose to leave GG's origins a mystery until she got to know her better.

GG swept her hand around the room and explained that when they had a "meet and greet" she liked to leave plenty of room for her patrons and her girls to move around and mingle. That explained the refreshing lack of clutter in her expansive living room. She said that clients at first liked to keep their distance, not wanting to feel as if they've just gotten into bed with everyone in the house. The girls needed to be able to stretch out, to let the men look at them and decide which one they wanted. They also loved the mirrors in the room that revealed what was happening from moment to moment.

GG led Melisse to an elegant divan, where they sat down in front of a silver tray containing small bowls of deliciously spiced pretzels and snacks. They began sipping iced teas that had been brought in by the housekeeper, in glasses with tall spoons. It was the first time Melisse had seen "simple syrup" served in a small glass pitcher, and she used it to sweeten her tea. Elegant and gracious rituals would eventually become the norm for her, but on this day, it was a first.

"Do you have a home, people, parents? A project, school, a boyfriend?" GG asked suddenly, and Melisse was taken aback by the directness of the questions.

"Um…sort of," Melisse replied, scrambling for a good answer.

GG looked at her intently. "Why are you really here, young lady? Apart from the money you can make," GG added with a brief smile.

"I'm not sure *why* I'm here," Melisse admitted honestly. "I feel something inside me that says I need to upgrade my life, get back into school and stop working at strip bars! It's killing me, physically and spiritually. Does that answer your question?"

Upgrade my life? By starting work in a brothel?

"Yes, dear, more than adequately," GG replied. "Now, I'll talk a bit if you may allow me. You said one thing that told me all I need to know about you. You said that strip bars were killing your spirit. I believe, my dear, that the *Divine* brought you here on a special assignment! Some people think *we* are the sewer of the society, but I say we are *not* the sewer: we are the *saviors* of society! Just imagine a world where horny men everywhere are unable to get their needs taken care of! It would be *a disaster out there*, wouldn't it!"

"Oh yes."

"Well, I believe that God brought some of us down to the earth to care for the lonely men who need our services. And we will be rewarded for it, in the end. *We* are His fallen angels, sent here on an earthly mission, should we choose to accept it. We are spiritual beings, children of God, having a human experience as divine courtesans. We were sent to comfort people, and *for this* we are well paid for our time. This is a divine calling, my dear. Never forget it, and never question it."

Spicy Secret: The Divine speaks to us in unexpected ways, through unexpected people, and in all kinds of unexpected situations.

"Yes," Melisse said. "Yes, yes, yes, yes. I've been waiting to hear that for a long time."

Melisse caught a look at herself in one of the large mirrors. GG said, "You're a pretty girl, Melisse, no question about that. I don't even need to see you undressed to know you have what it takes physically to become successful. You're not the typical high-end call-girl type, that tall, model-y kind of girl, but let me tell you: the short Napoleons of the world would just adore towering over you! And *they're* the ones with all the power and the money. I'd call you our 'Living Doll.' You could be *spectacular*.'"

That beats Strawberry Shortcake.

"With your personality, you could go a long way. Beauty gets the men in, but after that, it's all about character, education, bearing, and charm. That can keep them coming back. For years. The question is: Are you strong enough to take on this responsibility?"

Melisse sat quietly, contemplating this. *Am I strong enough yet?*

GG said, "Let's go upstairs and see the bedrooms."

They climbed the stairs together to get to the most mysterious part of the house.

"Now, let me show you around. We have five bedroom suites: Peacock's Lair, Zen Retreat, Tropical Heat, Paradise Found, and the Honeymoon Suite."

Melisse drank in the drama of the various room decors as GG led her through the bedrooms and the en suite marble bathrooms on each floor. Melisse asked her lots of questions about how the rooms had been designed, and GG seemed delighted that she was genuinely interested.

> **Spicy Secret: When outfitting your "lair" for sensual business activities (and unless you are prepared to do a lot of laundry or send it out), it's a good idea to invest in anything but white, pale, or solid-colored sheets. Go for high-quality, colorful floral or other patterned "flat" (not fitted) sheets. The patterns clean well and hide the inevitable stains from sweat, oils, and lubricants… And flat sheets enable you to stack them one on top of the other for easy changing between visitors.**

"You know," GG explained, "I just wanted to create a place where my girls can feel dignified and the clients can feel glorified. A bit bigger than life."

And at that moment, Melisse felt as if she really was a fallen angel who'd finally found an earthly home.

GG led Melisse down the hall back to the staircase, hesitating for a moment, then feeling it would be OK.

"Would you like to come up for a hot tea?" she asked. "It *is* tea time." Melisse got the impression this was a rare occurrence, the inviting of someone to GG's apartment. "Oh yes," she said, "I'd love to."

They went up another flight of stairs, and GG confessed, "Sometimes I think the only reason I started this house of pleasure was to have an excuse to decorate it!" she laughed, and then, out of the blue, "Do you feel at home here?"

"Oh yes! Well, it's so…*pretty* here. And luxurious. It's exactly the way *I* would have decorated it, and in that way I feel very at home here, but…"

"But," Gillian interrupted gently,"you're probably thinking there's just something about having sex with all these men for money; it kind of turns your stomach when you really think about it, despite all the comforts I've provided here."

GG's housekeeper ran down the stairs carrying a basket of laundry; she nodded to them.

"Yes. I guess so. I wish I didn't…" Melisse apologized.

GG motioned with her hand as if to say, "Don't apologize." She opened her door with a series of keys and they went in. Melisse was definitely on a roll. Now, she sat down on a nearby red chenille chair.

While GG excused herself to make the tea in a small kitchenette off the parlor, Melisse looked around at the red walls faux finished to look like suede, and covered with gold-framed landscape paintings. Every surface was covered with framed photos of GG as a younger woman on what appeared to be many different exotic travels, and often with distinguished-looking men.

Later, as they sipped a wonderful Earl Grey tea with lavender flowers out of unmatched elegant china cups, GG asked, "What are you thinking, dear?"

"Well, I've always been so fascinated by prostitutes—excuse me, *courtesans*—and now I'm finally here and I believe I could *try* to become one, but I don't think I can go through with it. You know, I never do anything I don't want to do until I'm *ready* to do it!" Melisse was suddenly out of breath.

GG stood and put her hand down firmly on Melisse's shoulder. "Melisse, please calm down. Nobody's going to tie you to a bed and make you do *anything*."

Melisse breathed in deeply and let out a long sigh.

GG went on, "It's not like the movies. We're not into white slavery here. Many ladies choose this for their life very deliberately. They're the ones I call 'my angels.'"

Then, to her shock, Melisse heard GG say, "Melisse, dear, I don't want you stepping in here again until you're absolutely sure you're ready. Some girls I allow in because they're finishing college, or starting a business, or wanting to pay off some debts, but you're not any of those things yet… Not even *you* really know why you're here yet. You're all of what? Eighteen years old?"

"Yes…"

"*Mon Dieu*, going into The Life now would ruin you. Forever. I could never live with myself."

All the stress of the day—getting ready for this important interview and facing the possible realization of her personal dreams, finally caught up with Melisse, and small tears ran down her cheeks. She rubbed them away with the heels of her hands as GG handed her a soft handkerchief embroidered with "GG."

"You mean I can't work here now?" Melisse asked incredulously, the letters embroidered on the handkerchief blurring as her eyes filled with more tears.

"No, I'm sorry," GG said firmly. "It's not time…"

"But I thought you liked me! And I like you," she added shyly.

"It's not a question of me liking you, which I do, very much," GG said sincerely. "It's just that you're not well enough educated in life—yet! You don't know the secrets of seduction or how to deal with men because you haven't had much life experience. And from your tears, I can see that you can't control your emotions fully. And *that* means you won't know how to control men, which is essential to your well-being as a professional."

As Melisse sniffed, GG went on, "And, you don't have a real dream yet to keep you going so you don't piss away all the money you'll make! That's the worst thing that an escort can do: piss away all the money she earned lying on her back, kissing disgusting men she doesn't love, spending the best years of her life servicing horny men who don't really give a damn about her. I mean, I'm saying it like it is!"

She didn't know it at the time, but Melisse would keep this handkerchief all her life, considering it a treasured possession and a reminder of GG's restrained advice in the face of Melisse's youthful foolishness.

GG smiled over at Melisse and finally Melisse took a deep breath and smiled back.

"You're right," she admitted reluctantly. "You're right. What should I do now?"

"Of course I'm right!" GG laughed. "I'm sixty-something years old. I know everything by now. First, you must get yourself back into school and get out of those depressing dance halls or strip clubs or whatever you call them. See more of the world, and when you're ready, I want you to come back to me a *cultivated* woman."

Spicy Secret: The more you have to offer, the more you'll receive in return.

"But…I don't have the money to see the world…"

"Bah! The money. This is America! Go get yourself some student loans, get a part-time job. *Read*. Learn! I'll be waiting for you if you want to come back, but you need to make it on your own. That way, what you'll offer my men will be more substantial. I want you to dazzle them with your intellect, your knowledge, your humor, your sexual prowess. Learn some languages, study literature, the cinema, massage therapy, and whatever you do: get some great oral skills! That means: conversing *and* blow jobs. That's how you get—and keep—the great clients, those with the ability to really change your life with their money, or their power, or whatever they have to offer. Clients don't want to be bored with some vapid model."

"Really?"

"And when they love you, they give and they give big. Even though they might not be able to carry on a traditional relationship with you, or marry you, men who love and value having you in their life will always find other ways to show it, by helping you."

> **Spicy Secret: Beauty is a marketable power. Enhance it. Preserve it. Showcase it. It's your "stock in trade" until someone discovers your inner beauty, intelligence, and your caring soul. And those things outshine all others.**

"And…" GG hesitated a moment, as if she wanted to say something but couldn't because it might hurt.

"And…" Melisse asked, "what else?"

"Dear, I don't want you to think I'm shallow. But you must *look the part*. If you come back, I want you to get a chin implant and put in some bigger breasts, but not too big! You need an eye job to open up those eyes and some liposuction on your tum and bum. Then, go fix your teeth. Your nose, it needs smoothing out. And perhaps decide on just one hair color," she said with a final wink.

God, that's what Candy and Raven told me on my first day dancing!

As Melisse sat there, stunned by GG's inventory of her lacks, her mentor-to-be added, "Don't worry, I'll set you up with someone good when the time is right. It will take a few months to make your transformation complete, but once you're in here, you'll pay it all off within a year. Just focus on getting yourself a good education, and the world will be your oyster."

Melisse sat silent, dumbfounded by this new turn of events.

"Will you do those things for yourself, my Living Doll?"

"Yes, I will, Ms. Gladly."

"Call me GG," she heard as the older woman rose, clearly signaling farewell.

GG gave Melisse a warm and knowing look and then walked her to the door, where she took her into a motherly embrace.

"See you back here for teatime in about five years, *darling*."

CHAPTER 14

From Temp to Temptress

Five years would pass before Melisse saw GG again. She had followed GG's instructions to the letter, learning word processing as a marketable skill so she could leave topless dancing behind. She found a day job as a temporary secretary, roving from company to company like a ghost. Eventually, she made enough money to pay her own tuition to a small liberal arts college, where she took evening courses. Every free moment not spent preparing for her courses was spent "becoming cultivated" by teaching herself French and Italian, and she devoted a significant amount of her time to studying the worlds, places, manners, and ways of the rich. She lived for the moments she spent at the library sifting through fashion, business, and travel magazines, as well as visiting the great art museums of New York City.

One renowned museum even gave her a part-time weekend job as an usher for its concerts and art history lectures. This work introduced her to the world of classical art and music (and sometimes she assisted at the museum's extravagant galas and fundraisers). The job exposed her to the wealthy, fashionable, and glamorous women who attended, whom she studied carefully for every nuance, as if they were people from another culture and she was an anthropologist studying (and hoping to copy) them.

> **Spicy Secret:** "'Glamour' is assurance. It is a kind of knowing that you are all right in every way, mentally, and physically and in appearance, and that, whatever the occasion or the situation, you are equal to it."
> —Marlene Dietrich

But for her, most of her day-to-day work life (apart from her courses and the great museum gig) lacked luster. She hated the offices in those cold skyscrapers she ascended to after scurrying underground in the subway like a rat. Then, when she arrived, there'd be the petty politics at each company, as she suppressed her personality to fit into corporate life. She cringed when being announced to her ever-revolving cast of fleeting employers, like a sandwich that had just arrived at the front desk: "The temp is here! Where should I put her?"

Melisse was able to move out of the Hotel Sixteen and rent a small apartment in a nice part of Brooklyn, where she lived alone. GG had suggested she find some lovers to practice her sexual skills on, and her handpicked suitors were always eager to stop by to enjoy her seemingly insatiable desire for sex. Little did they know that they were short-term practice models to achieve her long-term goal—getting back to GG and entering The Life.

During that period, which GG would teasingly call Melisse's "promiscuous years" (with a wink, of course, followed by, "You went from temp to temptress in five easy years!"), Melisse made a major discovery.

> **Spicy Secret:** "The hardest task in a girl's life is to prove to a man that his intentions are serious."
> —Helen Rowland

She discovered that most men seemed to secretly want *something for nothing,* and if they could get it that way, they would. If they could get sex without actually having to invest themselves financially, emotionally, or time-wise, they would do whatever it took to get it—until they got it. And then they'd disappear for a while, until their appetites brought them back.

So when Melisse was ready to move on to bigger things, she knew it was time to turn the tables on them.

It was time to make them pay.

Spicy Secret: "There's a trick to the Graceful Exit. It begins with the vision to recognize when a job, a life stage, a relationship is over—and to let go. It means leaving what's over without denying its value."
—Ellen Goodman

CHAPTER 15

Opening Night

It was summer, and a few short days after her graduation from college. Melisse walked slowly down the block of imposing Upper East Side brownstones and their flowering, sheltering trees. It was early evening, and the front bushes were in bloom, the air thick with jasmine-scented humidity. Melisse tried to capture her last few moments before going inside GG's House of Pleasure to give herself up to The Life.

She and GG had spoken, and GG had agreed she was ready to begin. As she looked up at the townhouse, Melisse thought, *Let me in, old house. I've done my time. I graduated from college with honors. I tried life in corporate America for five years and now I want to be my own boss. And I want to be glamorous. I want sex with strangers who pay, exotic travels, control over my schedule, big cash money, and all the freedom and adventures it can bring. I want to be myself, to be what I've always known I am: a jet-setting temptress at heart. Let me in. Now, old house!*

She punched the correct code into the system and was buzzed through a heavy door into the inner vestibule. The unforgettable scent of GG's favorite French Cire Trudon "Abd El Kader" candles wafted their signature scent of mint, ginger, tea, and tobacco into her pores.

A voice came over the intercom. "Helloooo? Melisse? Do you have our code word for access today?"

"Yes," Melisse smiled. "Rambunctious!"

"Correctimento!"

A minute later, a pretty Asian face peeked out of the front door, and Melisse was greeted by Kin, GG's faithful assistant, who managed the house. She was an efficient Japanese girl seemingly just out of college herself. She was reserved, quiet, and smartly observing it all.

"Welcome to our little Shangri-la!" Kin said. She rushed Melisse into the foyer, then sent her discreetly back past the Living Room to the changing/waiting room. There, Melisse changed into a cute little black cocktail dress, black lace thigh-high stockings and garter belt, lacy black panties, and a matching demi-cup bra. Kin brushed Melisse with some sparkling powder and handed her a lipstick to gloss up. Melisse felt as if she were backstage at a theater preparing for a major performance.

"Just jump into it. Don't think about what you're doing. You'll be fine," Kin said breathlessly, as if she herself was about to embark on a dazzling adventure. Melisse looked down at her bare feet. "Oops! I forgot to bring my shoes!"

"Oh, who cares? Go without shoes! It's *charmante*." She brushed some rouge and a shimmering "veil" powder onto Melisse's cheeks, and sent Melisse off to the Living Room. "You look gorgeous!" Kin assured, and Melisse marveled at her kindness. She must have known how nerve-wracking the first night was. Melisse would never forget Kin's first small kindness.

"Just get out there and work your stuff. You're shy and pretty, just like GG said—a 'Little Doll!'—so don't try to be something you're not. Just be yourself."

Spicy Secret: Fashion is nice, but how you carry yourself counts for so much more.

The Living Room was every bit as beautiful as Melisse had remembered, only the atmosphere was sexier on this day, with a variety of women sitting provocatively on the couch and chairs, disco music playing in the background. A heightened sense of flirtation was in the air as the other girls leaned forward in their chairs, giving their undivided attention to a good-looking man in stylish clothes who occupied one particular wingback chair. Later, Melisse discovered it was called "the hot seat."

Spicy Secret: "All the world's a stage, and all the men and women merely players…" —Shakespeare

The women took turns introducing themselves, then looked up when Melisse walked into the room and sat down shyly on the edge of an empty chair. It seemed rather natural that a new girl they'd never seen before had walked into the room.

Melisse's short black cocktail dress seemed kind of stiff in contrast to their long, sparkling slip dresses.

"And this is…" Kin began as all eyes went to Melisse.

"I'm Melisse," Melisse said softly, not looking the man in the eye. She could already tell she didn't like him or his arrogance. He was the kind of man she instinctively knew would end his session by saying something like, "Don't you think you should be paying *me*?" But she thought, *Well, girl, this is what prostitution's all about. You have to jump in, because if you find reasons not to sleep with all the guys who come through here, you're never going to make any money!*

"I'm afraid I didn't get your name," Melisse addressed the man. "I'm sorry, I wasn't here when you came in." She said it as if she was late for a class and missed the introduction of a new subject.

Spicy Secret: Even when he is paying for your company (or on a regular date), it is up to the man during an introduction to make you feel secure, wanted, and welcome. Give only as good as you get during an introduction. If he gives nothing, give nothing in return and ignore him. Or simply leave the premises. He's just taking up space and not worth the negative experience that will inevitably come next.

"Tom," he said curtly.

"Hi, Tom. I'm Melisse," she said, leaving her seat a bit and extending her hand to him, which he shook weakly. That was awkward. *This is a brothel—not one of the offices where you temped!*

"I'm Melisse, Tom," she repeated.

"I got that the first time." He snickered a little at Melisse, her awkwardness, her tiny size, her imperfect looks, still untouched by a surgeon's instruments.

"Melisse is new here," Kin said generously, "She's from California and…"

"Skylar," Tom interrupted, nodding with ownership at a tall, voluptuous blonde, an indication for her to take him upstairs. They stood up before Kin could finish her sentence.

"Thanks, ladies," he said, turning his back to all of them. It was as if he knew whom he was going to see when he first came in, but wanted to put them all through their paces so they could drool over what a fine specimen he was. He probably thought he was the one exception to the myth that "only ugly men who can't get laid visit brothels."

> **Spicy Secret: All kinds of men visit brothels and hire girls, not just nerdy, ugly, and socially inept men. This includes the handsome, arrogant ones who are such assholes that they can't get laid anywhere else—not even at home. Like their stinky garbage, most of their wives would gladly pay to have them taken away.**

"Asshole," Kin said when they were out of earshot. She took his drink back to the bar and dumped it out in the sink, pinkie in the air, trying not to touch where his mouth had been. She looked upstairs, as if addressing him. "Prickisan. They're *supposed* to tell *me* who they want to see, in my ear or in the other room. Where does he think he is—a *trailer* in Nevada?" The others seemed to agree.

"Even at a trailer in Nevada, he'd have to be a little nicer about how he goes about choosin' someone," Livia, one of the girls, said knowingly, as if she'd worked in Nevada at the Bunny Ranch, the well known "legal" brothel.

Spicy Secret: Following protocols and practicing civility is very important in the Wild West of the adult entertainment business.

The remaining girls went back to slouching or lounging. Melisse just felt relieved that she had some more time to take it all in.

"No manners," one girl sighed, pulling a magazine out from under the cushion.

"Seen him," another said. "He thinks he's pretty hot stuff, but he hasn't got a clue. He's about this big and…" She made a relentless back-and-forth motion with her little pinkie to symbolize both his size and sexual technique. "The poor fucker has that short-man-small-penis syndrome combined with a strict anti-tipping policy. I wouldn't see him again if he paid me."

"He sure seems like he's got a chip on his shoulder," said Julia, a pre-Raphaelite British brunette who had slipped on her burgundy cat-eye glasses after the happy couple left the room. Melisse guessed her to be a singer/songwriter when she took a guitar out from behind the bar to strum on while they all talked.

Then Livia—who was gorgeous, with cocoa skin, saucers of hazel eyes, and curly hair extensions down to her ass—added in a Southern drawl, "Yeah, good-looking guys like that never tip, plus the goddamn arrogant attitude. I'll take a nerdy Jewish lawyer any old day. Nobody ever got rich stiffing waiters, hookers, or taxi drivers."

"Guys with chips on their shoulders always want to do it the whole time from behind," Julia complained. "I think it makes them feel like big cavemen." She imitated a Tarzan accent. "Me got hard-on. You get on all fours. I pull hair. Me come in four seconds. Me don't tip."

The girls all laughed, but Melisse's eyes widened. Kin saw the fear.

"No, honey…aw, look at poor Melisse…" she giggled kindly. "She just means doggy style—not anal. Two completely different things. We don't 'speak Greek' here, if you know what I mean. Not that anyone will admit to. And that hair-pulling stuff? Well, it's just a game the girls play to get the guys to come off quicker, right, girls?"

"Yeah," Livia said. "Sweetie, if you want a guy to get off fast *and* think you're the greatest, just say stuff like…"

Livia turned over on the couch and stuck her rear end in the air and held her hair back and imitated exactly how she did it, breathlessly and with wild abandon. "…like this: Fuck me, oh, fuck me, ah, like that, yes, yes, fuck me, ohhhhhh, FUCK MEEEEEEE!"

> **Spicy Secret: There is something so visually and physically stimulating to men about the doggy-style position, combined with "Fuck Me!" that it's one of the most powerful offerings in a professional's physical repertoire. It's simply because most modern men are descended from dogs and for a few delicious moments it reminds them of their true nature. And also, dogs like to obey commands from their masters. Woof!**

She turned over and they all laughed. "Now you practice it, Melisse!"

Melisse smiled shyly and then gave Livia a winning rival performance. When she was done "coming" she found herself, for the first time in her life, laughing hysterically in a room full of women who would become her friends, her friendly competitors, and sometimes her fake lovers for the next two years.

The doorbell rang and they all quickly arranged themselves into "Living Room Mode." Kin led the client into the room and Melisse observed just how a client was secured by a crafty lady in the midst of some heavy competition.

The man came into the parlor in his gym clothes (a visit to the gym being a common alibi for men deluding their wives). Before even introducing herself, Livia said suspiciously "And where have you just been?"

"I've been to the gym," he said, putting a squeeze of lemon into his sparkling water.

"Oh, yeah? Well, you look like *some* days you go to the gym and *some* days you set about gettin' yourself into some trouble. Imagine how exhausted you'd be if you were doing the same workout all the time! Do you sometimes have to watch exercise videos on rainy days when you can't make it to the 'gym'?"

She managed to get him to laugh, and Melisse did, too.

"Hey, exercise videos can be sexy! What's *your* name?" he asked.

"I'm Livia, and this is Melisse."

"I'm Bill," he said.

Kin had told Melisse that after they introduced themselves, they were to take turns introducing another girl in the room until everyone was introduced. So Melisse said, "Hi, I'm Melisse, and I'd like to introduce you to Julia…" and then Julia introduced the next girl, and so on…

"So where do you work out?" Livia asked Bill, seemingly interested in physical fitness. He only had eyes for Livia, so the other girls backed down in their seats.

"New York Sports."

"Oh, it's nice over there," Livia said enthusiastically, making it obvious that Bill was her "catch of the day." She added, "There's one machine—lordy!—that cycling machine gets my crotch all in an uproar!"

He laughed again and began eyeing her up and down. She moved around here and there in her chair so he could look at her (the girls weren't allowed to get up and parade around too much; it was considered too competitive). Then he looked over at Melisse, but she just grinned at him and looked back over at Livia as if to tell him, *You should pick her—she's fantastic.*

> **Spicy Secret: Acting bitchy, proprietary, or preventing the advancement of other ladies, whether in a brothel, an office (or anywhere else) won't get you very far for very long before someone stops you (or punches you). Help other women get ahead in The Life, and you only help yourself.**

"You look like *you* get plenty of exercise," he said to Livia.

"Oh...I work out once in a while...thank you. I do Brazilian butt lifts—and that's a very nice compliment coming from someone who goes to the gym as much as you do!" Then they both broke out laughing. They had become very familiar very quickly.

> **Spicy Secret: Expert working girls (and successful people in many other fields) use a combination of subtle physical and psychological techniques, like "mirroring," "subliminal hinting," "eye play," and good old-fashioned flattery to lure in their fish. If you study a wonderful psychology called NLP (Neuro-Linguistic Programming), and/or the books of Leil Lowndes, you, too, can become an expert angler, salesperson, or communicator.**

Bill called Kin over and in a whisper asked if it would be all right to spend some time with Livia. She nodded excitedly. Livia then walked him to the bottom of the stairs and said, "You go on up to the Zen suite, and I'll be right up, OK, baby?"

When he was safely upstairs, Livia came over to Melisse and said, "Shit. Go to the gym. Like I don't get enough exercise fucking everyone around here."

Then she asked, "Melisse—you gonna be OK down here by yourself? I mean, if you get to go upstairs...?"

"Yeah, I'll be fine. Just watching you has taught me a lot already."

"Well, this ain't the half of it—but you'll see as you go along. I think you're going to do just fine. Don't forget to watch the clock. Straight girls aren't used to watching the clock," she laughed, reaching into her evening purse. She added, "Don't give them a minute more of your time than you have to. They'll try to get away with all kinds of things. Remember, this is a business you're conducting, not a relationship you're having."

> **Spicy Secret: Money can be lost and found again. But you can never get back your time. So don't let clients—or men—waste that most valuable commodity.**

"Thanks," Melisse said, making a mental note.

"Damn," Livia said, "I almost forgot to lube up! He'll think I got wet downstairs just talking to him." And with that, she lifted her skirt, held it under her chin, took down her panties, pulled something from her purse and rubbed a dollop of something called WET into her panties. "Ah, ah," she said, grimacing as if it was burning hot. "Yeast infection season. If it ain't one thing, it's another. I get zits down there, ingrown hairs, an itch, I run to the doctor. You know, you can't go spreadin' stuff around. It's not right, and GG would have a hissy fit. Doc's like, 'Livia, what are you doing back here?' I'm like, 'Doctor, doctor, is it herpes?' He's like, 'Damn, girl, get OUT of here. You don't have an STD, you've got a *worrywart*. I don't want to see you again this summer!' Ha!"

Livia rolled her eyes up in consternation. Melisse giggled at this strange new camaraderie. She had always been so shy about personal hygiene but she supposed there was no room for that anymore. Livia pulled her panties back up, let her dress down, and ran up the stairs for her session with…

"Kin! What's his name again?" Livia whispered to Kin from across the room.

"Bill!" Kin shot back.

"Thanks, got it!"

CHAPTER 16

Jack the Bat

The girls were still upstairs entertaining as Melisse sat by herself in the Living Room thumbing through a *Cosmopolitan* magazine. Kin told Melisse somebody would be coming over soon just to meet her.

"It's Jack the Bat. He's a little weird, but totally easy." The butterflies in her stomach fluttered and Melisse decided to move over to the piano. She sat doodling there, playing bits of all the classical songs she could remember from her childhood piano lessons. Before she knew it, Kim walked a man in to meet her.

"Melisse, meet Jack. Jack is an old-timer here—all the girls love him, don't they, Jack?"

He nodded proudly. Melisse was embarrassed that he'd caught her playing, as if a snippet of a Mozart sonata was something very personal from her past.

Kin winked at her and Jack came over to stand close to Melisse. "Hey, keep playing," Jack said. "You're a cute little pixie!"

She looked up at a short man with bushy eyebrows and a beaked nose and dark, longish hair circling a bald head in a style that reminded her of a circus clown. He wore a fine suit with all the trimmings. *Oh, God, he's going to be my first. I guess he's OK; there's nothing mean or menacing about him, so I'll be friendly to him. I'm here to please him and he's here to give me his money. I just need to remember that. And he already has one redeeming quality—he just gave me a nice compliment.*

"I bet you're wondering what other instruments I might play," Melisse said with a seductive grin that plumped up the apples of her cheeks.

"Yes. Usually people who are talented in one art are talented in something else," he agreed with a mischievous wink.

She smiled knowingly. She liked that he was interested in the arts. She gave him the old up-and-down glance that she'd seen so many men give women but never the other way around. She liked how the rules of etiquette were turned upside down for women like her in places like this.

"I play a great skin flute," she said matter-of-factly, rubbing her finger up and down over the zipper of his pants and looking up into his eyes. *Oh, my God, I can't believe I just said that. And did that!* It made her start giggling, it sounded so silly. But this was a performance, after all.

> **Spicy Secret: Most men these days have a high threshold for dirty, naughty, and overly sexy teasing and talk, especially just before—and in—bed. What feels and sounds utterly and completely crazy and ridiculous to** *us* **sounds completely normal, reasonable, and extremely enticing to** *their* **ears. Blame it on porn.**

"Oh, yeah?" he chuckled awkwardly, holding her hand to his crotch lightly.

"Yes, sir. I'm a regular little 'Liber-raunchy,'" she giggled, referring to the famously flamboyant pianist, Liberace. *Where did that come from?*

"Oh, you are?" he said, raising his eyebrows. "Can I take you upstairs—uh, Liberaunchy?"

"Suuuuure." *And here we go!*

> **Spicy Secret: "Act well your part; there all the honour lies." —Alexander Pope**

What she remembers about that first session is the tallness of the door to the Peacock's Lair and the huge fake Ming vases flanking it, the tall peacock feathers bowing to their entry, making her feel as if she and Jack were in Alice's Wonderland. She was inspired by the drama of the decor, pretending to herself that she'd done this a million times. She led Jack by the hand into the room and looked around.

The walls were covered in a rich teal fabric flocked with subtle feather patterns hanging from floor to ceiling. A rug with a feathery pattern in spice colors of cayenne, cumin, and saffron lay on the floor. The furniture seemed inspired by colonial Indian antiques, in dark thick woods. Silk potted fan palms were under-lit and cast strange shadows on the high ceiling. GG's tropical bouquets were composed of tiger lilies, birds of paradise, and heavily scented hibiscus. It was heady in there!

She undid the many buttons on Jack's shirt to expose a flaccid pale chest, then got on her knees and slid off Jack's loafers. She looked up at him, her eyes wide like a doe's. Her small hands rubbed the inside of his thighs and she pressed her nose through his pants to his hardening cock. Leaning in, she rubbed her face around the fabric without getting lipstick on it and heard him sigh contentedly. Inspired, she continued her seductive journey, first helping him out of his clothes and watching as he gamboled over to the bed. He climbed in to lie naked on the stack of pillows, his small member standing up independent of his reclining body.

She went to the armoire where a stereo was hidden and opened it, turning up the music a bit. She clicked the CD to her favorite Sade song: "Never as Good as the First Time." Then, as she came around the bed, she grabbed Jack's hands and looked intensely into his eyes.

> **Spicy Secret: The ability to look a man right in the eyes and hold your wanton, sexy gaze there for a significant period of time (without flinching) is akin to seducing with intent to ravish. You'll soon have him hypnotized, at which time you can easily plant any thoughts, commands, or wishes you want into his mind.**

"May I put on a little show for you?" she asked sweetly. It was the most power she'd ever felt in her lifetime. She was the boss here, earning outstanding money. He was looking to her for erotic authority, practically trembling at the promise of the pleasure she would reveal to him.

She possessed the singular ability to wrap all his senses with an indelible lust, and at the very least, remove him from an ordinary existence so he could enter a rich, sensual world. Her own experience, however, would sit more permanently in her memory because Jack was her first john. She would tell him afterward that he had been her first trick, believing it would please him immensely.

Why do I care so much whether I please him or not? she wondered, then realized that she was teaching herself, as she went along, how to be a good courtesan.

She came in close and leaned over, whispering in his ear, "May I… undress myself for you?" He nodded enthusiastically. She turned to look back at him, and walked slowly to the middle of the room so he'd feel as if he were watching a private sex film. When she came in close again, she would step right out of the movie and into his bed.

> **Spicy Secret: Men are visual creatures, plain and simple, and you don't need to be drop-dead gorgeous to get—and keep—their eyes on you. If you want to cater to their primary modality, then give them a good, colorful, pretty show leading up to a "final reveal,"and they'll be happy to show you the world. Better yet: dress to please yourself and show *yourself* the world!**

She began to think: *What is it like to be him? If I were him, what would be turning me on right now? What does he mostly want from this experience?*

It was decidedly antifeminist to her, to think only of *their* pleasure and to view herself as an object for men to be pleased by. But this was business. And doing business wasn't political or personal. It was a world unto itself with its own set of rules, procedures, and traditions.

Instead of experiencing her own pleasure, she found herself observing herself with a three-hundred-and-sixty-degree view, as if she were a piece of merchandise in a shop window. Or, more specifically, a "piece of ass" being assessed and viewed from every angle.

But how many women in our society display themselves or treat themselves like a piece of merchandise to be objectified, even though they aren't actually for sale and get no tangible benefit from doing it? How many women lived first to please and appease others, before pleasing themselves?

It did thrill her to think that this way of life permitted such a blatant, fleshy form of satisfaction for the parties involved. Stripping certainly hadn't. A voyeuristic, merely flirtatious striptease was simply an appetizer for the libido. Now, she was also providing the main course.

Later, she would treat her sexuality and sensuality as if she were a master chef, proud of her cuisine and wanting to share it with high-paying patrons who would look forward to tasting it, and reserve well in advance in order to sup at her table.

Prostitution seemed much more serious than topless dancing, of course. Its directness—the confident assumption that each participant would emerge gratified, either sexually or financially—left room for all kinds of other, deeper urges to arise.

But one day, she would discard these thoughts entirely and conclude that prostitution was a poor substitute for the sensual experiences that could only be had between two people deeply in love.

She smoothed down the crepe of her black dress, slowly unzipped it, and let it drop to the ground, walking away from it as if from an afterthought. In turning her back to him, she revealed the creamy crescents of flesh on her thighs edged in lace, the black stockings and lacy garter belt accentuating the way her ass curved out gracefully from beneath.

She was proud of the way she looked in her lingerie, though her body was not yet the perfection it could be. She saw herself in the large mirror that stood alongside the wall by the bed. Her breasts seemed ready to pop out over the top of her lace bra as she slid the straps off her shoulders and dropped it on the floor. The black silk patch of her G-string, no bigger than an eye patch, shimmied over light, short golden hairs she would later be advised (by a client) to shave completely.

> **Spicy Secret: Laser hair removal is totally worth it in the end.**

She took everything else off and left her panties on. She was in command of the room and had captivated his attention, imprisoning his body in a fiery circle of desire and lust that could only be broken with the meltdown of sexual release.

She saw her face in the armoire mirror. Her eyes slanted up ever so slightly and she'd lost a little of the overall fleshiness of her teenage years. Her chin and cheekbones led to pale cornflower-blue eyes and the puffy pillow of her lips. She had a sly smirk that said, *I'm willing to do just about anything—for the right price.*

"God, you're pretty," Jack said.

"Thank you, Jack," she said softly. Her first compliment received as a pro hit her like a teenager's first toke of grass. She looked down at herself for a moment, then looked up at him and reached her hand into her panties and said, "God, Jack, I'm getting soooo wet down there, in my magical little spot—hee-hee!"

> **Spicy Secret: If you're not naturally wet, or never going to get wet with a guy, then sneak a little water-based lube on your fou-fou before your date or appointment. Men feel flattered and potent when they see you're seemingly excited, even if it's ridiculously unbelievable because they haven't done a darn thing to help get you there.**

It wouldn't always be so, the nervous wetness, but she thought, *Why not take advantage of the situation and knock the guy's socks off?*

"Jack, my snatch is so tight and hot and juicy I don't think I can keep it from you any longer…" She came in close and guided his hand down under the fabric. He reminded her of a blind man the way he looked up at the ceiling and, closing his eyes, felt around.

"Oh...God," he sighed, as she felt her pussy nearly grab on to his finger. "It's so tight!"

"Just think about how good your cock would feel inside there."

Spicy Secret: Sometimes it's good to point out the obvious in plain language as an enhancement to the experience. You're only saying what he's thinking.

Jack took his hand out of her panties and breathed in its scent, then he put his hand on his straight-up cock and it disappeared into his small, fast-moving fist.

"Jack!" she said jealously, pushing his hand aside, then lowering her voice. "That's enough of that. You're not ready for that yet. When the time comes, *I'm* going to do that *for* you."

"No, you don't understand. This is *what I like to do*," he sighed.

Spicy Secret: Let clients do whatever they like to do most with their time, as long as it's not hurting or abusing you.

He smiled gratefully, but put his hand right back on his cock. She wondered if the other girls worked as hard or as devotedly as she did, or if they would have let him jerk himself off on his own in two minutes flat. He didn't seem interested in full-on sex, so she didn't need to push herself on him. There'd be "fuckers" aplenty (as she would soon learn the clients were called who had full-on sex, and not some noninvasive variation of foreplay or fetish).

Jack grimaced and moved his hand rapidly, choreographically almost, as he shook his penis, stroked it, slapped it, did all kinds of nutty things to it while he cupped his balls in his other hand and got lost in his activities.

Jack, you're not paying attention to me.

Spicy Secret: You may think the appointment or date is all about you. But when it comes right down to it, it's all about him. Successful working girls know this and keep their (sometimes big) egos in check.

She stood with her hands on her hips and looked down at him, amused and relieved in a way that her tasks seemed to be over for the time being. But she thought of what she could do to heighten or intensify the experience.

She got on her knees on the bed, next to him, and leaned over him.

"Suck my gorgeous little tits, Jack," she said, holding them up for his perusal and what she suspected would be a delicate tongue. He tried, but he was pretty caught up with himself, his eyes closed tightly, his lips pursed.

"Melisse…" he stammered (jerk, jerk), "wanna…wanna see something I bet you've never seen before?" (jerk, jerk).

"Yeaaaah…" she said breathlessly, as if she were as involved as he was. "Show me something I've never seen before."

"OK." And with that, Jack made a great effort to swing his legs up over his head, finally hooking his feet into the railing of the iron bed.

"Hold my legs up there," he gasped, "and push me up even more when I tell you to."

She held him there. She was curious now. *This must be the "bat" part.* She was almost in giggles. She dared not think of what he was going to do.

"Watch this…NOW, Melisse…" he moaned. She pushed him up as instructed.

"Aaaar-uuuh—uhhhhhg!" Jack opened his mouth and shot his pale yellow come into it, lapping around the edges of his mouth with his creamed tongue. "Mmmmm…" he said as she let his legs down gently, hoping his back wouldn't crack.

"Oh," she sighed, "look how yummy you look."

God, that's disgusting, she thought. *What am I doing here?*

Spicy Secret: *De gustibus non est disputandum.* That's Latin for, "There's no accounting for taste."

Almost immediately, Jack was up and at 'em in the bathroom, standing on his tiptoes, washing himself off in the sink. Melisse leaned back on the pillows and sighed. She turned on her side and looked at herself in the bedside mirror.

I'm finally, and officially, a hooker. I just did something that's turned me into a hooker. I'm now one of the most socially maligned creatures in the universe. Wow. I don't think it's something I can reverse or forget, nor do I want to right now! No, I've labeled myself forever. It's the label I've wanted for so long: call girl, goddess, temptress, courtesan—whore? No, I'm not a whore. A whore is someone—anyone, in fact—who does something they really don't want to, or wouldn't ordinarily do, just for money.

I'm doing exactly what I want to be doing.

Kind of.

Jack came out of the bathroom to dress himself and paused to look at Melisse looking up at herself in the ceiling mirror.

He snickered a little as he tied his tie. "Kin told me you were brand new to the business, and it's obvious you're not. You're just too good at what you do. You've done this before!"

"Have not, Jack," she sang.

"You have, too," he sang back, pointing his finger and pulling on his pants.

"Will you come back and see me?" She leaped up to make sure his shirt buttons were all done up. "You know, Jack, *every time* with me is like the first time—at least it feels that way for me," she went on eagerly. "And I'd love to see you…"

Spicy Secret: Avoid "upselling"—i.e., asking a client, or even a boyfriend, to call or come back and see you after he's been "drained." It sounds too much like a nagging wife or a whiny date ("Will you call me again?"). After they've come, the game is over for most men. They'll be back in touch when their balls and brains (and we hope, hearts) have filled up again. For some, that means a few hours; for others, a few weeks (or years).

He was eager to get out of the room and get on his way, but he turned to say, "How about same time next week? I'll tell Kin to book it on the way out."

And then he'd cancel it the next day to spare her feelings. *Variety is the spice of life*, was his motto. But Melisse didn't understand yet exactly how these clients' minds operated.

Spicy Secret: The world of the courtesan is filled with men proffering hot air, false promises, and broken agreements. When you learn to rise above it all by virtue of your own propulsion, you'll soar like a bird.

"OK!" she said. "Can't wait! I'll be here for sure then. You're my first regular!"

"Take it easy, kid," he said, handing her a tip. He left the room and descended the stairs. She looked around as she dressed and glanced at the clock. Livia had said to be sure to watch the clock. Not even twenty-five minutes had elapsed and she was already downstairs where an envelope with her fee would be waiting. And she had a repeat appointment booked. Things were looking up!

One thing she knew for sure: her envelope would contain almost as much as she'd have made in a whole week working in a boring office, *including* the commute. Here she could be a star and wear almost anything (as long as it was sexy) she wanted!

She suddenly remembered to ring the bell for the housekeeper to come and change the sheets and garbage. The girls were to wash off thoroughly with soap and water, always make sure their breath was freshened again and their hair fluffed up again after matting down against the bed. GG made sure there was always a "freshen up" tray of supplies for both the men and women on the bathroom counter.

And GG was often teased mercilessly by the girls about her obsession with stocking the "right" toilet paper.

> **Spicy Secret:** Word to the wise: when perusing the toilet paper options at the store, always choose the strongest (not the softest) that money can buy. Nothing screams "amateur" like a lady "getting into position" with white paper crumbles decorating her "crevasse." And if you're going to be "on the go" around town, then carry a stash of your own along to avoid any embarrassing incidents due to subpar TP that may be lurking in the hotel or public restrooms.

As Melisse went into the grandiose bathroom, she thought, *God, he never even touched me and I just got paid. I was nice to him, made him happy, and now I have some money. By the end of the week, I'm going to have myself a whole lot of money...*

A newfound sense of joy and an odd sense of security embraced her as a greedy excitement funneled its way into her brain. Like many who had come before her, sex for money—big money—was like a drug.

And she was now hooked.

She danced around putting her stockings and lingerie back on, hurrying to get downstairs quickly before she missed another man and another dollar.

> **Spicy Secret:** "(Greed is) the lust for comfort, that stealthy thing that enters the house as a guest, and then becomes a host, and then a master."
> —Khalil Gibran

CHAPTER 17

The Mole and the Weasel

After a short dinner break on her first night at GG's, Melisse was late getting into the Living Room. She was late because after Jack the Bat, she'd been chosen by a very handsome, young-ish ER doctor who'd spent most of the time kissing and hugging (and then fucking) her as if they were boyfriend and girlfriend. While it was pleasurable, Melisse was still a bit confused by the instant intimacy of the whole experience, but she just "acted as if" and carried it all off like a pro.

"You're an awesome little GFE," he said, while spooning behind her in the bed of the Zen Retreat as the minutes ticked on and then she went into "overtime." The housekeeper must have been busy and failed to give her "the knock."

"What's a GFE?" Melisse had asked innocently, honestly not knowing the lingo just yet.

"Girlfriend Experience—like being with a girlfriend—like we're in love." Then suddenly, "How old are you, anyway?" he'd asked.

> **Spicy Secret:** "How old are you?" is a ridiculous question during an appointment (or while on a regular date) and you'd be well served to never answer it unless your life depends on it. It's none of a man or client's business if he is attracted to you. Your age is completely irrelevant to the experience you've been giving him if he's been having a good time.

"I can tell you one thing. My birthday is going to be this weekend!"

"No kidding! What will you be doing to celebrate?" he asked, and when she told him that absolutely nothing was planned, he volunteered to take her out to a fun restaurant in Little Italy that was famous for the waiters singing and patrons dancing—on the tables—after being stuffed full of pasta.

"We could have a sleepover at my place after," he said hopefully.

"I can't see people outside the house, sorry. House rules and I'm true blue to GG. But we *could* have dinner. I'd *love* that!" she said sweetly, sincerely believing that this darling man who'd just had her sucking his cock for a half an hour, then pounding her for another half hour, would still want to take her out, even though sex wouldn't be on the table.

"Sure! I'll make a reservation for 8:00 p.m. in your name!"

"Goody!"

Needless to say, Melisse showed up at the restaurant that weekend, dressed up and looking forward to a romantic birthday night out in NYC with the cute ER doc…only to wait and wait for a guy who never arrived.

As she walked through Little Italy alone that night, tears welled up in her eyes as she thought of some of the sincere friends she could have spent her special evening with. Even talking on the phone long-distance to friends and special family members would have been more gratifying than waiting futilely for some lying sack of shit she'd met in a brothel, whom she'd never see again.

As Melisse approached the Living Room after her dinner break, she saw two men—one rounder, older, and taller than the other. The other was much younger, sharper, and shorter. They reminded her of a fat mole and a skinny weasel. The Weasel was the one talking animatedly, and Melisse came into the conversation a little late.

"Yeah…we snuck out. My wife just had a baby a week ago and there's a baby shower for her tonight. She had a girl."

Livia and a new girl—a gorgeous redheaded Marilyn Monroe look-alike named Shishapuss—were the only girls in the main salon. Shishapuss, perhaps a full decade older than Melisse, had an extraordinary presence about her that nearly lit up the room. She and Livia were nodding and faking smiles. Melisse could tell that the girls didn't think it was funny or amusing or admirable that these guys were stepping out on their wives and bragging about it, especially the one who'd just had a baby. The men didn't seem to feel guilty about it in the least.

Melisse was pretty sure that they weren't living in "open" marriages, and their arrogance and sense of entitlement made her squirm. But she was already learning to keep those feelings to herself.

Kin said, "And here she is now—our Melisse!"

"Hello," Melisse said breathlessly, sitting down, catching a long, lascivious stare from the short one. Shishapuss gave Melisse a little wink. She then tugged down on her right earlobe, jingling her bejeweled earring. She did it twice for effect.

"Lenny and Ziggy want to have a party with all three of you ladies—isn't that fun? I'll get the champagne open!" Kin said excitedly, going to the bar.

Melisse looked a little pensive. This would represent her first orgy.

"It's all right. I'm a really nice guy. I don't bite," the ferret one said sweetly, but in a fake way. "Come on…come and join the party!"

"OK…"

> **Spicy Secret:** "The louder he talked of his honor, the faster we counted our spoons." —Ralph Waldo Emerson

> **Spicy Secret:** When a man goes out of his way to tell you (for example, during a pre-screening or an introduction phone call) how nice he is, or what a gentleman he is, or how generous he's going to be… he almost always ISN'T. Time to hang up and hide the spoons.

Kin gave the go-ahead. "You kids go on upstairs to the Honeymoon Suite. The house is closed now, so you have the run of the place."

Lenny, the ferret, almost sprang up the stairs while the rest of the group got up to follow.

Melisse had just sat down, and already she was up again.

"Man," Livia said, hanging back with her, fanning her skirt as if it were on fire. "Whew—no rest for the wicked, huh, Melisse?"

Shisha just walked by elegantly, her nose almost in the air, leading Ziggy, the nearly drunk mole, past them by his dick. She had quickly undone his zipper and it was now sticking out through his pants. Like a dog on a leash, he obediently followed behind her luscious, outrageously curvy hips and tiny waist, enhanced by a clinging black sundress of sheer stretch lace with a teeny-tiny black G-string beneath.

Melisse watched, fascinated, as Shishapuss effortlessly navigated the staircase in four-inch black patent-leather platform pumps while never letting go of Ziggy's divining rod of a cock.

Ziggy the Mole looked like he was ready to get down and lick her heels as Melisse suppressed a giggle. Livia just shook her head and rolled her eyes at the outrageous scene.

"Shishapuss is just the bomb," she said admiringly. "You can learn a lot from Shisha."

"Why do you call her Shishapuss?" Melisse asked.

"Cause she's got a smoking-hot pussy, like a little tiny pipe, *and* she's shaped like a shisha base."

Shishapuss overheard this and looked over her shoulder while leading Mole up the stairs.

"It's called a *hubbly bubbly*," she said in a fake British accent. "And many have smoked at it and become *totally high*," she said with a flat diva delivery, while Livia and Melisse broke up behind them.

"And a few have even gotten *burned*," Kin said, with a flat delivery and a smirk as she looked up from her job of clearing glasses.

Things happen fast in a brothel, especially the first night. You're swept up into the action and you lose yourself for a while. And then every night becomes like this: a new set of players who join in to interact and play with a revolving cast of beautiful women.

Weasel, the younger, shorter, sharp-suited man, took Melisse by the elbow and backed her up against the wall in the hallway before they even got to the Honeymoon Suite. He kissed her on the lips and stuck his tongue deep into her mouth. Revolted, she forced herself to kiss back. Nobody had told her that men might try to kiss her. At that time, she didn't know that she didn't have to agree. Melisse was focused on doing the job right, never suspecting she was giving too much.

Weasel pulled away and began tearing off his clothes as he entered the room, tossing them everywhere and then grabbing a glass of champagne from a table. Melisse followed, drawn to the dusty rose walls, plush carpeting, and softly lit, pale wood built-ins. It was like a film star's private dressing room. A huge bed loomed above, two steps up on a platform. A hot tub, too, was already bubbling away.

The girls undressed the men, then the men undressed the girls. Melisse stood back and watched. The men arranged and sniffed lines of coke off a mirrored tray before jumping into the tub. The girls joined them in the Jacuzzi. "Well, aren't you coming in?" they invited.

"I sure am!" Melisse said as she dropped her dress and got one last comforting whiff of her perfume before she eased into the tub.

The men were already receiving belly rubs, while the girls were getting their nipples soaped. Despite the cozy scene, Melisse was still thinking about the wife who had just borne one of these men a baby. Here he was on the night of her baby shower, sitting in a Jacuzzi with hookers!

> **Spicy Secret: Never underestimate a horny, dishonest, and selfish (or sex-addicted) man's ability to abuse a woman's trust to disgusting degrees. Shocking but true, he will be quite unsentimental about cheating on her during special occasions (like her giving birth or while she is visiting a dying parent) and sacred spaces**

for his convenience (like his home, feeling free to do it with other women in the marital bed when she's away, "to save money on hotels"). He'll give these things no weight in his quest to satisfy himself and then chalk up his bad behavior to his feeling "neglected."

Melisse stood at the stairs of the Jacuzzi as the water swirled around her hips. She wanted to focus on the beauty of the other girls in that bacchanalian reverie, but like a small shark, the Weasel zoomed in.

She looked into his eyes and looked away. The overweight Mole was displacing all the water, and the men looked like ugly beasts in a fountain of smooth-skinned goddesses.

As the girls surrounded the men, they rubbed them all over, cooing, "Look how Livia's tits are bobbing."

Melisse sat up against the side of the tub. "Melisse could stand up in here and it'd come up to her neck," Livia teased.

"Very funny," Melisse said. "I like being small—you wouldn't believe the positions I can get myself into." Weasel was nibbling on her ear. "Mmmmm, are you trying to steal my earring?"

"No, steal your virginity."

"Ha! Really?"

"Yes, Kin told me you're brand spankin' new to the business."

Well, if that makes it a little better for you…

She dried off and went over by the bed. Two men and three girls. Emptied champagne glasses, bottles of lubricant, the condoms, high heels, everything in the bed felt like a slow-moving sex barge.

"Hop on!" the fat man said to the round-hipped Livia. She tromped on him and rode him like a horse, a bored expression on her face. The Weasel, who had been fucking Shisha from behind, pulled abruptly out of her and moved over to Melisse.

It was the first time Melisse had ever seen other people having sex "live" right in front of her. She felt her pussy pulsating with excitement, despite the fact that these were two of the ugliest men she'd ever seen in her entire life.

Shisha scowled at the Weasel behind his back, pointing and mouthing the word *asshole*. He tore off his condom and threw it on the floor, then poured himself more champagne without offering Melisse any, and she *wanted* some.

> **Spicy Secret:** Watch how men you don't know well handle the after-dinner "drinks and dessert" portion of a date. In a restaurant, after dinner, if he asks the server for the check *without first* checking in with you to see if you'd like some dessert and tea or coffee, expect minor—or major—problems up ahead.
>
> If a worldly, sophisticated man doesn't offer to indulge you in a little dessert and hot drinks to extend his time with you (even if he doesn't care for any himself), there's something wrong with him!
>
> No dessert? No mint tea or a cappuccino? He's a withholding douche bag waiting to happen. Run to your nearest sweet shop.

"Let's go to the other room," he said. They walked down the hall into the Peacock's Lair. It was dark teal everywhere without lights, the Devil's cool womb.

"What do you want to do?" Melisse asked as Weasel faced her.

"This," he said, and guided her hand to his pencil-thin penis.

"Oh." She reached for the condom that would be kept in the inlaid wooden box on the bedside table.

"Want me to suck you a little bit?" she asked, hating every crass, unromantic word of it, yet knowing this was the language he expected—and liked—to hear.

"No, why bother? Let's just do it."

"OK." She rolled the condom on him and slathered herself with lubricant. Then she rolled onto her back and spread her legs wide enough so she might avoid feeling him. *I haven't found one nice thing about this man, and now he is inside me and I feel nothing...*

A suitable amount of time elapsed and so she stiffened her hips, scratched Weasel's prickly back, and faked a powerful Harvest Moon, Earth Mother, Goddess of Fire orgasm, joining in the chorus of the girls she heard next door.

> **Spicy Secret: Once again, your loud (and sometimes loudly faked) orgasm may sound like total bullshit to your ears, but to him it might as well be Verdi's** *La Traviata* **(or his favorite rock and roll song). When faced with a client who is eager to please you, don't let him down, audibly speaking. There is one great solution when faking so you don't disturb the neighbors: at the height of your "passion," simply press the pillow into your own face as he pounds away at you and scream the words, "You are such a bad lover!" into a pillow. He'll hear "rad" instead of "bad" and everyone will be happy, including your neighbors.**

After she recovered, he said, "Get on all fours."

She turned over on her paws and got into what she thought was the "lion" position in yoga. He punted her like a little cork and slid in and out. She sighed and rolled her eyes in the dark and rested her head on a pillow. *Is this what it's going to be like, Melisse? It's only the first night. Is this what you want? A lifetime's worth of dream dates like this, all lined up ahead of you?*

She remembered to muster up an, "Mmm, yeah, feels so gooood!"

"Hold on," he said, and she heard him moving around behind her, half-in, half-out.

"OK," he said at last.

They went back to what they were doing before, and nothing felt different, only his hip strokes were getting more rigid and uniform, quicker, harder, like he was about to come.

"Uuuuh-uh-uh-uh." He came with little aftershocks, tremors of oversensitivity.

She turned over and fell onto her back, on the pillows formerly occupied by Jack the Bat. Her stomach turned thinking of Jack's come shooting into his mouth. Now, Weasel was standing, smirking contentedly. His penis was bare and dripping.

Shocked, Melisse clutched at herself to see if the condom was somehow left inside her. No, but she was dripping with his come. The condom was nowhere to be found. She turned the lamp up a few notches while he made a show of blindness.

"Where's the condom?" she demanded.

"Uh, I don't know," he said innocently.

She looked around the room, and there it was, torn off and abandoned on the floor, way over in the corner.

"How did *that* get over *there?*" she asked, furious, revealing that her former turn-on act was all a ruse.

"Uh, gee…"

She flashed back to a night a few years before when a man she already knew well enough had date-raped and degraded her after refusing to wear a condom. Now, simmering rage reached a boiling point inside her, yet again. Being raped, whether violently by a stranger, or "gently" by a so-called friend, had the same effect on her as it did on any other woman: that feeling of having been stripped of her human dignity. For a long time after it happened, it left her with an indelible mark of sadness, fear, and lack of trust. Worst of all, she still blamed *herself* for even letting a man like that into her orbit.

How ironic that she found herself here, *now*, in a supposedly super-controlled situation where men were supposedly screened and on their best behavior, yet here she was again: in a similar circumstance of someone doing something to her without her consent. It had echoes of that other violation, yet it was new and different and now tinged with the strange new element of money changing hands.

If this is how it's going to be, I don't want it, she realized. But what could she do? She vowed to herself from now on to *always, always pay attention*!

Spicy Secret: In "doggy" (or any other position, for that matter) reach back several times during intercourse, as if you're grabbing or stroking his cock, but in reality you're checking to make sure that his condom is securely on and properly lubed (because when they're dry, they break easily). The vast majority of male clients are good guys and would never take their condom off on purpose, but sometimes condoms have a rubbery mind of their own, so remain *en garde*.

He pointed into the other room nervously. "I'm going back in there," he said.

"Fine," she said icily. "I'll be in there in a minute." She looked at the wet spot on the sheets, got up, and rang the bell for the housekeeper. Then, she climbed into the sage marble bathtub, ran the tap, and washed the HIV and the herpes and the HPV and the gonorrhea and the chlamydia and most likely, nothing at all, off herself.

A more cynical, experienced girl would have kept reaching behind her to make sure the condom was on securely, not trusting a crass, impulsive man like the Weasel, but Melisse was clearly just off the banana boat.

This is it. The end of the night. You'll go home after this. Get your money first. You've earned it.

She held her roiling stomach, wondering if this horrible turn of events meant that she should leave for good, say good-bye to prostitution and go back to working in offices.

It's not as pretty as you thought, is it, Melisse? Is it time to come up with a new dream? No! I'll make it pretty; I'll make it into what I want. Now, I've got to learn what to avoid. Avoidance is OK. It's called "screening." I don't have to see anybody I don't want to. I'll avoid the young, the arrogant, the ones who use language to degrade, not to play... I don't need them to make money. Even just one trick a week will suffice if it lifts me up instead of drags me down. I already have one nice booking next week: Jack the Bat!

She stopped herself from sobbing. Someone was patting her back as she squatted in the running water, scrubbing at herself with a bar of soap as she held back tears.

It was Shishapuss. "You OK, honey?"

"No…"

"I was trying to tell you. I know him from another house. Everyone outside of here knows him. You know, I don't just work *here*. I hustle it everywhere I can. But please don't tell GG that."

"He tore off his condom and came inside me…"

"Of course he did, honey."

"Is this what it's going to be like every night here?"

"Ohhh, noooo…not at all. They're usually more afraid of us than we are of them. They're all soooo nice, such nice guys, really. Just a few assholes here and there, and even *they* are pretty harmless. You'll get to know how to handle them."

"Thank you, Shish…" Melisse said, screwing up her face once again, trying not to cry.

"Don't mess up your pretty eyelashes and mascara over him. He's not worth it. He's nothing. He's the turd of an ant." Melisse held back a sad giggle.

"He's a parasite in the turd of an ant," Melisse confirmed.

"Yes, that's right. He's the…I don't know how you get any smaller than a parasite in the turd of an ant!" she laughed.

Then Shisha leaned down and in her high, sweet, breathy voice, said in Melisse's ear, "Here's what you're going to do about that little prick," before whispering further instructions.

CHAPTER 18

The Oscar-Winning Performance

Melisse opened the door to the Honeymoon Suite and saw the two guys and the two ladies still in orgy mode. The women seemed totally fed up with these two bozos. They weren't the usual fare, that was for sure, but Melisse was too green to decipher that.

Ignoring them, she went to her pile of clothes and slid back into her dress. Clothing was power in a room full of nakedness. Melisse strode over to the Bose sound machine and cut the music on all of them, mid-fucking, just like in the movies when "the party's over."

Then she walked right up to Weasel. Everyone stopped what they were doing to look at her.

I'm a star; I'm holding center stage, she thought with some satisfaction. She got so close to Weasel that he moved away nervously, but there was no stopping her now.

She found her power voice, putting away the idiotic voice that previously giggled and said stupid things to get through the night.

> **Spicy Secret:** Sometimes it's necessary to "dumb down" to fit in or create a good chemistry with what a client wants or needs. But most of the time, it's best to just be yourself (even if you're a bit serious or reserved). Somewhere, somehow, someone will love what you have to offer, and those with discerning tastes especially appreciate an "authentic" woman who doesn't hide her intelligence.

"You know, *honey*, there was a reason why I wanted you to wear a condom tonight," she said in a no-nonsense voice. "You really assumed a lot of risks when you walked into a place like this. It's a *whorehouse*! Or haven't you noticed? So when you decided to tear off your condom and come inside me and *expose* yourself to a girl like me, did you *ever* think about the consequences?"

Everyone looked terrified and wide-eyed. Silence. Weenies softening.

"Uhhhh…" he said nervously.

"So let me tell you a true story about me…" she continued.

His face filled with dread.

"Last summer I was living in Chicago and I was walking in the park and guess what? I got raped—no, that's too nice a word for it. I got *sodomized*. I got butt fucked, for those of you who only know slang. Some big guy just grabbed me and dragged me off into the bushes and that was it, man.

"I won't bore you with all the details, but this guy was, like, two hundred and fifty pounds, and when he was holding me down with his arms as I was trying to fight him off, I got a glimpse at something *I'd* certainly never seen before. What do you think that was? His arms were covered, up and down, with *track marks*."

Weasel's eyes widened.

"Shall I go into further detail? Oozing, raised, *infected* track marks… This was a mean, mad drug addict."

"Oh, God!" Shisha sighed dramatically. "Melisse! That's so awful!"

"Tell me about it. I'm just glad to be alive. So when he was done beating and then raping me and right before he left me for dead in the bushes, I heard him say, 'Little bitch. Your timer just got set.'"

"Oh, no," Livia sighed with sympathy.

"Jesus fuckin' Christ," the Mole said.

Then Melisse poked the Weasel's chest with her finger, hard. "And so *that's* why I wanted you to keep your condom on tonight, you fuckin' prick! Before you took your rubber off, you didn't even stop to think that I might be HIV positive?"

The lights in the room seemed to flicker. Melisse detested telling this story, for in telling it so intensely, the lie became a part of her, as if it had really happened. The other girls were twisting uncomfortably in the background, but Melisse went on staring at Weasel.

"No way," he said, trying to seem controlled, yet trembling and clutching his gold chain with a cross suspended from it. "Then why are you working *here*?"

"*Why not* here? This job is fine as long as everyone wears a condom. I make enough money working a few nights so I can rest most of the week. Do you seriously think I could ever go back to some nine-to-five job when I don't know how much longer I have left? I'm so exhausted these days I'm lucky if I can just get out of bed in the morning. This doesn't demand very much of me and it's over very quickly, and that's good, because I just want to live the best I can now. My medications are incredibly expensive."

"Have you gotten tested?"

She mimicked his whiny voice. "'Have you gotten tested?' So what…?"

Then she raised her voice to the rooftop.

"So when you fucked me without a condom, you'd know that your precious little shit-eating self would be safe? Who gives a damn about *you*! Do you seriously think one girl in this place gives a rat's ass about *your* health? You're a big boy. You knew what the risks were when you came in here. You should have known what the risks were when you took your little condom off and decided to put your little pencil dick in *here*!" she screamed, pointing to her vagina.

She then stepped closer, leaning into his ear. "Lenny, I just think you should know. I'm one of those white, middle-class HIV-positive women who looks healthy, but who's really not. But now you know the truth—I have the HIV virus, honey, and I'm heading toward full-blown AIDS. And you probably are, too, now."

She stepped away and said, "You should be very careful around your new baby, and you'd better find some way to avoid having sex with your wife for a while. But oh, I forgot, it doesn't matter anyway, right? She was big and pregnant last week, so she's the *last* person you'd want to have sex with! I mean, why make love with your little wifey who just shit out a kid for you, when you can sneak into the city…to go bareback with HIV-infected *hookers*…on the night of your wife's baby shower!"

At this, Weasel turned to his buddy. "Shit, man. Let's get out of here. This got fucked up. I'm truly fucked."

"You're not fucked, honey," Shisha said calmly. "You're just a fucker."

"I'd say he's a *mother*fucker," Livia chimed in. "One. Big. Motherfucker."

The guys dressed in a hurry, left the room, and ran down the stairs.

Livia grabbed her clothes and gave Melisse a half-sympathetic look before sliding out the door.

Livia would find out later that it was all a lie, and she'd respect her more. She'd whisper to the other girls who worked in the house about Melisse's incredible performance that night, for years to come.

Shisha was sitting on the bed, dressed again. She silently clapped her hands and blew kisses over to Melisse. "Bravo!" she whispered conspiratorially as she took Melisse's elbow and the two walked down the stairs to face their naughty "clients" in the Living Room.

As the two men cashed out and prepared to leave, Melisse and the other girls sat on the couches, waiting to get paid and scowling at the offender. The guys handed around their tips. Melisse found that Weasel had given her an extra-large tip.

Suddenly, GG was standing there in the hallway, blocking the men's way out. She looked like a guardian angel, wearing a silky white seventies-style caftan dress with winged sleeves.

Spicy Secret: If you save a quality fashion piece long enough, it will eventually come back into style. If you buy well, it won't ever go out of style and you can wear it forever, even to look chic at your own funeral.

She nodded at Melisse, signaling that she had heard about most of the confrontation, either from Ruby the housekeeper, or perhaps from the yelling downstairs and then eavesdropping at the door, or watching it all play out on a hidden surveillance system. The important thing was, she was there.

The men moved to leave the room, but GG blocked the door. She had a friendly look on her face. "Gentlemen, did you have a nice time?" she asked graciously.

They looked at each other and shrugged. "I know it's late. And we know you live out of town. But you've simply had too much to drink. We cannot allow you to be out on the roads or trains like that. So you'll be getting a ride home tonight with our house driver. Please go downstairs. He's waiting for you!"

"But…the car is…"

"Oh, no, no. I *insist*. We don't want any DUIs now. I've set it all up. I know where you *live, remember*? Your car is safe at the parking garage, is it not?"

The men seemed pleased enough and hurried out to the foyer. GG opened the door wide and motioned for Melisse to come and watch. Standing outside next to his long white Cadillac was Nate, the bouncer from The Pussycat, Melisse's introducer to GG, and GG's all-around fixer/errand man/hush-money transporter.

He grinned up at GG and winked at Melisse, then looked at the guys in a friendly way. "Go ahead, guys. Jump in." The way he said it, this was a kind offer they really could *not* refuse.

The men went down the stairs, got in silently, and they all drove off.

"Where are they *going*?" Melisse asked.

"Oh…Nate is such a dear. He'll be taking them on what we might call 'a little joy ride.'" GG sighed and then adopted a genteel tone, as if she were an elegant tour guide describing a fine night out.

"Nate has an old cop friend in the Bronx with a proper basement facility where he'll take the guys…to have a drink, get high, you know…to relax and meet some underage strippers for a private lap dance. But the evening will take a different turn when the skinny one who compromised you will suddenly find himself in a "bar fight" and have his ass kicked around, his face bloodied *just a bit*, and perhaps a tooth or two knocked out, while his friend watches helplessly. And then before you know it, they'll be back in the Caddy on yet another delightful adventure. They'll find themselves dropped off, lost and scared shitless at three in the morning in an area of the Bronx that has…how shall we say, *yet to gentrify*. Perhaps they can find some shelter until sunrise in a crack house."

The whole description had Melisse laughing nervously, and wonderfully. *Good riddance.*

Melisse knew their first stop well. Tony's Wedge. *God bless handsome Tony.*

"And...when Lenny comes looking for his car, which Nate will have asked him to point out so he could generously pay his extra garage expenses for the night, the car will sadly, not be found. You see, Nate seems to have a friend in the "towing" business. In fact, Lenny's new family-size Mercedes will soon enough have a new identity entirely and eventually be enjoyed by someone in South America. And, of course, the proceeds from the "sale" of that vehicle will go to you, Melisse. That should pay for any esthetic improvements you may be considering. We should know by next week what it fetched."

"Wow, thank you!"

"*De rien.* It's nothing."

GG closed the door behind her. "You can be sure they won't be pulling *that* shit again."

> **Spicy Secret: Men with no manners (and women in the business with no morals or ethics): think twice before screwing over other girls and their bosses in the sex biz, whether it be with violence or even the arrogance of writing "bad reviews" that destroy or disrupt her business. You'd never guess how well-connected some sex workers are to "friends in high (and low) places" (like the CIA, Mafia, lawyers, private investigators, and anyone else who can fuck up your life). The girl might not be that mad at you, but her "friends" in high and low places may be extra pissed when you hurt someone they love.**

Melisse followed GG upstairs to her private apartment, where there was a large envelope stuffed with a normal week's worth of income waiting for Melisse on the console table, even though Melisse had only worked one night.

"So how *the hell* did this happen? You were supposed to protect me!" Melisse demanded, sipping from a glass of chilled dessert wine GG had poured out for her—several times already.

"Protect *you*! *You're* the one who's HIV positive, fucking around in my house!"

For a moment, Melisse thought GG was serious. Then she let out a big guffaw. "Ha! I know that's not true! I know we just tested you last week. You were brilliant, young lady. An Oscar-winning performance! From now on, please use that talent of yours with the clients, but in more constructive ways."

It annoyed Melisse that GG was seemingly trying to make light of the situation.

"How did they get in? I thought this was supposed to be an airtight operation!"

"These men were absolutely *mistakes*—I don't know *how* they got in here! Kin and I have never seen them before! They were *not* my clients! I want to KILL them! There is something very off here."

"I thought you said you knew where they live."

"I should. But I don't."

"They weren't your clients?"

"No, please," GG said, slugging down Melisse's glass of wine. "They slipped through. Somehow they had the right door code, the right phone booking pass code, but they weren't on the books as members when we finally looked them up tonight. They slipped through." GG slumped down on the couch. "I'm…how do you say? Freaked out. But Nate will scare some sense into them."

"I agree, from what I know of Nate," Melisse concurred. "So their little 'joy ride' tonight isn't *just* about avenging me? It's about making them too scared to ever talk about *you* to anyone?"

Melisse was shocked at her boldness, but tonight had brought out her fighting spirit in a big way.

"Well, it's both. We're killing two shit birds with one stone."

GG took Melisse's hands in hers. Melisse, after everything she'd gone through, was a bit reluctant to be affectionate this evening.

"I'm so sorry; I've lost your trust, but I will earn it back. I'm not in the habit of letting something like this ever happen to one of my girls.

I'm sure you're probably going to be fine and we'll test you again in a few months and you'll see…you'll be fine. I'm sorry it was a bad first night for you."

Then, smiling, she added, "All this drama means all the rest of your nights in your career are going to be fabulous. Smooth sailing, you'll see. Your baptism by fire is now over!"

Melisse smiled weakly. GG had probably seen enough in her time to know that this was true. GG poured a little more wine into Melisse's glass. Melisse tried to lighten the mood by recounting the funny thing Shishapuss had said on the way up the stairs, and how she had referred to it as her "hot burning hubbly bubbly pipe."

"*That's* Shisha. You'd do well to make her your best friend in The Life, Miss Melisse. She's worked with me a long time, and I know her to be a very sensible, sensitive person. She'd never do you wrong, and she knows everything there is to know about being a good courtesan."

"I'll think about it. Thank you."

"No. You'll do it. It was not a suggestion."

Little did Melisse know that GG would cry herself to sleep that night. She was devastated by the fact that Melisse's first night had ended so badly. After all the years of worrying about her girls and her operation, moments like this were rare, but they deeply affected her.

She'd always believed that one day she would have to answer to God at the Pearly Gates. Not for being a madam, but for the unforgivable sin of making a bad judgment that might cause one of her young ladies to suffer even one moment of pain or physical hurt.

Contrary to what so many thought, this business at the very high end was a relatively safe haven for the women. The well-heeled clients were, for the most part, nearly always on their best behavior with the girls.

When GG was done crying over the incident with Melisse, she cried for the way she woke up every morning, alone and without an adoring man to cuddle her. How had a beautiful, accomplished woman such as her come to this? She cried about staying cooped up in her house and giving up her world travels in the name of running a business. She cried about the stress hormones she felt coursing through her veins the minute she woke up in the morning, and when the phones rang off the hook as she tried to match all these people up and meet their high expectations for what "her girls" would supposedly offer (especially the ones spread the world over who catered to her "Other List").

Who wanted to cuddle an old madam living on the top floor of New York's most legendary bordello? And why hadn't she walked away long ago?

Spicy Secret: "If you must play, decide upon three things at the start: the rules of the game, the stakes, and the quitting time." —Chinese proverb

GG was so caught up in her addiction to handling her business in The Life that she kept it hidden away from almost everyone. Little by little she had retreated from society. Malcolm was the exception. He was a brilliant British client who attempted to sincerely befriend her and whom she ultimately hired as a highly discreet and well-connected consultant. He helped her clean her money, pay her taxes, and diversify her investments outside the United States to be square with the powers that be.

Now she rarely left her house, had no friends except Malcolm and her girls, and had become a prisoner of the limited thinking of her own mind. She had always dreamed of retiring to the beautiful old restored plantation-style beach house she owned in Barbados.

Barbados.

It was always there, beckoning to her with its shiny wood floors, white ceiling fans, and plantation shutters facing a huge wraparound porch.

But GG was like a gambler who knew she should get up from the table soon, but was too much into the game now to leave: *Let's play just one more hand.*

It's time to let go and retire. You've had enough.

As she fell asleep, she reached up for her cat and found him sleeping near her head. His warm presence soothed her thoughts as she said her nightly prayer.

"All that I have, all that I need, all that I want…comes to me in the perfect moment and in the perfect way by divine grace. And so it is."

Spicy Secret: "Let go and let God (or whatever God means to you personally)." There is a higher power that is always at work in our lives. If you hand over your cares to this power before you sleep, you'll sleep better knowing it's now being "handled" in ways and means that you might never have conceived of. Visualize this higher power as a master dry cleaner who can accept all of your dirty laundry and return it back clean and pressed the next day.

CHAPTER 19

A New Best Friend

Back downstairs, Shishapuss was the last one in the waiting room. She was wearing her casual street clothes, which gave away nothing of her smoldering secret lifestyle. She was waiting to make sure Melisse didn't have to leave alone on her very first night in The Life as she had once had to do.

Shisha graciously offered to take Melisse out for a bite at the corner Greek diner before they made their separate ways home. Over Chicken Caesar salads, Shisha said, "Don't feel so bad. Things like this happen to all of us sooner or later. That was about the worst it's ever going to be, as long as you stay careful and you keep working on the high end of things."

Melisse sighed. "Thank you. But it's really all my fault. I wasn't watching what he was doing."

"Melisse, it's not your fault! It's not about reaching back there and seeing if the condom is on. It's all about how you *carry* yourself. How you…*comport* yourself. And *that* determines if they'll try to disrespect you or not."

"Comport myself?" Melisse said.

"Yes. Can I tell you something, girl to girl? Even in a whorehouse—*especially* in a whorehouse—if you allow people to treat you like shit, shit is *exactly* what they'll think you are, and shit is exactly how they'll treat you. When he had his tongue shoved down your throat and you didn't like it, was a good time to tell him to back off and that you have limits, or else you'll kick his ass (which you have to say in the sweetest way)."

Spicy Secret: "Respect yourself, and others will respect you." —Confucius

Spicy Secret: "No one can make you feel inferior without your consent." —Eleanor Roosevelt, *This Is My Story*

Shisha continued, "Couldn't you just tell that those guys were assholes when you first met them in the Living Room? I mean, they talked the talk, they walked the walk, and they stank the stink of the breed we've all come to know as 'the asshole client.'"

"Yes..." Melisse nodded.

"But didn't you see they'd be assholes in the bedroom, too? An *asshole* in the Living Room is an even bigger *asshole* in the bedroom! The same social rules that apply in real life also apply here, but they're on 'high speed.'"

"Hmmm?"

"Let's say, for example, you had a first date with a straight guy, not a client, and you saw he was a douche bag, or let's say he treated the waitress badly or he talked to you rudely. Would you have had a second date with him?"

"No, not anymore," she agreed. "But I *used* to do things like that. I used to feel *lucky* if someone, even some turd, wanted to have a second date with me. But things have changed."

"Didn't we all let men walk all over us at some point in our lives before we 'woke up'! You're too nice—and that's fine to be nice—but if you project that doormat thing too much in this biz, every cock-sucking john in the world will come out of the woodwork to wipe his feet on you. Believe me, Melisse, it takes one to know one. As a former doormat myself, I'm here to tell you that those days are over for me."

"Yes, they're over for me, too. What kind were you? Of doormat, I mean."

"I was…a red shag. And you?"

"One of those wiry brown ones, the kind that looks like Dachshund dog fur," Melisse offered, which made them bust up laughing.

"OK, continuing on! Well, OK. So in the Living Room, it's like your first date where you watch him and interact with him. And the bedroom is like your second date, when you sleep with him. It's the same process as dating; it just goes a little faster and you have to put up with people you wouldn't ordinarily date or sleep with. When you see that they're unpleasant, you need to keep an extra eye on them!"

"But I thought I was supposed to accept them if they're clients."

"No! If none of the girls wants to be with someone because he seems like an asshole or he's been one in the past, that man will sit in the Living Room and get frozen out by the girls. It's like pro baseball down there. The girls have signs and signals when a guy comes in. Didn't you notice us all signing? Didn't you see me signing to you about him, with my earring?"

"Huh? There was signing going on?"

"Yes! Didn't they show you? God, I guess Kin forgot to."

"So how does it work?"

"OK. If he's been a real jerk before, like talked badly to one of the girls, or just been unpleasant to be with, one of the girls will do this…" Shisha pulled down on her right earlobe several times. "Or if he's just an exhausting never-ending fuck, like a real pounder, which some of the girls can't handle because they want to keep their energy going for the whole night for other clients, or maybe she has a special date, then they'll go like this…" Shisha rubbed her hand across the bottom of her nose several times.

"No way!"

"Yes way. If nobody wants to see him, he'll leave because nobody will go upstairs with him. GG runs a clean house. She doesn't care who stays or who goes, if that's what the girls decide! If he can't get laid, then he's come to the wrong place."

"But what if *nobody* wants him?"

"That almost never happens. Because someone is there to make money and will put up with whatever the issue is. Usually a mature woman like me, who can verbally whip his ass around the block. They know not to dare mess with me. Some of these guys, they say some shitty thing to try and put me down but I subtly get them back with something I might say. So they find themselves bleeding after the appointment, but they don't know where or when I stuck the knife in, you know? They just know their ego has been damaged."

"And they have nobody to blame but themselves," Melisse chuckled. Then they sat silently for a while, finishing their salads.

"Most of the guys are soooo, sooo nice, Melisse. Soooo nice. But sometimes you get one. Like last week… You know, GG always markets me as this extremely intelligent, bombshell diva of a woman. Great. OK. So this guy asked me, 'If you're so smart, why are you doing *this*?' I mean, come on, how low can you blow?"

Spicy Secret: "The moment you feel you have to prove your worth to someone is the moment to absolutely and utterly walk away." —Alysia Harris

"Ouch."

"Ouch is right. But I zinged him back. Don't you worry. Just remember, the whole reason most clients go out of their way to insult us about being pros is because deep down they feel bad that, for whatever reason, they have to pay for sex."

"That might be why, but it's still not right for them to take it out on *us*."

"No, and when they do, you have to decide: take their shit and let it go, *or* set them straight. Immediately. Before they perpetuate their evil. Just nip the insults in the bud and dish something back."

"Ha! I had one tonight already. I was going down on him and the guy grabbed my head and said, "I want to watch how *a real pro* does it."

"See? There you go. He just *had* to point out to you and remind you that you're a prostitute so he could feel superior."

"So what should I have *said*?"

"You should have said, 'Ohhhh, yes, baby. I *am* such a big big whore, I just luuuuuv to give head to johns like you. I love that you pay me for sucking you off.'" Shisha laughed. "And then show him your teeth, like you're going to bite it off, and snarl at him. But then just continue sucking until he has one of his low-pressure ejaculations. But no cuddles after! He didn't earn those cuddles from you by being nice."

"Ah, I see…"

"See? This is obviously a man who has to put his balls up in a jar when he gets home. Just feel sorry for him. I swear to God. He'll come back to you looking for more because you didn't let him break you. And he'll be nice the next time."

Spicy Secret: "Is this her fault or mine? The tempter or the tempted, who sins most?" —William Shakespeare

"I think I met someone nice tonight," Melisse confessed, alluding to the cute client she'd just had her first Girlfriend Experience with.

"Don't go any further," Shisha said, holding up her hand. "Listen, serious business. Some of the guys, when they see that you're new, will use you up and toss you aside if you let them. You're only here to give them one thing: the pleasurable use of your body *for a limited amount of time* and *maybe* a little bit of your mind, whatever you're willing to share. Don't *ever* let anyone have more than that. They get to screw your body, not your mind, and whatever you do, *don't* give a client your heart or your precious time for free, even if you're tempted. *That's* dangerous territory. Never. Ever. Go. There. *Unless* you love him *and* he's prepared to whisk you off your feet, take you out of The Life *that very day*, and make your life infinitely better."

Melisse felt herself blushing, thinking of the ER Doc she'd entertained this evening whom she'd agreed to meet with on the weekend for her birthday dinner (and who would never show up).

She nodded, understanding now and wondering how she could have been so naive. Still, maybe the Doc was different. She was still willing to find out. Melisse knitted her brows (this was before she discovered Botox).

"Ohhh, honey," Shisha sighed, putting her hand over Melisse's. "I just feel so bad for you. But this condom thing is never going to happen again."

Then, with a wide grin, Shisha ordered a piece of New York cheesecake with strawberries on top for them to share, and told Melisse some of the secrets of the ancient hetaerae, French courtesans, and modern call girls.

In the quiet booth at the back of the diner, she taught Melisse how she could work all month long, therefore not losing income to Mother Nature (by using the controversial practice of taking birth control pills all month without "the pill break"). Or how, even while she had her period, she could continue working by using slightly moistened natural sea sponges tucked inside her, just for the hour when she would meet a client. He'd never feel a thing—as long as she remembered to take the thing out before the date turned into a bloody horror movie!

She even described to Melisse how to fill the end of a condom with water so that men who liked to get "rimmed" or "around the world" (licked around their assholes) could feel just like she was using the tip of her tongue.

> **Spicy Secret: "Rimming" for real is more of a specialty service, not typically expected of ladies of the evening. But for those willing to do it (for those clients who love and request it) the service can be a real money-maker (because you'll charge a supplement for it). Since not everyone does it, they'll be extra-loyal and repeat visitors. If you like licking assholes, this is the way to go.**

Shisha taught Melisse how to get up properly from a bed (using her knees and feet for leverage first before rising), as she was going to be getting in and out of beds a lot more than the average person over the course of a day.

She taught Melisse to never, ever allow a client to do her from behind without propping herself up on several pillows first. "It's a very good way to hurt your back and go out of commission for weeks," Shisha counseled.

"And if you never want a condom to break on you, remember the words of the famous watercolor artists: 'Always keep your palette wet. Where lube is concerned, too much is never enough.'"

> **Spicy Secret: Use water-based lubricants ONLY. Never use anything else or allow a man to massage you "down there" with vegetable or mineral-based oils, as nothing weakens or breaks down a condom faster than oil.**

As they sat talking, it was like one of those "pre-honeymoon" talks big sisters used to have with their clueless little sisters back in the 1950's. Except that the "wedding night" had already taken place in GG's Honeymoon Suite.

Melisse thanked the Lord for big sisters like Shishapuss.

"If you don't mind my asking, what was your breaking point?" Shisha asked Melisse. "Everyone has one. That moment when you decide you're going to sell your body."

While Melisse saw the stripping episode as a gradual softening of her mind towards the whole idea, she confided that her *real* breaking point on the road to GG's had happened when she was raped by a jerk she had thought she knew better. She recounted to Shisha how he lured her to his apartment with an invitation to travel together, and then when she merely asked him to wear a condom, he had humiliated her by forcing himself on her without a condom as she screamed, scratched, and cried for him to stop.

He'd answered by pinning her down on the bed and pumping her hard, saying, "I bet you're sorry you told me about your little fantasy of becoming a whore. How do you like it? Wanna go to France *now?*"

He'd groaned like a beast, and then nearly kicked her toward the bathroom where he told her to "Go wash off the evidence. And if you report this, I'll cut your tits off."

At some point during the telling, Shisha had grabbed Melisse's hand and held it tight. Melisse only noticed it when she came to the end of the story.

"Shisha, in that moment, I vowed that nobody would ever just 'take' from me. From then on, they would have to pay for it. And here I am."

"Here you are." Shisha listened, sadly shaking her head. "Honey, one night we're going to go on a special mission and teach that guy a lesson!"

"OK!" Melisse agreed, not really believing Shisha, but Shisha was the kind of woman who always meant business and kept her word; Melisse just didn't know that yet.

"Listen. At GG's you have the luxury to be choosy about who you let into your experience. And GG doesn't want us to be unhappy. But that doesn't matter. *You* don't want you to be unhappy. So don't ever do anything you don't want to. They're like buses, these guys—other clients always come along. That's the one great thing about this business: in any economy, in any big city, there's always plenty of business to go around. *If* you're good-looking, smart, and sweet girls like us."

"Oh, well, thank you!"

"You're welcome."

"And you? What are you doing it all for?"

"I'm an actress, but I never wanted to be a *starving* actress. I feel I've been playing this role for a little too long now. I could retire on this role alone. I'm ten years already in this business and I save virtually every penny."

"How do you do it, I mean, stand it?"

"I like to think of all these tricks as performances, and I'm the star of a big Broadway play. Sometimes the session is an afternoon matinee, sometimes an evening performance. And everyone wants me to play a different role for them. Very rarely do I ever get to play myself. But that would be nice. I'd like to go out on my own sometime, but the houses provide a constant stream of clients and income."

"If you go out on your own, maybe you'd get to finally play the fabulous Smoking-Hot Shisha."

"Smoking-Hot Shisha. I think I'll use that…" she mused, then held a finger to her arm and hissed, as if she were too hot to touch.

> **Spicy Secret:** Don't be surprised when you find "performing" to be exhausting. It's natural to feel drained, tired, and a little out of sorts after "being on" and "putting on a show" for a few hours (and for some, days) without a break.
>
> Don't let the "travel companion" or "all day/all night" clients stage-manage your show. Carve out (and negotiate for) some precious "alone time" in advance of your "theatrical" engagements.

CHAPTER 20

Put a Little Love Into It

In the months that followed, Melisse often thought of all the men (and, in fact, kept a detailed list of them) she had been upstairs with. Precious few of them were men she would choose for herself, but if she learned to accept them, maybe she could pretend desire as effectively as Shisha, Livia, and the other girls. She was never going to get many clients if her negative thoughts about them showed in her face or in her body language.

She realized that if she wanted to make money, she had to accept these men. She could replace her lack of desire for them physically with respect for them as human beings, which was worth a lot more in the long run than just acting horny, no matter how convincing.

> **Spicy Secret:** "A stranger is just a new friend you haven't met yet." Once past your security clearance, it's best to approach and speak with new clients as if they were old friends. They've taken the (often) bold step of reaching out to you. Now it's up to you to take them the rest of the way.

The "exchange"—which occurred in private—always had a theatrical element to it. Both participants simply suspended their disbelief for an hour or two while they hooked up. But if she wanted to be a first-class courtesan and a real success in The Life, Melisse knew she'd have to offer something superior, something more *real*. She'd have to offer "love" in some form or other.

So she decided to love her clients on some level, to accept and care for them while she lived in their fantasy world. She would conduct herself with underlying love instead of underlying disgust or hate or a spirit of manipulation. She suddenly remembered a saying from childhood that was appropriate to her situation: *Find something nice about a person, even if it's just one thing...*

It was the one redeeming thing about each man that would release her fears and her dread and her disgust. She would also be able to tame the hurtful accusations she could make against herself for choosing The Life. And hopefully, this would be the alchemy that could turn her tarnished hooker's heart to pure gold.

Spicy Secret: Act "as if"—and thus, it shall be.

One night many months later, Melisse sat with GG as she did her paperwork. "I'm just going to love them, whether I really do or not," Melisse told her.

"That's well and good," GG said, "but don't love *them*. Love *yourself*. Show great care for yourself first, otherwise you'll have nothing left to give *them*."

During her fully paid week off following "the first-night incident," Melisse enjoyed her sudden windfall, but she could also see that this business had the potential to drive her nuts. She began attending a spiritual center GG suggested to her to keep her balanced.

There, during a workshop, she had been asked to write a letter to herself in the future, to the woman she would be one day, looking back on her life from the perspective of a much older, wiser person.

After much thought, Melisse made this journal entry while sitting in a Soho café with a glass of hot apple cider:

Dear Melissa,

I am you, but in the future.

Oh, the lessons you are learning, young lady. It's taking time and tears to learn this particular kind of physical and emotional endurance, I know, but I can tell you that it will be worth it. You didn't arrive on this path for no reason.

Simply put, one cannot be squeamish in this timeless, ever-evolving business of being a pleasure-giver. Only when you learn to accept human nature and all its sticky gray areas can you proceed gracefully to become a "provider," someone who takes care of men who come seeking satisfaction—in one form or another—from you.

Once behind those closed doors and atop the pretty linens, you will be faced with a man who is in essence a spirit struggling to feel free under the weight of his physical body, all his collected memories, his earthly pursuits, his responsibilities, and his many possessions.

Remember: he just wants to feel free of everything and to live in the present for a short period. You can facilitate a temporary escape into pleasure and passion and the satisfaction he's craving, but never believe you are responsible for anything more.

Keep it light. You're an entertainer, a healer, a giver of what is missing, and you will be the source of many men's warmth in a cold, harsh world where each is struggling in his own way.

Don't feel bad about what you're doing. Be proud.

You're an angel along the way for him. Just as there are angels along the way for you.

For as long as you remain in the erotic profession, you are fulfilling a special assignment. Just know that every fallen angel, no matter how negatively she is perceived by others, or even herself, is still a child of God.

And so there is meaning and purpose to what you are doing.

Just go with it. Go with the flow and see where it takes you.

CHAPTER 21

Shame on Shamus

It was well over a year after Melisse had been initiated into GG's House of Pleasure. By then, Shishapuss and Melisse were working together in the house and had become good friends and respectful colleagues, even if Shisha was far more popular and established in "the business" than Melisse.

Now, on Halloween night, the two young women had just finished an evening of work at GG's. They sat together in the back of Nate's old white Cadillac with the dark tinted windows, which was now parked in front of a nondescript building in Murray Hill. It was rare these days to see Nate, Melisse's old bouncer friend from The Pussycat Lounge (and the man who'd introduced her to GG).

Nate seemed to be brought around only on "special occasions," like when naughty clients needed to be dealt with, large sums of money needed to be moved about, or when girls needed "favors" or secure transportation (if "party favors" like recreational drugs were going to be involved).

Nate was always well paid because he kept his mouth shut and got things done. And tonight, according to Shisha, was a special occasion, *and* a night of getting things done.

A few minutes before, Shisha and Melisse had slid into the back of Nate's Caddy wearing completely outrageous S and M dominatrix outfits they'd rented for the night in shimmering, slithery leather, complete with tall boots. Their faces were shrouded by black leather masks and hairpieces (Melisse was a redhead for the night and Shisha was a blonde, in a divine role reversal). But the costumes and masks did little to hide the fact that two beautiful women sparkled beneath them.

They'd met Nate discreetly on a corner near GG's house before being driven the short distance to Murray Hill. Nate had only turned around and given Melisse a kind, knowing nod "hello."

"Shisha baby. Strawberry Shortcake. How you two pretty girls be doin'? Long time no see."

"We're good. But we're on a mission tonight," Shisha said in a businesslike manner. "It's what I told you about before."

"Gotcha," Nate said, having been briefed completely.

"This needs to be neat," Shisha insisted tersely as Nate pulled into traffic.

"I'll be right here, ready to roll, and you got me on the line," Nate said, pointing to a mobile phone on the center of his console.

Before they knew it, they were parked around the corner from their destination.

"Are you ready?" Shisha asked, taking Melisse's hand, which was covered in tight leather gloves pulled over even tighter rubber gloves.

"I think…" Melisse hesitated. "Are you *sure* I can't be recognized?"

"There's no way. Remember—we're not doing anything *really* bad. It's not exactly against the law to do what we're about to do."

"And we break all kinds of laws already, anyway…"

"Right," Shisha chuckled. "Well, speak for yourself."

"And this motherfucker has it coming. It's long overdue. I can't thank you enough for pushing me to take care of this, Shish…"

"Don't mention it. It's nothing. I love missions like this. And you're not going to speak, so he'll never know it's you. I'll be doing all the talking. But you'll be taking care of the details. Like the…" Shisha pulled out a big plastic bag full of mushy dog shit.

"Oh!"

Even though there was no stink because it was sealed in a ziplock bag, it still made Melisse cringe as she transferred it to the purse she had strapped around herself. She needed both hands free for what she was about to do. The shit still felt warm, and given its bulk, it had come from a large dog, maybe a German shepherd or a Rottweiler.

"Running with the big dogs, Shish?"

Shisha snickered.

"My neighbor now thinks I'm crazy, by the way. I mean, I'm out there asking him if I can clean up after his big dog with my own little plastic sack."

"What did you *say*?"

"That I need fertilizer for my sick fern! Like, 'Scoop, scoop! Zip, zip! Thanks a bunch! My fern will be so happy.'" Shisha laughed.

"And…" she said, pulling a stun gun from her purse, "if things get a little out of control with this one, it's just a little old zap…to his balls. I'm sure it won't come to that."

"Yeah, just a little zap'll do ya. I am glad we're doing this," Melisse said shakily.

"It's what friends *do* for friends."

Melisse never stopped marveling at Shisha's ability to finesse just about any situation. And she never stopped marveling at her friend's ability to keep her word. On their first night out for dinner together, before they were even close, Shisha had pledged that she and Melisse would one day avenge this particular little crime of Melisse's "youth" that had gone unpunished.

And tonight was the night a little bit of justice would be exacted.

They didn't even know if the guy would be home, but Shish had paid Nate to do some recon on the guy's usual habits, and it seemed likely he would be home. It was worth getting dressed up, getting Nate on duty, and gathering up some big dog's shit to do what she had to do.

Suddenly, Melisse was climbing the same stairs that, seven years before, had led her to the most degrading, upsetting night of her life. This man had lured her there with a proposal for a romantic trip, then forced himself on her against her will as she screamed and cried for him to stop. Afterwards, he treated her like a piece of garbage before she managed to run out of there to safety.

And now, Melisse felt the same fear, horror, and disbelief (that one human being would do that to another) flashing through her body all over again.

The girls knocked, and he answered.

It was surprising that a date rapist would still be living in the same apartment. You'd think that someone like that would get in trouble sooner or later and have to move around a lot, but Shamus was still there, a pale, middle-aged sloth consuming—or make that binging, or over-dosing on—porn, watching TV, or whatever it was that misogynistic, socially retarded cowards did on Halloween night when they couldn't get a date (or a rape) in New York City.

"Trick…or treat?" Shisha said, holding out a small empty shopping sack and smiling wide under her black sequined cat-eye mask.

"Well, well."

"Do you have some candy for us, baby, or…uh…maybe some booze?" she asked. Melisse stood by, smiling wanly.

He chuckled, looking the girls over in their outrageous outfits.

"Candy is dandy, but liquor is quicker," Shisha said in a sexy, suggestive manner. "Happy Halloween. Can we come in?"

"Uhhhh…yeah!" He laughed. "Who sent you?"

"Can't tell you."

"This is a strip-o-gram or something, right?"

"Something like that."

"Well, I can find some candy. Or liquor. Come in!" he said.

The girls stepped in and looked around. *This is too easy.*

"Do you have any roommates?" Shisha asked.

"Oh, no. It's just me here," he said, scrounging in the small kitchen for a bottle of something and three glasses.

"No dogs here? I love dogs," Shisha enthused.

"No, unfortunately," he said, returning with a bottle. "But I act like a dog sometimes. Anyone like doggy?"

Even Shisha in her fakery could not laugh at his lame sense of humor.

He poured out the drinks and shook his head. "This is kinda crazy. Wow, what a Halloween. Who sent you girls? You're hookers that someone sent over here, right?"

Melisse and Shisha pretended to giggle.

"Something like that! We did say 'trick' or treat. Tricks are better, right?"

"Ohhhh, yeah," he concurred. "Listen, was this prepaid? Because I don't usually pay for…"

Shisha couldn't help but roll her eyes as Melisse dug her gloved fingernails into the couch.

"It's all set up," Shisha nearly hissed.

Melisse and Shisha had agreed they wouldn't drink whatever was offered, but just fake that they were drinking. Who knew what might be in the drinks when a guy like that was offering.

"Your little friend doesn't talk much," he said, snuggling in by Shisha.

"She's one of those strong, silent types of dominatrixes," Shisha said. "She took a vow of silence. Not from pleasure; just from talking."

"I see," he said, his eyes lingering over the leather clinging to their thighs.

Melisse nodded and smiled behind her mask, looking over at the bed where she'd been humiliated. It appeared that he'd never even bothered to freshen up his bedding since that time.

What a loser.

She began to feel excitement boiling up inside her like a tidal wave, knowing that he was just about where they wanted him.

After a little more small talk after he'd downed most of his drink, Shisha said, "Honey, would you like to play a little? Let us put on a little show for you?"

"Ohhhhh, yeahhhhh," he said. "Is it OK if I get naked first?"

"You wanna be naked for your dance? Suuuure!" she said, talking to him like a five-year-old. And before they knew it, he was buck naked and sprawled on the couch with a boner, like some lap dance client. Melisse wanted to vomit at the sight of him. What made out-of-shape men who obviously never made a damn effort at exercise think they had a right to sprawl?

You've heard of "urban sprawl?" Well, there's human sprawl, too, and it ain't pretty.

"Wow, I gotta thank whoever sent you girls over to make this a Halloween night to remember."

"That we guarantee!" Shisha said firmly. "Hey, can I put on our music, baby?"

"Oh, yeah. Do whatever you want, girls."

Shisha looked at Melisse, rolled her eyes, and pulled a portable speaker out of her purse and hooked it into her phone. She turned it up very loud, so that the neighbors wouldn't hear his voice.

It was Queen's "Another One Bites the Dust." On repeat. Over and over.

Shisha really was a good friend, Melisse thought. She always thought of everything when it came to special occasions. Christmas, Valentine's Day, and all the major "family holidays" when the clients usually disappeared off the radar, always found Shisha planning something nice for them instead of staying home alone.

"I need to tie you up for this, sweetie!" she said matter-of-factly, dominatrix style. Well, not exactly. A true dominatrix wouldn't have told him ahead of time.

"Ohhhh, yeah, great! Whatever you want," he said, walking over to a dining room chair. "When a beautiful woman tells me what to do, I comply, man."

Melisse felt like gagging.

"Get the rope," Shisha commanded, and Melisse pulled the soft but strong ropes out of Shisha's large purse. Shisha had shown Melisse how to expertly truss him up to the chair so he wouldn't have any extra "collateral" damage, like cut off circulation, bruising, or telltale marks when all was said and done.

Shisha double-checked Melisse's work. Shamus's hands were disabled and his feet were tied correctly to the feet of the chair. Yes, indeed, he was now basically immobilized.

If Melisse had her way, this asshole would be hogtied on the ground with his ass in the air, so they could rape him repeatedly with an outsize dildo, but the girls had agreed not to do something that could get them into *serious* trouble.

"Ohhhh, sweetie, you're so gonna enjoy what's coming to you," Shisha said, as if she were going to lavish his cock with pleasure all night long. And then, "Pop!" Shisha said softly, which was Melisse's reminder that she should pull out the prepared syringe from her purse and stick him with it.

Shisha stood in front of him, slowly zipping down her leather jumpsuit to reveal the cleavage of her luscious breasts encased in a skin tight, hot-pink bodysuit.

"Hmmmmmmm, what do you think? Like 'em?" she asked proudly.

"Wow!" he uttered, mesmerized. "Nice rack." And then, "Huh?" He winced suddenly as Melisse gave him a small jab in the upper arm with a needle dose of a mild sedative capable of knocking any aggression out of him.

He suddenly went a bit slack-jawed, but his eyes registered that he knew he'd been had by his two "trick or treaters."

"Baby! Don't you know? It's payback time!" Shisha hissed.

"Whaaaa?" he said groggily.

Melisse's heart pounded. An instinct rose up in her to just strangle him then and there, but that would be going a little "off plan."

"DD," Shisha reminded, like a surgeon asking for a scalpel.

A scalpel could work, too. Melisse could just slice off the tip of his nose. Melisse looked into the face of this man who had assaulted her and almost felt sorry for him. What kind of low self-esteem and hate and sense of entitlement must a man feel that would compel him to hold down and rape a tiny, trusting young woman?

Perhaps he'd grown up and moved on, but there was still a ghost of the young Melissa left in that apartment, and Melisse was there to retrieve that young woman in her loving arms and get her out of there safely once she'd corrected this situation once and for all.

"DD!" Shisha said, slightly annoyed.

DD? Oh! Doggy doody.

Melisse reached into her purse and pulled out the sack of dog shit.

Shisha grabbed Shamus by his hair and pulled his head back suddenly, so he wouldn't bite.

"Now, this won't hurt a bit. We're not here to hurt you, baby, just give you a little dog treat."

Melisse opened the ziplock sack as the offending scent wafted over all of them in a shit smog not even a dog lover could love. Melisse held her breath. Shisha wriggled her nose as Melisse handed over the open sack.

"Something just for you, baby! Time to eat shit!"

"OHHHH NOOOOOO!"

"Oh, yes. Good times—open up!" Shisha said, expertly grabbing the plastic sack and smushing its contents into Shamus's nose and gaping mouth.

"AAAARGHHH…OHHHHH…"

"Delicious, isn't it? Smells so good. I know it's an acquired taste, but we thought it was time for you to try something new and different. This is a shit pie! A *tarte de merde*. Like it? Mmmm…"

Melisse chuckled, despite herself.

Shisha kept forcing the shit into his mouth and then forcing his mouth closed with her leather-clad hand, which pressed down on his nose.

Melisse watched, fascinated by her reaction to the scene. It was so… satisfying.

"Swallow!"

"NOOO!" he said, gagging, swallowing nonetheless, then gagging again, as if he wanted to vomit.

"Yes," Shisha growled. "You motherfucker." He was seemingly choking on the bulk of the shit being force-fed into his mouth.

"Breathe, you prick. Through your nose. Now you know what it's like to have something stuffed inside you that you don't want there. It's a great feeling, isn't it!"

He was gurgling and gagging and his eyes were wild as he strained to be released from his ropes. But the drug cocktail was doing its job, and he was still paralyzed from its effects.

Small tears formed in the corners of his eyes. Whether butt fucked or forced to eat shit, it was time for this man to know what it was like to have his dignity and choice suddenly stripped away with no alternatives, just as Melisse had learned while becoming his unwilling victim.

"Oh, yes, delish," Shisha said, slamming another hunk of shit all over his face and smushing it over his forehead, down and up his nose, and then wiping even more by force into his mouth.

"OH yum yum yum yum yum…" she said, as if feeding a baby.

"Eat up."

Gurgle. Choke. Gasping for breath.

"It's time you learn what it's like to be forced to do something against your will, honey. And eating shit is a good place to start," she said authoritatively, calmly.

Shisha stood back and admired her work. His eyes pleaded with her as he took a big gulp of air and finally spit out, "Why me, you fucking cunt?"

"Why *not* you?" Shisha tilted her head. "You've heard of vigilante justice? Well, let's just call this…*shitilante justice!*" She laughed as she quickly discarded the dog bag and gloves in another plastic sack in her purse, pulled on another pair of gloves, and made a quick clean-up check around the premises.

She unplugged the music and neatly threw the apparatus into her big purse.

Done.

Melisse took everything except his glass to the sink and rinsed them off thoroughly. She let the hot water run over them.

Now go in there and wash off all the evidence. That's what he'd said that night when he was done with her as he made her sit in the bathtub.

Yeah, I'll wash off the evidence.

Melisse returned to the scene, where their mark was moaning softly.

The two women then stood in front of him. He was still tied to the chair and not going anywhere soon.

Shisha said, "Isn't he cute? He's still got a shit-eating grin! I think he needs to stop smiling so much. Here you go, babe," she said as she slammed a ball gag into his mouth and tied it tight behind his head. "Now," she said, wagging a finger at him, talking to him like a schoolboy. "This is just a reminder that I don't think you wanna be telling anyone about what just happened to you. The person who sent us to you doesn't like you very much, and this is just a little message… you know, a little 'amuse-bouche' from her to you, to let you know not to *eve*r fuck with her again."

"Aaaargh!" he choked from behind the gag.

"What did you just say? I can't understand you."

That made Melisse chuckle again.

Shisha continued. "OK, so it's a message not to fuck with her—or *anybody*—ever again!! Got it?"

He gave a spineless nod.

"Let's go," Shisha said, the boss of this night and Melisse's very best friend in the world.

Melisse lingered behind for a moment while Shisha checked to make sure the hall was clear.

"Trick or treat, baby," Melisse whispered softly in his ear, before the girls slipped unseen out the door and disappeared into the night.

Spicy Secret: Revenge is a dish best served cold (or in this case, still steaming).

CHAPTER 22

The Last Teatime

It was already Melisse's second Christmas Eve at GG's House of Pleasure. She would later come to think of her two years at GG's as her "finishing school" period in The Life. And after two years of working together, GG and Melisse had become special friends. Although the normal boundaries of respect were still in place, there was definitely a special understanding between them.

Perhaps Melisse reminded GG of herself when she was a young woman working for the famous Madame Claude in Paris. Or perhaps it was simply that Melisse was excellent company for the older woman. After all, Melisse happily climbed up the many stairs of the bordello to take afternoon tea with her mentor in GG's apartment before the real action in the house began.

By now, GG had introduced Melisse to Malcolm, her VIP client who liked to act out his special ball-twisting, jealous rage fantasy. As GG's business consultant, he visited often from London and usually stayed at the Waldorf Towers or the Four Seasons.

Now, it was an incredibly snowy Christmas Eve. There were no flights for the day going back to the UK, and so Malcolm called up GG to request a long, late afternoon date with Melisse until after dinner.

As Malcolm waited for GG to pick up her phone, he watched the snow accumulating outside his window at the Waldorf. It reminded him of his visits to snowy Moscow in the dead of winter to track down hackers who had broken into a private bank's system in New York. They had altered the bank's internal system, to electronically pretend they were bank clients, and managed to wire eight million dollars to their account in Moscow. The New York bank had hired Malcolm to go and get it back, using "whatever means necessary." He had done so after a tremendous struggle.

Now, his thoughts turned to the vivacious blondes he'd bedded with his substantial "finder's fee" after tracking his prey during those months in Moscow. Still, none had satisfied him as Melisse did now, but his needs were not as specific back then.

Spicy Secret: For men with very specific fetishes and fantasies, finding "The One" who can satisfy him perfectly without extra drama is priceless.

"Hello, Malcolm!" GG said, coming on the line in her singsong voice, returning him to the present. "It's Christmastime in Manhattan! Shall I send over your darling present early?"

He didn't know that Melisse was sitting with GG now, enjoying tea in her private parlor. "Yes, please! I adore her!" he replied with undisguised eagerness.

"OK. She'll be there at 4:00 p.m. I know. I love her, too…" GG said, looking at Melisse. "I love her like my own daughter."

Melisse felt a warm flush upon hearing this, and Malcolm asked something on the other end.

"No, no. I can't talk about that right now. She's here with me; she'll be there at 4:00 p.m. You should see the fur-trimmed snowsuit she's got on! *Very* sexy."

She chuckled some more, but it was a mysterious and reserved chuckle full of nervous energy. She bid Malcolm adieu and clicked off. A serious look crossed her face, and when she noticed Melisse looking closely at her, she simply flashed her a smile.

As Melisse and GG sat waiting for her to leave for her appointment with Malcolm, they ate chocolates from a beautiful box covered in gold foil.

"So…" Melisse said, pouring out some more tea, "I'd like to know one of *your* spicy secrets, Ms. GG…"

"Ah! A spicy secret question!"

"Is there anything in your life that you never did professionally, but really wanted to?"

"La Fantasia," GG answered quickly.

"La Fantasia?"

"Yes. It's my vision for a club like this, but more of a private retreat, set aside in a country setting. It's completely feminine and designed more like a spa, with Jacuzzis, gardens, spa treatments… But only for women, completely secure, hidden away behind high walls. I see it as a private estate staffed by men—straight men, handsome men, darling, charming, service-oriented men who know what they're doing and don't mind doing it! La Fantasia will be a place for women where any fantasy, any desire can be…"

"Discreetly fulfilled," Melisse said. Excitement stirred in her solar plexus and she felt small goose bumps appear on her arms. She suddenly pictured La Fantasia as clearly as if it were her own dream.

Spicy Secret: "Hold fast to dreams, for if dreams die, life is a broken-winged bird that cannot fly." — Langston Hughes

"You like that? Isn't it a delicious idea?"

"*I love it!*"

"I'll never get to do it at this point. But I'll transfer my dream to you, to hold as your own if you ever want to take it on."

"It seems like a wonderful idea!" Melisse said. "Imagine a place where any woman could go and be totally physically pampered and satisfied without any complications, without fear of being discovered, without worrying if she's beautiful enough or skinny enough or whatever enough…as long as she has the means…"

"Yes, this was my dream at one point. I just got too busy and too big for my britches catering to *men*. But *someone* needs to create a retreat like this in a beautiful part of the world for women only. I'm sure it would be a big success. But it would need to be a very *discreet* success."

Melisse nodded. *Why not me?* There was a calm inside her now. Before, she had been searching for that special something, a project she could devote her life to besides travel, eating well, and being a courtesan. Being a courtesan couldn't last forever.

"It'll never work in the States," GG said. "Maybe France or Italy, the Caribbean, *anywhere* but here."

"Yes."

"Yes?"

"I love it. I accept your gift. La Fantasia is now my dream."

"La Fantasia is yours." GG smiled. "It is a special assignment transferred from me to you, and you shall fulfill it within your lifetime."

And with this, GG rose and went to a jewelry box hidden inside her dresser drawer. She brought out a dazzling gold ring with a raised floral design of rose gold and yellow gold, with a small round-cut diamond at the center.

"Give me your hand," she told Melisse, reaching for it.

"Really?" Melisse lifted her right hand up to GG, who took her ring finger and slid the ring on. It fit perfectly.

"With this ring, we agree that the dream of La Fantasia has now been conferred from me to you. And you are now duty bound as my favorite protégée and close friend to carry out the creation of this secret refuge for women, hereto known as La Fantasia."

Melisse nodded in solemn agreement, admiring the striking looking ring.

"I do agree to carry out this dream," she confirmed.

"And what else?"

"I agree never to get married under false pretenses."

"You're full of promises on Christmas Eve," GG laughed.

Melisse, the girls, and GG had often discussed this phenomenon of the pampered wife who knowingly marries for money, then proceeds to neglect her husband. It was a common old story among their clients, a story that always managed to get both madam and girls riled up.

Melisse would hear this story or a variation of it many, many times as her career progressed: the story of the men who continued to pay for their wives' lifestyles, providing them with a home, social status, bills paid, and every luxury desired; meanwhile, the same woman would refuse to give him a cursory blow job or a back rub or an erotic cock rub from time to time. *Nothing. Nada. Niente. Nulla*!

These couples would live together like roommates, with him going for years sometimes without sex from his wife. The poor man would continue busting his ass every day, commuting to work to keep up their lifestyle, paying *her* bills, raising their children, and secretly dying from the lack of affection and touch.

Yet he'd feel that he would break a heart or a home if it was discovered that he had finally ventured outside to get what he needed from a professional, and then found that he couldn't live without her secret support.

It might have provided GG and the girls with business, but it still broke Melisse's heart every time a sincere man broke down and told her his dilemma. And the part she always wondered about, but never knew, was whether the wives were having intense, secret love affairs on the side, the kind that went on for years, which made the women indifferent to the needs of their men. Who knew?

GG would always say, "*Those* are the real whores! They may call *us* bad names, but if you want to call someone a whore, look at women who take advantage of a situation like that! They are soooo much smarter than we *romantics*. They have set themselves up well…but believe me, living like that is no life…"

"I agree. When there's no attraction left in a relationship but you stay for his money, the status, and the security—yet you don't *even* want to touch him," Melisse would add, "much less look at him naked. Spare me!"

"Never," they would say in unison. "That will never be us."

"I'd rather work by the hour than work by the life," Melisse would say.

It would become her mantra during her career as clients came along who tried to convert her into their girlfriend. They had no understanding of who she was as a person and were unaware that she was giving a performance and didn't feel the same. Many were just looking for a pretty doll they could "love" or even marry until her human frailties began to reveal themselves. It reminded her of people who bought a cute puppy from the pet store, got it home, and then realized they'd signed up for way more than they expected.

Spicy Secret: If you marry for money, you'll earn it every day.

Her favorite answer when clients tried to date her "on the side" or keep her with them "off the clock" was a quick reply she'd learned from Shisha: "Listen. I'm sorry, but I don't get paid to stay; I get *paid to leave*. If I stay on with you for free, then that will make me like a girlfriend, and that is exactly what you are paying me *not* to be. Because once you have me for a girlfriend, then you'll be on the lookout for someone else just like me—someone who'll fuck you without ceremony and leave."

GG would say, "We do what we do by the hour or whatever. And then we go home. *Fini*. But you, Melisse, if I ever hear that you married someone for his money, I will kill you!"

"Oh, don't worry. I promise not to! And what about you, my friend?" Melisse would tease. "You've still got a trick or two up your sleeve."

"Nobody's asking for my hand in marriage right now. I'm a little busy, you know. I'm juggling a lot of men...*on the phones*..." GG laughed, the beautiful, worldly, wise laugh of a woman still gorgeous and comfortable in her own skin, despite being a world-class madam with more stresses than most women could handle.

Then GG would qualify it all with, "Melisse, let's stop judging the people we're dealing with—the guys and their wives."

Spicy Secret: While it's often tempting for pros to analyze why men are "stepping out," it's probably better to be more like a bartender and just "shut up and serve the drinks." As long as nobody drives home drunk while under your watch, their motivations are not your business.

GG got excited and went to a shelf containing all her favorite spiritual books. She put on her glasses, which hung on a chain around her neck, and turned to a bookmarked page in *Course in Miracles*. "Here it is, Melisse. I love this one."

> *As you see "your brother" you will see yourself.*
> *As you treat him you will treat yourself.*
> *As you think of him you will think of yourself.*
> *Never forget this, for in him you will find yourself or lose yourself.*

Melisse loved it when GG shared her beliefs with her. For all her mother's cramming of religion down Melisse's throat, she had never "shared" with Melisse the beauty of her faith, like GG did.

"You're right. And let's remember, there are two sides to every story. There's the gold digger's side, too. I mean, I'm sure they have their reasons for marrying for money instead of love."

"Yes. If only we could hear both sides, I am sure we would have a different point of view. But the point is…*not* to have a point of view… about anything…just stay open and remain without judgment."

"So we shouldn't listen to either side?"

"Don't need to. Just be present, that's all. Believe in their good, whoever they are, whatever they're doing, whatever side they're on…"

Then the phone rang. It was GG's "offshore" assistant asking a question somewhere in Singapore, GG's Asian base of operations.

As Melisse had gained GG's trust over the years, she had learned that GG was controlling a vast, worldwide operation of four hundred girls awaiting assignments in many foreign countries. This little red parlor on top of the bordello where GG sat was headquarters for a worldwide pleasure network of beautiful, willing women in every civilized country where rich, lonely men sought comfort.

GG huffed to the person in Asia, "Then tell him to screw off. I don't have anyone 'on' right now in Tokyo. It's late there now and I'm not waking up my best girl just because Funsaki is drunk again and wants to go off singing at two o'clock in the morning!"

The assistant said something on the other side.

"Who? No! She can't. She just got home at midnight from that other one, Yamaguchi, didn't she? Let that little Sinatra pickle in his own sake! He needs to learn how to book in advance. This is not a take-out restaurant. These are beautiful, accomplished women with *lives*."

She hung up the phone. "Jesus Christ, they drive me crazy. The Asian billionaires really feel entitled. Karaoke—at two in the morning! He wants a girl to go listen to him sing Rod Stewart. A little Japanese man singing "Do Ya Think I'm Sexy?" One of the girls told me he has a sparkly Michael Jackson glove that he likes to wear."

"Oh, God!" Melisse commiserated.

"One young lady said that she and this Mr. Funsaki flew to Macau so he could gamble, but as soon as they got into the room, he got drunk as a skunk and was wiggling his little worm around for her while dancing around in a pair of purple spandex pants. Can't people just *act civilized*?"

Melisse giggled hysterically and GG guffawed. Here they were, the sacred and the profane, alive and well in GG's house!

That Christmas Eve afternoon before leaving for her meeting with Malcolm, Melisse walked over to the mirror and checked herself out in her tight, shiny black snowsuit. It was hugging every curve, and it looked good.

"Are you going to be OK if I go? It's Christmas Eve and all," Melisse asked GG. "Shisha and I are supposed to go out for dinner together later. We're having a 'white elephant' gift exchange."

Melisse giggled, knowing they were to exchange gifts that clients had given them over the year but that they didn't really like or want to keep. Melisse had a broom that a client in the housewares business had brought her. She'd marveled at the absolute ignorance and cheapness of the gift, yet tried to see it from his point of view. Who knew what Shisha would have!

Melisse stood with the broom, which had a big red bow on it. She was sure she'd get some good comments from Malcolm about it, and maybe she'd even *use it* on him!

"Why don't you come along? Or we can bring something in here to eat with you," Melisse made the offer, though she felt bad knowing that the last place Shisha wanted to be on Christmas Eve was the brothel.

"Oh, no. Not tonight. You girls go enjoy yourselves. I'll be fine. You'll see," she said. "This year, I do really want you to take two weeks off for the holidays."

"Two weeks off! Are you unhappy with me about something?" Melisse gave her an anxious look.

"No, no, my dear. Sorry for the last-minute notice; I just have a ton of things I need to accomplish. Sometimes I need to sequester myself to do it, you know? Everything is going to be fine," GG said. "And get that hood on. I love how it looks with that black fur against your blonde hair."

"If you say so. Are you sick, GG? Slipping away for a facelift... *what*? Because I can come..."

"God, no! My facelift was four years ago, and anyway, it's wasn't a lift; it was a fat transplant! Don't worry about me; just go enjoy yourself and take a little time off."

Melisse gave GG a hug goodbye. It was a more significant hug than usual.

"I'll be seeing you," GG said. "And I'll be sending some outcall clients your way—no worries about the time off; just carry on. The Universe provides!"

Melisse nodded and padded downstairs. There was no more time to chat about it. She got into her fur-lined snow boots, grabbed her "working purse" and the broom, and disappeared into a flurry of slowly falling white flakes, trudging toward the Waldorf Astoria and her date with Malcolm.

CHAPTER 23

The Waldorf Walkabout

After her long afternoon date with Malcolm, during which he enjoyed his balls being alternately beaten and then brushed with the rough edges of the bow-tied broom, Melisse slinked back through the lobby of the Waldorf in her sexy snowsuit and her furry boots. She admired the velveteen flowery chairs and swirling rugs and potted palms and marble pillars. But like animals camouflaged in a jungle, many sets of male eyes followed her, some glancing up suddenly, some already staring. It was like they *knew*. She made eye contact with them, too, but continued on the short journey to the exit on the Lexington Avenue side of the hotel.

The first few days after Melisse had started turning tricks at GG's, she suddenly felt like a psychic who could pick up on all the hidden signals between men and women that she'd never noticed before. She was tuned in to a strange sexual bandwidth that vibrated at its own frequency, one that only a few people could tap in to. It had added a lot of new "noise" in her life, and this hotel lobby was very "noisy."

She stepped onto the escalator that led into an express passageway that crossed the length of the hotel and felt someone get on behind her and walk up to the step just behind hers.

"Are you available tonight?" a voice asked. "I know we've never *swept together* yet, but…"

That's bold, she thought. *How does he know?*

"Very funny…"

She turned to look at him. The man looked harmless enough—an older man, well dressed, kind looking. It would be one of the first times she ever worked "rogue" outside of GG's. But with two weeks off from the town house, a little extra cash wouldn't hurt.

He made a good offer for a half hour of her time and she nodded. She wasn't too proud where money was concerned. Who knew when she would have the power to make money so easily again? GG always reminded her about that. Turning down perfectly decent work on account of too much pride, GG said, was an insult to every poor prostitute in every third world country across the globe, some of whom were forced to work as sex slaves. They would have begged and cried to have had such work as Melisse, such freedom to choose their clients and at such high prices.

> **Spicy Secret: Being a female isn't the same for everyone in the world. Many women suffer from oppression, heartbreaking poverty and the absence of freedom and rights, not to mention paralyzing threats of violence and danger that our privilege and placement make it nearly impossible for our pampered brains to truly conceive of.**

Melisse would finally "get it" one day in the future when she would get a firsthand glimpse inside the seedy underbelly of India and Asia, where women worked for almost nothing. Later, she would visit the Middle East and hear the stories of the abused foreign domestics whose passports were locked away and were forced to service their bosses who "paid" them in food!

In the end, the sad lives led by third world prostitutes made her feel ashamed that she wasn't doing more with her life and education. Yet she just kept on working, not knowing for sure what she wanted to do, and feeling that in a sense, she was already living out her "calling" by caring for lonely men.

> **Spicy Secret:** "Pursue some path, however narrow and crooked, in which you can walk with love and reverence." —Henry David Thoreau

But tonight, there was a different feeling, having "acquired" GG's dream for La Fantasia. Though still a bit out of focus, it was as if there was a new lighthouse somewhere in the distance, and if she headed toward its beacon, everything would be OK.

Now, she and the stranger from the escalator arrived at his room. He opened the door and without much conversation, she gave him a significant look, zipped down her snowsuit and stepped out of it, revealing a racy black lace teddy beneath. He directed her to lie down on the bed and unsnapped the crotch of the teddy, revealing her to be pink, perfectly waxed, and shaved. She pulled part of the covers around her top half; the room was quite cold. The man obviously hadn't expected to proposition a woman on the escalator and then bring her to his room.

He proceeded to lick her the entire time. His joy in life was eating pussy, which became clear. He didn't even want to come himself or even touch himself. He just loved to lick, suck, gently nibble, probe, and otherwise devour her with his tongue and lips until she was straining with the pleasure of it, going to the edge, where he would pull back and then start again, bringing her to a higher edge. He gained a feeling of power in giving a woman that much pleasure, and he was well practiced and intuitive at the skill of cunnilingus.

> **Spicy Secret:** There exists a select, secret society of men out there (call them the "Cunning Linguists") who love going down on women so much that they would gladly spend all their time giving a woman oral sex. Meet one, and you'll know it right away because he won't let you go until he's felt the power and pleasure of making you come on his face.

Many men were this way, Melisse had discovered at GG's. They derived great pleasure from giving to women, and the love of eating pussy always seemed to indicate a man who was also generous in myriad other ways.

She was enjoying the experience, and as she lay there she thought about the power of her beauty. How amazing to have a strange man see her from afar, want her, and chase her up an escalator, then pay her well to give her pleasure. Possessing that kind of beauty was something relatively new to her. Earlier that autumn, she had undergone a complete transformation from a "cute" girl to a very pretty, symmetrical, and sexily curvaceous woman. Her expertly executed surgeries and dental work (and their recoveries) were painful and expensive, but turned out to be an aesthetic and commercial success for her. They were perfectly natural-looking enhancements and would turn out to be one of the best things she'd ever done for herself.

Her self-esteem had ascended to a new level, giving her a better command of herself in the Living Room, which translated into more clients, a better income, and a better experience with clients who treated her with more deference because she carried herself with more confidence.

However, during the course of her metamorphosis, she had developed a raging crush on her single, young surgeon, Dr. Markstein, whom she now considered a god for having transformed her.

She had embarrassed herself by calling him up one day and asking him on a date. She didn't know if she had misinterpreted his sweet behavior as real-life flirting or just an excellent professional bedside manner, but it had inspired her to see if there might be a future with him.

After the worst part of her surgical healing was over, she'd gotten up the nerve and called him at his office one afternoon and asked casually, "Would you be interested in taking me on a date?" She was still insecure about herself, and she'd never been on many dates to begin with, so she had no idea that calling up and asking a man, particularly her cosmetic surgeon, out on a date was the kiss of death! And he already knew she was a professional escort (not his thing), so her offer was especially pathetic and futile.

"Uh…" he countered. "I don't think my girlfriend would like that. You wouldn't want to tangle with her."

"Oh!" Melisse said. "Well, I give it three months. Good-bye, Doctor."

She'd hung up mortified at her rude insult, and embarrassed and mystified at herself for her lack of finesse (she hadn't yet read the book, *The Rules: Time-Tested Secrets for Capturing the Heart of Mr. Right*, which would become her private bible for handling instincts like this one properly).

> **Spicy Secret: Call girls get crushes, too. Sometimes, even on their clients! But the same rules apply to call girls that apply to you. So, to borrow from the excellent book by Greg Behrendt (which should be considered required reading for every woman): If he's not calling or tracking you down for a date, then "He's just not that into you."**

Now, lying in the Waldorf Hotel room being licked by a total stranger whose name she did not know, she thought, *Did all that general anesthesia and my new look go to my head when I felt compelled to call Dr. Markstein?*

Meanwhile, the stranger was licking her more aggressively, bringing her closer, so she tried to put the uncomfortable thoughts of the doctor out of her head, but couldn't. She still wasn't over her feelings for him, so she imagined that this man was actually her adored doctor, and focused on having an orgasm.

"Ohhhhhh! Yessssss!" she gasped, grabbing the man's hair. She ruffled it and told him he was really, really good at what he was doing.

> **Spicy Secret: Men literally lap up positive feedback. "Be hearty in your approbation and lavish in your praise." —Dale Carnegie**

Then she turned her head aside for a moment after she came, as the old familiar wave came up, bringing tears to her eyes. She knew now that her cosmetic surgeon would never have a thing to do with her because of her profession, and mourned what seemed to be the hopeless situation of her love life. Was this how she wanted to live indefinitely?

Before she knew it, she was back in the Waldorf Hotel's public areas, trying to get outside to Lexington Avenue. But since she was thirsty and it wasn't time to meet Shisha for dinner, she stepped into the Bull and Bear bar on the street level, sat down self-consciously, and ordered a bottle of water.

Another pleasant-looking man was sitting across the bar, staring at her. He made a motion to ask if he could come over and sit next to her, she nodded, and they made small talk as she waited for the inevitable invitation.

"Are you, by chance, *working*?" he asked. "And I don't mean sweeping up," he said, looking over at the broom and its red ribbon.

"Yes." She smiled and named her price. "Is that gift OK with you?"

"That's fine," he said. "You enjoy your water. I'll pay the check, and we'll go out separately. I'll be waiting for you in Room 704."

Melisse marveled that she had only begun her walk through the Waldorf a short time ago. Yet before making it to the other side of the building, she had received two quality propositions, even while wearing a snowsuit and furry boots!

Life is definitely better when you're a prettier woman, she thought later as the man pounded her from behind and she saw her money stacked on the bureau. The pounding vibrated something loose in the core of her being, however, and she felt the loneliness of another transaction with another stranger entering her body, one who would soon send her away.

She hugged the pillows beneath her (just as Shisha had taught her in order to save her back).

"Come for me!" she eventually demanded as he grabbed her hips, lifted her up, and fucked her for all she was worth. "Pound me! I won't break!"

> **Spicy Secret:** "Pound it, baby, it won't break!" or "Unload it, right there, baby!" are commands that are as useful when directing construction men working in your house, as they are for clients who you'd like to come—soon.

I am not a body. I am free. She recited these words to herself again and again—it was one of GG's favorite sayings culled from *A Course in Miracles*.

The man worked out all of his pent-up anxiety, his rage, his sadness, and his lust as he pounded Melisse and then came in a loud burst of pleasure. Melisse kept hold of his hands around her waist as they collapsed together on the bed. *He shouldn't feel alone or abandoned in this moment; it's the holidays, after all,* she thought. *And if I get up immediately, he will. I will stay here.*

He tapped her a little on her hips.

"That was great, thank you," he said. It was another way of saying, "Thanks for the fuck. You can get out now."

> **Spicy Secret:** No matter how much men adore them, hookers are always paid to leave. While many men are cuddlers after sex, some are decidedly not. If you can, know who wants what, and make your exit sleek and hasty when you know he's the kind who wants you out. Like, yesterday….

She removed his condom gently with a Kleenex, as she had been taught, and brought him a warm soapy washcloth.

"Wow! Full service! Thanks," he said. She smiled, went back to the bathroom, washed, got into her snowsuit, powdered her face, and combed out her bed hair. Then she was out the door, her fee tucked in her pocket.

Again, she attempted to have a drink at the Bull and Bear, this time a hot chocolate to fortify her for the battle for a taxi, as heavy snow was now covering the streets. She "scored" again, was approached at the bar with an offer, then capped off her night in the room of a man visiting from Florida awaiting the recovery of his wife from a round of cosmetic surgeries.

The lucky lady's "tune-up" was her fiftieth birthday present from her devoted husband. At this very moment, she was getting a top-to-bottom makeover with a renowned surgeon (but *not* Dr. Markstein).

Melisse would never forget how the man looked at her as she lay down before him, (as his wife lay in a recovery room in a posh nursing center uptown), saying, "You know…she's gonna look great when this is all done. She's a beautiful woman to begin with. But there's just nothing like screwing something…I mean, someone *strange*—know what I mean?"

Something strange.

His words made Melisse hurt inside for all the women in the world who desperately tried to please their husbands, spending billions on their collective beauty enhancements. These wives put up with their husbands' bad breath, their lack of finesse, their boring lovemaking and unskilled hands, meanwhile yearning for more and better, but being too loyal to start an affair.

And as their reward, they were cheated on when their supposedly devoted hubbies chose to plant their cocks inside a hooker (or two). Melisse knew it was all meaningless physical activities to the men (because the men really loved their wives) but most of the women outside her profession would never, ever understand that.

But to have the selfishness of men *at their worst* boiled down to one shitty sentiment like this man's, whose cock was now inside her, it was appalling.

Something strange.

Melisse wanted to get up, get into her snowsuit and boots, and leave this asshole. But she stayed. Her "new and strange" body lay there limp with hate until it was over and she collected her money. The man didn't even notice that Melisse wasn't enjoying herself. He hadn't even given her his name, or asked hers.

When she had the money in her purse and her gift broom in her hand, and was partially into the hallway where he couldn't take a swipe at her, she turned to him and said it.

"Oh, by the way, you really should do something about those big bags under your eyes. Maybe a little surgery there? And a penis implant. You could really use one. You'll look great after, I'm sure. But even so, your wife will probably be thinking how nice it would be to be with a new, different cock, something younger. You know—someone *strange*."

Melisse didn't know what came over her, but she just wanted her words to sting, and make him aware of his completely inconsiderate behavior in light of his pretty wife's condition.

"Filthy cunt!" he said, slamming the door.

"Asshole!" Melisse screamed back, slamming her be-ribboned broom against his door.

> **Spicy Secret: Before you take it personally and get upset with a man for cheating on you, realize that from his point of view, 'strange stuff' isn't always better stuff. It's just strange.**

She realized that, as an esteemed guest of the hotel, this nameless guy held all the cards, and by wandering in its halls, she was a trespasser. She made a quick diversion toward the fire escape staircase and quickly made her way down to another floor. God forbid he'd call hotel security, which could easily be waiting for her at one of the hotel entrances. Melisse's heart beat fast as she found her way to safety on the street outside.

> **Spicy Secret: Doing outcalls to upscale hotels is almost never a problem with hotel security for the well-dressed "trespasser" who looks as if she belongs and knows exactly where she's going. A smart girl will have the guest's name and room number memorized, in case she is questioned. And in a worst-case scenario with tight hotel security, she can always call from the lobby and ask the gentleman to meet her downstairs and accompany her up.**

She couldn't miss Christmas Eve dinner with Shisha! God forbid!

It was just about the last time Melisse would ever work in that manner, picking up total strangers in a hotel lobby or bar. It wasn't her style to be with people who hadn't sought her out because they knew she was special. She wanted them to eagerly anticipate the encounter, like enjoying a fine meal after reserving it well in advance. Dealing with "impulse shoppers" was definitely not her style!

> **Spicy Secret: A pretty, kind, sensual, giving woman is someone to be savored, treasured, and highly valued. If you choose to exchange your charms and time for cash or other considerations, place the highest possible value on them. Be patient, stand tall, and let those who can appreciate you find their way to you. The market will always pay you what you're truly worth: high fees, high respect, and high appreciation. Pro or non-pro, don't ever settle for less.**

Picking up random strangers in hotels also felt immoral, Melisse decided. There were always men harmlessly sitting in a lobby or a hotel bar, traveling away from home and wife on business. But by "strutting her stuff" and purposely tempting them to act in ways they weren't planning to…well, it was like entrapment, which made her feel guilty.

In fact, it seemed wrong to tempt, seduce, and charge hapless men who weren't seeking her out. She vowed to herself never to do it again.

Unless, of course, it was an offer she couldn't refuse.

> **Spicy Secret: If "working hotel bars" is not really your style because it feels skanky to go upstairs with someone you just met, one variation is to never go upstairs with anyone, but simply give any gentlemen you chat with (at the bar or in the lobby) an elegant business card with a special web address and secure access code. This way, your face is not all over the Internet, the potential client has already seen you in**

person (and you've "met" him), and he can "visit" your web page later and get to know you (and your rates and expectations). Let the man call you for a chat on the phone, followed, perhaps, by an appointment.

Just another option for the enterprising woman who needs to keep a low profile but wants to supplement her life with a bit of pleasure for sale.

Later that night, Melisse and Shisha greeted one another at the festive restaurant in Greenwich Village that they'd chosen for their annual Christmas Eve Indulgence Dinner (the one where they ordered whatever they wanted off the menu and gorged on endless goodies), followed by a return to Shisha's apartment for an overnight to catch up on romantic comedy movies. The next morning, they would find that Santa had stuffed a large bottle of each other's favorite perfume into their Christmas stockings.

Each was shocked to find that during their "white elephant" gift exchange, they gave each other identical brooms! It turned out that the same client of GG's had seen them both earlier that year and bestowed each of them with a gift broom from his housewares business.

After being seated in a banquette and about three glasses of pink champagne in, the two women sat musing over their white elephant gifts.

"Wasn't that thoughtful of…whatever his name was?" Shisha said. "It truly *swept* me off my feet," she sighed dramatically, pouring them another glass of holiday champagne.

"I was positively *bristling* with excitement when he gave it to me," Melisse concurred in a spicy tone, first sipping and then guzzling down her drink. "More, please."

"I can only hope that next year he'll bring me a coordinating dustpan," Shisha suggested wistfully as she poured out more. "I would so love to have one to go with my broom."

"Speak for yourself, bitch. This one is mine. And I fully expect to *clean up* with him."

"Really, now, get *a handle* on reality, girl. He's mine and you know it."

CHAPTER 24

The Disappearing Madam

Several days into Melisse's forced Christmas vacation, she was stopped in her tracks at her local newsstand. On the cover of the *New York Post* was a photo clearly showing GG's town house accompanied by a headline, which read:

"Lux Bordello Bust: The 'Manhunt' for Missing Madam." In another city rag it read, "House of Pleasure Mistress Disappears Without a Trace."

Melisse was shocked, but she suspected that GG had probably known about the impending raid, which was why she had given Melisse the weeks off. Then she thought about Malcolm's strange behavior and his significant wink when he'd said he was on a job in New York to help a client "disappear," and would be "orchestrating something for someone."

Melisse stayed calm, but couldn't resist trying GG's phone. She got an answering machine, the line sounding as if it rang through several others before reaching the machine, like a strange new forwarding system.

Then Melisse's phone rang. It was Malcolm, who didn't have her private home number. Apparently, GG gave it to him.

"Melisse, it's Malcolm. How are you, dear?" Without waiting for an answer, he said, "Listen carefully. Call me back on the number I gave you, but do it from a pay phone, okay?"

Melisse immediately went outside, found a corner pay phone, and dialed the number. Malcolm picked up. "Your company is desired at the Four Seasons Hotel this evening, as soon as you can get there. Please arrive well before 8:00 p.m. at Room 1401. Please be discreet, and make sure you're not being followed. Speak to no one about this. Oh, and there's no need to dress up," he chuckled. And then he clicked off. Deep down, Melisse knew that the "GG's House" part of her life must now be over, and she already felt nervous about what to do next.

That night at the Four Seasons Hotel, Melisse was stunned to find GG in Malcolm's room waiting to greet her. Melisse noticed that she had set up a litter box for her cat in the room's buff-colored marble bathroom. Given the cat beds and cat toys all around, the cat obviously reigned over the entire hotel room, decorated in tones of taupe, gold, and cream.

"Melisse! Get in here!" GG grabbed her into a hug. "Can you believe it?" She seemed astonished, yet thrilled by the situation. "I'm finally going to go to Barbados to retire! It's the Universe at work. It was time for me to let my business go, and the Universe just put it all in motion for me. When I first heard I was under surveillance and the bust was imminent, I was terrified! But then I thought *it's time*! Thank God for Malcolm here... He's helped me get out of it with everything *all wrapped up.*"

They both looked over at Malcolm, who sat on the couch watching TV. He waved at them and went back to watching his program.

"But what about Kin and the girls? Aren't they in big trouble?" asked Melisse.

"We knew ahead of time how it would play out from a contact on the police force. We also knew approximately when the bust was going to take place. So this week I kept a minimum of girls in there, and hardly any guys were let through. It was all sort of an act to keep the Commissioner happy so they can look like they were doing their jobs. I paid the girls who were there very well, to just be there and go with it. I also left some cash "gifts" in there so the cops working the bust could feel good about it all, and not be too hard on everyone. It was slaps on the wrists all around, not even misdemeanors…and… you see how it works? Everyone's a whore for money in one way or another…"

Malcolm chuckled. "I'm one! I'm the first to admit it!"

GG, now excited, led Melisse over to sit next to her on a chair while she settled on the couch in front of the TV next to Malcolm.

"You're not going to believe what Malcolm engineered for me! I mean, I've been a law enforcement 'person of interest' for some time, apparently. They don't really give a damn about the house. What they're *really* after is my international operation. It has generated quite a lot of…offshore revenue…and the players are powerful. It would be great for people higher up in our government to be able to threaten them…"

"Threaten? Try bully, extort, or blackmail!" Malcolm said.

GG continued, "But they'll never touch it. We just needed something to ensure that they didn't seriously go after that, because it would be…"

"Oh, that would be bad," Malcolm piped in.

Malcolm put his arm around the back of the couch. He and GG were clearly comfortable old friends and confidants.

"Your friend GG here has expertly manipulated the media. Many influential people tonight will be shaking in their boots. *Nobody* will want GG to get in trouble, and *everyone* will see to it that she is able to disappear quietly and retire."

Melisse looked at GG, amazed by it all. But she wondered where it would leave *her*. Where would she work? What would she do? The idea of going independent and using her own apartment to conduct business had been brewing for some time. But was she ready? She supposed the Universe was guiding her along, too, with this latest development.

But how? She now had the resources, the great credit, and the right documentation to rent her own working apartment in the city, but she'd been dragging her feet (afraid) to take the first step, and GG's place was "home"…

As if she were reading Melisse's mind, GG grabbed her hand and said, "Melisse, don't worry about a thing, my dear. Tonight you will leave here, and tomorrow you'll go to this address." She handed over several sets of keys and a piece of paper. "There at space 405 you will find a package. There will be some very detailed instructions in the package."

Malcolm said, "A large package, if I dare say—like mine!" he laughed.

"Oh hush," GG continued, "I just need to ask you one favor. It's a little unusual, but you may be pleasantly surprised!"

GG scooped up her fat orange cat up from his place on the floor by the couch. "I need you to adopt Butterball. He needs a good home and you're the only one I'd ever trust to take good care of him. If I took him to Barbados, I'm afraid he'd run away or get lost! If he goes with you I will rest easy, knowing he has a good mom and a good *home*," GG said, giving her a significant look. "A nice apartment where he can stretch out…"

But Melisse already knew the answer to this new challenge and answered it painfully. "I'm sorry, GG, but they don't allow pets in my building!"

Malcolm smiled. "Melisse…go to space 405 tomorrow and you'll see that taking Butterball won't be a problem." At this point, Melisse couldn't wait for tomorrow morning to go to this mysterious space 405.

GG nodded. "I always knew you'd be special to me, and I always knew we would be friends. There you were, eighteen years old, looking like something the cat dragged in. You were so sincere about following your strange dream of becoming a pro, and now look at you! Big adventures await you, my dear. Do you promise me you'll travel and see the world?"

"Yes! Absolutely!" Melisse didn't have to think twice about that.

"I just want you to always stay in touch and let me know how you're doing."

"Of course I'm going to stay in touch! You'll need updates on Butterball!"

At this, Melisse took Butterball into her arms and cuddled him. She loved cats, and believed that feeling of love was the purest she had ever known. It had been too long since she had their friendship in her life. She sat down on the couch and Butterball sat on her lap, contentedly purring as she petted him.

She would give him a purrever home, indeed.

Spicy Secret: When all others desert you, your Butterball will still be there.

CHAPTER 25

The Interview

"It's coming on!" GG squealed and Malcolm turned up the volume on the TV.

It was the highly respected news magazine show, *60/60*, hosted by Pamela Maller, a woman with a blonde bouffant hairdo, and Lou Strouds, a bald man with dark, short sideburns.

Voiceover: "And now, a special segment—we've got more on the mystery of Manhattan's 'Missing Madam'…"

Visual: *The host, Lou Strouds, and GG walk through the brothel.*

Pamela Maller: "Interview with a Madam."

Visual: *GG Gladly and Lou stand proudly in front of the town house.*

Pamela Maller: "For the last twenty-three years, GG Gladly—not her real name, we're sure—has discreetly reigned as New York City's premier madam, running the most exclusive brothel and outcall service in town. You'll get to meet this elusive lady and hear what she's got to say about prostitution, life, and love."

Visual: *Lou Strouds and Pamela Maller, now back in the 60/60 news studio.*

Pamela Maller to Lou Strouds: "How did you enjoy meeting the madam and touring the house, Lou?"

Melisse let out a snort of laughter. "Like he's never been there before!"

Lou to Pamela: "It was interesting. She took me on a rare odyssey through her world. You'll see her place and her girls as I ask intimate questions about the world's oldest profession."

Pamela: "Even more remarkable is the timing of the interview. "GG's" was shut down only a few days ago, and GG is nowhere to be found. So this footage is certainly important."

Lou: "Yes, I think it's the only interview she has ever granted. It's truly an exclusive."

Pamela: "It's going to be an eventful hour. I can't wait for your interview. First up: Where Are They Now? Victims of the Khmer Rouge speak out."

"They always leave the sexy stuff for last, as a tease," Malcolm said. Melisse, Malcolm, and GG sat around the TV for the next hour, eating room service snacks and drinking champagne and watching the show, waiting for the final segment on GG. Finally, it arrived.

Pamela: "Welcome back. Well, Lou. Prostitution. It's the world's oldest profession and one lady has been keeping it alive and well in New York City for the last twenty-three years—and even before that—working on her own, traveling the world as an in-demand self-described 'courtesan/healer/therapist.' She's GG, New York's reigning luxury madam."

Lou: "I found her to be refreshingly benevolent, modest, honest, a bit spiritual, and almost guru-like. The girls had nice things to say about her off camera, too. Not what you might have expected from a high-powered madam! I was actually surprised."

Pamela: "Her girls seem a cut above the usual…"
Lou: "Oh, they are…"
Pamela: "But it's still prostitution."
Lou: "Yes."
Pamela: "And we're going to examine that question. Is prostitution more acceptable, more palatable to society, when it's off the street, exclusive, and high priced? Or is it destructive to marriages, communities, public health, and the lives of these girls, as we suspect it

might be, no matter how it's packaged? Tonight, we'll hear a madam's point of view."

Visual: *Interior of GG's Living Room. Pan over antiques, couches, rugs, bar, girls milling about in the background, the sound of laughter, glasses clinking, men's voices. GG is seen from behind, walking around, wearing a Chanel suit.*

Visual: *Lou sits down in the "hot seat."*

Lou: "Uh, gee, GG, I'm nervous." (He chuckles nervously)

At this point in the show, GG and Melisse were guffawing about Lou's feigned discomfort in the "hot seat." He was so used to the "hot seat," in fact, that it had his butt marks imprinted on it.

Visual: *Girls' legs and sexy shoes atop couches and chairs, faced toward Lou.*

GG (with face hidden): "We always try to make our clients feel comfortable. This is an exclusive club where our members can make themselves at home. We offer our clients a drink, conversation, we throw in a little humor, and before he knows it, he's totally relaxed, he's chosen his companion, and he's ready to go upstairs."

Visual: *Upstairs bedrooms. GG leading Lou through each bedroom. Camera pans beds, hot tubs, mirrors, etc. GG lies atop a made-up bed with a white feather boa around her neck (but we cannot see her face).*

GG: "This is what it's all about, Lou—comfort, luxury, transcending the ordinary in a peaceful, clean setting."

Lou: "GG, do your clients transcend the ordinary sexually here, too?"

GG: "Sex is never ordinary. I don't care how long you've been doing it or who you've been doing it with. When you fuse your body and sometimes your soul with another person, you are transcending the ordinary. I have many, many couples, husbands and wives, who come here to experience sexual transcendence together. For a night, the women will fulfill their fantasy of being a highly sought-after prostitute, and their husbands or boyfriends will play the role of an adoring customer, paying tribute to them. The women enjoy getting more in touch with the sexual goddesses they are."

At this, Melisse looked over at GG. "That's not true! You totally lied to them!"

GG shrugged. "It was my chance to start a new trend. It could add new life to those old, tired relationships."

Malcolm chuckled. "Now every miserable couple will be calling up for a weekly shagfest in their local bordello to spice things up. And frigid wives will now command top dollar for a reluctant fuck, thanks to you. Excellently done!"

Lou: "Doesn't that get expensive? For married couples to come here?"

GG: "Not as expensive as a divorce."

Visual: *Interior of the Honeymoon Suite, with Lou and GG beside a bubbling Jacuzzi and a cold bucket of champagne. Girls splash around, blurred out in the background, giggling.*

Lou: "What about diseases, GG? Doesn't that ever cross anybody's mind?"

GG (stroking the tub): "Why, no! I know that Jacuzzis can be breeding grounds for germs, but I'd like you to know that we keep this Jacuzzi *very* clean. My housekeeper has been with me for years. Sometimes we get in here in our bathing suits on Saturdays and Wednesdays and scrub it together. We really go above and beyond to wipe out germs."

Visual: *Lou just looks dumbfounded.*

Visual: *Interior of the Peacock's Lair. Lou and GG sit cozily together on a love seat. Several foreign presidential Christmas cards sit innocently on a table in the background.*

Lou: "What kind of man comes to a place like this, GG?"

GG (looking through a large black ledger she suddenly pulls from her purse): "Um…let me see. Well, we get all kinds: mostly capitalists, industrialists, newly minted Internet millionaires—but they're just kids. Ah! Nobel Prize–winning scientists, self-help authors, Olympians—we like those. But here I see we do get a steady stream of politicians—senators, lobbyists sweetening deals in here. Hmmm… ah, yes, a president or two have graced us— before they took the oath of office, of course. You know, people love to 'congregate' here, so we get those too…I mean, Congressmen. We are fully equipped here. I provide a fax machine, an Internet station, *and* we have security cameras in all the rooms recording everything, you know…for our peace of mind…"

Malcolm guffawed. "'We have security cameras in every room'! What are you, nuts! That's not true!"

"Of course not. You know me better than that. I'm just trying to put the fear of God in anyone who would prevent my smooth passage into retirement."

"Fear of God is right! Some people are shitting in their pants tonight."

Visual: *Lou and GG outside the girls' pink marble bathroom. The girls are in lingerie, putting on makeup and rushing around, blurred in the background, getting ready for the evening.*

Lou: "What kind of woman chooses this way of life to make a living?"

GG: "Some of the smartest, most enterprising, most ambitious, and spiritually advanced women you could ever hope to meet. They all have goals and dreams, and this way of life gives them the time and money to attain them faster.

"Lou, tell me: Do you really think a woman should just give away sex for free on the third date to someone she barely knows and isn't sure really loves her? How many men are sitting there on a date calculating, 'Well…I spent six hundred dollars on dinners in the last three weeks trying to get this woman into bed…and it's really time that she slept with me. And if she doesn't sleep with me tonight, I'm not going to call her again or spend any more money getting to know her.' See?

"We women feel that. And the smart ones figure out that if he wants sex without love, without a real commitment to their love or friendship, then he should pay the six hundred dollars and get what he *really* wants from a professional!

"In my girls' cases, many *were* that girl on that date until they got fed up with that cynical system we call 'dating.' Unfortunately, it seems that dating is a social ploy used to justify many men's search for sex without love or commitment. These women have decided they'd rather just have the six hundred without dating and all the games and talk of relationships from men who really just want sex."

Lou: "That sounds so cynical, so jaded."

GG: "Well, let me finish. They've decided to let true love find them when it's time, when it's right, when they are financially or professionally independent and can make decisions about relationships that are not based on financial security. Meanwhile, they are paying their way through school, through world travels, through business start-ups, whatever they want."

Lou: "Hmmmm…an interesting take on things. And what *about* true love? Do you *really* think that after a few years servicing men in here, they can still believe in that?"

GG: "Fervently. It's all any of them ever talk about while they're between clients."

Lou: "Last question. How have you managed to stay in business so long? There is no record anywhere of you having been arrested on charges of pandering or promoting prostitution. How do you avoid the police?"

GG: "First of all, I don't promote prostitution. What I promote is *pleasure*. There are many lonely people out there in dire need of pleasure, men and women alike. Many men simply don't have the social skills or time to woo women. They're shy, they're too busy, whatever, so I provide an appropriate outlet for them to satisfy their basic need for pleasure."

Lou: "With beautiful women. For large sums of cash."

GG: "With beautiful women, yes. And any cash they receive is simply a tribute. But all women are beautiful in one way or another. Every girl has something special about her."

Lou: "Okay, back to the police. So…?"

GG: "I believe in two things that have protected me all my life: the first is tithing. It might surprise you, but I give 10 percent off the top of everything I make, back to God. I believe this has made me a rich woman. I have always paid my taxes, which is another form of giving back. And second, I give to the people who protect us, here in the city. We give generously to the Police Scholarship Fund, the Fireman's Fund, and any charity related to the police or the firemen."

Lou: "So you pay off the police?"

GG (**with a twinkle**): "I didn't say that, Lou. Don't put words in my mouth now. I give generously to the organizations that protect us. I also give to the good Italian families who make sure things run smoothly…you know, things like taking out our garbage and handling our security. Things just go smoother when you are friends with Italians."

Visual: *Lou and GG stand together at the grand piano. A hired pianist plays some Gershwin in the background. GG finally has her moment and sings her off-key favorite, "Someone to Watch Over Me," for her TV audience.*

"Bravo!" Melisse and Malcolm clapped when the show faded to a commercial.

GG sighed. "It had to be done. I hope I did the right thing."

"It was brilliant," Melisse sighed. "You dropped just enough hints. And the song at the end…perfect."

"GG, you have firmly established yourself as New York's favorite madam of all time…a legend…never to be seen or heard from again," Malcolm confirmed.

Melisse's last night spent with GG was coming to a close. The two friends got Butterball into his travel bag and loaded Melisse up with his litter box and food. GG began crying as she put him into the bag and looked into the netted window of the sack.

"Bye-bye, my little Butterball. You've been a faithful friend and an excellent companion through thick and thin. I'm afraid our paths diverge here. And now you will go with Melisse on a new adventure. She'll be the best mother you ever had! She loves cats and it's her dream to finally have another one! She will be a much better mother than me…" GG began, sobbing.

"No, don't say that," Melisse gently chided her.

GG embraced Melisse. "I won't say good-bye. This is *not* the last time," she said, as she pulled away, sobbing. She recovered a bit and said, "Don't forget about finding love! Give it away sometimes, Melisse! Don't make *everyone* pay. You'll know when you meet the right one. You'll want to quit all this for him. If so, go for it. *Go for someone who gives you good sex and treats you well.* Those are the only two requirements. Everything else is negotiable."

GG shut the door and then opened it again. "Come over here!" she whispered. "Sorry, Malcolm, this is just between us girls."

Melisse approached. "And La Fantasia! Do it!" GG whispered. "Don't forget about that!"

"Never! It's a done deal!" Melisse pointed at her ring as GG shut her door and leaned against it on the other side, terrified of what her life would be like without the routines of madaming.

Malcolm folded Melisse in a big bear hug at the door. "I'll tell you where she's living in Barbados when the time comes. Tell no one. And Kin is also in on things. She'll take over running some of the international business for GG. GG wants the girls to be able to keep in touch with their house regulars, privately. But Kin will have all the details. The girls are set. I daresay, rather well."

Melisse nodded. "Kin's an excellent manager. No worries there."

Malcolm saw her out. "And I'll see *you* in London, one day soon. I'll send you a round-trip ticket at the earliest."

"London?"

"Yes. I won't be coming back here much anymore, but I'd still love to see you if you'll have me. I'd like to be your first 'international' client."

"Of course!"

After one last hug with Malcolm, Melisse descended in the grand elevator of the Four Seasons Hotel with Butterball in his sack. She felt the hefty weight of all her new responsibilities.

"I think it's just you and me now, Butterball," she sighed.

And to her delight, he meowed.

> **Spicy Secret: When it's time for a new beginning, bring along a furry friend who needs a home, to take good care of you, and you of him/her, and you'll never feel too lost or alone.**

CHAPTER 26

The Wonderful Gifts

The day after Melisse and Butterball said good-bye to GG and Malcolm at the Four Seasons Hotel, she found her way to "space 405," which GG and Malcolm had told her would have further instructions for her in a package. It was, in fact, space 405 of a parking garage on the Upper East Side, off Madison Avenue and rather far from GG's town house.

Melisse was led to space 405 by a handsomely built garage attendant, Gabriel, as his name tag read. While following him and his cute ass across the lot to the space, her eyes widened as she saw the curvy shape of something hidden beneath a thick canvas zip-off cover, custom made to fit whatever was beneath it. Melisse stood wide-eyed, smiling incredulously.

He smiled. "What, you never seen your car before, miss?"

She smiled back. "Hmmm…it's been a while…"

He carefully zipped down the cover and gingerly slid it off the car. Melisse started breathing faster. It was a dark green English sports car, a little roadster…a Connaught Green Morgan convertible. It wasn't that old, but it was made to look antique with a wood frame carved into the distinctive Morgan curves and engineered to give many years of driving pleasure, if not a lifetime.

The attendant rubbed his hand lovingly over the car. "Niiiiiice… right?"

"Niiiiiiice is right." Her heart beat faster.

He took the key from her, unlocked the door and opened it. She stepped over and got in. She sat down, unbelieving, in the driver's seat.

"You wanna take her out for a drive?" he asked.

She thought, *Yes*! but then realized that she didn't know how to drive a stick shift. "I do. I really, really do. I just…ummm…not today." She needed to get some driving lessons on a stick shift—enough so she could race this on FDR Drive or out in the country without ruining it.

Stick shift lessons tomorrow, she thought, her mind abuzz with the pleasure of owning such a fabulous vehicle.

"I'll be out front when you're ready. I'll zip everything up again, don't worry about it," he said and went up the ramp on foot.

Normally, Melisse might have been thinking of other things that Gabriel could unzip for her, but today she simply sat, dumbfounded, inside the beautiful gift. Apparently GG had bought it on a whim. In the time Melisse had known GG, she had rarely left her house. She hadn't even known GG had a license!

Malcolm had mentioned there would be another package in "space 405," and she reached over and opened the small glove compartment, where she found a thick envelope rolled up inside. She pulled it out.

As Melisse read through the documents in the package, her esteem and respect for GG grew even more. GG was indeed an organized woman who had left no detail unattended for Melisse. Her generosity seemed to know no bounds. She had been preparing for a long time for her "sudden" retirement and to gift Melisse with a big boost in The Life.

GG had arranged for Melisse to have a long-term, nearly "forever" lease at a very low rent for an apartment located nearby. GG would be paid the rent at a discreet offshore trust, which officially owned the apartment. This apartment would become Melisse's "lair."

GG had generously included power of attorney documents giving Melisse limited powers to handle GG's affairs as they related to the apartment. And in the package was a document showing that the building was actually a condo, a pet-friendly one at that! GG noted that it would be far more comfortable for a courtesan to live there than in a nosy, overly posh co-op building.

Melisse marveled as she read that the condo maintenance had been prepaid for ten years. This ensured that if anything happened to GG (or Melisse) and her offshore trust could no longer pay the maintenance, Melisse would still be fine.

In her letter to Melisse, GG mentioned that Melisse should have her life together enough to leave the apartment in ten years' time anyway if she wanted to. Or she could stay, if necessary. There was a sublet clause included, just in case Melisse ever hit upon hard times and needed to sublease the apartment as a source of income.

Apparently GG had kept the apartment as a "bolt-hole," a guest suite for some of her visiting girls from out of the country, and as a secret rendezvous for her best girls when they needed to see very high-profile local clients who could not be seen arriving at a hotel room or, God forbid, in the bordello.

The Morgan was a gift GG was handing over to Melisse with a signed gift tax return dated one year earlier. The registration and car insurance had been changed over to Melisse's name. This had been done a year ago in case GG's assets were seized in the coming year for any reason. This way, the car would not actually belong to GG, but to Melisse.

What thoughtfulness! Melisse marveled. Even the name of the space holder for the garage had been changed over to Melisse, and prepaid for a year.

"Your insurance and garage is paid up, my dear, but please remember to tip the garage guys each time you take the car out, and at Christmas," GG had written in her instructions. Malcolm had clearly gotten this all done seamlessly. In fact, Melisse was already the "owner" of the Morgan and "residing" at the address of her new apartment and "receiving" her electric services and mail there.

So GG knew…for a year…that she might get in trouble…yet she was so calm, letting Life have its way with her. Melisse walked up the ramp of the garage and handed Gabriel a nice tip. "See you soon!" she said, envisioning the day she would get behind the wheel of the Morgan and spirit herself off to the countryside or the beach on an adventure.

Apparently, it was time to step into her new life as a courtesan.

Spicy Secret: "Do not go where the path may lead, go instead where there is no path and leave a trail." — Ralph Waldo Emerson

As she walked down the street with the keys to her new apartment, she felt that surge of relief some feel when they can finally leave Brooklyn and become a Manhattanite—living on the Upper East Side, no less, a short walk from Central Park.

Living well in Manhattan had always been her dream when she was growing up in rural California, and now she was actually living it. She would become an exclusive independent courtesan, eventually traveling the world, an elegant and gracious lady whose base was the greatest city in the world.

She gave no thought to the unpleasant things this elegant, gracious lady would have to participate in, the sacrifices she would have to make, or the loneliness that would come when she established herself as an independent courtesan.

> **Spicy Secret: While it doesn't have to be this way, the nature of high-end hooking has an insidious way of preventing sex workers from the true pleasures—and potential heartbreak—of "real" long-term romantic relationships. It's challenging for a woman deeply entrenched in The Life to mature emotionally, given her daily task of creating and maintaining temporary, "idealized" relationships in "fantasy scenarios" under "perfect" conditions.**

Now, Melisse opened the front door of her new apartment and stepped inside. Her new "stage" was a beautiful vintage space with high ceilings, wood floors, marble mantel fireplaces and a view to a back garden. She grinned—this would be such fun to decorate! It wasn't a huge, sprawling place; the size was just right for her taste.

Melisse sat down on the wood floor in a state of utter gratitude. It didn't make Melisse sad to think that the new apartment was just another, more private, more isolated variation on life in GG's bordello. Instead of coming and going, as she had at GG's, separating from her roles and going home at the end of the night to just be Melisse (a girl with a double life living in Brooklyn) Melisse would be living in the Manhattan apartment 100 percent of the time.

In fact, she was ecstatic about the possibilities it would afford for her life and the "better use of her time" it would allow by eliminating her commute.

> **Spicy Secret: Like any self-employed consultant making business decisions and arranging her daily schedule, a professional temptress must always ask herself, "What is the best use of my time?"**

GG had thought long and hard about making it so easy for Melisse to fall into a life where she would be "on" more often than not. It would take tremendous discipline for Melisse to make time and space for herself because the money was always too good to turn down.

Being on call all the time would become her lifestyle, just as it had for GG when she'd lived in the apartment as a swinging call girl after returning to the U.S. after a successful stint as a "Claudette" in the famous Madame Claude's clique of girls based in Paris.

It's OK. Melisse will find her way, GG had told herself as she signed Melisse's "lease" and then forged Melisse's signature one year before Melisse would step foot into the apartment.

> **Spicy Secret: "Without mysteries, life would be very dull indeed. What would be left to strive for if everything were known?" —Charles de Lint**

CHAPTER 27

Life in the Lair

It wasn't long after she moved into the apartment that Melisse launched a major advertising campaign for herself and became a highly sought-after "VIP companion." She knew from GG's that location and ambience were hugely important to clients, and these qualities would keep them coming back for more.

With this in mind, she made her new home look as if it had been there forever, patina-ed and antiqued and poshed-out in a kind of soft, feminine, pale flowery perfection, filled with reflective surfaces and fresh roses and fragrant lilies, fine candles, luxurious towels, sheets, and, of course, Melisse: a work of soft sculpture unto herself. The decor made her clients feel coddled, comfortable, and steeped in well-being.

GG had always had a land line phone line connected into the apartment. It would now ring occasionally with referrals originating from GG. These were GG's old clients from the international side, visiting NYC or on their way in, and were now Melisse's for the taking if she picked up the phone, or decided to return their calls.

But to develop a more local and loyal clientele, Melisse advertised herself fairly honestly and accurately in the upscale magazines and newspapers around town that permitted such advertising. She even ran an ad in the Yellow Pages. The Internet was really just in its infancy in those days, but it would soon explode into becoming THE place for men to search for ladies of the evening. And Melisse took advantage by being at the forefront, aggressively marketing herself on the Net, even if it seemed like blatant self-promotion.

Spicy Secret: Don't worry too much about your blatant self-promotion in the adult entertainment business. Nobody ever died from it and, in fact, the ladies in question laughed all the way to the bank (while hoping nobody would recognize them).

Melisse always stayed in touch with Kin, who would eventually become a close friend, her paid "personal assistant," her cat-sitter, and her most-trusted confidant in the business, in addition to Shishapuss, who was her only true "big sister" in The Life.

So Melisse hired a company to build her a website filled with beautiful photos and tantalizing descriptions of herself, offering clients "the ultimate in warmth, charm, and pleasurable possibilities…" She would eventually produce a short, tastefully provocative video ad, and was one of the first in her profession to do so. The use of something so evocative was highly motivating to men who were seeking what she offered.

To screen her clients and avoid ever having to talk to the wrong ones, she devised an elaborate call-in system whereby they could listen to a prerecorded message in her own voice. In it, she introduced herself and reassured them of her sincerity and high quality. The men could not help responding to her high, childlike voice saying:

"I'm wholesome-looking—but not too wholesome, if you know what I mean. I love to see you have a good time and I possess a delightful giggle. I like to take my time and I do my absolute best to help you have a warm and wonderful experience that hopefully you'll want to repeat—again, and again…(giggle) and again… I'm very selective about who I meet. I'm looking to meet a gentleman who is kind, genteel, generous, and easygoing, a man who can truly appreciate someone sweet and accommodating like me. In return I offer a nice time and my utmost discretion…"(and on and on)

After they listened to Melisse's introduction, they could call a voice mail system to introduce themselves by name, with details on how Melisse should return their call.

Spicy Secret: Remember, you choose the clients—they don't choose you.

Spicy Secret: The pro's recipe for success: the harder you screen your clients, and the higher the fees you ask for, the higher the quality of the clients you will attract. And high quality clients offer nicer experiences. The nicer the experience that you have, the better your reputation is, and the better your reputation is, the more regulars you'll have, and the more income you'll have (with less stress).

The inverse is also true and leads to disaster: bad/no screening and low rates can lead to low quality clients, which results in bad/dangerous/demoralizing experiences, which leads to a bad attitude/bad health/bad reputations…Bad reputations lead to a lower income/necessity of seeing even more bad/unpleasant/low-balling clients…you *don't* want to go spinning into that vicious downward spiral.

The "security system," as she called it, and the one she taught other girls how to create, protected her from wasting her time speaking to "jerk-offs" (men who would call in with no intention of making or keeping an appointment). It gave her more mobility, too—she could make arrangements from anywhere she wanted as she wasn't tied to picking up a phone, not knowing who was on the other end.

She concluded that what made a lot of girls turn mean, impatient, and snippy was having to pick up a phone *cold* all day long and talk to men playing games, like asking a girl what she looked like, and what she would do for them. With a few slick moves, she'd avoided having to sit through inquiries from socially retarded men with nothing better to do than waste her time and, worst of all, the constant hang-up callers. Then, too, there were the men (and other women) who, once they had a lady on the phone, spewed out filthy wishes and curses. Ugh!

> **Spicy Secret: Even though "call girls" are called "call girls," the best ones spend very little time on the telephone, and certainly never pick up calls without screening them. Voice mail was made to protect you from the astounding amount of meanness, time-wasting, and stupidity on the other end of the line. If you follow a "system" to the letter, you'll only need to call back those potential clients who actually book an appointment and show up on time and often with a gift!**

> **Spicy Secret: Don't use the voice mail system or texting on a mobile phone as your "go to" number in your promotions, or for conducting business. Rent a stable, solid, inexpensive voice mail number from an established company that can give you a number that can follow you anywhere (and easily alert you on your mobile when you have a message waiting). God forbid you ever lost your phone or mobile phone account—you'd be up sex creek without a paddle! Just get an independent voice mail number instead.**

When she has to meet new clients, Melisse never deviates from one rule: apart from her "pre-screenings" (calls, email introductions, etc.) she always meets a new gentleman in a public place first—for a drink, a walk, a chat, *something…* It's the one rule that has saved Melisse from being killed, raped, arrested, or otherwise compromised. Nor would she invite anyone directly to her home without meeting them first.

By meeting new potential clients in public first, she gives her instincts and intuition a chance to assess the fellow. Years of this has honed her ability to know both from the voice on the phone, and then first impression in person, whether he's a safe bet or not. What she finds there never lies. And sometimes, when she's found something that sets off an inner alarm, she'll walk away. With elegance, of course.

> **Spicy Secret: When meeting a client in public before your appointment, if you don't like the looks or vibe of him, it's better to walk away—and maybe give the person in question a "sweetener" (like a hundred-dollar bill) and an "excuse" ("I'm sorry, I just ate something before we met and I suddenly feel like vomiting! Could we re-book later? I'll call you!").**
>
> **When you don't like what/who you see/feel during your "meet and greet," it's better to give up an appointment and be safe and maintain your privacy... than be sorry and have some freak know where you live.**

Her philosophy was that if she was at all nervous about meeting someone in public, she shouldn't be going in the first place.

It was quite an art, the screening of potential clients over the phone, and then vibing them out later in person. It was much more than that, however. It was the art of staying alive, being pleasant, and staying in control of herself and her life.

Excellent screening, in her opinion, was the most important task of her career, and *everything else* was secondary.

Melisse's Pro $ecrets for Staying Safe and Problem-Free:

> **Spicy Secret: A stranger (or a strange client) may just be "a friend you haven't met yet." But NEVER let strangers into your home or into your heart OR give them your address until you've met them in person and felt totally comfortable in their presence.**

Spicy Secret: Don't give out your full home address by phone, email, text, or otherwise to a stranger (or even a long-term client). You never know who (a murderous wife, a private investigator) may one day be reading that communication and can use it to track you down. Break the contact info down into small bites in different places.

Spicy Secret: When you first meet a client in person and you're comfortable, give him a piece of paper with your coordinates, such as entry codes, unit numbers, etc. But let the details be vague enough (or arrive in separate pieces) so that anyone else who may someday find that piece of paper cannot come and find YOU.

Spicy Secret: When inviting a client to your location (in a larger city or apartment building), go in separately after the first meeting with a delay of at least five minutes. Never be seen with gentlemen going into your place of residence if you can help it. This is to prevent your neighbors, building superintendent, janitor, management, or others from suspecting that you are a successful companion with many clients. Over years of seeing many men in the same location, this act makes all the difference.

Spicy Secret: If you're just a non-professional woman who enjoys a variety of men visiting you, then this MO (modified, perhaps) is still a good idea! Erring on the side of discretion is the sign of an evolved and sophisticated woman. When everyone—friends, neighbors, family—knows your intimate personal business, they have potential control over you. You can maintain your power and privacy by keeping yourself and your activities more mysterious.

Spicy Secret: In places where "entertaining men" is not exactly legal, always remember on the holidays (or sometimes every month) to tip or gift generously your building management, the superintendent, the maintenance men, or anyone else who might "know your business" and who may be allowing you to "get away with it" anyway. They deserve your appreciation.

CHAPTER 28

Lilies, Orchids, and Roses

After her screening process, and when Melisse *does* finally let a vetted stranger into her lair, he gazes around delightedly at the pale soothing yellows, the vases of fresh lilacs on either side of the bed, the inviting couch where he will sit and wait for her as she prepares his drink. The romantic music soothes him as he catches a glimpse of her in the mirrors polished to the ultimate reflection, as she slips into something skimpier and more beautiful behind a gilded screen in the bedroom… All of this contributes to getting him excited in a gently accelerated manner.

> **Spicy Secret: Creating the right ambience with decor is (nearly) everything in the life of a temptress. Don't underestimate the power of creating a feminine environment—with paint, fabric, pretty furnishings, home fragrance, and the right music—to skillfully seduce the men in your life.**

His cock is usually hard by the time she emerges to sip from her own drink and pat him higher and higher on his leg as she disarms him animatedly with whatever "small talk" she fancies.

> **Spicy Secret: Spend the time, however long it takes, to make your guest feel comfortable. Don't watch the**

clock (or even have one in the room) and don't "stack" your appointments too close together, which can lead to disaster. He should have the impression that you've got "all the time in the world" for him (because many will extend their appointments when they have that impression).

She will never "compete" with him in terms of knowledge or intelligence, but will subtly let him feel that he is "superior" and "a king" in her lair. Then, she will engage him in conversations that reveal a deeper level of interest and caring about him on a much more personal level than he may be used to in his daily life.

> **Spicy Secret: "A 'gossip' is the one who talks to you about others; a 'bore' is one who talks to you about himself; and a 'brilliant conversationalist' is one who talks to you about yourself." —Lisa Kirk**

While conversing with him, the straps of whatever gown she is wearing will have a way of sliding down, the fabric exposing the dusty rose of her nipples right before she takes him, or he takes her, into an embrace or a long round of kissing. She may, with the shyer clients, ask, "Can I interest you in a…massage…or something like that?"

> **Spicy Secret: When your guest is a bit nervous, a great question to ask is: "Were you nervous about meeting me?" Once he admits it and stops hiding his discomfort, or talks about why he's so nervous, this always leads to him loosening up and having a better time.**

She will slowly seduce him while straddling his hips, opening her lips for a kiss if that's what he wants, and then when he can't stand it anymore, she'll undress him and gently push him onto the bed, where she'll lead him in that naked dance lying down, starting first with a slow, strong massage (the one she will entice him into giving *her* so he can savor her curves). This will make any resolve he might have had to last a long time soften like warm putty in her hands. She'll keep things moving, though, while allowing him to linger over every detail of her body. Then, she'll indulge him in a long, languorous blowjob of subtle differentiations in all the ways she takes him into her mouth and teases his cock with her tongue.

> **Spicy Secret: Once again, excelling at oral sex is a skill set that can change the course of any woman's life. If you truly want to please your lover and keep him enslaved to you, don't neglect to give him this "gift" as often as possible and with as much gusto as possible. Smart move: when you feel the instinct rise up to whine or complain over petty "nothingness" (the kind that ultimately turns you into a nag in his mind) just stuff his cock into your mouth for a while instead and show it some love. You'll stop talking, potentially save your romance, *and* he'll give you whatever you want in the end…after he's come, of course!**

Then, she'll take a lick around his balls that always has him sighing for more, and that brings him to the edge, but never takes him over… Finally, she'll make a formal but enticing ritual of slowly rolling on a high-quality condom while grabbing the base of his cock.

> **Spicy Secret: Lambskin condoms could be considered the ultimate and most pleasurable type of condom available. However, they are not proven to truly protect against STDs. They are expensive and look strange, but the enhanced pleasure they allow (while still being relatively safe) is worth considering for boyfriends and special clients.**

Finally, she will allow him inside her, but only so far. And then little by little, she'll writhe and move her body in every mode and position of pleasurable movement, pretending to come several times (or coming for real many times if her client knows what he's doing!) until she gives him final permission to fuck her hard, and with no reserve, until they both come.

"Just let yourself go," she'll urge. "Give it to me!"

> **Spicy Secret:** Depending on culture and circumstance, some clients and men in general need a little extra "permission" to enjoy themselves guilt-free in bed. Think how great you'd feel if a lover said, mid-passion, "I want you to enjoy yourself as much as possible; don't worry about me. I love to see you receiving pleasure, so just let go…"

When she's done with him, and he's exploded in a massive crescendo of pleasure, he's had her so many ways he can't remember which he liked best, only how seemingly quickly and wonderfully it all ended. And after bringing him a warm, wet towel, she'll give him a long, professional-level massage over his entire body with her strong hands (even his scalp if he wants it), followed by a final delicious rub of his feet. It is her tradition to rub their feet with a peppermint-infused oil at the end.

> **Spicy Secret:** Rubbing a man's feet with confident hands (if he's not ticklish, that is) is addictive to just about any man and certainly the second-best way to his heart. While you're lazing around watching TV with him, put yourself to good use and rub his feet. It's a lot easier to get control of the remote and watch what you want while you're altering his state of mind with a good foot massage.

Then, Melisse offers a sweet bit of teasing, some complimentary conversation about his great performance, and then a hot tea or a glass of wine, a hot shower, or something else that gently signals that their time is coming to an end.

Melisse will slip away to the bathroom for a few moments to freshen up and check her messages, slide a colored gloss on her lips, spritz on her glorious perfume (if he can be exposed to perfume), then pull a brush through her messy hair. Finally, she'll hide her lovely body with a beautiful silk robe and a darling pair of golden slipper sandals that match her decor.

For her, these interludes are a series of elegant, gracious rituals in a world she has created to cocoon herself, and her clients, in a universe away. It is a padded place that protects her (and them, for a few moments) from the world at large.

Melisse always remembers the words of Madame Claude, who passed them down to GG: "You are not selling sex, you are selling an experience." And Melisse sought to make each experience as deliciously capricious as observing a butterfly aflutter in her beautiful garden.

There would often be clients in the afternoon, or a dinner date with a client, or perhaps dinner out with another jewel in the necklace of her escort friends (many of whom went independent after GG's shut down). Perhaps there would be a trick or two turned gently in the dark of night at one of the luxury hotels, for good measure.

Some clients just came and went, of course, and it was to be expected. But others remained quite loyal, smiling in anticipation as they walked quietly down her hallway, often bearing gifts, as she peeked out her door to let them in.

Melisse has now come to think of her level of prostitution as just another social institution that exists in the world, like marriage or motherhood, or anything else women choose to undertake with devotion. She has committed to excelling at this career, and has found there are good and bad aspects, pleasures and pains involved. Ultimately, it's all a learning experience.

Before bedtime, the events of her days and nights spiral into memories and meditations on all the intriguing, potentially inspiring things she has learned and heard. She tries to forget the calculating pleasures she has sold and the unwanted touches she has endured, particularly those slithery tongues pushed down into her throat that day. She can't bear when they do it, but the deep kissing is part of being a total Girlfriend Experience. It's an expected feature of her offerings.

She considers what the clients bring to the experience as being the same as what a reader brings to the absorption of a science-fiction novel. "The willful suspension of disbelief" is alive and well in the hearts and minds of every client seeking out the GFE.

> **Spicy Secret: When deciding to offer the "GFE" (versus a more straightforward sexual servicing) be prepared for the added anxiety of now catering to needier clients with higher expectations for "romance, passion, and girlfriend-like affection" from their experience with you. GFE could also stand for, "Gee, I am Fucking Exhausted!"**

She hopes all the day's chitchat and the memories of the ho-hum lovers she so willingly engaged with will blow away like a fluff of cotton. But they don't. It all rests deep in her subconscious. She tries to forget the little lies she lives with by busying herself with her travel plans, her bigger-picture plans for La Fantasia, and the juggling of her portfolio of suitors. Particularly the VIPs—those who book her for longer travel, or to accompany them on their vacations.

There were certainly plenty of precious men, and those "Near and Dear" that she didn't mind seeing at all, those who were a delight to entertain. They were all gentlemen, consummate businessmen, citizens of the world, and great conversationalists, the kind who brought wonderful gifts like lingerie, jewelry, or even gold coins ("for your security") and lay back and let her take over, asking only sweet things of her. One liked to share poetry with her, quoting Roethke in his "gift" card that contained her payment: "She taught me Touch, that undulant white skin."

One wanted only to hide away from his job in the mad, noisy pits of Wall Street and nap, curled up with her in the late afternoon after the market closed. He liked her to open the windows so he could hear nothing but the birds chirping.

Another asked only to have his legs and feet tickled with the tip of her feather duster. One of the funniest, a skinny young Chinese man, brought a music player and asked to perform his ritual "Macarena" dance for her while wearing a cheerleader's costume, having Melisse lie down on the floor so he could dance over her and lift up his skirt for her. Then he'd dance and strip down to a pair of black panties with gold lamé hearts which, once pulled down, revealed special messages scrawled for her on his butt, in indelible ink. Her giggles watching him dance over her as she read his body graffiti only turned him on more.

Some of them asked what really turned *her* on. She tired of that question and wanted to answer it by saying, *Falling in love with someone nice who I am attracted to, who could take me from this life, or inspire me to quit—that would turn me on…* but it's not something you say to a client.

"Just put a big stack of cash on the bureau and take a hike—that'd really turn me on!" she'd laughed once, coming up with funny ways of answering that particular question as she sat at the sidewalk café during an impromptu meet-up with GG's ex-girls discussing business.

What Melisse couldn't answer without sounding too sappy was what got her wet for *real-real*: the fantasy of sleeping with her ideal mate, the one who would know her completely and love her without restraint. The one she could have *fun* with. *I need someone with a big heart, a big mind, a big… I need someone who's going to blow my mind and rock my world and blaze my body… I wonder, is that just too much to ask? No, I hope not. I have at least as much to give, but in different equivalents.* Yes, she was good, and smooth—she gave the clients 100 percent of herself when she was with them. The time came and went fast for a man, as if he'd slipped inside a dream fantasy. She felt she occupied the secret satin-surrounded chamber of their hearts where they could retreat. If they left her apartment and hadn't "thoroughly" enjoyed themselves, from nervousness or otherwise, she gave them express permission to think of her, later, in their wet dreams.

> **Spicy Secret:** Always end your appointment by saying you'd love to see the man in question again (if you really would; otherwise don't bother). That little bit of extra reassurance upon their exit is part of the courtesan culture, as men can sometimes be plagued by insecurities, particularly if their "performance" didn't match yours, or if they are usually rejected by women.

After the door closed behind them, she looked back into the beautiful rooms she had created five years before and wondered, *They come here, but where can I slip away to?* But she kept working like a dog. Her dilemma, the one of so many in her business, was that she feared it would all go away. She had vague feelings of guilt about what she was doing. Was it unfair of her to use her beauty and cleverness in this way? No, it wasn't. Even the worst critics, if they could see inside her life, would say that she earned every penny taking care of, and "providing" for, lonely, horny men who were often neglected by the very partners they'd hoped and originally believed would provide them with physical affection.

Like the famous song said, she felt they were "Lookin' for love in all the wrong places," and she was just one of those places. Lucky for them, she was the best possible place of all the wrong places.

When her clients left, she was gloriously alone again. But as she got busier and busier, more and more popular, The Life began to slowly, imperceptibly close in upon her. Her time between appointments got shorter and shorter, and there was even less of her to go around. She stretched out her natural well of affection and charm, and the ball of light inside her began to grow dim. She was going to exhaust her essence, and perhaps this was what GG meant once when she said she'd gotten "caught up" a long time ago during her time in Paris, and for a long time couldn't remember who she really was, what she really wanted. But Melisse was keeping her sights set on her dream for La Fantasia.

She'd created a "well-lubricated" mechanism to live her life well and give her the financial fuel to go toward her dreams with a certain pride and with panache and aplomb. And true to what GG had taught her, the more she had to give, the more she got in return.

She consistently knocked her clients out with her warmth, her sexual prowess, and her ability to create a subtle emotional longing for more time with her. Despite her rough start, she had finally become a master artisan in her craft.

Spicy Secret: "Mastery, to whatever degree your circumstance allows, is determined by a handful of choices repeated daily." —Chris Matakas, *My Mastery: Learning to Live through Jiu Jitsu*

And indeed, she took great pride in sharing her craft and commanding high prices for her expertise. Now, after many men, many interludes entertaining in her lair, and many "outcall" excursions to visit those whom she'd cultivated in various countries, here she was, sitting on a private jet, flying across the ocean to go entertain one of her most challenging clients to date: Sheik Jazzy. The sheik was an oil-rich ruler of a small Middle Eastern territory known as Wadijazzizi.

I've become a Pleasure Consultant!
An Ambassadress of Pleasure.
A Jet-$et Temptress.
A woman of easy (but expensive) virtue.
Lord help me.

THE PRESENT

CHAPTER 29

Flying the Even Friendlier Skies

We now find Melisse sitting in a sleek jet, zooming through the air headed for Dubai and her kooky client, Sheik Jazzy.

Melisse wakes from her musings about the past, which (together with a small piece of an Ambien) had eased her into a deeper sleep after she first boarded Jazzy's jet. Now, after flying for several hours under Halima's faultless piloting, Ahmed the cabin attendant serves her a wonderful dinner while she watches a movie. After dinner, he comes along with a tempting piece of cheesecake covered with strawberry sauce.

"A piece of cheesecake?" he asks with a gleam in his eye.

"Uhhhhh…" she says, wanting to bury her face in the delicious creamy confection. It's definitely an "off diet" item.

> **Spicy Secret: "I saw it, I smelled it, I tasted it, I wanted it, and then I ate it…and now I wear it: on my hips."**
> **—Aunt Fran**

"Take it away," she commands with a smile and a wave of her hand. Ahmed returns to the galley at the back of the plane. Still, she can't stop thinking about it—the way the berries were glistening, the way the sweet cheese was so fluffy…

Suddenly, she pushes the service button.

"Yes?" he asks, appearing again.

"I will actually...*have* the cheesecake," she confesses guiltily.

A sad, sorry look crosses his face.

"What?"

"I'm so sorry. I ate it. There was only one. And you said you did not want it. So I ate it."

"You ate it!?"

Then he breaks into a laugh. "Haaaaa! You are too easy. I'll be right back with that. We have a whole cake in the back."

"Bring two then. I need to balance out both hips if I'm going to do this right."

Spicy Secret: "Too much of a good thing can be wonderful!" —Mae West

Eventually, Melisse feels the inevitable drowsiness (and sugar crash) that crossing time zones brings on, and goes to the bathroom to prepare for bed, as always removing her makeup before sleeping and patting on a powerful moisturizer.

Then, she enters the darling special compartment of the plane built expressly for a good night's sleep. She closes the door, removes her dress and jewels, and crawls between the soft, cool sheets of the spacious bed. Stretching out luxuriously, she quickly falls asleep from the comforting vibration of the plane barreling through the air.

As they approach Casablanca, the early morning light comes through an open window in the bedroom area. Melisse is sleeping on her side, partly out of the covers and still drowsy when she feels someone gently slide in beside her, pressing against her warm, naked body. Melisse presses back, knowing from the silky-soft skin that it can be none other than Halima.

Halima wraps one leg around Melisse and cups one of Melisse's breasts in her hands. She softly pulls Melisse's hair aside and begins kissing Melisse's neck as she slides her hand down Melisse's stomach. Then, she reaches down to play with Melisse while she is still half-asleep.

"Mmmmmm..." Melisse moans.

"Jazzy sent me as your gift to warm you up this morning…" Halima whispers.

"It's a lovely gift," Melisse sighs as Halima's fingers gently probe her, lightly brushing across her clit.

The next thing Melisse feels is Halima's soft hair on her thighs. Melisse half opens her eyes and notices a small glass bubble in the corner of the room, where Sheik Jazzy must be watching or recording remotely. Even though this is a performance, Melisse decides to forget about it and just enjoy it.

Halima spreads Melisse's legs as her tongue lightly dances over Melisse's clit for what seems like hours on end. Melisse wants to come, but she's yearning to feel Halima's pussy lips rubbing across her pussy lips, all of her weight on top of her, the heat and wetness mingling into the orgasm Melisse feels welling up inside her.

Reading her mind, Halima jumps on top of Melisse, rubbing her large breasts on Melisse's and pressing her slick pussy into Melisse's. Melisse spreads her legs as Halima gets between them and presses her pussy lips deeper into Melisse's, then rubs her up and down vigorously with her body.

Melisse feels as if her clit has turned into a giant throbbing cherry, every sensual movement of Halima taking her to bursting point. The feeling of Halima's large breasts grazing her nipples takes her over the top, and they both climax with total abandon, hidden in the quiet chamber of the plane's bedroom.

The performance over, Melisse covers them both with a sheet and they settle down to get some sleep, Halima leaving things to her handsome co-pilot.

A few hours later, there's a knock at the door and Halima rouses Melisse and gives her a sly smile in the shaded cabin. She whispers in Melisse's ear, "Sorry for waking you. Sheik Jazzy's orders, you know…" as she turns up the lights and pulls up the window shades.

"How well I know…" Melisse practically yawns. God, the "schedule" is starting already. Early, too.

"Yes?" Melisse says to the door, half-asleep.

"It's me, Ahmed."

"Well, come in, Ahmed."

"Hmmm, I guess I'm going to have to leave you now," Halima says mysteriously. "*Someone* has to fly this plane, and it might as well be me!" she laughs, gathering her clothes and covering herself up so Ahmed can't see too much. He stares, trying to get a good look at his pilot, but his hungry gaze intensifies when he closes the door behind Halima and sees Melisse wrapped in a sheet.

By now, Melisse is exhausted from the trip and the lovemaking with Halima, but being Melisse, she's also hot for whatever Ahmed wants to give her as long as she can just lie back and enjoy him.

"I need to have you," he says, undressing quickly. "Now! I haven't been with a woman…"

"I know," she interrupts, pulling the sheet off her body. "You don't have to tell me. Just…" And with this, she lies on her back and spreads her legs apart (in the direction of the camera, of course).

"Come inside me, now!" she demands, still wet from Halima as he dives toward her. He has undressed so furiously, Melisse doesn't even have a chance to check out his cock. He enters her hard, without any foreplay, without any fanfare, just shoving his cock inside her—and it is one of the hardest she's ever experienced.

Melisse relishes the feeling of a desperately horny man pounding away inside her after being in Jazzy's prison for years. Despite his status, Ahmed takes a long time to release all his pent-up lust. He must have jerked off a whole lot in the pokey, she thinks.

But it's nothing to be annoyed about; Melisse just lies back and enjoys his relentless return to life on the outside—or rather, inside.

After a while, he slows down, his cock swelling even more because he feels he wants to let it blow. Now, he is balancing himself on his arms, easing his weight off her and letting his cock and hips do all the work.

Melisse is so turned on by this hard cock slowly entering her and then exiting, and coming back for more, that she grabs his ass and yells, "Fuck me hard until you come! Please, Ahmed!" she begs. "Lean down on me, put all your weight on me, and just grind me down into the bed."

His face clears, and he looks as if someone has given him the best Christmas gift ever. "Yes!" he says, and buries his face in the pillow, presses all his weight down, and pounds her. His cock is now deep inside, with her hands guiding his ass up and down. It hasn't escaped Melisse that this will make a nice little video for Jazzy, but at this point, she couldn't care less. She feels release coming as her pussy starts to pulsate faster and faster again, this time with that fabulous feeling of a hard cock ramming deep inside and massaging her clit at the same time.

She wraps her legs around his back, tight. "I'm coming!" she yells, her pussy finally exploding in a bomb of pleasure.

"Ohhhhhhh!" Ahmed yells with her, releasing his load.

Melisse starts laughing once she catches her breath. "Welcome to the mile-high club, Ahmed," she giggles.

"Oh, my God, it is excellent to be a free man again. Peace be upon Sheik Jazzy for releasing me into his service on *this* plane."

Melisse leans up on one arm and strokes Ahmed's chest. She takes the sheet and covers their heads to prevent anyone from picking up their voices.

"If you don't mind my asking, what were you writing bad checks for that got you in trouble?"

"I never did that," Ahmed asserts. "I would never do such a thing. You see, I was the sheik's sports car mechanic at one time and he asked me to buy a new transmission for his broken antique Ferrari. He wanted to exhibit it at the antique car show in California. I had authority over the car collection and I sent a check to the parts vendor, but the sheik's secretary had not put enough money into the account at the bank to cover it and…"

"The check bounced."

"Yes, and it delayed everything. It made it impossible for Sheik Jazzy to display his car at the show, and he was very angry."

"I see. So he jailed you for bouncing a check. Basically, it was one of his own checks, from his own accounts, that he bounced."

"Yes. I did three years' hard time! OK, it's a bit like staying at an American Howard Johnson hotel, with a private chef and a gym. Still, it was three years without…" He gives Melisse's body a lingering once-over. "And," he adds, "there was razor wire outside the building, above the tennis court."

"I get it. What a nice guy." Melisse sighs as she cuddles into Ahmed's arms for a bit of a snooze.

"Well," Ahmed says, smiling, "at least he was nice enough to let me fly with *you*."

CHAPTER 30

Jazzy in Dubai (by Way of Paris)

After her lustiest flight on record, Melisse finally lands in Dubai, refreshed, renewed, freshly spritzed and showered. She is greeted by an efficient airport assistant who stamps her passport before leading her to a waiting silver Bentley, shimmering on the tarmac. The chauffer will take her on to the Burj Al Arab hotel, where she will meet Jazzy. In the past, she'd taken a helicopter, which landed her like a bullet on a bulls-eye on top of the Burj Al Arab's helipad, but she'd put the kibosh on that, politely asking Jazzy if she could just take a car instead.

Between the night spent in the jet and the wind generated by the copter, the journey always seemed to wreak havoc with her expensive blow job (the hair kind, that is) and it made her "halo" extensions feel like they were going to lift off and take flight, too.

> **Spicy Secret: For those of you with thinner hair, a good hairpiece (like a 'halo') or high-quality hair extensions of a length similar to your own hair looks lush and sensuous (when cared for properly, i.e., curled with an iron) and are an excellent investment (until men want to run their hands through it—and they usually always do during lovemaking). Best approach: wear your piece out to dinner, or upon arrival when you need to 'woo.' Then, "go natural" once you're in the bedroom. Men are never as picky as you think**

they will be about your hair. They're just counting on having a good time sexually, and your "big" hair is the least of their concerns when they've got you nailed beneath them.

She was grateful for the drive from the airport to the hotel; it gave her time to "get into character," which was necessary when she was about to give a week-long performance akin to *Cats* (if the star of the show were a tomcat expecting nonstop pussy in heat) meets *Joseph and the Amazing Technicolor Dreamcoat* (if Joseph were an oil-producing tribal ruler with a penchant for top-shelf vodkas and Russian hookers).

In the world of modern-day courtesans and jet-set blonde escorts from the West and Russia, Dubai is a lucrative touring stop for high-end sexual providers. It is also a worthy destination for the upscale buyer of sex. But both parties must be careful in their communications, arrangements, and in-person meetings in order to weave through the potential legal minefield known as "the moral police." Though trouble is unlikely, it's best to fly very, very low under the radar. For the tourist and connoisseur alike, Dubai offers a veritable buffet of women for swarthy lovers of exotic "blondes": British, American, and Eastern European women bold enough or connected enough to find work there in a safe and discreet manner.

Dubai is at a crossroads of the Middle East, where wealthy men, normally following a strict religious regime in their oil-rich (but dry) countries, can come to relax their morals and splash around in the forbidden mix of alcohol and erotica. Anything goes, as long as it is done discreetly in hotels or hidden behind high walls, where the glossy image of Dubai as a world-class shopping, dining, and family amusement destination will not be tarnished.

"Miss Melisse," however, is not on tour in Dubai. She has been invited as a desired guest by the eccentric, infinitely rich, if badly mannered (she calls it "hootless," as in, "He doesn't give a hoot if he acts like a hyena!") ruler of a small kingdom.

She personally finds Sheik Jazzy's nonstop party nearly intolerable and invariably exhausting. But there's something oddly lovable about his endless fascination with relatively harmless new fantasies, games, and adventures. He's a guy who's comfortable in his own skin and he's incredibly generous. She loves the bottomless well of money and gifts he brings to their "relationship." And this is an integral element that helps finance her dream, La Fantasia.

> **Spicy Secret: The quirks and things that annoy you about your most challenging clients will be your best teacher. They have arrived in your life for a reason. In Melisse's case, by dealing with Jazzy, she is learning patience and stoicism, while stretching the limits of her creativity.**

So here we find her once again on that dusty drive from the Dubai airport, marveling at the terrifying driving of not only her chauffer, but also everyone else on the road, darting in and out of traffic and accelerating at insane speeds when there's a brief clearing.

As Melisse looks out the tinted window of the Bentley and breathes in the luxury that it symbolizes, she marvels at the strange serendipity that first brought her into contact with her host. It was in Paris…two years before…

PARIS

Her first meeting with Jazzy had occurred one evening purely by accident. Melisse was simply relaxing and listening to romantic piano music at the bar at the George V Hotel in Paris. It was the night before a client was to arrive at the more modest La Villa Hotel in Saint-Germain-des-Prés. She had arrived early to enjoy a free day in Paris before her one-hour blow job (the blow job that was to end all blow jobs) the next morning. The gentleman felt that receiving such a service would calm his nerves and enhance his negotiating abilities that day in "the most important meeting of his life."

"And here I thought the most important meeting in your life was the one with me!" she'd teased during the spice-up call when he booked her. She'd thought, *What an utterly ridiculous waste of money. But if he's going to waste it on someone, who better than me!*

> **Spicy Secret: A man in possession of a high amount of "disposable" income is often in need of a pretty, curvy receptacle for it. Try to lay hands on his throwaway dollars, but without appearing "trashy."**

Her presence at the George V Hotel bar that evening felt a bit like a field trip to observe others of her kind in their natural habitat. This was a bar well traversed by discreet, worldly courtesans and well-heeled European call girls on the make. Melisse knew she would at least feel comfortable among her own as she "people-watched."

As soon as she sat down, a drink arrived for her, a glass of pink champagne, which delighted her. When she asked the waiter who had sent it over, he pointed to a tall, wiry, long-bearded man wearing a dark-gray pin-striped suit, enhanced by a crisp, white, cuff-linked shirt.

She lifted her glass to him to say "thank you" and he nodded back, asking in sign language if he could join her at her table. She nodded, secretly wondering if he was one of those elusive "unicorns" described in hushed tones among her jet-setting courtesan friends. "Unicorns" were men of power, status, or wealth whose desires and resources could change a girl's life infinitely for the better. As the man drew closer, she noticed that his cuff links were of dazzling square-cut diamonds and sapphires, the suit and shoes definitely hand-tailored in London, and the toes-out walk (or waddle, to be precise) was very Middle Eastern—from an emirate, to be precise. Melisse had observed it all before and knew all the signs of a wealthy Arab out of his regal robes and feeling free to indulge his appetites.

"Hello," Melisse nodded, smiling.

"Pretty lady, you come up to my waist, but I think we will fit together very fine," he greeted her, smiling from ear to ear. Now Melisse, after four years of entertaining the rich, knew that the more unusual a man's conversation opener, the wealthier he was likely to be.

Her companion clinked his glass to hers. "Cheerios!" he said. "I collect these Disney cartoons, you see, the original drawings from the Walt Disney collections. And you remind me of my Tinker Bell figure. I want to take *you* home with me."

"Well," Melisse replied coyly, "I'm not sure that will be possible. We don't know each other very well yet, Mr....?"

"Emir Abdullatif ibn al-Jazziz of the Kingdom of Wadijazzizi. My home is a privately annexed emirate found at the far edge of Um Az Zumul. It is pronounced *oom-az-oomul*, like 'I'm an asshole' and I produce a rich crude oil that is now flowing like a motherfucker."

"Ah...Ooom an Azhool...it sounds very nice," Melisse said graciously.

"It's not. It's a fucking pit of sand and snakes, but I have made it a home..."

In the course of their conversation, Melisse learned that Jazzy's home was a large palace property surrounded by lush golf-course-like gardens that dropped off into dunes at the high retaining walls.

According to Jazzy, there was nothing much in Wadijazzizi apart from the low-level compounds where the oil laborers lived, a track and soccer field, one rather pathetic-looking jailhouse set far out of town, and a small main street of shops and services for the laborers to purchase Jazzy's overpriced groceries, international phone calling services, and his *Daily Gazette*, a rant he published every two weeks that "reinterpreted" world news items.

But Jazzy was smart in the ways of business—somewhat of a futurist who knew his oil may one day run out—and he had become an environmentalist who ran a self-sustaining palace where nothing went to waste, including the shit of his pet pigs, which he developed into fuel. His "Pigpoo" technology was a patented power system that environmentalists the world over were apparently clamoring to learn more about.

"A pig fuel?" Melisse asked, apparently fascinated, as if Jazzy had discovered fire.

> **Spicy Secret: Whatever boring thing he is talking about or working on is the most fascinating, interesting, and mind-altering concept, idea, or project you've ever heard of. You can't suck up enough of his knowledge of steam turbines, the derivatives market, or the plight of the last remaining Amazonian indigenous peoples. "Amazing! Tell me more!" you say, while trying to keep your eyes from crossing.**

And then Jazzy recounted how he'd developed it with the help of a sexy Western female university scientist named Debra, who was naive enough to apply for the Royal Wadijazzizi "work/live scholarship" he offered. And, of course, it involved a stay in his palace compound.

Once their important work together was done, Jazzy tried to convert Debra into one of his "palace entertainers" via a lucrative contract—but Debra, totally against such frivolity and sensing impending doom, used her satellite phone to get an human rights organization involved and hightailed it out of Wadijazzizi in an American military helicopter during a rooftop rescue.

As Jazzy told it, he and Debra were sunbathing nude on the roof at the time (the only way she could convince him to let her up there for her pre-scheduled secret rescue) and Jazzy was left jumping up and down, screaming, "Debra! Debra! I was falling in love with you! You were the smartest woman I ever met!"

"My kiki was swaying in the wind because of the force of the copter and…and…it's like an elephant trunk, you know, and the Americans were laughing at me!" he seemed to cry, before cracking up. "That

Debra was a real ball-buster. She broke my heart…" He grabbed Melisse's hand across the table. "Comfort me, Melisse…"

And then he tickled her palm with his middle finger while giving her a salacious look.

"Tell me more about your life, Emir…" Melisse said, returning the tickle.

Jazzy continued, "Well, my helicopter gets me quickly into Abu Dhabi for supplies, and when I want to have fun I go to Dubai. Or I come here to Europe for some—um—cultural exchanges."

"Ah! So what cultural exchanges have you planned for this trip?" Melisse asked, almost afraid to hear the answer. "I know there is a new exhibition that just opened at l'Orangerie…"

"Well, I am going tonight to the girlie dancing show at Le Crazy Horse. I like the places that have the smaller breasts on view in the show. It makes me feel very Frenchie. And if I am lucky, you will join me and then we will go to Pont Jarretelles afterward for some *one leg up*."

Melisse smiled and nodded. "One leg up? Pont Jarretelles?"

"Yes, you know…" He made a little motion with his hips. "It's a little, what they call *exchangiste* nightclub for rich and sexy swingers. I will keep my pants on and you will keep your dress down, but in the dark we can still be doing a little…" He made a strange hip-rocking motion. "In fact, I have already booked us a table."

"Ah…I see." Melisse smiled. She decided to go all in. "Emir…?"

"Call me Jazzy."

"Jazzy, I have a secret confession to make. I've always wanted to be a dancer at Le Crazy Horse! I've always fantasized about what fun it would be to live in Paris, work there in the evenings, and be part of this magical place. So I am so excited that you will take me there tonight!"

> **Spicy Secret: Men who pay you to entertain them love "secret confessions." Make them up if you have to, but keep 'em coming, and the wilder, more unlikely, or impossibly outrageous, the better.**

"That is very wonderful!" He seemed genuinely pleased, then sat sipping from a drink Melisse would eventually know to be called the Sazerac. It was a sort of cognac cocktail laced with absinthe. His palate was very sensitive, and he knew whether or not only the best ingredients had been used, and if they weren't, it was sent back. She would also learn that the same went for sending back his girls.

Spicy Secret: "(Absinthe) makes the heart grow fonder." —Jason Webley

He took a sweeping look around the bar. "These women are all like skinny stripper poles, like the ones they dance on in America. I am seeking a small woman like you tonight, a Tinker Bell girl, to play some magic upon my cock with her pixie fairy dust. And in return I will sprinkle her with gold dust, if you can be understanding what I mean."

"Well, Emir al-Jazziz..." She hesitated.

"I wasn't for sure if you were for sale, or what," he interrupted. "It's very hard to tell when I am outside of my own lands. Western women are very confusing. Everyone on the street is looking like a *sharmuta*, but almost nobody is actually for sale."

"I am not for sale," she said, her mind racing. "I am..." *Do I tell him I AM for lease, or...? Maybe I shouldn't let him know I'm already working as a professional escort. He'll like it much better tonight if he doesn't know the truth, and thinks he's made friends with a non-pro.*

"Yes? What?"

"This would really be a first for me, you know. Giving myself to you, for a...for a..." she stammered innocently "a consideration..."

"So you are not for sale, but you are for lease."

"Uh...yes."

Spicy Secret: "Lend yourself to others, but give yourself to yourself." —Michel De Montaigne

"Oh, darling, there is no need to talk of all that. Just know I will take care of you very well. I know I am taking up space in your evening, but I would be grateful if you would join me."

"Oh, no! I'm enjoying myself! I don't get out much and I'm enjoying just *talking* to you. But I hope…there could be *more*…" she said shyly yet seductively.

He sighed and seemed happy with this. "I am wondering if you will do the anal way of sex with me later?" he asked. "I want *prime access* to your asshole."

She coughed a little into her pink champagne and downed it. She pretended to act shocked, but this was a normal request she'd come across often among her "darling Arabs," as she liked to think of some of the sweet and gentle, super-generous "back door boys" she'd carefully screened, met, and cultivated during August holidays in Marbella.

They were more about relaxing and having fun all day and spending evenings filled with music, food, and friendship, than shoving cocks up her ass. And when they eventually did, they were gentle and obedient, and she *did* kind of like it, when it was done right. Sometimes they were so cute and the rear entry made her so hot, that she begged them to make regular love to her…but the answer was "no" and she respected their reasoning. Many were happy to make her come with their talented hands instead.

"Hmmm…I'll have to think about it." She smiled shyly at Jazzy.

> **Spicy Secret:** Try to say "yes" to your man's playful or sensual requests as often as possible, but when you want to tell someone "no" (to harmless things only; i.e., when someone asks you on a date and you don't want to go), just say, "Ohhhh…not yet" or "Not now" or "You never know," or "I'll have to think about it," which is a much softer way of saying "Never" or "No."

> **Spicy Secret:** When agreeing to do anything in "real" life, let your yeses mean "Yes" and your no's mean "No." You'll only drive yourself and others mad if you say yes when you really felt like saying no.

That was the first time someone had come right out and asked her for anal sex so directly. It was not on her usual list of offerings back in the U.S., but he was a potential unicorn, and if he was gentle…

"Ummmmm…hmmmmm…I can't make any guarantees about this style of…"

"Pleeeeeease? How do you say? Pretty please with sugar on top of me?"

"I don't know…it's not my usual thing…" she said, knowing that the rich always want most what they think they can't have.

> **Spicy Secret: Always leave some sensual act, fantasy fulfillment, or detail about yourself supposedly "out of reach" and "off the table" (like cookies in the jar for little boys), which keeps men striving to reach into your cookie jar. And don't hesitate to slap their hands when you catch them trying to sneak a cookie.**

"You will like it with me! I am not just ramming it in like a motherfucker."

"Jazzy! That's naughty! You stop that talk right *now*; this is not really up for discussion," she said fake-firmly.

He leaned in close and spoke in a more salacious, yet oddly sweet way about the matter, which assured her that even if it did occur, it would not be a thing of huge regret. She wouldn't have to go to the hospital from being torn apart by some madman ripping into her ass.

She leaned in to listen.

"I like to take my time. I go very, *very* slow. I can take all night, if that's what you need. I know the muscles in this special place like to get…relaxed. So I like to rub gentle all around the circle of your asshole, with my tongue first, and then when you are happy and begging me for more, then I use something bigger. My finger, and then two of my fingers so your asshole will be ready…and then finally…I simply ease my long willy inside…little by little, sneaking it into your asshole… You will not even know I'm there."

"Yes, I understand... Hmmm..." she said, acting as if she were totally innocent, had never tried anal sex, and that the way he described it was having a "corrupting" effect on her.

Spicy Secret: "Innocence is one of the most exciting things in the world." —Eartha Kitt

"Look. I have aroused myself," he said, taking a large linen cocktail napkin and placing it over his lap. It seemed to tent up a bit but nobody was around very close to notice. "All of this butt-talking gives me a willy."

He took a large wad of cash out of his jacket pocket—together with its bejeweled money clip—unclasped the clip of her Kelly bag, dropped the cash *and* the jeweled clip in, and tidily locked the purse back up. He'd obviously had practice navigating a fine handbag like hers.

"Hermès," he noted. "But yours is looking a bit worn. We will go shopping for more if you come to visit me in Dubai," he said. "I like to spoil my entertainers."

"So what is this gift for, exactly?" Melisse asked.

"It is your taxi fare and spending money for the evening tonight at Le Crazy Horse and the Pont Jarretelles club. If we like each other, I may allow you to spend the night with me back here."

"I see," she said, seemingly still mulling over his offer. Certainly that one wad in her purse was more cash than she'd ever earned in a night, not even counting the jeweled money clip. Who knew what that was worth!

"If I may ask," Jazzy went on confidently, "what size shoe do you wear? Sometimes I like to buy shoes for my special friends."

"Size six!" she answered, perhaps too quickly.

She sensed that this one "unicorn" would be a handful, but she also knew that if she played her cards right, she could take a wild ride on his golden horn until his magic carpet led her to the perfect property and all the start-up capital she needed for La Fantasia.

Spicy Secret: Showing reserve and exercising restraint, and not seeming too eager to please—i.e., the "I can take it or leave it" attitude—gives you that air of exclusivity and unattainability that keeps the high-end man coming back for more.

CHAPTER 31

On "Le Crazy Horse"

A few hours later, Melisse and Jazzy sat cozily in a red velour banquette at the famous Parisian Le Crazy Horse cabaret show. Under a discreet, glossy black raincoat, she'd worn a Betsey Johnson black lace bustier, which tied up at the back with hot-pink ribbons. She wore a matching short black lace skirt, made full by a black-netted crinoline beneath. The skirt just covered the tops of her black-lace-topped, thigh-high stockings, held up by a Lise Charmel black lace garter belt trimmed with tiny pink satin roses.

A tiny black G-string went over the garter belt because the whole contraption was very difficult to undo and redo in the *toilette*s or in a swingers club. Melisse wore an elaborate jet-black-and-hot-pink bejeweled barrette in the shape of a camellia, which held her hair back to one side in a 1940s-style wave. Art deco earrings in black onyx stones cascaded down the nape of her neck.

Jazzy gazed at Melisse with a combination of curiosity and approval. This little minx was so unlike most of the women he usually "contracted" with when he was in Europe. Most were moonlighting lingerie or fashion models introduced to him through an iron-fisted, velvet-gloved British madam known only as "Maggie." He'd met Maggie (and driven her nuts with phone calls) through a small ad in the *International Herald Tribune*, and he'd been doing business with her for years. But sometimes a one-off with a surprise *sharmuta*, or pro, added a bit of spice to his life.

And this one was a bit spicier—and spunkier—and more excited by his irresistible presence, than the dull-witted, jaded, and bored-looking dates who usually accompanied him around the European capitals.

It was obvious that Melisse hadn't spent a dime of his money clip gift on any last-minute shopping in the nearby designer boutiques. Her whole getup had a "vintage" look, and for some reason he found it endearing. It reminded him of the photos of the pinup girls he had admired, tucked into some books shipped to him from a naughty friend in England when he was a kid.

Melisse noticed that a waiter seemed to be at their sole beck and call. He kept pouring them glasses of champagne from the ice bucket nearby while a dapper "plainclothes security" bodyguard watched over them from a short distance away.

"Maybe you could still dance here at Crazy Horse," Jazzy said, twirling a finger around Melisse's long hair as he sat with his arm around her.

"I'm not tall enough and my breasts are a little too big. They want all the girls to be *coupe de champagne* size and…"

"Let me see," he said. Like the tentacles of an octopus coming out of nowhere, his hand cupped her left breast and squeezed it through the corset.

"Mr. Emir!" she squeaked, only partly in mock distress.

"What? Am I doing something bad?" Melisse hoped the lights would lower soon, as she could feel herself blushing.

> **Spicy Secret: One of the most challenging aspects of being an escort is handling the desire for PDAs (Public Displays of Affection) from some clients who are clearly inappropriate for you (i.e., much older, or weird looking, etc.). Mortifying when everyone in the room stops to stare at the "odd pair," figuring, "She's obviously been hired," as they kiss or hold hands in the corner. A nice way to put him off this is to say, "Please, let's not make all the lonely people in the**

room jealous by making out in front of them!" or "I just saw a beautiful woman in here looking you up and down like a piece of meat. Let's pretend we're 'just friends' and see if she'll come over and try to seduce you. What do you say?"

He removed his hand, looked at her, and sadly shook his head. "Oh, it is very sad, Melisse. Really, this is a very broken dream. Your boobies are way too big. They are more than the small handfuls that are required here at Le Crazy Horse. I'm afraid you'll have to…"

She braced herself for what she knew must be coming next and took a sip of her champagne.

"Go back to America. There they like the mother cows to have very large titties for much drinking of tasty milk, filled with cancer-causing hormones."

"Ah, yes. That must be why our twelve-year-old girls look like they're eighteen," said a smiling Melisse, matching his tone.

"I've noticed that! I have to watch myself when I am in the States, that I am not trying to fondle the little teenagers with big boobies. I do not want to get arrested in America. Then I would have to make a deal for diplomatic immunity with the President of the United States. He is always depending upon me to put in a nice word for him at our annual meeting of the filthy-rich 'towel heads' who jointly decide the price of oil. I would not want to embarrass myself before these clean and politically correct Americans."

Jazzy guffawed devilishly at this image, swilling down another sip of the Cristal.

"Oh, Emir," she said, preparing him, "it seems to me that whatever little girls you might try to seduce will be much more mature than you are."

"You know, sweetums, from across the room tonight without my glasses, you yourself looked like a little girl. But then when I got close, I saw that you are like an old lady. But I decided to keep you anyway so I can check out this little pussy, like a kid at a carnival attraction. I want to see what an old prune looks like!" And with this he made a prune face.

"What!" Melisse screeched. "You insulting butthole!"

"You started it, my dear."

"I am not even thirty yet!" she lied. "And fifty is the new forty, which makes thirty the new twenty, so go screw your…" Then she saw that he was laughing, having "zapped her," as he would say later.

"Let's change the subject, Jazzy, and go back to your milk cows, or whatever."

Suddenly, he reached under the table and groped around her garter belt and crotch, looking for her hidden riches. He liked what he felt.

"You are not a prune. More of a peach. I feel peach fuzz."

Then he gave her a naughty look before the curtains parted and the cabaret show began.

Melisse rolled her eyes, laughing at her new, super-rich client's crazy way of expressing himself. She then enjoyed every minute of the first half of the expertly choreographed show, which was both tasteful and teasing.

"I have a special surprise for you," Jazzy said during intermission, as he used his bare hands to pull apart a steak and devour a plate of fries, licking off his fingers.

Melisse had dabbled with a shrimp cocktail, not wanting to eat anything heavy that might upset her stomach and disturb her upcoming financial windfall.

He signaled for the waiter to deliver a lemon-garnished finger bowl to clean his hands. "I hope you don't mind, darling, but food, especially meat, just tastes better when I eat with my hands," he said as he cleaned his face with a linen napkin that had been dipped in the lemony water.

"Oh, that's very cave-manly!" she said, looking away and rolling her eyes.

"I love Omaha steaks from America, and the Garrett popcorn from Chicago. Can you bring me some on my jet when you come to see me in I'm an Asshole?"

"Why, yes!"

That was promising.

It was still intermission and Jazzy now sipped a glass of champagne. He looked at her and commanded, "See the man who now approaches? I wish you to go with him."

"Where? And what about you? Are you staying here?" Melisse asked, noticing a very attractive man approaching in a tuxedo. She checked out the man and decided he wasn't going to be a problem, but was curious as to what was going to happen next.

"No, no. I don't like to ruin for myself the fantasy of the dancing girls in the backstage. If I see them without their costumes it makes me very sad. It is like believing in your Santa Claus. But I want *you* to visit the backstage, so go on! It will be fun, and then…"

"And then?" Melisse asked, rising from the banquette.

"And then we will enjoy our very own show," he said smirking.

Backstage was bustling as the set was changed and the girls left their dressing rooms after changing into their next costumes. They moved quickly to leave time for a cigarette break, and the hair/makeup people were freshening everyone up as they smoked.

The tuxedoed man leading her to a private dressing room was friendly. He described everyone he saw to Melisse while greeting everyone whose path he crossed. He was obviously a high-level manager of the show.

"Hello, Francois!" some of the girls cooed as they passed by.

"*Ou est Matilde?*" he asked one of them.

"*Matilde ici!*" Matilde yelled as she came out of the shadows. She was a flaming-red-haired woman in a flamboyant, printed smock with pockets holding makeup and hairbrushes. He took her aside and whispered in her ear, and she nodded and looked Melisse up and down.

"Please, if you will. Go that way. Matilde will be helping you prepare."

Melisse hung back, grabbing Francois's arm.

"Prepare? For what?"

"Yes. It's the Emir's orders. When the boss says jump, you jump. When the boss says dance, *you dance.*"

"*He's* the boss?"

"He's one of them. The Emir is a chief investor in the club. He also co-owns many grand hotels in Paris! He keeps all of us in business when things slow down; as you know, tourism is so mercurial… Anyway, *bon chance,* Melisse! I'm sure you will be *merveilleux!*"

"Unbelievable!" Melisse murmured, half-excited, half dreading her time on the stage of Le Crazy Horse, as Matilde quickly applied some false eyelashes and very intense white stage makeup, followed by copious powdering, blushing, and eye-shadowing.

As Matilde finished up Melisse's lipstick, the dancers' chief choreographer quickly briefed her on what to do next. It was almost time to go onstage, and Jazzy's eyes—and all other eyes in the club—would be on *her and her very rusty sexy dancing*!

"…and then…when zee dancers separate…it will be your time in zee spotlight! Enjoy it! This costume is fitting you perfectly, but the shoes—amazing! We are lucky tonight!" The choreographer said, giving her one final appraisal.

"Amazing!" Melisse gasped at the perfect fit of the beautiful blue satin tango shoes, which left the chances of her falling slim to none.

"Ha…it's no accident. *Actuellement,* Sheik Jazzy had them sent over a few hours ago just for you. Just remember…you know…to slowly, slowly remove the wings, with zee music…revealing what is beneath it…this body…you are a beautiful little woman, Melisse… This is the time of your life, and you are so lucky to be sponsored by this crazy sheik! Go out there and enjoy!"

Melisse looked down hopelessly at her bloated belly pooching out of a royal-blue lace bodysuit. She sucked it in. The corset-like bodice went up only to her bare breasts and didn't cover them, and its underwires pushed up her boobs out of the corset.

She turned into a mirror and saw the back of the bodysuit disappearing into her butt cheeks. The costume was topped by a detachable sequined cape, shaped like huge butterfly wings in variegated shades of blue.

Melisse was to follow the classic striptease hip movements and the burlesque traditions of "less is more." Fortunately, she had studied them years ago at burlesque shows on her nights off in New York's East Village.

She was to keep her breasts shrouded by the wings and only do "peekaboo moves" during the music, but as the tempo intensified, she was to reveal more and more until the end, when she spread the butterfly wings while facing the audience, so they could be treated to a full-on view of her bare breasts. Then, when she twirled to bow, she would reveal her huge ass (as compared to the tiny asses of the usual cast of dancers at Le Crazy Horse).

Melisse was more nervous than a virgin at a prison rodeo as she stood at the edge of the stage waiting to go on. Just then, Matilde approached her with a couple of "sparklers" shooting off sparks. "Here! I almost forgot! These are for the act!"

"What should I do with these?" Melisse asked, taking the sparklers.

"Dunk them in the bowls of water just off the stage when you are done, right before you start le grand finale!"

But I'm afraid of fire!

No matter. Before she knew it, the music of "Sex Bomb" by Tom Jones began and spurred her into giving a fun performance. Melisse was slinking out onto the center of the stage, smiling, dancing with sparklers, then peekabooing her breasts, then throwing off her wings, and then shaking her tits to a room full of applause. It all went off without a hitch.

> **Spicy Secret: "You've gotta dance like there's nobody watching, love like you'll never be hurt, sing like there's nobody listening, and live like it's heaven on earth." —William W. Purkey**

As Jazzy watched Melisse's dazzling performance, he was thrilled by her youthful exuberance, combined with a seeming mastery of the seductive and striptease arts. At first, given her classy and reserved demeanor at the bar, he'd thought she would be like a shy librarian who wouldn't know a damn thing about dancing for a crowd! But a little voice inside him suspected otherwise, and now he had confirmation…perhaps her every move, every word had been as expertly choreographed as this show tonight. If so, she was a true artist and worthy of his patronage.

Spicy Secret: "When she raises her eyelids, it's as if she were taking off all her clothes." —Colette

He was pleased to see the crowd stand up, clap, and whistle in appreciation for this surprise star of the show! Jazzy also rose, whistling and making a special whooping sound that nomadic sheepherders only make in the desert during a wedding.

Little did Jazzy know that Melisse had studied a lot of Mae West, seen Dita Von Teese, and had even learned a thing or two back at Tony's Wedge, that hole-in-the-wall strip club in the Bronx as an eighteen-year-old topless dancer.

And Melisse, like a heroin addict shooting up again after years of being stone-cold sober, was really enjoying herself, smiling and then running backstage, feeling goose bumps covering her body as Matilde threw a robe around her and embraced her.

"You didn't tell us you are a dancer!" Matilde marveled.

"Bravo!" Francois said. "Incredible! How fun! Can you come back sometime?" He smiled. "Please! Come back again to us, anytime!"

Melisse laughed, knowing that after this, if the rest of the evening went well, she could indeed come back anytime she wanted to, and if their time at club Pont Jarretelles proved "over the top" for Jazzy, she'd be going other places someday, too, like La Fantasia.

There was only one thing she wasn't sure about: this anal sex she'd sort of "promised" him tonight. She sighed.

Spicy Secret: Sometimes you just have to get what you want through the back door.

CHAPTER 32

Pont Jarretelles Swingers Club

Jazzy held Melisse's hand in the back of his armored limo as they made their way toward the Pont Jarretelles nightclub.

"Are you having fun tonight?" he asked.

"Oh, yes." She smiled, squeezing his hand. "I love surprises!"

"Ha! *Now* you will need more surprises!"

Melisse turned and looked at him with amusement. "Are you afraid you won't be able to keep me interested without them?" She knew this was bold, but something told her he would appreciate her bluntness.

They'd already had a round of mutual "insults," so she knew she could take things pretty far.

She was right. Jazzy's next question was surprisingly touching. "Tell me something honestly, Melisse. I know I am not Mr. Universe. What kind of man do you…think about…when you, you know… touch yourself…?"

"Ummm…well, I think of someone like you, with your kind of looks!" she said, not very convincingly.

"Really? Please, let us have some honesty between us. Go on. I want to hear it. You like, ah…like a Tom Cruise, a *Top Gun* type?"

"Ha! NO."

"What about a Brad Pitt? A George Clooney?"

"God, no."

"Tell me what you like, then," he almost pleaded.

"OK. When I can't find a tall, lean guy like *you* in my imagination while I touch myself…then I don't have anyone at all."

266   LANTANA BLEU

Spicy Secret: When men ask probing questions about their looks, skills, or otherwise, remember that flattery is like icing a cake with frosting: you can never lay it on too thick.

"Please, lady. Let us have more honesty between us. Tell me something that is not a big load of horse doo-doo."

"OK. I'll tell you something: I just luuuuv bald men."

"Ah! Bald! I will shave my head immediately! You are a strange girl, Melisse," the Emir observed. "I have never met someone like you before. How many boyfriends do you have? Fourteen?"

"I don't have anyone. Only *you*." Melisse leaned in and put her head on his shoulder. She felt Jazzy melting a little.

Spicy Secret: Most clients love the concept and idea of exclusivity but the reality is they wouldn't know what to do with you if they had you all to themselves. They also *like* knowing you're a "little bit slutty." Walk the line by giving them your undivided attention, and never talk about your other suitors, but then wow them with a physical prowess that can only be attained through erotic adventures with a variety of men.

"You are too good."

"Ha! Look who's talking. How many wives do *you* have?"

"I have three wives. And I try to treat them all equally. My wives are always fighting and scratching each other over who will get to spend the night with me! I am supposed to give them each a night, but sometimes I make like a fun little competition, so one can get extra time with me. It is quite gratifying to my ego to see them haggling over my stiff willy like a cut of good meat in the butcher shop. Not that they know anything of this grocery shopping."

Melisse laughed at this. *Yeah, right.* "Maybe someday they're going to chop you up into three pieces! Winner gets the best piece of Jazzy!"

"Each piece of that piece will be long. And all pieces of me are great prizes," he said with total seriousness.

Spicy Secret: Whenever men are indulging in bragging or tooting their own horn about some amazing thing they did, just back them right up. Even if it's true, they're telling you because they feel insecure deep down, and it's your job to give them a boost.

"Ohhhh...well, then, I do feel lucky tonight," she said, squeezing his hand again.

"You're not feeling lucky tonight, you're *getting* lucky tonight," he said with a slight snarl.

"Hmmmm...I can't wait," she cooed. The limo was stopped in front of a beautifully lit French restaurant, where the tables were doubtless decorated with candles and small bouquets of flowers. *Oh to be inside, holding hands and talking with someone I could adore.*

"Now, my Melisse, since it will take some time for me to win your love, I will just have to win your lust tonight with my cock missile. I am going to land it deep in the crack of your asshole. Then it will be exploding..."

This again? Can't these guys think of anything but themselves and their cocks?

"Oh, dear. Are we almost there yet?" *The big barkers never have any bite.*

"Yes. Put this on," he said, handing her a beautiful female Venetian eye mask.

As she did so, he put on a matching male eye mask.

"I must protect my identity. Everyone in the European media follows me and suspects me of being a bit naughty when I come here to Europe. But nobody knows for sure, and nobody can ever catch me. And nobody knows I am *this* naughty. Except for you. And I expect everything that we do will remain a secret."

"Of course, sir," she said crisply.

"Otherwise, I will lock you up in chains and leather in the private jail in my palace."

"Understood." She nodded. "Actually, that sounds very sexy. Do you really have a private jail?"

"It is more like a hotel suite made of leather and equipped with racks and bars on the door."

She looked over at him with a suspicious look on her face.

"I am kidding." He smiled beneath the mask. But somehow she knew he wasn't.

"You go in first without me," he said as they arrived at the club. "I need to make a little call. We're on the list," he said. "And Rachid, my security valet, will walk you to the door. And then he will walk you to the table. And Rachid will never leave your side until I am present."

"Understood."

With a guy like this on the chain, you'd never need to worry about your personal safety. Melisse was starting to like this rarified lifestyle of armored cars, security valets, and…leather dungeons?

Pont Jarretelles, a cozy nightclub for those with erotic predilections (or an interest in watching others who did), was hidden away close to the priceless works of art in the Louvre. It housed its own works of art: beautiful, sexy creatures of the night enjoying themselves, seeing and being seen in the posh, velvety, candlelit, hopping boîte.

It reminded her of a turn-of-the-century bordello boudoir, oozing sensuality with the most seductive music possible, perfect for inspiring spontaneous seductions.

As they sat down at a reserved table, she was delighted to find a bouquet of gorgeous red roses lying there, just for her. There was even a small card, which read, "Melisse, For you, with all my love…" *That* was classy. And then she read more: "Let's go deeper tonight."

Uggggg!

Despite the man's incongruities, she was enjoying her newfound "red carpet" treatment while dashing out and about with Sheik Jazzy. Yet no amount of red carpet or red roses was going to ever make her genuinely physically or mentally "attracted" to him for a serious relationship.

And no amount of Jazzy's red carpet treatment would diminish the dark circles she would have under her eyes when her American client showed up tomorrow in Saint-Germain-des-Prés. He was due late the next morning at "their" hotel, expecting her to arrive bright-eyed and bushy-tailed with his "lucky blow job." It would be a challenge to conceal that she'd been out partying the entire night before. But she *might* be able to pull it off if Jazzy was gentle tonight and let her get enough sleep. Maybe she could keep her hair in front of her face, as she felt her jaw almost falling off while blowing the guy for a solid 30 minutes til he spurted in a geyser of corporate ecstasy all over her neck.

Couldn't she just leave a lucky rabbit's foot or a four leaf clover on the guy's pillow instead?

> **Spicy Secret: If a client has reserved your time, it should be set in stone, regardless of his status in your ever-shifting hierarchy of men.**

But what if Jazzy wanted her to stay with him for breakfast through another day? She'd have to say she had an important doctor's appointment the next morning…then go back to her hotel to blow the American and return in time for lunch with Jazzy…

> **Spicy Secret: When juggling your schedule to accommodate multiple clients, consider yourself blessed with an abundance of more business than you can handle. No worries, though: the Universe usually has a way of balancing everything out to make your schedule work seamlessly and appointments dovetail nicely. It's not "in the nick of time," it's "in the prick of time."**

Hmmm…experience told her it was quite possible to pull it all off.

Spicy Secret: Where there's a weenie, there's always a way.

At that moment, Melisse decided to switch from the ever-flowing champagne to pure, cold Evian water. Meanwhile, Jazzy had switched to a fine port, which he swilled slowly and enjoyed, knowing each sip was bringing him closer to the hoped-for access to Melisse's ass. They sipped at their drinks and enjoyed the scene.

"Do you think *he's* handsome?" Jazzy asked of a smallish, milk chocolate/café au lait man walking by slowly. The specimen in question was a short, bald man of African descent with lean muscles and a yoga body wearing a tight, silky black T-shirt and black pants with an elegant belt. "He's got something you like—no hair!" Jazzy laughed.

"He's fine," she said, trying to seem disinterested. *More than fine. Too fine. Way too handsome and modelesque for me.* But too short to be a fashion model, so he was *just right*. Delicious, in fact. He looked like someone about to become a famous R & B singer, like an Usher—those eyes, that facial structure, the perfectly proportioned body. Guys like that usually never took a second look at her, and she often wished they would.

"He's fine, but I'd rather have *you*," Melisse lied.

"I'd like to watch you seduce him. Let's see if you can do it," Jazzy said.

"Jazzy! NO! I'm *your* date…"

"You don't understand me yet. I *like* this type of kinky thing. It turns me on to watch my woman having a good time. And however that good time happens, is just…" He shrugged his shoulders. "C'est la vie. Things happen. I cannot have sex in the normal way in your—how do the French say it—in your *fou-fou,* your *minou.* Your *vagina,* as you Americans call this little miracle of human anatomy… It is against my morals."

"Really?"

"Yes. I *do* have morals but I do not know where they have gone to at the moment," he said, looking around like he'd lost something, and then laughed.

> **Spicy Secret: "Lead me not into temptation. I can find the way myself." —Rita Mae Brown**

Melisse chuckled. "Are you sure about this?"

"I know you would want *me* to have a good time, too. If I could. But I just enjoy watching you, and later we can see what fun we can do."

Wow, Melisse thought. *A "no sex" client with millions to burn. I've truly hit the jackpot. What's the catch?*

> **Spicy Secret: Sometimes the "no sex" clients are a lot more trouble than you'd expect. Their creative alternatives to intercourse might include head games, elaborate fantasy scenarios and/or "substitute" activities that give you lockjaw or carpal tunnel syndrome.**

"What if he's with someone? That wouldn't be right. Or what if he's gay?"

"I'm *sure* he's not," Jazzy said. "Gay men don't come here. Now go on!"

"Really?"

"I'll be tracking you. I want to see how a woman more ugly than the man she's after can get him and drag him back to the private area back there."

"More ugly?" she asked, appalled.

"Less attractive?"

She snarled out a sigh. "You really think I'm ugly?"

"Oh, did I hurt your feelings? You're not a fashion model, let's put it that way. But you're cute. What they call a 'natural beauty.' Like I told you, you're like a Disney character. I am so boring with models!"

"Bored. It's 'bored.' Oh, please. Beauty is so subjective, Jazzy. *Some* people think I'm very pretty."

"Really? Who? You told me you don't even have one boyfriend!"

Melisse pretended to act defeated. "You're right. Nobody finds me attractive enough to date me. You are the first in a long time."

He patted her on the back. "I know, huuuuuney. I am happy to make your night."

Spicy Secret: Men who are extremely attracted to and intrigued with a woman will often toss out mild insults to see how she reacts. If she doesn't take the bait, she's a keeper (and they'll probably cut out the teasing, too).

"Now go and see if he's gay or not by taking him in the back room. In front of me. I want proof."

She felt the small sting of his insult and the buzz of challenge in now having something to prove. But then Melisse realized that it was probably just another one of his "zaps."

She slowly got up from the table. "You really want this?"

"What do you think?" he said, smiling beneath his mask. "Do you think I play games?"

The incredibly handsome man stood by a small bar area. Melisse approached tentatively, feeling Jazzy's eyes watching her through his mask. She got as close as possible to him and smiled shyly. He seemed a bit annoyed at first, but then saw that she was wearing an intriguing mask and a cute outfit covering her pretty curves.

He spoke to her in French. "*Ça va?*" he asked.

"Hi," she said shyly. He looked over her shoulder quickly, at someone.

"Hello," he said, smiling now, switching into a charming Parisian accent. "Charming mask. So few wear them here. You must be famous."

She chuckled. "No…I just…like to have my fun anonymously. *Completely* anonymously."

"Ah, you want to have fun! May I buy you a drink?"

She smiled. "Yes, please." But as they waited for the bartender to pour a couple of Kir Royales, she felt nervous. She decided to be forthright. "You see that man sitting behind us? Don't look now, but he is also wearing a mask. He would like me to seduce you, but I told him I think you must have a girlfriend here. You are so handsome. It is impossible that you would be here alone. Or, you are gay."

"No. There is no one with me right now and I love women. I am not for a man. Women only, let us be clear. I am alone and I am here for the same reason you are. I would love to go to the back *chambre* with you. You are beautiful. I love…the *petite* woman…the way she feels so…small…"

"Please. The gentleman I am with is a *merdier*." (A bullshit maker, someone who likes to create drama where there is none).

"And so what are we going to do about him?" he asked, laughing. "Will we satisfy him, give him what he wants?"

"I need you to act like you are rejecting me at first, but be very dramatic about it. In a few minutes, gently push me away. Then I can go back to him pretending I feel rejected so he can comfort me. He can feel like the better man and I can get on with my evening and go home with him…"

"How bizarre!" the man said suddenly as the Kirs appeared.

"What?"

"Sheik Jazzy just called me to come over here to seduce *you*. I 'cater' some of his parties in Wadijazzizi; I fly in the girls, I bring special boys, etcetera. For him, it is like importing French cheeses. And he asked me to come here tonight to be with *you*."

"Oh, he's very resourceful, isn't he? So…let me see if I understand… you are *working*?"

"Yes, of course," he said. "I am…*just a gigolo*," he sang, referring to the song popularized by Louis Prima. "But don't tell *him* that I told *you*."

"Just a gigolo? *Mais, c'est tout!*" Melisse said, switching into French. "What's your name?" Melisse asked, happy to know a cute, straight gigolo she could potentially pull in on some of her "couples" requests.

"I am Patrique. Cheers!" he said, clinking champagne glasses with her.

She sipped hers quickly and felt another delicious shot of alcoholic comfort go right to her legs, numbing out any remaining nerves about "performing."

"Can I lead you back to the pleasure room now, Miss…?" he asked, searching for her name.

"Melisse," she said. She squeezed his hand, feeling a wonderful excitement at the prospect of going to the back with someone so darling that she would have chosen him in a heartbeat. "Sorry, I'm a little, um, nervous."

"Say no more, Melisse. We are here to work, but we can enjoy, too. We will make a good show," he said like a fellow craftsman, squeezing her hand sweetly in return. He whispered, "I find you incredibly sexy, *by the way*."

Melisse's ears tingled. Was he sincere or just doing his job?

Spicy Secret: Be wary of the man whose game is as good as yours. There can only be competition, and then— a winner and a loser ahead. Which will you be?

And with this, Melisse shot Jazzy a nod and was led to a special back room, where more obvious erotic encounters took place. Here, couples sat enjoying the ambience on chaise longues and velvet-covered mattresses, to be watched by others with keen interest.

Jazzy was one of them, and rose to follow them, keeping a discreet distance. He took a seat in a chair that had been ribboned off with a RESERVED sign.

In the *very* private area, decorated by more soft, cushiony lounging areas and fewer tables, Patrique lay down with Melisse on a round bed covered with a white silky sheet and red rose petals. A small crowd formed around them, watching as he kissed her neck for a while, his hands gently caressing her over her corset, her stockings, and her legs. Then he stood, his chest puffed out like a peacock, and began undressing.

Patrique made a dramatic show of removing his belt, undoing his pants, and pushing them down over his athletic legs. His body, covered only by his silky shirt and underwear, was a beautiful light brown, firm and smooth. He pulled his T-shirt slowly over his head to reveal a sleek, strong physique that could only be obtained by a precise amount of slow and meticulous weight lifting, combined with Pilates or yoga and punctuated by a measured amount of "pulse" running on a treadmill. When he pulled down his underwear, there was a small gasp in the room.

Now *that* was something you couldn't get by working out!

His was a magnificent cock straining to rise and become vertical—a beautiful tool of pleasure glowing in the candlelit room.

Melisse tried to ignore all the people watching them, including Jazzy. Thanks to her eye mask, she felt completely anonymous and secure. She left everything on but her panties, making a pretty show of indicating that Patrique could slide them down over her garter belt.

Just as she'd done at Le Crazy Horse cabaret, she left a little more to the imagination by leaving on her skirt, stockings, and bustier. Meanwhile, her "audience" could see very well that her pussy was completely bare and ready for Patrique to enjoy.

Through her mask, Melisse turned to her left and saw that Jazzy was in a prime seat for the show. His hand ventured discreetly toward his crotch, rubbing himself gently as he watched Patrique's face go under Melisse's skirt. He lifted it up toward her stomach to reveal her lace garter belt as his tongue roved all over her soft pink flower.

She groaned as his tongue found its way to her most pleasurable places, varying the amount of hardness and softness of his probing tongue as he licked around her clit, darting lightly over it, and then circled wetly and gently around it before giving another quick dart over it again, like a painter making quick strokes as accents. He alternated this by using one hand to apply light pressure over her entire vulva, vibrating it slightly as he licked away.

She'd never felt anything like this before! *This is what you get when you're with a pro.* These particular accent strokes sent waves of pleasure through Melisse, and she surrendered to the knowledge that strangers were watching her in a public place with an attractive man—a man who would eventually fuck her as only an experienced gigolo could. It was one of her hottest experiences on record!

She moaned loudly for her audience's benefit, noticing how her sounds of pleasure blended in with the sexy music playing.

And it was Jazzy, her erotic benefactor, who had provided all of this for her. *Who is servicing whom here?* she wondered as she succumbed to waves of pleasure.

Just when Patrique's tongue brought her so close she was ready for him to enter her, he stopped and stretched his naked body over her clothed body. Again, he kissed her neck, now running his fingers through her hair. Some of their admirers watched, barely able to breathe, their heads tilted ever so slightly, waiting for Patrique's cock to slip inside her. This was, indeed, "living art."

"Take off your skirt," he whispered in her ear, and she obliged, unlatching it in the back with a deft hand. He pulled it down and away from her legs, revealing the curve of her hips as they flared out from beneath her bustier and the lacy garter belt.

While she had distracted the audience with her skirt removal, he'd discreetly rolled on a condom, and then, when the skirt was off completely, he pushed her legs into the air and placed them around his neck. He slowly pushed his cock inside her, making a show for everyone of its length, girth, and the slow and pleasurable disappearance of it into Melisse.

"Oh…God!" she moaned, almost destroyed with pleasure.

He began pumping her with a slow, steady rhythm, matched to the music. With every delicious slow pump, he brought her closer, but this position wouldn't really make her come, and she wanted to come "for real."

She motioned for him to take her legs down from around his neck, and she wrapped them lightly around his thighs.

"Patrique, please just fuck me slow."

"I'm going to go slow. They need a long, slow show here…"

"Whatever you want…oh, it's so good!" she sighed.

So for the next half hour, as people milled around, coming and leaving the room, he rocked her slowly, sometimes exiting her completely, then diving it in deeper the next time, but always using the same, nonstop, slow beats.

Melisse couldn't count how many times she came, thanks to the perfect rhythm of his perfect strokes, moaning as loud as she wanted to against the music. They seemed to inspire other people as the room filled up with other couples having sex in various stages of undress. Some were pinned against the soft walls eating one another, some straddling each other on couches, while some couples shared the few round mattresses in the chamber.

By now, Jazzy had come to sit next to her and held her hand and stroked her hair as Patrique continued to give her his cock. Her hair was matted with sweat, and Jazzy was gratified to know that he had a satisfied, now *docile* woman on his hands.

Finally, Patrique could not resist her any longer, and looked up at Jazzy.

Jazzy nodded. "I wish for you to take off her top. Then, you may finish."

Patrique pulled away from Melisse's body for a moment as Melisse sat up and Jazzy helped her undo the pink ribbons of her bustier. Once loosened, he pulled off the lacy piece and held it like a prize as her breasts went free. She lay back down again as Patrique came to her breasts and sucked on her nipples gently.

Jazzy nodded down at Patrique and lightly touched his own cock through his pants. Melisse reached up and rubbed Jazzy's cock lightly as he held her hand. As Melisse looked around at everyone either having sex or watching her having sex, it made her hotter and hotter.

Patrique lay atop Melisse again, and this time spread her legs a little wider beneath him. She wrapped them around his back, knowing that a hard ride was in store.

The excitement of their watchers was so hot and palpable, you could almost hear them panting as Patrique proceeded to pump Melisse hard and fast, driving his cock deep inside with relentless strokes. He had only one goal in mind this time, as she was completely spent and exhausted from coming far more often than she was used to.

It was his turn now. He pulled out of her, tore off his condom, and let out a moan like Tarzan as he felt his jizz coming up and out through his cock in an explosive geyser of supreme pleasure.

"Aaaaaaaarrrrrggggh!" Patrique groaned, spewing his come all over her belly and between her breasts.

They lay together in a sweaty heap as the small crowd around them applauded. Jazzy snapped his fingers and the waiter who'd been on "standby" for him rushed over with a platter holding two towels, which Patrique took to gently clean off Melisse's torso, which now resembled a creamed confection.

Melisse leaned back, closed her eyes behind the comfort of her mask, and smiled. *This was truly a night to remember!*

"Happy?" Jazzy asked, squeezing her hand. She nodded.

But it wasn't over. She remembered that Jazzy wanted her ass. And at this point, after giving her a mini Adonis to attend to her, he could have whatever he wanted.

But he probably knew that already.

Once back in Jazzy's suite, Melisse agreed to give Jazzy "prime access to her asshole," as he'd so elegantly described it. He'd popped a Viagra when they'd left Jarretelles, but when they finally got into bed, he was nearly half-asleep from drink and the late hour, and could barely speak.

As he tried to delicately impale her with his quasi-hard penis, she pushed back on his every approach, making it seem that she was just very tight, making it nearly impossible for him to enter from that approach. He wasn't rough or demanding sexually when it came to performing, and eventually gave up and fell asleep in a Pernod-induced stupor.

This would become his usual pattern, as she'd learn over the course of time. Hope sprang eternal when it came to his dream of anal sex with Melisse.

It was the first and last night that Jazzy would experience the wonders of Viagra with Melisse. She'd "handled" the situation for her future travels to Dubai by having a contract vitamin company whip up some placebos that looked exactly like Viagra. Once she gained access to Jazzy's bathroom on some pretense, she'd swap out the real stuff for her custom-made placebos. He never noticed the difference or seemed to care much that the pills weren't working for him. He was just happy hoping—and drinking.

Normally, she would have felt guilty and immoral doing such a thing (after all, she believed that her mission as a courtesan was to give sensual pleasure). However, in Jazzy's case, she concluded that he was one man who was much better off without a woody! The potential side effects of mixing Viagra with all his other concoctions of pleasure—strong cocktails, Cuban cigars, and who knew what medicines—could harm the guy! He was worth more to her alive than dead, after all.

The next morning after Pont Jarretelles, an early morning visit to her guest bathroom in Jazzy's hotel suite had already revealed an incredible envelope with a jaw-dropping amount of cash for her (inside a shopping sack filled with various Hermès perfumes and assorted French goodies from the neighborhood boutiques). He (with the help of the hotel's concierge) had prepared it for her as her "gift" for the night they'd spent together.

But she knew from experience with her sweet Arabs that it was always better to get the envelope while also giving a story of why you need the contents inside. In this way, she would spare their sensitive pride from anything too harsh or transactional, as in "feeling like a client," and instead, cultivate within him a sense of caring generosity.

Melisse had learned early in her career that rich Arabs didn't like tidy transactions, preferring to be parted from their pocket money with long, sad stories, well-lubricated with copious feminine tears.

So while they cuddled in the morning and she sensed that his mind was turning to other matters and it would soon be time for her to leave, she looked up, gave him her "sad face," and said, "I don't want to trouble you with this…"

"No, huuuuney, go on!" he said, fully expecting to enjoy a bit of "theater" as she proceeded to tell him that her short-term Paris vacation apartment rent was due. "Today! Can you believe it?"

Spicy Secret: The most effective "sad face" involves turning out the bottom lip slightly while looking down and to the right.

"No! Really? Tell me more..." he mused, now understanding what a smart girl she really was, not to just "take the money and run." He would enjoy indulging her in letting her tell her "story." He was sure it would be a good one.

"Well, Emir... It's ten thousand euros per month for my rental and they locked me out yesterday for nonpayment! I've been having trouble with my online banking...which is why I was trying to spend most of the night at the bar downstairs until I could reach my banker...and you know...it's why I was so happy I could come stay with you for the night! And you fed me, which made me so happy because I was getting soooo hungry."

"I thought I heard your stomach growling!"

Her fake sad voice might have worked but her naughty smile gave it away charmingly.

A big smile crept across his face, and he seemed to be struggling not to laugh. "That is a very sad story. I feel very sorry for you. My sheets are probably so much nicer here than what they give you in a cheap ten-thousand-euro-a-month apartment!"

"The sheets gave me a rash." She turned over so he could get one last luscious look at her ass. "Right here, on my bottom!"

"Oh, you poor thing," he said, rubbing her butt down. "Does this home also have a terrace with a view of that horrid thing? What's it called? The Eiffel Tower?"

"Yes!" she said, pretending disgust, half smiling. "When I want to sleep at night, the light show of the Tower is disturbing me! And during the day...this big monstrosity, this Eiffel Tower, is throwing a little too much shade on my big terrace with the flowers. And the fountain is noisy. So I have to go into my solarium on the other side, for shade."

"They should move that Tower out of the way for you. I will tell them to take it out."

"Thank you! I hope I can finally get to sleep in that hovel!"

"You poor thing. I hope they at least gave you running water in this flat. Is there a rain showerhead?"

"No. It's just a jet massager, like, jets of water coming out from every direction. It's a true Vichy spa shower but, you know, it feels more like a 'bitchy' shower to me…I am a simple girl…" she added demurely. "I really just like to rinse my hair with bottled Evian water… *but they forgot to deliver it*!" she whined.

"Awwww…I hope your shower was not squirting out too hard and hurting these big nipples!" And with that he pinched one really hard as she made a faux slap at his face. He took her by the waist back down on the bed as they both cracked up.

"I am having much fun with you," he said, cuddling her. "I wish to see you again—in Dubai. Soon!"

"Thank you for my gift, Sheik Jazzy. It came at just the right time and it will really help me with this crazy apartment rental problem I am having today."

"Awwww…" he smiled.

"You saved my life," she said, doe-eyed, giving him a final hug.

Later in their relationship, on the rare occasion they ever had to discuss the unpleasant matter of her fee, he would use the term "foreign aid" to ask how much he should wire into her bank account to make her blissfully happy and eager to visit him again. He was happy to support the small foreign country known as "Melisse."

> **Spicy Secret: Use euphemisms when referring to payments: call it a gift, a tribute, a donation, a consideration, or a token of appreciation…but never call it what it really is: pay for play.**

Before leaving, Melisse visited the guest bathroom and tucked her huge envelope filled with "foreign aid" into her purse. After she freshened her lipstick, they said good-bye at the door.

> **Spicy Secret: Leave the discreet collection of your "gifts" or envelope until the last possible moment if you trust the person you're with. And NEVER count money out in front of *anyone*. Money doesn't exist, remember? You don't want to give the impression that you like the money more than the man.**

Before she left, instead of handing him her elegant business card (which would give away the fact that she was a consummate call girl) she dictated all of her numbers and email address to Jazzy. She watched patiently as he entered all her numbers into his mobile phone under the category, "Gift Baskets."

Now she knew he could find her the next time he wanted another helping of the goodies in the "gift basket" named Melisse.

"This was the best gift basket ever!" he said, hugging her good-bye, then grabbing both her cheeks in his hands and leaning down and sliding what felt like a cold, electrified eel into her mouth for a few moments of…*eel kissing*?

Melisse tried not to let gagging get in the way of a memorable good-bye.

"Bye, darling Jazzy!" She whispered before scooting out the door and into the elevator.

Once downstairs, Melisse looked at the time as she stepped outside the hotel and into the fresh buzz of a spring morning in Paris.

Just in the prick of time.

She nodded/winked/smiled/tipped the doorman who got her into a taxi headed to Saint-Germain.

Her estimated arrival time to "the good luck blow job" and her client's arrival from the U.S.A? Twenty minutes and counting!

She hummed that old Frank Sinatra song on the way.

Luck be a lady.

THE PRESENT

CHAPTER 33

Jazzy at The Burj Al Arab Hotel, Dubai

Whenever Melisse was in Dubai and approached the iconic Burj Al Arab hotel, the sail-shaped tower seemed to rise from the flat landscape of the beach like a cock at full mast. This was a beacon of hope for her, and every time she saw it, she knew she was financially one step closer to seeing her dreams come true.

The Bentley entered the driveway leading out to the hotel, and Melisse's thoughts turned from her first meeting with Jazzy in Paris to her immediate challenge: keeping him happy now that she was back in Dubai! She saw the hotel in the distance, where she would yet again spread her magical pixie dust on Jazzy.

As the car pulled up the drive, she saw him, all in a dither, nervously excited in his royal white robes: Jazzy was waiting for her. She was one of the few in the world who knew that he was hiding an outrageously long, perpetually limp dick under all that garb. His weathered face was topped by a traditional head dressing, like a long turban with a black band, all very formal-looking and officious. A dirty smirk rolled across his face when he saw his own silver Bentley with dark tinted windows roll up, containing his prized girl.

She took a deep breath. *Here we go again.*

Spicy Secret: No matter how much you may secretly dread spending time with someone you have no chemistry with (but who loves you anyway), simply "reframe" the experience as entertaining a patron who is making a donation toward your dreams and goals (whatever they may be). And every donation counts.

Melisse quickly peeked inside her bag before she exited the car. Ah yes, thank God she'd remembered the blue placebo pills that resembled Viagra. As usual, she planned to switch them with the real thing later when she found Jazzy's Viagra container upstairs in his Dopp kit. By the time he wanted to get hard, when he was in the dim lighting of his suite's marble bathroom (the size of her entire apartment back in New York), he was usually too cross-eyed drunk to notice that the pills were a slightly different shape and shade of blue than the real Viagra.

The door of the Bentley opened and Melisse carefully stuck out a leg. A hotel greeter hoisted her up and out onto the driveway.

It's showtime!

Melisse exited Jazzy's Bentley and was quickly guided by his "handlers" all the way through the lobby of the Burj Al Arab up to their adjoining suites.

Jazzy had discreetly nodded and smirked at her as she passed him and breezed into the hotel. He would soon take a separate elevator up to join her for what he called the "welcome warm-up"—a time when she would appear in costume so they could act out a fantasy. The costume always had to be something new and different, one he'd never seen before—a high school cheerleader, a rock star singer, a goddess painted with gold, a naughty librarian, and the like.

Melisse had to keep notes on what she had or hadn't worn yet, and what fantasies she hadn't served up yet to entertain Jazzy. To make efficient use of her time, she'd bought about three dozen of the cheapest, tackiest, wackiest costumes and props she could find online, and created sexy scripts for them to play. This was so that she wouldn't have to spend her precious time and mental energy before every trip figuring out what getups to bring for him.

Spicy Secret: "Think ahead. Don't let day-to-day operations drive out planning." —Donald Rumsfeld

A few minutes after she arrived, she'd already changed into her first costume. Jazzy knocked on the door of the bedroom in her "wing" of their adjoining suites. She had prepared for the "welcome warm-up" by wearing a Harley-Davidson getup, including a leather G-string and bra, leather chaps over tight jeans, and a small motorcycle jacket, fake tattoos, and a bandanna.

"Jazzy!" she squealed, as if a war had separated two lovers for a decade and now they were reunited.

"Oh, my little minx, here at last," he sighed.

He sat down on the bed and slathered her with a disgusting, probing tongue kiss, which she returned while grabbing his arms in an effort to seem like she was grabbing on, but really she was subtly trying to push him and his tongue away.

He, of course, took this as her way of holding him closer for a better smooch.

"And how has *he* been?" she asked, with the utmost concern.

She reached down for his crotch, hoping to distract him from her lips.

"He is a hard, hot rod today." He looked her over with an air of approval.

"Vroom, vroom…" she snarled. "Can I hop on your crotch rocket, big bad moto-daddy?"

"Oh, that is very exciting, baby. I promise to give you the ride of your life as soon as possible, but first…?"

Melisse had grabbed him around his neck and was nuzzling him in his favorite place with her teeth bared. He shuddered with excitement.

"Oh my God, this is a very good warm-up. But I have something very special I must ask of you," he said, pulling away. "Today is the last day I am entertaining my friend Simo here in Dubai, you see? He is the minister of finance and new technologies for a small Arab kingdom. We are distant relatives but he is very powerful—in fact, he is a royal, and he may do me some favors for my environmental research in using my pig shit for fuel and…I need you…"

"Yes…?"

"Well, I would like to offer an interlude with *you* as an incentive." He said it as if she were an imprinted logo pen or one of those toothbrushes they gave away at the dentist office.

"An incentive. For your *pig poo cause*? With *a royal*?" she asked incredulously.

He didn't answer, and it was part of the job (which she was paid exorbitantly well for) so she asked, "Is this Simo a nice man? A gentleman?"

"Oh, yes, I swear on the fat body of my dead queen mother. I am almost jealous how much you will like him and he will like you. But I must give him a going-away present, and *this* is the man who has everything! He is a prince, but he works. So I want to give him *you*—but only for an hour. You are my most prized possession, and for this I will give you something extra."

"All right, Jazzy. But I'd much rather be with you. Anyway, what should I wear?"

"Go as you are!" he said, sitting down on the bed. "And rock his world. Just zip up your jacket, put on your sunglasses, and the other guests in the elevator will believe they are looking at Madonna."

"Ha, Madonna! Right. But Jazzy, I prepared a little dance for you. It's to an American rock and roll song. Shall I do that, too?"

"Oh, yes. He has never seen anything like this. He doesn't get out much in his country. He is a very straight man. You may need to overpower him with your vixen ways…" He grinned.

"I get it. When do I go?"

"Now! He is downstairs in his suite waiting for you!"

Melisse made a move to grab her handbag.

"But!" Jazzy said. "*Do not* make sex with him."

"Don't have sex with him!?"

"No. I would not be able to stand it. Just *tease* him. He must only get a small taste and then be jealous that you are for me and not for him. And then when I *really* need something from him, I will offer you again—for e*verything*."

"If you don't mind my asking, what do you want from him, exactly?"

He coughed and then said, "I want to attend a major technology trade show he holds every year in his country. It is a most prestigious exhibition…"

"Yes, *and*…?" Here it was. It was sure to be something ridiculous.

"And I want to set up a pigpen to display my albino potbellied pigs as part of the interactive display for my Pigpoo technology."

"*Interactive*?"

"Yes. I am willing to rent an entire section of his convention center for my booth, so I do not know what is the big bloody deal! But his people are saying no, that my project won't fit in with the software companies and that it will be stinky and slippery. And someone in his circle even said it was 'a shitty idea.' But Simo has the final authority over the exhibition, and what he says, goes."

Hmmmm…it sounds kind of like children's Science Fair politics meets Dr. Dolittle, meets "4-H," and shoveling a whole lotta manure.

"So *that* is why I need *you* to go down there and give *him* a *boner*. Then, after he gives me my booth and the show goes well, I'll send you again to *bone* him. As a thank-you."

"Jesus fucking Christ, Jazzy! There's no need to use such crass terms! Do you think I came here to do your bidding?" Melisse practically screamed across the room as she pulled a brush through her locks and adjusted her leather bikini in the mirror. The nice thing about having half a floor was that you could get very pissed off (and sometimes even throw things, like shoes, at your client) and nobody would ever hear.

"Cool your jets, baby. He is a nice guy. Just go down there and do as you're told, give the man a great show and give him a nice time. Get me my pig poop booth!"

"Oh, God," Melisse sighed. That's glamour. *Now I'm a negotiating piece in a battle over a pig shit presentation!*

"What is Simo's room number?" she asked, officially annoyed.

The fortunate thing about Jazzy was that the more visibly annoyed he made Melisse, the more he was turned on by her. He loved that she could freely display her angry side to him (and she kind of enjoyed it, too), with the accompanying slew of naughty words and scolding he knew she dared not use with anybody else. It was all part of the fun she was paid to give him.

"The goddamn fucking room number of this guy? Jazzy?" she said, finally losing her cool (for real, this time).

"What room number? He has a whole floor unto himself! Not like me, some peasant who is merely having half a floor. *This is a man to be reclined with*! I'm telling you!"

"Reckoned with."

"That is what I said."

> **Spicy Secret:** Be flexible about making new friends through friends. You never know if your next referral (as long as it's a quality referral) could be the next great love of your life, your greatest client ever, or someone who'll offer you an exciting new adventure.

CHAPTER 34

Simo the Excellent

Melisse was led into Simo's sumptuous suite/apartment/floor by an assistant who said, "I present you, Your Excellency, with…the lady!" (because Simo wasn't supposed to know her name) and then he walked out without turning his back on Simo the Excellent.

And he *was* excellent.

Simo was surprisingly young, maybe in his late thirties with beautiful silver hair around his temples, the only feature revealing his slight maturity. He was way too good-looking to fit into the usual stereotype of a Finance and Technology Minister. But Melisse supposed anything was possible in this part of the world. He actually had the kind of looks that made her salivate—dark, on the shorter side, lean, swarthy, a shadow of a beard, with warm brown eyes and very short hair. He was the Arabian version of Tom Cruise she would have loved to see rise from Ali Baba's magic lamp to grant her three wishes: his cock, his tongue, and his heart! What a coup!

Simo approached Melisse in a friendly way, opening his arms for a hug. She had imagined she'd be meeting a man shrouded in robes. Instead, he wore a simple pair of jeans and a black T-shirt. He was also barefoot.

"Hello, my lady."

"Hello…your…Handsomeness," she smiled.

"Call me Simo, please," he said with a soft English accent as Melisse hugged him, breathing in an extraordinary fresh and almost pure scent of what might have been expensive cologne composed of amber and hints of vanilla and lemon.

"Can I offer you a drink?" he asked. "I'm having an aloe vera juice for my health, and honestly I cannot wait til it is finished, but you can have whatever you want. A real American iced tea?"

"An iced tea?"

"It's Tetley. I love Tetley, freshly brewed. Sweet and with lots of ice and lemon! I discovered this drink in Charleston on a visit once. My assistant now brings the tea bags for me wherever we go and he makes it *perfectly*."

"Mmmmm…"

It was an enticing offer, to sit down and have a nice beverage and talk about Charleston and all kinds of things with him, but she thought better of it.

"May I just have a glass of cold bottled water?"

"Whatever you want!" he said, going over to the minibar, which was not so mini. It was more of a maxi bar, taking up an entire corner of the living room, and embedded with a large-screen TV.

> **Spicy Secret: "Whatever you want," or its cousin, "Anything you want," may just be the best three-word phrase a man can ever utter to a woman, beating out the overused (and often underperforming) "I love you" by several points because of its tangibility, its inherent promise of things to come, and its sense of generosity and freedom.**

"Do you know why I am here?" she asked gently as he returned with her glass.

He looked her over. "You *might* be here from the Harley-Davidson dealership about a new bike?" he laughed. "Ha! No worries, I know that Jazzy sent you as a…"

Simo seemed suddenly unsure how to phrase it.

"I'm a little gift. Here's to new friends," she said, clinking her glass to his. She was feeling so shy, nervous, and excited about getting close to this man that she forgot to laugh at his Harley joke.

"Do you have something I can play music on?" she asked, and he led her to the stereo system, where she set up her music.

He sat down on the couch and relaxed back into it as AC/DC's song "You Shook Me All Night Long" began playing.

Melisse started slow, loving the music and the lyrics so much (and knowing she was about to be indulged by one of her cutest "clients" on record) she eventually let herself go completely as his smile encouraged her onward. She pulled him up and they moved around the room, dancing to the music together, him stripping off her Velcro chaps, her stripping off his T-shirt, her throwing off her boots, then shimmying out of her jeans, then pulling his jeans off him, tossing aside her bandanna, and then landing on the floor with him. She ruffled her loose hair in his face, and then found herself writhing on her knees before him in only her leather string bikini.

When the song hit its stride, she jumped onto Simo and began gyrating over his black bikini underwear as she felt his cock straining to be released from its confines.

When the music faded away, she was in his lap, hugging him around the neck as he wrapped his arms around her. She was out of breath from her gyrations, feeling her breasts heaving against his muscular chest.

She briefly wondered if he had a wife or was single and had a girlfriend—or wanted one. In fact, a deeper part of her imagined her being his girlfriend, being loved by him, traveling with him to beautiful places.

But then her reverie dropped off at the thought of that great divide in society—especially *his* society in the Middle East—where "bad girls" like her slid into the abyss of extreme categorization. There were no gray areas where bad girls were concerned.

Spicy Secret: "Every girl wants a bad boy who will be good just for her...and every boy wants a good girl who will be bad just for him." —Unknown

She was Simo's girl right now, behind closed doors, and that would have to do.

"Wow!" was all he could say, thrilled, as he began to kiss the nape of her neck. She enjoyed feeling the slightest bit of stubble on his chin lightly grazing her face. Then, suddenly, he scooped her up off the floor and carried her into another room, where a huge bed was centered, surrounded by floor-to-ceiling glass and views of the Arabian Sea beyond.

Simo slowed things way down by stripping off his underwear slowly for Melisse as she stood and watched. His delicious-looking cock was rock-hard, hairless, and outlined by a blazing orange sunset. She went to the bed and lay down as he came and joined her on the stark-white bed. He gently tugged at the strings of her bikini top and bottom, releasing them and sending them to the floor, leaving her completely naked.

When Melisse felt his gentle kiss, she loved how he softened her lips by gently parting them with his. His fingers traced down her breasts and gently rubbed around her nipples. When he moved down below, he slowly entered her with his fingers, running them in a circle around her clit. He did this patiently, with all the time in the world to please her, until she was soaking wet, writhing in pleasure and begging for more. He then guided his cock to the places his fingers had just been, and she enjoyed the feeling of its wide head gently pressing over and under her clit, rubbing and thumping against it. She felt her legs spreading as he rubbed his shaft up and down in a straight line over her wet, hot zone.

Then, instead of going deeper, he raised himself up and brought his cock up to her mouth, where she sucked it eagerly, imagining what it would be like to have it inside her vagina.

"Jazzy asked me not to make love with you," she confessed breathlessly in a moment when his cock was not in her mouth. She so wanted Simo to press his cock deep inside her then and there, but she should play by the rules. "I was only supposed to come in and tease you for an hour or so…"

"Do you *always* do what Jazzy says?" he asked as she licked him up and down and then sucked at him again, as if her mouth were the ultimate little pussy grabbing at his engorged cock, barely able to contain it.

> **Spicy Secret: When it comes to managing around some of the more possessive, ego-driven, jealous, or controlling men/clients who will inevitably enter your orbit, why not behave just like they do? That is: Do whatever you want when they are not around because what they don't know won't hurt them. The men you contract to play with have no "claim" on you unless you've agreed to something exclusive and are being taken care of accordingly.**

He moved his cock away from her mouth and lay on top of her, kissing her on the mouth again, this time more forcefully. She felt his cock begging for entry by pressing into the tight door of her lower lips.

"I won't tell if you won't," he said as she felt his hands spreading her thighs apart as she yielded. He eased himself down and began lapping at her clit with a talented tongue, then took her vulva into his mouth and suctioned it hard, using his entire tongue to rove even harder over it. She gasped in pleasure…she was so close to coming. He stopped.

He moved once more to get on top of her, his cock was closer to entry. "What do you think?"

"Ohhhhh, yessss…" Melisse sighed as he slowly eased himself in, barely moving. She enjoyed the feel of her pussy lips stretching around him and the easy, confident way he barely moved his hips, which allowed her to savor every tiny movement of his cock as it pushed in and out of her.

He kissed her lips and her neck artfully and sensuously the whole time they made love. For one moment, she actually forgot he was a "client," she so enjoyed the feeling of his whole body merging with hers, and especially his lips as they communicated something "more" behind the kiss.

Is there really "more" here, or am I just kidding myself?

"Do not worry about neighbors or staff. There is no one here to ruin our pleasure," he assured in a whisper. "We can stay forever."

If only!

Simo stayed inside her, calmly pleasuring her, stopping and starting, taking a little break outside her at times, as if he had all the time in the world. It had become impossible for Melisse to detect how much time was elapsing, but she trusted Simo not to get her in trouble with Jazzy.

Melisse enjoyed the absolute calm, quiet, and setting sun coming through the window as Simo slowly and sweetly moved his cock inside her, building and building her whole body up to a climax. It seemed to go on forever. And then, she was moaning with abandon, her pussy spasming in one long aria of pleasure just as he exploded inside her as well, gasping with relief.

Simo gave her the ultimate honor of turning her over and pressing his beating heart to her back. He held her, spooned into a cuddle, his arms wrapped tightly around her with an affection that lasted twice as long as the sex had.

He buried his face in her neck and clung to her, almost as if for dear life, and the way he hugged her was so loving that it filled up a particular hole that was always left open in her soul.

She'd finally met a client with whom she experienced "perfect chemistry."

Melisse knew it was crazy and greedy, but she felt a deep yearning to have this, or this guy, in her life *for real*, for always…

She savored a few more stolen minutes with this prince, or this minister, or this sultan…whoever he was… She didn't even know his full name. All she knew was that Simo was a delicious specimen of a man and a spectacular lover. He'd managed to extract from her a reminder of her pure desire for a true lover she would never have to get up and leave again.

She felt a tear gather at the corner of her eye and fall down her face where Simo supposedly couldn't see it. But he had, as the tear had landed on his arm.

He also knew he would never forget her. He'd never had so much natural fun with a woman in all his life as during their short-lived dance around the living room of his suite. How strange to think that two strangers could meet and become instant playmates with no more than a few words spoken between them. He really didn't want her to leave.

She wiped her eye discreetly, then slipped out of bed to collect her scattered things before changing in the guest bathroom.

"Don't go!" he moaned as she walked away.

It was certainly one of the sweetest phrases she'd ever heard out of the mouth of a "client."

She looked in the bathroom mirror and smiled sadly.

Crying after sex. Ridiculous.

When she emerged, Simo was waiting on the living room couch, back in his jeans, with two tall glasses of real Tetley iced tea set on a silver platter, along with a side of extra ice, lemon, and simple syrup.

Oh, and a box containing an exquisite pair of ruby and diamond earrings she would treasure forever.

Both the delicious, refreshing tea and the earrings were a simple act of graciousness she would never forget.

And from a man with whom she felt "perfect chemistry" yet knew nothing about. And whom she would never forget.

As they sat sipping their teas after she thanked him profusely for the earrings, she asked, "What *time* is it? I've lost all track…"

"Two hours have passed," Simo said, smirking guiltily.

"Oh, my…" She sucked in her breath. Jazzy wouldn't like that.

"I already took care of it," Simo assured. "He's happy. I would never compromise what you have going with him by keeping you too long. I understand why you are here," he said with a small look of regret, as if, *I wish we could have met under different circumstances.*

And she knew instinctively that if the assurances came from Simo's mouth, it was so.

She loved how plainly he spoke, and the sentiment beneath his words. How unlike a spoiled royal he was to have taken into consideration her precarious position and ensure that she didn't misstep.

"How can I ever see you again?" he asked. "I don't even know your name… Where do you travel? Where do you live? Where do you spend your summers? Who *are* you? What do you like to do? What *do* you do? What are your dreams, your projects, your needs…? How could I ever help you?"

"Please." She put up her hand, trying to stay calm. "I can't talk about all that right now. I'm just a girl from New York City…"

"A wonderful girl, he smiled.

Spicy Secret: Despite the heat and warmth of love igniting, don't give men everything they want, even if it's just information they're after.

Her heart beat frantically as she tried to savor this moment. There was always that one delicious moment in the beginning of a relationship when a man adored you madly, and she wanted it to linger forever in her memory.

I'm falling in love with him! Against my better judgment. I feel like I've just taken a drug that's now running through my body and I'm powerless against it. What would he ever want with a girl like me? I can't help how I feel. No…it's just a crush: another handsome man who couldn't care less about me. It's just a game.

THIS IS NOT LOVE AT FIRST SIGHT!

You bet your ass it is, the voice of GG, somewhere in the distance, reminded her.

It was an experience of pure, perfect, romantic and physical chemistry, the elusive gift she'd searched for all her career (all her life in fact) and had never, ever, found.

But could there be something intellectual, something emotional, between them that could thrive? There was no time to find out. Not now, anyway.

Her heart pounded. It was decision time. She didn't want to hand him one of her business cards, as that would reveal just how commercial she really was. In his presence, she hated who she was, commercially.

She was flustered, so unlike her, and grabbed a pen and small piece of hotel stationery from the end table. Then, she wrote down her first name, "Melissa," and her private phone number, but she did it so fast and nervously, her hand shaking, that she forgot to give an email address. Later she would wonder if she'd even written her phone number correctly. She tore off the paper and handed it to him, thinking: *He'll never call; he's just enjoying seeing yet another girl lose it over him.*

"I must be going," she said matter-of-factly yet full of regret.

They stood up and she hugged him with everything she had. She pulled away, feeling like crying again. *What the hell?*

"I'm sorry; this is awkward. I actually *like* you! And I don't even *know* you," she admitted. "I just like being *around* you."

"I like you, too!" he smiled. "I feel something, too. I'm not supposed to, I know! But I *do*."

"No promises?" she said, heading to the door without turning her back on him, taking him in for one last time. *Love at first sight—so that's what it feels like.*

"No promises," he agreed. "Although I'm not averse to promises," he smiled.

The front door opened slowly, as if by magic, but it was only Simo's assistant, waiting to escort her back to her floor.

"See you again sometime," she nodded sadly.

"See you again…No, wait!"

He strode closer and took both of her cheeks lightly into his warm palms. He pulled her face to his chest and planted a kiss gently on top of her forehead and held her close to him. She savored the feeling of his sweet lips bestowing his final farewell.

It put her into a bit of a daze. No man had ever given her a kiss quite like that on her forehead. It felt so protective, almost fatherly, and extremely benevolent. That, as much as their lovemaking, had shaken her to her core.

He pulled away, looked her in the eye one last time with a small nod, and then turned around and walked away.

The assistant touched her lightly on her elbow to indicate it was time to return to reality. But just for a moment, Melisse was lost. Totally and completely lost.

Spicy Secret: Being a parting gift for a prince can be such sweet sorrow.

Spicy Secret: If you're lucky in The Life, you'll meet a client with whom you absolutely fall in love, and it can happen in a split second. You will feel that love acutely because it's in such a stark contrast to the day-to-day "grind."

If it happened to the *Pretty Woman*, it can happen to you.

Keep the faith.

CHAPTER 35

The Funfest

Melisse returned to her suite in time for a long soak and to "calm down" from her interlude with Simo. She lolled in an outsize tub decorated in what appeared to be gold tiles and poured in a huge amount of bubble bath infused with argan and fig oils blended with rose essence.

Then she put on a sleek cocktail dress and descended to meet Jazzy for dinner in the hotel's fine seafood restaurant, where they would dine against a backdrop of aquariums filled with exotic fish. He had arrived before her and already had the caviar and champagne waiting (with a grateful smile) and did not seem to be upset from her having overstayed her allotted time with Simo. In fact, she would learn later that Simo had granted Jazzy permission to bring his potbellied pigs and a model of his energy combustion system to the important trade show in Simo's kingdom.

"Sit down, honeeeeey; let's celebrate!" Jazzy said, as a server poured out their champagne, which fogged and bubbled and was the usual start of many "they" would enjoy in a night. Melisse appeared to be drinking along with him by taking many tiny sips, while Jazzy put back more than seemed humanly possible.

> **Spicy Secret: When your alcoholic client says, "Bottoms up," it's not going to be about your bottom. It's going to be about whatever he can lay his hands**

on to drink during your date. And once he's drunk, depending on how he handles his alcohol, he can be very unpleasant or embarrassing to deal with. **You must decide if you're willing to entertain and enable friends like this. If you lay down the law about drinking in your marketing, men will usually prioritize shagging over boozing.**

"I hope you don't mind that I told Simo that you are my *exclusive* plaything," Jazzy said casually. "And that I am thinking of marrying you one day because I have grown so attached to you. And you to me."

Motherfucker!

"Why would I care?" Melisse said nonchalantly, holding in her rapid breathing and wanting to stab his neck with the tip of her high-heeled shoe.

Now Simo will never call.

She excused herself suddenly and escaped to the ladies' room for a "breather"—one of those moments with Jazzy when she found it necessary to escape to a private toilet stall (complete with its own sink and mirror, of course) where she could curse the life she was leading. She tried not to vomit, tried to get hold of her breath and focused on just getting through to the next compartment of her day.

But this particular 'escape' to the ladies' room was worse—and different—than all the others that had come before. This time she allowed herself to sob, and to hell with her mascara. She sobbed with abandon until the gracious bathroom attendant knocked softly on the door of her 'rest-room.'

Melisse knew she musn't keep Jazzy waiting.

"Is everything all right Madam?"

"No, it isn't," she sniffed, blowing her nose into a tissue.

"May I help you with something?" the attendant asked outside the door, concerned.

"This is just not something anybody can help with," Melisse whined. "But thank you anyway." She looked through her tears into her purse for the tools to doll herself back up before returning to the theater of her life.

Spicy Secret: Life up close sometimes resembles an inch of a woven tapestry, with no reason or art to the stitching, and certainly no clear image to decipher within. But viewed from farther away someday, you will see the whole picture and the beauty of your story, and how this one little thread was a vital addition to the masterpiece of your life.

Upon her return to the table, Melisse had recomposed herself and commented lightly upon the beauty of the decoration on the elevators, which looked "Arabo deco" to her. Jazzy reminded her that in the age of art deco, Dubai was just a dusty field where his nomadic ancestors picked at carcasses by fires fueled from camel shit.

Of course, he snorted after he said, "*Shit*." He couldn't resist saying, "Bet that camel *shit* smell got their appetites going! Do eat up, Melisse! They flew this caviar in for your roving tongue to enjoy. The tongue that will soon be licking *my balls.*" She winced at his gross sense of humor (especially in contrast to Simo's genteel, classy mannerisms) and thanked God that the walls of the banquette were high and that nobody else could hear their conversation. She did notice his two bodyguards roll their eyes as they looked away.

"Jazzy," Melisse said, gritting her teeth. "I've had just about enough of your *shitty* language for one evening. I am up to my neck in animal *shit*, between your pigs and the camels. Right now I would just like to eat a civilized meal. Can we do that?"

"Yes, of course, darling," he said, guiltily, unable to resist a smirk.

"Thank you," she oozed sweetly. *Who else has to have conversations like this with a client?*

Ah, silence. For a brief moment.

He was obviously frustrated from not having played with Melisse for a while, and knew that she'd been with another man—even if he didn't know to what extent. Men were definitely harder to deal with when they were this way.

Spicy Secret: Due to their distant lineage to dogs, the same rules of training a dog apply to training a man. If you want a man to behave well, it's best to exhaust him with play first before attempting to teach him new or better tricks.

To reward him for shutting up, she took a delicate spoonful of the caviar and savored it as only a lady could, slowly licking up the spoon as if it were a beautiful you-know-what (all the while, looking into his eyes). Jazzy watched admiringly, and she suspected he was already thinking of ways to enjoy her after their sumptuous meal.

He'd mentioned marrying her, which meant nothing by now, as she was quite used to this "fantasy" of his. He loved to discuss what it would be like if she lived with him in his palace on a daily basis, and all the fun they would have. As far as she was concerned, it was all "hogwash"—like pig feed for his fat ego.

As they proceeded to eat and drink their way through a ten-course "tasting menu," their conversation was peppered with his nasty teasing of her (and her witty comebacks), and his spicy propositions (and her seemingly lusty acceptance of them, knowing his cock would never get enough lift to impale her in all the places and ways he was fantasizing about).

They shared tales of their travels, and while Jazzy often descended to the downright vulgar, Melisse remained always the lady—except when he managed to piss her off, of course, but that was always dealt with in private. And then, what a show she gave! Jazzy had nothing on Melisse for creative cursing. Even his naughty parrot, Pasquale, would have blushed. Jazzy loved watching her tirades and temper tantrums, which was why he tried to annoy Melisse whenever possible.

And it was this entertaining dichotomy between the lady and the witch that kept him inviting her back, and why she now found herself about to embark on another round of Sheik al-Jazziz.

Spicy Secret: The recipe for success in The Life is to look like an angel, act like a lady, think like a man, work like a dog, fuck like a bunny, be strong like a warrior, show the patience of a saint, have the discipline of a nun, treat the man like a god, and wield all the trickery of a devil.

As she rode up the elevator after dinner for about an hour's worth of "naptime with an octopus" before a long night of partying, she knew exactly how the trip would turn into another exhausting week. Though she never indulged, she could see why many call girls working at her level needed coke or pills to keep them going all night.

Instead, she fueled herself solely on her ambitions and a desire to make as much money as possible in as short a time as possible. And she took about thirty vitamin supplements and prescription-grade "natural" enhancers and hormones each day, to gain more energy, stave off aging, fight down illnesses like flus and colds (bad for business) and to get a deep sleep, even if the sleep was only for a few hours if she had to entertain all night.

With all these vitamins, if she had to give some kinky client a "golden shower" he'd think she was a "fallen alien" and not a fallen angel, given the DayGlo green pee from the supplements! And in NYC when she was really "oversubscribed,"—i.e., overbooked but doing it anyway—she'd tuck into a local medical "infusion center" that offered an IV hookup to an energy-giving cocktail of vitamins and nutrients. After a "hookup," she'd be good to go for another day until her schedule would allow her some downtime.

"Doping" isn't just the realm of Olympians. Sexual athletes need all the help they can get, too!

Spicy Secret: Seek the advice of a qualified, nature-oriented physician before going on any anti-aging, energy-boosting, hormonal- or body-building regimens combined with exercise. Though supplements

are not regulated by the medical authorities, there are risks and side effects involved in taking them. Get help, blood tests, and advice first, to do it right. Then stick with it. The results could be fabulous!

The previous "Funfests," as Jazzy liked to call her visits, always took place in one of the Burj's massive suites, where the decor was like living inside an exploded mandala, a kaleidoscope of color reflecting on floor-to-ceiling glass and mirrors. Jazzy had insisted on inviting live bands to serenade them with loud Arabic music, bringing in dancing Thai and Indian girls.

Jazzy never touched them, only watched. He once confided to her that the beautiful belly dancers bored him. He'd seen them all his life. What he *really* liked was African-American music and hip-hop dancing à la "Baby Got Back" by Sir Mix-a-Lot. Jazzy liked the dirtiest, funkiest rap music he could find, and Melisse indulged him by bringing him the best examples she could find of this urban American art form.

Unfortunately, during Funfest he enjoyed playing them at maximum volume. Melisse had a pair of flesh-colored earplugs which she often wore when they went to clubs or even in the comfort of Jazzy's suite when he played his music. It helped save her hearing, and she could also hear less of his bullshit when he started rambling incoherently when reaching maximum intoxication.

But on the night of this particular discussion about his taste in music, he had launched into a ridiculous rap he had apparently ad-libbed. "I like jigaboo booty, like some real ghetto ass, gettin' down and dirty, dancin' to a nasty rap…"

"Now Jazzy, that is not politically correct," Melisse had scolded primly.

"I want to go to America to this dangerous ghetto place they are always talking of, and find a big mama for me. A big mama to squeeze my face between her big boobies and then I want to shoot my wad in her big buns," Jazzy had slurred. "Will you take me there, Melisse?"

"No. You'll be going alone."

The nights partying with Jazzy were balanced by daytime visits to his desert falconry club for lunch, complete with his crapping shoulder birds. He'd pout and say that while the falcons were distinguished, he really missed his giant rainbow parrot, Pasquale, back home at his palace. Over lunch at the falconry club, Jazzy would regale Melisse with stories of Pasquale's exploits.

Melisse loved animals of all kinds, but Pasquale sounded like an out-of-control, potty-mouthed parrot that had lost touch with his purer jungle nature. She was sure Jazzy was of no help to him in becoming a respectable bird.

The "calm" nights were hours of storytelling, fortune-telling and card games conducted in Jazzy's native tongue, with a permanent, male-only group of local guest bullshit artists and "friends." The men sat in the living room all night enjoying an outrageous catered buffet and "open bar" as they regaled Jazzy with "Knights of the Roundtable" type stories, told in the slow, dramatic, old fart Arab style.

Melisse was responsible for relighting their stinking cigarettes and keeping the men in Scotch, strong, hot tea, and bar snacks while wearing a sexy French maid's uniform.

"You can look, but you can't touch," Jazzy had warned the men, as Melisse feathered his nose with her feather duster, which always made him sneeze (and then fart during the sneeze, which he tried to cover up with the sound of sneezing).

"I heard that, Jazzy," Melisse would chide, giving him a fake serious look.

When Jazzy was feeling generous, he made Melisse shine the men's shoes as they sat on the couch, all the while prominently displaying her cleavage. She did this all with a smile, sometimes spitting on their shoes to give them that real "spit shine."

Jazzy would then hand around hundred-euro bills to each of the guys so they could "tip" Melisse for shining their shoes. As they slid the bill into her push-up bra, they'd cop a little feel at the same time. They were kindly old farts and the tips sure beat her days scraping her knees while dancing on the bar at The Pussycat Lounge.

Spicy Secret: There's nothing like remembering how bad you had it in the "old" days to make you appreciate how good things are now (and sometimes vice versa).

Hey, it's a living, she thought while getting her tips and calculating how she would use the bonus money.

Then, on the "wild nights" she would sit through smoky evenings at nightclubs where she would assist Jazzy as he "interviewed" Russian working girls. The whole process resembled a bizarre, sexualized inquisition. It was as if a Russian bride/hooker agency were being visited by a (blind) horny census examiner stopping by on a drunken bender, with money to burn. Girls lined up for the opportunity to have a "shot" at the wily sheik who wore sunglasses at night to avoid being recognized. He groped them absently from time to time, before determining who would come back to the hotel suite for the rest of the party. It was well known among the towering, icy blonde working girls of Dubai that Jazzy's gig was "where the money's at."

He would pretend he was making a documentary so he could ask embarrassing sexual questions, followed by inviting all the "winners" back to the suite. And they were *all* going to be winners, but some didn't know that yet. Jazzy enjoyed spurring them on in "competitions," which sometimes resulted in catfights, to his delight.

"Look, Melisse...they are fighting over me!" he'd chuckle as one blonde scratched at another's face or tore off an enemy's hairpiece (and then lit it on fire with her lighter), or as one girl merely slapped another girl to get ahead in the line (which caused the ladies in question to be expelled from the club by Jazzy's bodyguards. One thing about Jazzy: he didn't tolerate cheating).

"I do see that they're fighting over you. You're such a prize," Melisse deadpanned.

Then, when they'd all been transported by several stretch limos back to the suite, Melisse took over, confiscating (and carefully labeling) their mobile phones for the night before making up ridiculous drinking games for them all to play into the wee hours. Melisse carried a classic Twister game with her in her luggage, in which the plastic base would be slicked up with oil. It would provide hours of viewing entertainment and giggles as Jazzy's female guests played naked, drunken Twister as Jazzy watched, tossing out euros, which they had to catch in midair while trying to hold their positions in hopes of being the one "winner" (as Jazzy determined) who would get a fat envelope of cash.

Toward the end of the night, Jazzy would just lie there nearly comatose, farting on pillows and sucking from a shisha pipe packed with Rif Mountain hashish. Meanwhile, a fat disco dancer wove around the room gyrating her hips and performed faked-up lesbo sex before him for what felt like hours on end.

Melisse, as the Mistress of Ceremonies, had to stay up all night till the party was over and the last hooker was paid in cash from the "fun money" envelope she was in charge of. Then, with the help of the "butler" for their suite, she made sure that the women went quietly as a group to a special back elevator that took them downstairs to a special, discreet side entrance (no dawdling) and from there to a waiting minibus that would deliver them safely to their homes.

Jazzy was indeed a "people person," but Melisse was decidedly *not*. In fact, all this was hell on Melisse, who apart from nights out in NYC visiting with her clients, normally followed a clean lifestyle of early to rise, early to bed, very little alcohol, a perfectly strict diet, avoidance of stressful situations and parasitic friends, and enjoying a smoke-free environment at home, along with rigorous fitness classes and yoga to relax.

> **Spicy Secret: A "dissolute," stressful lifestyle will age you, wear you out, and make you jaded and hardened faster than anything else in The Life. Unless you're being extremely well rewarded, it's best to "just say no" to people, substances, activities, and schedules that don't fit within the parameters of a "healthy, sane" lifestyle that will keep you rested and hydrated.**

> **Your health is the most precious asset you have, and you can't work without it, so decide on your priorities and pick and choose your "parties" accordingly.**

During Jazzy's "Funfests" in Dubai, there were always shopping trips to the big mall and skiing on the freezing-cold fake indoor snow bluffs at the mall's "slope," which she detested. The mall trips were sponsored by Jazzy with a special loaded credit card, the limit of which she never knew for sure.

> **Spicy Secret: Don't abuse your client's generosity by conducting a "mad grab" at the shops. Though money may seem "no object" to your benefactors, you're being watched—to see if you'll abuse their kindness. Either get clarification on what is possible and permissible, take them with you shopping, or show some restraint. But whatever you do, don't shock them with a bill or spree that went seemingly "out of control." And always, always buy them a little gift of some kind (with their money) to show your appreciation.**

During the shopping trips, she'd carefully choose a few investment-grade items like Chanel and Hermès bags, which she could easily sell back in the States on consignment at Michael's or Encore, for cash. And always, some lingerie she could "show off" for him later in private, in addition to a lovely evening gown or two (and matching shoes and a few small pieces of jewelry, of course) to wear to dinners out.

Melisse was happy with her own basic collection of classic designer bags, shoes, lingerie, and a few new things once in a while to freshen things up. She had learned that happiness was "being content with what you already have." And what she had were enough beautiful, high-quality, classic things to last a lifetime. The rest of the loot was just gravy—to help fund her "retirement" and finance La Fantasia.

> **Spicy Secret:** "Trying to be happy by accumulating possessions is like trying to satisfy hunger by taping sandwiches all over your body." —George Carlin

The other realization she'd had by this time was that *things* don't love you back. Even thinking about her new career dream (or retirement dream, depending on how you look at it), she wondered who would share it with her. She always seemed to draw a blank.

> **Spicy Secret:** Never attempt to make important conclusions or decisions when you are hungry, angry, or tired.

I'm just tired, she thought. *I'll get a vision of him when I get out of this place.* Her Prince Charming was a shadowy figure in the brilliance of the dream that kept her going, but she wondered who on Earth would want to participate in such a crazy operation as La Fantasia. Simo the Excellent? Certainly not, she thought.

Please, get those kinds of thoughts out of your brain.

But it was time to stop focusing on the nonexistent "him" in her future and focus on creating a week of wild wonders and festivities for Jazzy, starting with a fabulous night of partying that would take them who knew where.

The elevator doors opened. It was 11:00 p.m. And it was time to get to work.

> **Spicy Secret:** Life—and "The Life"—has its highs and lows. The best way to take advantage of the highs and minimize the lows is to manage your physical and mental energy before you burn out—or bottom out.

CHAPTER 36

Rocks Mean Business

A week later, as her time in Dubai came to a close, Melisse was focusing on getting downstairs and saying good-bye to Sheik al-Jazziz, who was waiting for her in the hotel lobby.

She would send Jazzy back to his homeland and his remote compound out in the desert (and the three wives, pet potbellied pigs, and his fifty "palace entertainers"), thinking he had had the time of his life. She would give him a romantic send-off and leave him panting for more.

Meanwhile, she might as well have been performing in a Broadway play for seven days straight with few intermissions. She was totally *knackered*, as they say in London—absolutely exhausted.

She couldn't wait to return to her life in New York and free-fall back into more conventional appointments with clients. She might give herself a day or two off and spend a day at the Peninsula Hotel spa, then have a quiet dinner alone at Le Bernardin with a book, feasting on a delicious lobster in a cream sauce, followed by a decadent dessert, before officially returning to her diet staples of salads and grilled fish or chicken. And pretending that desserts didn't exist.

> **Spicy Secret:** "Seize the moment. Remember all those women on the *Titanic* who waved off the dessert cart."
> —Erma Bombeck

But when she really thought about what lay ahead, she felt sad. There was no true love, no "real" fun at the end of the ride home in the private jet. This was her life—rather posh at times (and thankfully with no more work in offices to drive her to feeling suicidal), and every moment was geared toward fulfilling her dream of La Fantasia. She knew exactly why she was doing what she was doing, and what it would take to get there.

Melisse found herself once again descending in the Arabo deco elevator to exit the hotel, where Jazzy's security detail was waiting to escort her to another private plane home. She hoped it would be piloted by a different crew. As tired as she was, she wasn't quite sure if she was up for another day of aeronautical erotica with Halima and Ahmed. Instead, she would spend her comfortable hours on the jet sleeping and trying to cleanse her mind of the past events in this crazy week. She would certainly return home to New York City a wealthier woman, with yet another small piece of her innocent, romantic soul torn off and sold to the highest bidder.

She wore a long pink silk *abaya*, or caftan-style dress, embroidered with delicate silver flowers and tiny Swarovski crystals, which covered her body well. Wrapped around her head and circling her neck was a finely made cashmere-silk blend Hermès scarf in a subtle floral print.

The elevator doors opened, and she stepped out delicately, awaiting the Emir. Sheik Jazzy approached, waddling up, penguin-like, in his leather sandals under royal robes. He gestured to his two security men to fall back, then took Melisse to a secluded part of the lobby.

To her shock, he dropped to his knees, and she felt eyes and cameras everywhere focusing on them.

This was so very unlike Jazzy, who tried to keep a very low profile, watching her movements covertly in the lobby. He usually preferred not to make contact until they were cozied up in a restaurant booth, hidden away in their suite, or together in a dark SUV (for rides out to the desert to visit his falcons), the brilliant Bentley, or sometimes his tiny Ferrari.

Clearly, this was some kind of special occasion, one for which he could toss discretion aside—at least, most of it.

"Pleeeeeease, Melisse. I beg of you! Let's do what we talked about last night. Marry me!"

Forcing her hands not to shake, she took off her sunglasses and looked at him. "Your Highness Jazziz. It was so lovely of you to host me here and show me such a fabulous time. I really appreciate it…"

"I ASKED YOU TO MARRY ME!"

He was serious! She remembered him asking but had thought it was another game, and she had told him, "Let's talk about it tomorrow" (when he sobered up). Now it was the next morning and he was apparently still on this marriage kick.

"Jazzy, it's impossible. But maybe there's another way for us to be together."

Spicy Secret: When saying no to someone you don't want to disappoint, say it as if it pains you like a stab in the heart, but stand your ground. And try to offer other options.

The Emir opened his hand and produced a heart-shaped, palm-size canary diamond necklace. The rock was so large, so perfect, and so awe-inspiring that it could never fit on a ring, so it was suspended from a thick golden chain.

"Will *this* convince you?" he asked with a knowing twinkle.

She sucked in her breath. It *was* a substantial jewel, but… *What am I thinking?*

"I'll be good to you…" he taunted.

"No. Really. I can't. Absolutely not."

"Melisse, according to Wadijazzizi law—which I wrote, by the way—I can only have *one more wife* and I want her to be you. There are only four of these diamonds in the world! I want you to have this last one, as my wife."

"Well…that's nice and everything…but…" She motioned him to come closer so they could have an intimate conversation. She whispered, "But I have things I want to do with my life, you know? I don't want to be married…"

Melisse struggled with a way to be diplomatic. She wanted to be honest without rejecting the guy completely and losing him as a client.

"And, you know, call me uptight, but I can't share you with your three wives and your palace full of concubines, or whatever you call them."

"They're palace entertainers! Easily expendable. And my wives? Simply formalities of the state."

"Ah. I see. And what about *my* dream? You know…my sexy spa for women?"

"Oh, darling, I'll just buy you that bordello-whorehouse-whatever you want to start in France."

"Jazzy! Shhhhhh! It's *not* a whorehouse. Oh, you really irk me sometimes…"

"I'm just saying I'll buy it for you and we'll hire a manager to run it for you in France while *you* take care of *me* back home at Wadijazzizi. What do you think, snugglepuss?"

Melisse hated when he called her that!

"There's one other thing. Please don't take this the wrong way. It's very simple and most human beings can understand this: I'm just not in love with you …*yet*. I'm working up to that… I think we still need more time to discover each other."

He tried to mesmerize her once more with the palm-size, heart-shaped canary diamond, which she fingered fondly, but with detachment.

"Love is the most precious thing in the world, you know?" she tried to explain. "To be in love, to have a deep attraction and connection and rapport with someone."

"What is love? You wanna be *in love*? That's nothing! Don't worry about that part. I can make you fall in love with me when my Viagra finally kicks in and I can get a big stiff one and give you a good and hard shagging…"

"Shhhh! Please, Jazzy! At least I'm being honest with you."

"You *are* honest—the most honest woman I know. Which is exactly why you are my dream girl! I am so tired of being like the great emperor with his clothes off. My wives are all using me for my body."

Melisse nodded. "Oh, yes. I feel so bad for you getting so used like that."

He knelt again before her. "Can't you learn to love me, Melisse?"

Melisse grabbed his hand, pulled him up, and looked into his eyes sweetly in the biggest acting job of her career. God, she couldn't stand him! "Jazzy, not all fantasies come true, I'm afraid. But we can have lots of fun until you find yourself a proper wife!"

Spicy Secret: "All discarded lovers should be given a second chance, but with somebody else." —Mae West

"But I want to pop *your* cherry!"

"God! Shut up!" She couldn't help herself. "You're embarrassing me!"

He snickered. "You can go have that surgery on your V-G to make you like a virgin again and then we can be officially married and then my big pickle can pop that little cherry. We'll let all the blood spurt out and then we can show off your panties on a platter at our reception so all my relatives can see you were the *real deal*."

"Panties on the platter, eh, Jazzy?"

"Panties a la plancha! Served rare!" he said excitedly.

She thought she was going to vomit, but managed to control herself. She could barely restrain herself from running out of the lobby screaming.

Then, the instinct, that "voice of reason" inside her, urged softly: *Remember, dear Melisse. This cretin from a developing nation is only one generation away from the crude camel herders burning shit for fuel. He picks his teeth at dinner and farts to signal that he liked his food. He's rich from oil wells, but that hardly guarantees class. Do you think he knows anything different? Give the guy a break! He's paid you well and soon you can leave! It's not like you were here digging ditches.*

Melisse said, "Jazzy...innocence is in here….." She pointed to her head, "—and here—" to her heart. "But not here," she said, pointing to her hips.

"Yes, yes, yes. But I still want you for my wife. I must *have you*."

Spicy Secret: "Love does not claim possession, but gives freedom."—Rabindranath Tagore

Melisse turned toward the door, careful not to show her back to Jazzy. He was a royal, after all, but she walked backward as fast as she could, knowing his staff would get out of the way.

Jazzy followed her like a puppy out the door as she told him, "We'll discuss it on our next visit in London. Or in Cannes soon! For the film festival, like we talked about! We can play the Bunny Game and listen to your "Nasty Girl" music and…"

Then, Jazzy let out a mournful, spoiled, bratty sob, halting Melisse's escape as she dutifully stood still, admiring the tempest of the tantrum, which the staff teeming in the lobby pretended not to notice. It reverberated throughout the atrium of the hotel lobby. After a moment, she continued out the door, Jazzy following to the door of a silver Bentley limo held open by the bellman.

Gratefully, she slid in and rolled down the window as Jazzy stood sobbing outside. Then she blew him a sad, pouty, slow, lippy kiss.

His final act confirmed her need to get as far away as possible: he spread two fingers in a *V* by his lips and let his long tongue slide between them and wiggle for several salacious moments. Then, giving her a big wink, he confidently walked toward his waiting Humvee.

She sighed and rolled up the window. Then, lying down on the seat, unsure whether to laugh or cry, she did both.

Holy fuck, get me out of here!

CHAPTER 37

A Pleasant Homecoming

On the plane back to New York, Melisse was relieved to find out she had been assigned the "unsexy" flight crew. As much as she loved playing with lovely pilots and sex-starved stewards like Halima and Ahmed, after this past week she couldn't handle any more sexual stimuli. They'd have to strap her into her seat like someone gone off her meds in a sanitorium, not like the ladylike passenger they expected her to be. Once takeoff was over, she snuck back into her in-flight bedroom, closed the door behind her, and took what felt like a twenty-four-hour snooze.

As she fell asleep, trying to let go of all the week's "adventures," her thoughts turned to Simo the Excellent (the one adventure she didn't want to let go of), and the feeling of his arms around her and how she'd felt like a princess.

Let him go, too.

No!

When they finally landed in New Jersey, Melisse was reasonably rested, feeling almost frisky again, and her thoughts turned toward a "deeper relaxation." She considered who was on the agenda this coming week for work who might offer exceptional sex as well as excellent pay.

Darn! There was nobody good, really. There was Mr. Quint in a few days, always a delight but not exactly a hot date, and next week there was Mr. Funsaki, the Japanese billionaire with the teeny weenie who liked to sing karaoke.

Of course there would be new people calling in. She'd have to go meet them, which was always exciting in case one turned out to be a good lover—or even (hope springs eternal) her true love. But none of the "hot" clients she secretly preferred were booked in. There was no "hot stuff" scheduled—a professional call girl's ultimate delight, when great sex and a sweet guy blended with great money.

Perhaps she would have to consult with one of her "Category B's," but it always felt so strange to give them a booty call out of the blue, indicating that she was desperate. *No, that would never do.*

The irony didn't escape her. *I'm surrounded by men, yet sometimes I feel like the most desperate, horny woman on Earth, hoping for a good lay after all the bad ones.*

Maybe she'd just give one of her Category B's a call to come over for "bed and breakfast." Or maybe....

A driver and a black car were indeed waiting when Melisse left the tarmac and entered the small private jet terminal. Melisse gave him a knowing smile.

"Hello, Hakim," she said nonchalantly, but with a saucy smile, thinking, *Score!* Well, it wasn't a score, exactly. After his breakfast visit, Melisse had gotten an account with Hakim's car company, so she could always request him for her airport pickups.

One of the loneliest feelings she experienced on a regular basis was landing at an airport with no friends, family, or lovers to greet her. And having Hakim "on call" fixed that!

He smiled back and helped her with three huge suitcases filled with goodies from the shopping trips with Sheik Jazzy.

"May I ask you a question if you won't think I am being rude?" he asked as he tucked her into the backseat with a little pat on her knee, securing her into her seat belt. She nodded.

"Are you a drug trafficker? You seem to fly so much and you live so well."

She laughed. "No, Hakim. I'm a leisure consultant! It's a very special job but it is sooooo boring to explain. And...I'm a little tired now..." She winked.

> **Spicy Secret:** When men ask you questions you don't want to answer or that might infiltrate your game, play the "boredom" card. Tell him that (whatever it is) is "soooo boring" that "I don't want to bore you with how boring it is."

"OK," he said, giving her knee a squeeze and looking up into her eyes. "Whatever it is you do, I'm sure you're very good at it."

Soon, Melisse and Hakim were headed toward Manhattan. She looked at the island in the distance as they crossed the George Washington Bridge. Even as the years passed, it still felt like a mythical place each time she approached it. She could hardly believe that she was one of the lucky dwellers of New York City.

Hakim pulled up to Melisse's building and double-parked, then offloaded her luggage and, opening the back door, helped her to her front door. Melisse tipped him as she would any driver, even one who hadn't been her lover.

"Can I…?" He hesitated. Melisse smiled, already knowing the answer.

"You're double-parked."

"I know. Still…maybe we could…?" He nodded toward her apartment.

"Well, you could…you always could…but I would have to refuse because it is too last minute… so, do you have another idea?" she asked, reaching over and caressing his hand. "I loved the flowers you brought me last time…"

> **Spicy Secret:** Last-minute, hurried coupling is rarely an aphrodisiac. Have your man wait just a little longer to anticipate the event, and enjoy you when you're at your best. Meanwhile, they'll have time to please you, even if it's just in some small way.

"May I come over for breakfast again tomorrow morning? I will bring the champagne for the mimosas this time—and more flowers!"

What a lucky day! Her day off, with spice on top.

"Of course." She smiled, turning the key and pushing into her apartment. "See you tomorrow, Hakim. I'll be making a special omelet for you. Spinach, feta cheese, and tomato, with hash browns."

"Mmmmm...I cannot wait. I will be sleeping all night waiting for my...breakfast."

He gave her a quick kiss on the cheek and was off.

CHAPTER 38

Couch Boy

By the time a few days had passed, Melisse had recovered from her Funfest with Jazzy in Dubai. She buzzed around her apartment wearing a long satin dressing gown, preparing for a visit from her "Near and Dear" client Harold Quint, who was expected momentarily.

She was humming because breakfast with Hakim the day before had been extremely satisfying. As it was a "day off" and she wasn't in a hurry to go anywhere that morning, they had enjoyed a long, leisurely roll around her cloud-like bed, where they made love several times after breaks for eating, chatting, and getting to know each other better (without her ever divulging the true nature of her career as a "leisure consultant").

> **Spicy Secret: Your career as a call girl is on a need-to-know basis with most of the "straight" people you'll meet in life. So spend some time and energy coming up with a good "cover career" or business. Then, learn as much as you can about it in case you're asked about it (or choose something you already did in the past). If that's difficult, try becoming a "pampered divorcée," "living on a trust/inheritance," doing "ghostwriting," and "beauty/shopping consulting" or "moonlighting as a 'government' consultant" (or any other top secret**

profession you can't easily talk about). Cover stories are good to help you maneuver socially in the "real" world.

The morning was so good, she almost had a problem getting Hakim to leave! But he finally left reluctantly, and she enjoyed knowing she had given a deserving man a great time with no strings attached.

And it kept her mind from wandering back to Simo, who'd somehow in their short time together sparked in her a longing she couldn't understand.

> **Spicy Secret: Client crushes sometimes happen. It's how you handle them that counts. Enjoy feeling you're "in love" with and admiring someone, but until they return your affections, keep on with your life. When they're into you, you'll know it.**

It was time to get back to official business. Since his narrow escape from GG's bordello bust several years before, Harry Quint and Melisse had become regular companions.

Harry was the picture of predictability. Known as "The Hedge Fund Master of the Universe," he was still the best-dressed man in the city, and enjoyed celebrity status from counseling viewers on TV's financial news shows.

Mr. Quint (or Harry, as she'd begun calling him) was one of her favorites, and one of the few, apart from Jazzy, with whom she had shared her goals—specifically, La Fantasia.

Harry was someone of rare generosity. Everyone else Melisse met in high finance seemed to measure relationships with professional women in terms of: *I did this for you, now you do that for me;* i.e., *I brought you a gift, so you need to send me a spicy email to liven up my day...*or, *This is my fourth visit, so don't I deserve a discount?*

It always surprised Melisse that some of the richest men in the world still tried to negotiate with the upscale escort who played a central role in his private life. Fortunately, it was also interesting that so often, "middle-class" clients showed the most consistency and generosity, keeping their expectations for her time and attention in alignment with reality.

But Mr. Quint was truly a magnanimous, loyal, wealthy man. While he was way too politically conservative to invest directly in Melisse's La Fantasia project, he did try to support it little by little with generous gifts of cash. He also guided her along the way with business advice when she asked for it over the lunches or dinners they shared from time to time.

"Wanna go out?" he'd say, calling at the last minute, hoping she'd be free on a Saturday night, a time she'd confessed was lonely for her. Often on Saturday nights, after a fight with his wife, he'd be banished from the sprawling apartment located across from the Metropolitan Museum, and would go stay at his permanent suite at The Mark Hotel until things cooled down. Melisse often took him up on it because he was good company and she loved trying great restaurants.

For his part, Harry Quint enjoyed sharing fancy meals with a beautiful, smart woman he could easily talk to. But the one secret he'd never told Melisse was about Ruby, GG's housekeeper.

He'd feared that Melisse would tease him endlessly if she knew about his sexual interlude on a hot, vibrating dryer in GG's basement with Ruby. It had happened that winter during the day of the "pre-fated" police bust. It was an almost unavoidable consequence of an evening they'd spent together in the dark after they'd heard the cops making a commotion upstairs. Ruby and Harry had run down to the basement together and hidden behind the washing machines. They were never caught, and waited it out until the next morning when the coast was clear.

And Mr. Quint had never experienced such a "walk on the wild side" as he did during the spontaneous sex he'd had with this hot, saucy, pent-up cleaning woman, there in the forbidden basement of a busted bordello!

Ruby, to her delight, had soon after become the head of housekeeping in Mr. Quint's corporate headquarters.

When Harry strode into Melisse's apartment in his pale blue striped seersucker suit, a financial newspaper rolled under his arm, he was grinning mysteriously. He proceeded to unfurl the paper and opened it to an article, which he held up proudly. The headline read, "Dapper Master of the Markets Voted Best-Dressed Wall-Streeter (Again)."

> **Spicy Secret: Successful, self-made men can be proud of the oddest, seemingly most inconsequential things. But whatever it is, cheer them on if they choose to share their accomplishments with you.**

"*Mabrouk*! Congratulations!" Melisse said, giving him a hug. "Good morning!"

"*Mabrouk*? So now you're speaking Arabic? That sheik is taking over our lives. I can't believe you left me last week to go service that… Emir. That…"

"Oh, Harry, stop it! You have nothing to be jealous about!"

"Well, you come back exhausted every time you see him. What does *he* have that I don't?"

Melisse always giggled when he asked her this. "He's got a big mouth that never shuts up, a long, limp dick…and maybe a hundred billion dollars." She knew this would drive Harry crazy. Actually, she had no idea what Jazzy was worth. She just knew that the pay, the jewels, and the gifts were nice.

"Ah! Ninety-nine billion, two hundred million more than I have," Harry said sadly.

Melisse sighed. Rich men seemed to constantly compare themselves with other rich folks (except Jazzy, who didn't give a hoot). But as rich as most were, no one had ever discussed helping her get out of The Life and get on with something else. Still, these were clients, this was a business, not a charity, and each man was a step on the way to La Fantasia, *so* she was thankful for them.

For all their so-called overtures of "friendship," Melisse understood that she was a service provider in their eyes. An *intimate* one, to be sure, but just another "provider" in their universe. She was one who rendered intimate help and comfort, like a masseuse or a therapist, and she was well compensated for her skills.

> **Spicy Secret: Never assume you are more than you are to your clients. Know your place in their universe. Sometimes you're a star, and their world revolves around you. Other times, you're a strange planet they visited once and have no need to visit again.**

In the case of Jazzy, she knew she was quite central to his life, but not in a healthy way. She telepathically felt the weight of his thoughts about her from a great distance. Simply by reading the vast number of his rambling emails and listening to his controlling, obsessive phone messages, it was clear he was smitten.

Mr. Quint interrupted her thoughts. "You have a hickey on your neck," he pointed out. "Looks like someone had some fun recently."

Melisse covered it with her hand. She'd tried to hide it with powerful camouflage makeup, but nothing got past Harry.

"Harry!"

"What?" He shrugged. "Look. Even the great generals love to display their medals."

Harry began undressing, placing his clothing neatly on Melisse's wooden valet. "Hey, Melisse. Can we watch *Couch Boy* again?"

"Again?"

"Yeah, you know…it always gets me going."

Obligingly, Melisse went over to her TV armoire and popped in the DVD of *Couch Boy*. This was a graphic, though softly pornographic and charming tale, beautifully shot, carefully costumed, and well written—made for both men and women to enjoy together. It even managed to produce emotions (and heat) in its female viewers, which was why it apparently was a huge hit among women, who bought it anonymously online from the official *Couch Boy* website and had it delivered by mail to their homes.

Melisse looked at the DVD box and mused, "I wonder who he really is, this cute little actor who only refers to himself as Ronny Cockmeister? Hmmm, he sure looks Jewish to me. From the box, it looks like he's also the writer, the producer, the director, the editor, *and* the casting director...Oh, and...the direct distributor. He owns everything!" Melisse giggled. "Whoever he is, he's multitalented—he does it all!"

"You're telling *me* he does it all. In the movie, the guy is not only multiorgasmic, he's ambidextrous, bilingual, *and* polyamorous." Harry sat back on Melisse's couch and rubbed his cock while skipping forward to his favorite scene in the film, the one when Devin is auditioning for a role in the next Zorro film.

Melisse sat down next to Harry and took over rubbing his cock as they watched the film. She pretended to rub herself as she watched the darling guy, whoever he was. She had to admit, there *was* something about his charisma that made her feel a little tingly down there. She rubbed herself with a little more oomph, especially when Devin paraded around naked.

On Melisse's TV screen, Devin Wannabe stood in a closed office and read from a script wearing nothing but a Zorro eye mask, a red cape, and tight jeans. He used a fake sword to delicately push open the loose shirt of a pretty female casting agent as she sat unzipping his pants.

"Zorro" then ripped open his own shirt, and in a very bad Spanish accent said, "Oh, no, no, no. Feerst, I want to knohhh...if I geeve you vat you vant...what will youuu geeeve to me—like a job?"

In response, the casting agent pulled his zipper all the way down and took Devin's meaty cock out of his jeans. Harry sighed happily.

Melisse actually loved Devin Wannabe's cock because it was a shorter, thicker sausage version, not the usual "Big Long Thing" seen in porno films. Big Long Things turned Melisse off because she knew exactly how much they could hurt.

In real life, Melisse found that most of them usually ended up feeling like an overcooked calamari in her hand, without adequate blood flow to the peripheries. Once those big cocks were lubed up and stuffed inside her, they didn't feel like much at all since they didn't get that hard, and there wasn't that much room for movement, creating friction, or giving heat, especially with her tight, tiny size.

Big cocks were overrated, as far as she was concerned. It was the motion of the ocean, not the size of the boat that counted. Like a salty old sailor, she could speak intimately about that ocean, as she'd enjoyed (to varying degrees) many sails on many different boats.

Spicy Secret: A small skiff on a rocking ocean is sometimes preferable to a huge yacht chugging through a calm bay. Don't underestimate a smaller man's ability to maneuver his craft to please you.

But Devin Wannabe's cock was exactly what she would order from God to pleasure her every night, if one could make such an order (and she believed that if you asked the Universe for what you wanted, you *could* receive).

Devin's cock was very hard in every scene, standing rock-solid and straight up! Melisse secretly relished it when Harry wanted to watch *Couch Boy*, if only for another view at Devin's cock. But she would never watch the movie alone, unless she encountered dire circumstances, like a strike by her Category Bs!

"I'll give you three lines in my next pilot," the film executive said to Devin.

"That bitch! Only three lines?" Harry yelled at the TV. Then he calmed down as Melisse gave him an excellent combo hand/blow job while "Zorro" gave a good ramming to the casting agent on the floor of her office. The scene went on long enough and graphically enough that you'd have to be practically dead not to get excited.

After Harry came loud and long (at the same time that Devin and the agent climaxed together in the film), he collapsed onto Melisse's couch and blanketed his cock with one of her fine Turkish linen hand towels, pre-warmed on the bathroom towel warmer and moistened with a fine soap and spray of warm water.

"God, I would give anything to be a guy like that Devin Wannabe. Women doing me favors, throwing themselves at me…"

"I know," Melisse said, turning off the boob tube, which she only turned on when Harry came over for his DVD fix. "But you'll just have to settle for being richer than God."

"It never gets me laid, being rich. It's not like having a passionate love lay, you know? Have you had one of those lately, Melisse?"

Melisse stopped pouring more fresh-squeezed orange juice into Harry's glass of champagne and looked over at him incredulously.

"A *passionate love lay*? I vaguely remember something like that…" She sighed.

Harry looked at her expectantly, waiting for her to continue with her revelation (and maybe there'd be some spicy details!).

"But then I woke up from my dream," she deadpanned. The subject was closed.

Melisse handed Harry the crystal champagne glass filled with his mimosa, expertly rimmed with a bit of pink sugar. Mr. Quint had always admired her sense of domestic perfection. She sat down next to him and drank from a goblet of pure, fresh water from the five-gallon water dispenser in her kitchen.

Spicy Secret: For every glass of alcohol your man drinks, have two glasses of water and you'll be fine.

"You'll make someone a fabulous wife someday, you know that?"

"I'm not really wife material," she replied dryly, hating the idea of discussing alternate "roles" she could play in her life, especially when men started taking you for granted and you had to "babysit" them 24/7.

Spicy Secret: Consider this for a moment before you bitch and moan again about being single: When you're married (and faithful), the only difference between you and being a nun is one man.

"Why not find yourself a hubby among all your adoring fans and just be done with this?"

"Marry for money, and you earn it out over a lifetime of misery. I'd rather get paid by the hour than wake up every morning to someone I'm not totally smitten with."

"Ah ha! So you *do* believe in true love! You just confessed it without confessing!"

"I'm so busted."

Spicy Secret: "Wolves mated for life. Where was he? Where was the echo to her howl, her mate? Was there no other lone wolf, searching the hills for her?" — Andrea Hurst, *Always with You*

Later, while Melisse crouched down and rolled a lint remover up and down between Harry's pant legs, removing cat fur, Harry worked his cuff links. He was now in a hurry to go.

At the door, he turned and said, "I don't think you realize just how much you have to offer a man, Melisse."

She sighed. "Of course I do. That's why I charge so much for it!"

"Speaking of which…" Harry pulled an envelope out of his breast pocket. "Here's another little installment on the dream for La Fantasia."

Melisse smiled and impulsively hugged him. "Ohhhh, thank you!"

He looked in the entryway mirror and made sure everything was in perfect place again. "By the way, there's a special event on Thursday—a cocktail party for a hedge fund, a PR event for investors. Can you go with me and be my arm candy?"

Melisse hated any event where she might be required to make small talk, to be asked that horrible question, "What do you do?"

"Harry, you know how I feel about these things…"

"I know. I know. But it's a special mission. I've actually been asked by the SEC to wear a wire!"

"A wire? What's that all about?"

"They're closing in on a big huckster named Rosencrantz. He's been running a billion-dollar Ponzi scheme for many years and many people, mostly the "little" people who can't afford to lose their money, are going to get wiped out. The Bureau finally has enough data to stop him. The Feds, the SEC, the FBI, everyone is in on it. They just want me go to in there and ask him some questions to see what else they can get on record."

"How very valiant of you," she teased, but she was impressed, nonetheless, that her friend had been tapped for this undercover work.

"I do what I can." He smiled. "People make real money with *my* funds because they bring real returns. They may seem paltry compared to his, but they're legit. Rosencrantz's investment statements are worthless pieces of paper, and he's been suckering people for years. We need to stop him."

"OK, I'll go," she said, suddenly intrigued.

"Good. You'll feel like a James Bond girl. But you need to look the part. I'm sending you over to Luca or Valentino. Your choice." He reached inside his wallet and pulled out several stacks of crisp hundred dollar bills. "Go find yourself a pretty dress for the party," he added, sweetening the deal.

"Yes, sir," she said, smiling. However, she knew she would keep the crisp bills and find something gorgeous hidden in the back of her closet that he hadn't seen before.

She gave Harry a hug good-bye, wrapping her arms around his waist. "Remember, honey," he added, looking down at her and tilting her chin up, "you're always in my thoughts, prayers, and…?"

"Fantasies!" she laughed.

CHAPTER 39

It was the evening of the party with Harry, and Melisse picked out a dress from the back of her closet that he had never seen before. When she reached behind to access the special party dresses she kept in plastic, her hand grazed a heavy dress cover. Against her better judgment, she pulled the dress out of the closet and unzipped the cover to reveal a frothy, very pale pink wedding dress.

She looked at it, shaking her head as she remembered…

A couple of years before, she had worn the dress to her own beautiful wedding, right on the beach in front of GG's Barbados home. It had been a whirlwind relationship and engagement, which began innocently enough when Melisse had become fed up with her lack of a real social life. This was one of the sacrifices of being a hardworking courtesan. So she had ventured into the world of "straight" dating by creating a profile on a well-known dating website.

The profile described her as an adventurous, discreetly sensual woman working as a travel writer, sometimes invited to different destinations like overseas luxury hotels to write PR copy for them about her experiences.

The first attractive young man to respond to her profile and ask her out to a proper dinner had been "Davide," a transplanted Parisian and the youngest partner in a prestigious law firm in downtown Manhattan. He had swept her off her feet before she barely had a chance to lie and tell him that, in addition to her writing, she lived modestly on funds from a trust (which would explain her rather extravagant lifestyle).

Davide was dynamic and decisive, had been educated at the best schools, was raised in France with all the usual traditions, and was firmly rooted in "family values."

Naturally, his background made Melisse a little uneasy—he was way out of her league and she was not what one might call a "family person."

She liked the French part, however, and he was her ardent admirer. She also liked having a nice guy to date who didn't remind her of work. He took her out to nice places and seemed to genuinely care for her. It was worth it to give up clients on Saturday nights in exchange for the feeling of having a "real" life.

Of course, she kept her life as a courtesan hidden from him, and managed it all quite well. But little by little, it just got out of hand. He'd wanted to take her on dates during the week, and the impromptu suppers and overnights he proposed started to curb her business, her income, and her dream of starting La Fantasia.

Just when she was about to break up with him in the interest of getting back to The Life, he'd proposed marriage. She'd hesitated, tempted, but a long engagement with no guarantee at the end (meaning, giving up her courtesan work) would be a major disaster for her if it didn't work out.

> **Spicy Secret:** "Marrying a man is like buying something you've been admiring for a long time in a shop window. You may love it when you get it home, but it doesn't always go with everything else in the house." —Jean Kerr

She gave him a nervous look, and he begged her to marry him in a few months' time instead. "And I don't care where your money comes from," he had said breathlessly as he kissed her one night in front of her door.

She tried to explain that she lived off a "trust fund," which would cut off sometime in the next two years and seriously alter her ability to financially contribute. "Let us not speak of this. I have money enough for both of us," he assured her.

Davide was very sweet and modest, and as Melisse would find out later, he was heir to a huge fortune. His job at the law firm was viewed more like an internship to prepare him for the day he would run his überwealthy family's U.S. subsidiary, which required him to have substantial legal know-how.

Finally, she accepted his proposal without being truly smitten and before she knew it, she was being introduced to his highly cultured family, having lunch with his sisters, and practicing her French. She chose a gorgeous beach wedding dress with his mother at Vera Wang. Theirs would be an intimate destination wedding, and GG wanted to host it at her beautiful property in Barbados with a reception in her tropical garden.

"My Melisse is getting married!" she said proudly over the phone. "You'll do it here, of course, so I can host and witness this wonderful event!"

Melisse had explained to Davide that GG was her godmother and an extraordinary hostess who would create something memorable for their inner circle of family and friends. Davide had happily agreed, and everyone was excited about going to Barbados.

Melisse was absolutely thrilled with the prospect. She loved Barbados, and GG's villa was an intimate, dreamy retreat. She and Davide could honeymoon over on St. Barts afterward and enjoy a private romantic villa.

Sex with Davide was nice, but Melisse had secretly had better with a few of her clients, or even total strangers in random places. She'd certainly had better sex with a few flirty waiters in tropical resorts! Hell, she'd had better sex with herself.

Still, he was very loving when he pounced on her and then came a little too quickly, leaving her hankering for more. But it was really nice to feel so loved. He was financially successful, too, which would only get better. Both he and his family loved her, and that was what counted, didn't it?

"Have you told him yet?" GG asked. "The way you've been working, you're really 'out there,' my dear. Sooner or later, someone will recognize you…"

"I know. I'm just waiting for the perfect moment…maybe on the honeymoon."

There was a stony silence on the other end of the line. Then, GG blurted out, "The *honeymoon*! Are you nuts? You have to be honest with him, Melisse, and soon!"

"I know, I know. I'll do it tonight."

Melisse hung up the phone. She knew GG was right. She invited Davide over to her place for "the confession," gave him the news, and watched as it went over like a lead balloon.

Melisse promised to discontinue her work. After all, the wedding was getting closer, and she had plenty of cash to live on, so she stopped answering her phones and disabled her website. Davide was satisfied with her grand gestures, and he seemed buoyed by her impeccable honesty and the fact that she was now at his exclusive beck and call.

He began coming to her place at least three nights a week and allowed her to pamper him, getting a taste of what she would be like as a Tribeca loft wife. But strangely enough, after her confession, his flowers, gifts, and back rubs seemed to slow down, replaced by more last-minute "booty calls," more requests for blow jobs, more homemade Belgian waffles, and more "sex on demand" as the date of their wedding got closer.

He was gaining weight, while *her* bank account was dwindling. Ah, but it was a small price to pay for a life of security and respectability with a savvy Frenchman.

It was the most perfect Caribbean day for a wedding, and as the sun began to set, Melisse sat doing her makeup in an upper guest room of GG's traditional plantation-style villa. The villa was painted white, with pink bougainvillea spilling over from planters on every terrace.

There were wraparound porches on both the upper and lower level of the home. The place was set on a small hill, with the beautiful sand and surf of Barbados nearby.

The small wedding party of thirty people, mostly Davide's relatives, sat assembled on white church pews on the beach, brought over from a local church and festooned with tropical flowers.

GG sat with Melisse and admired her in the mirror as Melisse applied blush to her face. She wore a pale pink slip dress overlaid with crystal-covered white lace that cascaded down into a flared fishtail skirt.

GG wore a beautiful pale pink flowing caftan and matching bejeweled turban with bits of blonde curls framing her face.

"Gorgeous, honey," GG said. "Who knew? You're going to have a very enjoyable life. He's a nice guy."

Melisse was silent. She pulled on an elegant white sun hat and pinned it to her hair. It had been decorated with a flowing pink lace sash that matched the details of her wedding dress and cascaded down her bare back. A wedding day was no excuse to go without adequate sun protection on her porcelain-doll skin!

"Yes, he's very *nice*." She looked up into the mirror and met GG's eyes with a significant glance that lasted several seconds.

"A little *too* nice?" GG ventured.

Melisse nodded, thinking, *I'm going to cheat on him sooner or later and fall deeply in love with someone else some day, when he comes along. The sex is so unsatisfying and the "love" is so superficial. I love him, but I'm not in love with him.*

Spicy Secret: "If it is necessary sometimes to lie to others, it is always despicable to lie to oneself." —W. Somerset Maugham, *The Painted Veil*

GG turned away, holding her stomach nervously. She knew that Melisse was about to do something they had both agreed a long time she would never do. The thought of it pained her deeply.

There was a knock at the bedroom door. It was Davide. GG lifted an eyebrow. "Here's your chance," she whispered conspiratorially.

"Take it, or I'll jump off the balcony to my death!" She opened the door and stepped out quickly.

Davide looked at Melisse in the mirror. "Beautiful. You look beautiful, Melisse," he said sadly.

He sat down and took Melisse's hands in his.

"Listen…"

"What?"

"Darling, I just can't do this. I appreciate everything you told me a couple of months ago. I am grateful that you were so honest with me about your life as a woman of the evening. And, of course, I'm very grateful that you stopped seeing your *clientele*. I thought I could deal with it. I thought I was OK with it, you know? But obviously I was not, and I realized….I simply cannot do this."

Melisse began to sigh heavily, not knowing whether to cry or jump for joy. "It's our wedding day! Why didn't you tell me before, Davide?"

"I don't know. I'm going to be the bad guy here, the villain. I'm going to go out there and wait for you with the officiant. But I'm not going to go through with it."

"What?"

"Yes, I know. Everyone's here. People should not know why we're *really* breaking up. I mean, that I am breaking up with you because, you know, you were fucking all those guys. For money."

Melisse felt a stab, and then it all became clear. Exactly. What. An. Asshole. He. Really. Was.

Thank God this is happening now!

GG stood outside her door eavesdropping, thinking *Yessss!*

Davide continued, "So I'm going to make this easy on you."

"Oh, easy on me. Gee, thanks. And how are you going to do that?"

"I am going to wait for you down there, but then I'm going to take off when you start walking down the aisle. I'm going to take off down that beach and go to the airport, like some asshole who cannot commit. Because I cannot commit to you, to who you are, or what you were, or what you would be with me… It's impossible. It is something I completely cannot relate to, and if your secret ever got out, my family would never accept it, either. And certainly not our shareholders."

"Uh…your French family from Paris…they won't relate to the life of a high-priced courtesan?" she said. "Your father probably has someone hidden away in an apartment in the 8th arrondissement even as we speak. And to be sure, he is probably texting her right now, just as he is sitting next to your mother."

The comment made Davide wince. He *had* just observed his father texting and giggling about something, to his mother's annoyance.

"Perhaps. Anyway, the marriage is now 'off,' as they say."

He backed out of the room. "I'm sorry," he said. "I'm very sorry. I will meet you on the beach before I run away."

The door clicked shut.

Melisse heard the harp music beginning downstairs on the beach. It sounded like what they probably played at the pearly gates of heaven before the sinners got shut out and were sent over to Rock and Roll Hell.

Spicy Secret: If good girls go to heaven, and bad girls go everywhere, then jet-set temptresses are exploring outer space as their next frontier.

Melisse sat there stunned, listening to the harpist play "Clair de Lune." Then, she sighed and let her chin fall to her chest. GG came in and put her hands on her shoulders, smiling. She fiddled with Melisse's hat and the tiny silk flowers adorning the sash. She was almost giddy with joy.

"What are *you* so happy about?" Melisse asked.

"The good old Universe has just spared you a life of misery with some hypocrite who didn't love the *you* in you! And one who clearly didn't satisfy you *in bed*. I *warned* you not to do that! Remember when I told you I would kill you if you married for any other reason than love?"

Melisse nodded and gave GG a little smirk. "I guess I just saved your life, then. You told me you were going to jump from the balcony if I married him, so…I broke up with him! You come first, GG."

"Oh, you are a crafty little one! I have obviously taught you well to put a positive spin on everything. If I'd jumped, I would have landed in my pool, only to use my large breasts as a flotation device. Get back to work, Living Doll!"

Spicy Secret: "There is no more defiant denial of one man's ability to possess one woman exclusively than the prostitute who refuses to be redeemed." —Gail Sheehy

Melisse grabbed her mobile phone from her purse and tapped in a few passwords that brought "Miss Melisse" back to life again, in all her Victoria's Secret meets *Belle de Jour* glory. "I'll start answering my phones and turn my websites back on. Now."

Turning "Miss Melisse" on again felt to her like what a junkie must feel when getting a hit after a long break from using drugs. It felt so good, yet she was so calm—on a high just from returning to the life of a worldwide temptress. As her fingers worked over the keyboard, she felt the spice of The Life spreading back into her soul.

New adventures were just around the corner.

"Turn that site back on tout de suite!" GG said. "I wish we had this kind of technology when I was a young woman so I could appear and disappear at will!"

"It's so great..." Melisse mused, knowing that men the world over who missed her most would soon be jumping for joy as their screens lit up with the message, "I'm back!" sent from her database manager.

GG smirked. "But now, let's give Davide his show. First, we need *champagne*," she said, grabbing a bottle of Veuve Clicquot from an ice bucket she'd put next to the dresser, "in case of an emergency." Well, this certainly qualified!

The women were twenty minutes late for Melisse's wedding, feigning a wardrobe malfunction and sending "we're delayed" messages down to the guests through the housekeeper. They were actually sitting on GG's bed taking turns draining their glasses, re-pouring from the chilled champagne bottle and giggling.

"Here's to your continuing journey as a celebrated courtesan. Why waste your many talents on one ungrateful excuse for a man!" GG toasted. "You can now return to the life you know and were meant for!"

The women clinked glasses and guzzled.

Melisse really felt like crying. She was half-hurt, half-relieved, but she just kept drinking and giggling with GG.

Eventually, the two women descended to the beach, GG acting as that special family person who would "give away the bride."

As if anything were free in this world.

Melisse hid under the brim of her hat, smiling happily, as if this were the greatest day of her life. As the script had dictated, Davide would be waiting on the beach platform with the officiant, and Melisse would approach the wedding arch with GG, their filmy dresses flowing on ocean breezes. The friends and family smiled warmly as the women passed them, and Melisse waved happily to a few.

Davide stood there, stiffly uncomfortable and frowning slightly, like someone who was severely constipated.

As GG and Melisse got closer to Davide, they clung to each other, trying not to giggle. When they got close enough, Davide frowned, turned, and cut loose, practically tripping over himself as he slogged through the sand and hightailed it down the beach, away from the wedding, finding his way to the road and eventually heading back to the Sandy Lane Hotel. There, he would get a taxi and the next flight the hell off the island.

The small crowd gasped in shock and horror, then looked at Melisse for a reaction. Melisse pretended to faint, and slunk into GG's arms before falling onto the sand.

"Someone help!" GG cried. "Get her upstairs!"

She leaned down by Melisse's ear, pretending to try to rouse her awake. She whispered under her breath, "Did you see how he ran away, like his pants were on fire?"

"Liar, liar, pants on fire," Melisse said through her half-closed lips, trying not to giggle and snort.

Melisse smiled wanly. GG's houseman, Tandy, a native Bajan with a huge smile, came and scooped Melisse into his arms, spiriting her off to GG's suite on the top floor of the home.

GG told the catering manager to start up the reception and get the band going. She had paid for a party and a party they were to have! Who the hell cared if there was no wedding!

Once the party was in full swing and Melisse had supposedly "come to," the two women relaxed in the cool of the bedroom where, "Under no circumstances can anyone come in," GG ordered her staff. "Melisse is devastated."

In reality, the two sat on a couch getting drunker and drunker on a second bottle of Veuve Cliquot as the Jamaican reggae band played in the yard below. Melisse had never been so drunk in her entire life, usually limiting herself to one glass of alcohol at a time.

GG stood up unsteadily. "Let's really make their day. Let's give these people something they'll never forget. Here they are, acting like nothing happened, eating *our* food and drinking *our* wine after that little turd thought he was too good for you, when you were absolutely stellar by being honest with him. What a shithead!"

"Ohhhh, noo..." Melisse slurred. "GG, what are you gonna do...?" But she was too drunk to get up off the bed to supervise GG.

GG said, "I'll show you what I'm gonna do...I need to water the plants...!" She swayed up and out to her terrace and went to the faucet, turning on the big hose used to water her plants. Some of the water splashed on her, soaking her outfit. She muttered to herself, "Oops! Oh, well, it's just water. And someone should have shot a pistol after that young man, running away from Melisse like that. Instead, they all just sat there, the stupid farts!"

Melisse just lay on the bed and let whatever GG had in mind for them play out. She heard GG talking to herself and heard the water coming on, then saw it hitting the floor of the porch outside as GG tested the nozzle's On/Off feature. *What the hell was she doing?*

GG's eyesight was blurred now—she was totally sloshed—but she managed to turn the hose nozzle around until she found the "full power blast" setting. The water surged forward as GG stood on the terrace in her pink caftan and jeweled turban, turning the "gun" part of the hose out toward the guests below. Then, GG "pulled the trigger" and began spraying the water full-blast on everyone in the party, miraculously avoiding soaking her household help and the musicians.

She also tried to keep the water off the buffet table, in case she and Melisse got hungry later. She'd sprung for all the best vittles and was especially eager to taste the spicy chicken wings.

"Get the hell outta my house!" she screamed in a drunken slur. "The whole lot of you! It's time to go! Go back to your hotels! The party's over!"

She took aim at several key people, including the mother of the groom, nearly blowing her dress off, and then aimed at Davide's two sisters, who ran away screaming. There was a special butt blast for the ex-father-in-law-to-be.

Any remaining friends and family who weren't old or feeble were also treated to a power shower. She had "super-soaked" them all into a group of wet rats looking like hell for their escape back to their suites at the posh Sandy Lane Hotel.

Tandy, her houseman, just stood there shaking his head up at GG, trying not to laugh at the vision of GG's now soaking wet, transparent dress showcasing her "foundation" garments beneath. He went to the front of the home to the driveway and helped the disgruntled guests get into their chauffeured minibuses and leave the villa. This was indeed an evening no one would forget.

GG turned off the hose and headed back to the house, her wet clothes dripping water on the wood floor. She walked into the bedroom to put on a dry robe while Melisse laid on the bed, her feelings a jumble of shame, anger, and hilarity. The day had truly gotten out of control.

And that had been just what she needed.

"There," GG slurred as she returned from the bathroom, "that's that. They've all gone home. And it was damn time they left my nice villa—*The villa that pussy built!!*"

Spicy Secret: When someone pisses on your parade, give them a power shower.

LANTANA BLEU

Remembering this scene now, Melisse giggled, thinking of the "wetting reception," as GG now liked to call it. She put her wedding dress away and chose a dress for the Ripcore party. Then she sat down at her makeup table and carefully applied a fine line of discreet false eyelashes to her gorgeous blue eyes.

It was one of those warm evenings in spring, and she chose a simple royal-blue silk dress she'd had custom made in Singapore, with a fitted, boned bodice that gave a hint of cleavage and flounced out into a full skirt.

Spicy Secret: "A dress makes no sense unless it inspires men to want to take it off you." —Françoise Sagan

She donned an intricate "collar" necklace made of gold filigree, sparkling blue stones, and tiny pearls that reminded her of a birds' nest. She applied a buttery, glossy, pale rose lipstick that enhanced her slightly bee-stung lips. She still had a crush on her cosmetic surgeon, the one who maintained her "natural-looking," yet lush lips. But she kept her secret sadness at his long-ago rejection well hidden during her visits.

Melisse entered the closet reserved for "special occasion purses" and pulled out her darling blue sequined, heart-shaped clutch. She tucked in her exquisitely printed business cards and a few condoms, along with a travel-size bit of lube, and a smart travel container with a tiny toothbrush and toothpaste. You never knew what a night like this might bring, or who you might meet (besides your client—in this case, her wonderful Near and Dear Mr. Quint).

Would the party bring more money? Maybe a little love?

It always seemed as if the nights brought money. Well…that was always nice… but what about a little love once in a while, too?

If love were involved, I wouldn't need the lube in my purse.

If love were involved, I wouldn't ask for the money.

Melisse gingerly removed Simo's gift of the ruby and diamond earrings from her jewelry box and admired them, deciding not to wear them while she was working. As she chose something else, she felt a strange pang. She missed him.

Damn! This is ridiculous. Then she took one last look at herself in the mirror and tucked a small pack of her special oil-blotting tissues into her purse.

Your Simo the Excellent never called, did he? Her nasty inner bitch voice reminded her.

He's a prince or a minister of finance for a kingdom or…whatever! And he's probably too busy, Melisse's voice of reason countered.

Face it. He's "just not that into (a whore like) you." Can't win 'em all, can you?

Melisse sighed. *Keep faith, keep love. That's the advice Nate told me before I entered The Life.*

We'll see. It ain't over til it's over. I could wait a lifetime for a guy like that.

CHAPTER 40

Meeting Brahim

While Melisse was preparing for the investor's party in the comfort of her apartment, in another part of town, a lean, muscular "hot guy" (as Melisse would have described him) named Brahim Rosencrantz was racing up the stairs from a Manhattan subway stop. He emerged, barely winded, on the street and strode three blocks to the Ripcore Fund party.

Being late for anything was not his style. Not tonight.

Despite being dressed simply in black jeans, a clean T-shirt, and a pair of fine European leather boots, he was a standout from other male commuters. An intense charisma seemed to emanate from him, and women turned to watch him with decided interest as he passed them on the street, focused only on arriving at the party at least five minutes early.

Apart from his dark, masculine good looks, he was decidedly a one-of-a-kind guy. Although financially comfortable, he preferred living a modest, rather Spartan lifestyle. He was also a student of spiritual practices, but kept that to himself and a small number of close friends.

Quiet by nature, he spoke with care and intelligence when the time was right, and those who knew him considered his counsel invaluable, since he offered it rarely, but when he did, was unfailingly right. And whatever he offered was done with a sly humor that could make you smile days afterward.

On a more physical level, he knew that his jeans clung to his buns in a way women appreciated. Today, the front of his T-shirt read: "I like it. A lot." The back read: "The Ripcore Fund II."

His fashion philosophy was, "Keep it simple." He dressed in under five minutes, and usually wore a nice pair of jeans and a white shirt. He had also discovered the most expensive, deliciously seductive cologne a man could afford, and had stashed several bottles at home, just in case it one day became unavailable.

He was both predictable and unpredictable, and women were often at a loss to understand and keep up with him. It would take a special kind of woman to flow into his lifestyle. So far, he hadn't met one who'd lasted more than a month, to his regret. Brahim craved a partner, and he was nonjudgmental and thus open to any woman who captured his heart and gave him the freedom to be himself.

He was in his mid thirties and just 5'7". Filled with smoldering energy, he had a dazzling smile framed by dimples most women found "adorable." But such an impression was misleading: this man was as virile as they came. He had a strong jawline and slight hook to his fine nose, with thick, dark brows animated by warm brown eyes. His all-over tan came courtesy of his Israeli genes.

Brahim kept his head completely shaved and had no interest in growing a beard, both of which came from repeated confidences from his female friends, who loved the former ("My God, I love bald men!") and loathed the latter ("Itchy beards really turn me off!").

Because of his body's unusually high levels of male hormones, he wore a perpetual five-o-clock shadow, but it only added to his overall appeal.

All things considered, from his personal grooming (balls and cock area shaved to perfection to match his perfectly bald head) to his careful choice of words with the women he courted, he was a considerate—almost professional—lover, often slipping out unseen the next morning, leaving behind a sweet but definitive thank-you note (he carried his own letterhead in his back pocket for such occasions!).

Never one to hurt feelings when it could be helped (and always acting before women got too addicted to him) he'd often written a note saying he regretted having to cut short a "beautiful beginning" in the interest of avoiding a "sad good-bye" but "it was delicious while it lasted."

Brahim's mother, Rivka, was no slouch either, and had perfectly prepared her young son—with her unique sense of humor—about the mysterious ways of love, the qualities of beauty (often unseen, but still important) inherent in every woman, and the way to treat the women he would meet, even those he wasn't that interested in.

Yes, Brahim had been raised by a strong woman who believed that her gender deserved respect ("Revered, Brahim!" she'd often insisted), whether beautiful or homely, because of the womanly soul within, which was always beautiful, as it came from God.

While still a virgin, Rivka had defected from a strict Orthodox Jewish household in Brooklyn to hook up with Brahim's father, Bernie Rosencrantz, a born-and-bred Manhattan hotshot who swept her off her feet when he was twenty-four and claimed her as his bride when she was only eighteen. He told her on the day they met that he would one day be "a Wall Street King of the Universe."

Rivka, dazzled, had eyes only for Bernie, her passion undimmed by his physical appearance. Even as a young man, Bernie was borderline homely, with a bald head, a long, almost beaked nose, a wide mouth, and the longest fingers she'd ever seen (which he did put to very good use)!

Bernie, unlike the other boys her father had tried to foist on her, had big plans for his life, and he wanted Rivka along for the ride. Suddenly, life was taking a very interesting turn, and she decided she was in!

Rivka, by the way, was a zaftig beauty, a first-generation descendant of Israeli immigrants. She could have been a stand-in for Sophia Loren, and was secretly thankful that Brahim, their only son, had inherited all his best features from her. When he was born and placed in her arms, his beautiful swarthy complexion made her think of a perfectly formed loaf of warm wheat bread, just out of the oven.

"Abraham," she'd cooed. "We're in this for life."

When Brahim was a small boy, she saw him becoming "soft" because her business-obsessed husband was never around to be a good male role model. So she launched a search for a "manny"—a male nanny who could teach young Brahim how to be masculine.

An interesting fellow named Hamza applied for the job and Rivka could see right away, as she read through his application, that he would be perfect for the job. And she was right: it was Hamza who was responsible for Brahim being called "Brahim" instead of "Abraham."

When Hamza met the family, he was a recent immigrant from Palestine and a university student in his thirties taking an advanced degree at NYU. He'd lost both parents during a shelling of the city, and was seeking a new life in the United States.

"Leave it to a rich American-Jewish family with ties to Israel to take me in, give me a job, and change my life for the better," he often said, smiling ironically to himself. "Instant karma, I guess."

Rivka had found him through a domestic employment agency and invited Hamza to their Central Park penthouse to see how he related to Abraham. It was love at first sight: Abraham, upon seeing a guest in the apartment, had given the Hamza a sly smile from across the room and asked him if he would like to see his room.

When the two later emerged as best friends after a discussion of Abraham's butterfly specimen collection ("A true nerd in the making," Hamza had sighed to himself), Hamza offered Rivka an intense, rigorous summer program for her son. He would pick Abraham up for morning exercise in the park, teach him the essential sports, take him to museums and shows and concerts, and help him practice the three foreign languages he had been studying well before he hit kindergarten.

"So whad'ya think, kid? Do you want Hamza to come and visit you almost every day this summer and show you around?" his mother asked.

"Can we go out *now*?" Abraham had asked as his mother nodded and smiled, knowing she'd made a perfect match. "Just don't let the door hit your butt on the way out, Abe," she'd laughed. "And no shenanigans in the park!"

"Let's go," Hamza said, taking Abraham by the hand as the boy nearly dragged him out the door, happy to get away from his loving but often overbearing mother.

Once they got outside and into the park, Hamza had stopped Abraham abruptly, and it was a moment that Abraham would remember for the rest of his life.

"Stop right there, little guy. We need to talk about something."

"What?"

"Well, we need a special 'guy' name for you. From now on, I'm going to call you 'Brahim,' okay? That's a version of Abraham, which makes you sound like an old man in a robe with a beard. You know, Brahim?"

The boy chuckled. "Okay, sure. I'm Brahim. Nice to meet you. Hamza," he said, puffing out his chest.

"Yeah, you're a Brahim," Hamza had laughed, ruffling his hair. "Get a move on, Brahim. Let's go get a hot dog from that stand over there. You're not allergic, right?"

"A *hot dog*?" The thought had Brahim salivating. "No, I'm not allergic. My mother calls it junk food and it's on the list of foods I'm not allowed to eat."

"Yeah, okay. And if you tell her that we ate hot dogs today, I'll preserve you like one of those butterflies you have in your room! Like this—" he splayed out his arms and played dead "—with the pins and everything. First rule between us is: we don't tell each other's secrets. And second is, we eat whatever we want. After exercising. That's the first two rules today in The Man Code."

"The Man Code?"

"Well, yes! We have to have a Man Code between us, don't we?"

"Yes. Of course!" Brahim nodded, loving the idea. "We will have secrets and we will eat what we want. After exercising," he repeated, fixing his eyes on the hot dog cart, where he would soon commit his first delicious act of male rebellion and secret-keeping with Hamza—beginning with junk food.

Little did he know in that moment that he would begin a life-altering friendship with this hard-core, but learned and sensitive Arab. Hamza would love and mentor and coach the "fatherless" Brahim from boy to teenager, when he would be transformed into a nearly "ideal man"—that same rare gem who would one day be fortunate enough to cross paths with a gorgeous, independent woman named

"Melisse." By then, he'd have the balls and savoir faire to capture, fondle, possibly tame her and pin her down—just as he'd done with the beautiful butterflies of his childhood.

Today, as Brahim walks along 62nd Street toward the Knickerbocker Club where the Ripcore Fund Party is to be held, Brahim is fueled by his usual intensity. Fortunately, it's been tempered by a Montessori school childhood, summer theater camps, a fine classical high school education in an Eastern boarding school, and four years at Yale (where he'd studied finance *and* theater/cinema arts).

He'd always teetered on that seesaw between aggressive capitalism (his father's genetic influence) and the art and poetry of words, scenes, and subtext coming alive on film (his mother's artistic side).

To everyone's surprise—and his father's horror—he hadn't gone on to attend Harvard Business School to earn an MBA after college. He'd gone instead to L.A. to pursue his real passion—filmmaking—and the "other" passion he was too embarrassed to tell anyone: becoming a movie star.

During high school, Brahim had kept himself out of trouble and "in the money" by doing summer internships in the posh halls of investment banking firms (gigs financed by his father). His favorite "gig" of all, however, was watching from the pit of the Stock Exchange. There, he'd followed the fascinating fluctuations of world currencies and the fortunes of one particularly bullish trader named Paul who had been assigned to "show Brahim the ropes" as a "market mentor."

To balance out those harrowing market days, Brahim had attended as many theater classes as he could in the evenings to learn the art of improvisational comedy and acting.

Once settled in L.A., Brahim had secured a nice income for himself by trading in the foreign currency markets, and gradually amassed a small fortune that always felt too much like gambling earnings when the workday (or night) was done.

It made him very nervous.

So, having watched enough late-night commercials about real estate investing, Brahim took a portion of his profits and invested it in small fixer-upper houses in outlying suburbs of L.A. He would buy the homes "free and clear" at huge discounts from the banks or county tax collector, improve them and rent them out.

After thirteen years living out West, Brahim had developed a real estate portfolio of more than sixty rental homes that he owned wholly, and which he'd turned over to a competent management company to manage for him.

While he wasn't a mega-millionaire, his monthly net income had given him the financial freedom to pursue his dreams and to develop his "real" gifts and talents: screenwriting, producing, and directing small films. His greatest wish: to act on the big screen some day.

Not bad for a thirty-five-year old guy.

But there was one thing missing: a woman worthy of him, someone he could live for, love, be motivated by. Someone who had the special seductive powers to satisfy him and rein in his almost insatiable sensuality.

And not one of his many serial lovers had matched his appetites, or captured his imagination enough for him to consider easing into a more permanent relationship. There'd been no woman he could see himself waking up with every morning, happy with a warm snuggle when the sizzle and spice eventually wore off and the wonderful comfort of love, respect, and commitment took over. (Yes, Brahim was that rare man: one with realistic expectations about romantic relationships. Both his mother and Hamza had drilled this truth into him, so he wouldn't be shocked by the "honeymoon's over" feeling when it finally arrived. He'd even studied the book, *The Five Love Languages,* and well understood what it might take to keep a good thing going. He was more than willing—and able—to speak the five languages of love.)

But he hadn't yet met Melisse.

She was one of the few women who'd acquired the courtly skills, combining sizzle and spice *and* everything nice for a lifetime, so that when the right man came along, she'd be ready. "Honeymoon in the Afternoon" was one of her special menu items, after all.

Now, as Brahim approached the Knickerbocker Club, he prepared to step into his temporary new role as a hired gun for his father's investment business. He readied himself for this as if he were an actor preparing for a performance. For Brahim, he was entering a new "adventure"—one that had returned him to New York City for an undetermined period. This was a stint as a "consultant" (really a salesman) in his father's firm, Illustra Funds. And tonight, Illustra was hosting a party to launch the second Ripcore Fund, a hedge fund of mysterious strategies.

Those who enjoyed its double-digit returns spoke about Ripcore I in hushed, reverent tones. Now, Ripcore II was ready to take in new money from new "accredited investors" qualified by their wealth to invest in risky strategies with, alas, very little transparency.

His father had recently experienced some health setbacks. After the heart surgery that saved his life, he'd begged and then nearly bribed Brahim into returning to New York City "for a season" to sell the fund to "new money as only you can do." It would last "just until Ripcore II is flying, son, and then you can go back to L.A. an even richer man with funding for your next project."

Then, of course, his father had to add, "You owe it to me, kid. Payback time is a bitch, but I need you back here with me for a while, till I get my energy back after that 'surgeon' tore into me."

It was an offer—and a guilt trip—Brahim couldn't refuse. Fortunately, he was between projects and had the time. And New York was still "home," after all, offering up lots of potentially intriguing ideas, contacts, inspirations, and, if he got lucky, a woman or two (or more).

His producing successes until now had been with small, independent documentary projects, but they had garnered significant praise in the trades and excellent reviews for their originality and insight. Corporations and not-for-profits kept him busy with "private label" productions that he never lent his name to, but they paid well and kept him afloat as a filmmaker.

But it was his most recent piece—a short, dark, but emotionally gripping film about a Mafioso, called *Drowning Mr. Rat*, that was his first venture into producing one of his own scripts. Its popularity in film festivals had placed him squarely in view of major players in Hollywood eager to contact his agent to get a piece of him.

Still, he secretly wished they were coming after him for his acting. Well, maybe that would come one day...

Like him, his films were compact but packed a wallop. Anyone who paid attention to such things could see that Brahim was "on his way" in Hollywood...*if* he could keep up the pace and not get sucked too far into New York family dramas and the slick world of investment management.

CHAPTER 41

The Ripcore Party

Brahim knew he couldn't be late, especially since this was the first party in New York where he'd be hyping his father's new investment fund. He knew he wasn't dressed conventionally for the occasion, but he'd had his T-shirt custom made to say "I Like It. A Lot."

He had intended to create interest in his father's new fund and to get people to ask him questions about it—as in, "What is it you like so much?" He figured that if he was wearing a suit, he'd look respectable, but he'd just blend in. The T-shirt was a walking, talking marketing piece.

Once confirmed as a guest, Brahim moved into the posh, private Knickerbocker Club and noticed that his T-shirt was already working. Women began giggling, looking at him and then at each other, smiling delightedly.

Some of the men were staring at him, too, possibly envious. *Wouldn't it be nice to be able to just wear a T-shirt and jeans? Fuck all this formality!* he imagined them thinking.

Brahim didn't see his father anywhere in the main party room, and couldn't find him in the adjoining lounge where the buffet and the bar were located. Instinct told him to go back to the kitchen, so he followed a waiter scurrying away with an empty tray and entered the kitchen. It was abuzz with activity.

Ah, yes, there was his father with the catering manager, who wore a sleek suit with skinny pants, but appeared to be half-drunk. Bernie didn't notice that his son was standing behind him watching the whole scene play out, and continued with his rant. "We're feeding the classes here, not the masses, got that? Those little sausage things taste soggy! Do something about it!" he ordered the unfortunate manager.

The manager, in return, fired back in a heavy French accent, "Ahhh, I zeee…you weesh your 'pigs in blankets' to be wrapped in crispy, sexy sheets! Very well!" The manager snapped his fingers and two of the wait staff appeared at his side.

"Get all the *saucissons in croute* back in here and into zee oven!" He raised his hands dramatically, mocking Bernie. The two waiters practically ran out the door.

The manager looked around for his glass of champagne. "Aaaarggggh! We're having a culinary *crise*! I need a drink!" He guzzled from a glass of champagne he grabbed off the counter and assured Bernie that "Zee leetle swines will be sizzling in their blankets soon! Don't you worry, Mr. Rosencrantz."

Bernie just crossed his arms, disgusted that he wasn't getting the respect he deserved from the wise-ass French caterer.

"You're a putz," Bernie practically spit out.

Brahim started laughing and thought, *What a great scene for a movie.* He nodded at the manager.

"Hey!" he said, patting his father on the back. "DAD! How ya doin'? Long time no see." Brahim went in for a hug, but Bernie shrank back. He hadn't seen his son in several years, and wasn't prepared for a hug fest. Brahim felt his heart drop like a stone, but composed himself for his father's next comment, the predictable: "What the hell kind of suit is that?"

"You said it was a party. The invitation said it's a 'gay-la.'"

Bernie looked at Brahim's T-shirt. "I like it. A lot," he read aloud.

Brahim turned around to show him the other side, which said, "Ripcore Fund II."

"What is this?" Bernie protested. "I thought I told you to dress British and think Yiddish. You're here to impress and sell, remember?"

"And I will, Dad. You know, thirty-three percent of the people you meet are gonna love you, thirty-three percent are gonna hate you, and the other thirty-three percent don't give a damn. I'm here to convert the indifferent thirty-three percent of your friends into buying your fund."

Bernie looked at Brahim. "You're here to convert *sixty-six* percent. I want you to sell the ones who hate me, too. And remember, kid: there are no *friends* in this business. These people are investing in our fund because they're *greedy* motherfuckers. They want satisfaction. And believe me, if we don't provide them with great returns, they won't be your friend for very long."

"Got it, Dad."

Bernie pushed Brahim out the kitchen door, down the corridor, and into the party room, instructing him as staffers scrambled out of the way. "Get out there and start pumping the Ripcore. You've got exactly two hours to work your charms and round up some new investors. Anybody you find out is already an investor, just rave about how well we're doing and move on to the next mark. I'll point out the weak ones in the herd to you. Got it? Now, get out there," he repeated, shoving Brahim into the crowd.

Brahim could see the party wasn't even in full swing yet. "Don't you wanna have a drink with me first? Catch up? I just got in. It's been, like, *years*. I want to tell you about what's been happening with *Drowning Mr. Rat*."

"No, I don't wanna have a drink first and talk movies. This isn't L.A.," Bernie snarled in a loud whisper that sounded like Darth Vader. "I've got work to do and so do you. Go use those scripting and acting skills to accomplish something *real*...like making money for us."

Brahim felt a stab of hurt at this reference to his supposed "failure" in Hollywood. He'd had so many notable successes, and while not all were financially successful, he wasn't in debt and they had been artistically well received. But his father had taken no notice of those facts, despite Brahim having sent clippings and personal letters explaining things over the years.

There *had* been an extremely successful project about which he'd never told his father (of course, he'd found out anyway). Since that occasion, his father had continued to relish "rubbing it in" to this day.

It had occurred when Brahim had seen a sudden, almost dizzying drop in the value of some of his properties. In response, he'd swung into action and produced something more "commercial" in the entertainment business to help offset his losses before they snowballed. And that was how his one secret little sellout to porn had begun. To his amazement, it had resulted in the release of the underground, best-selling soft porn indie called *Couch Boy*, which Brahim wrote, directed, produced, and starred in, under the assumed name of "Ronny Cockmeister."

Apparently it was—and remained for a long time—a best-selling DVD among women between ages thirty and fifty. *Couch Boy* had garnered praise for its artistic approach to the usual "suck and fuck" scenes so common in the spicy movie business. Apparently, in porn circles, Brahim had single-handedly raised the usual "trashy" porno bar to a higher level with his first-class screenwriting, producing, directing, and acting skills.

He'd even starred in the film, and maybe that was a mistake, he thought afterward, but his ego had gotten the best of him when he decided to play the role of Devin Wannabe. Devin was the sweet, sexy, goofy young actor sleeping his way to success by systematically seducing Hollywood's high-powered female gatekeepers (in a wide variety of hot, fantastically shot scenes which showcased his body and sexual stamina).

Two years earlier, when it was first released, it was reviewed as a "symphony of seductive scenes," "sizzling with sensitivity" yet "alive with tongue-in-cheek (and other places) humor," and finally, "The only porn star you'll ever fall in love with."

In the flick, Devin ended up becoming an award-winning screenwriter when a powerful, much older famous actress fell in love with him, took him under her wing, and told him the truth about his lousy acting skills. At the same time (between long, seriously cinematic and graphic lovemaking sessions), she encouraged him to do what he really did best and become a writer.

In the last scene of the movie, all the women in the audience were in tears when it fast-forwarded to the future, when a more mature Devin (now an award-winning screenwriter) wheeled his actress lover, now elderly, down a beach sidewalk as babes in bathing suits walked by. He scooped her out of the chair, led her to a beach blanket, and kissed her passionately. This was the scene that had secured Devin's place as the sweetest, sexiest guy in porno history.

When Brahim is recognized as Devin while out and about in L.A., he simply denies it and says, "Hey. I get that all the time. But I'm not that guy. Wish I were, but I'm not."

"Now go chat up some of those gals," his father said, interrupting Brahim's thoughts and nodding toward a cluster of socialites. "You obviously know how to get what you want with that big swinging dick, don't you, Mr. Porn Star."

Great. Now everyone in hearing distance would know about Brahim's short-lived porno career. Being mocked by his own father during the first ten minutes of their reunion stung, but Brahim put on his game face and went to face the investors.

He believed that the law of karma would ultimately deal with those who belittled others, and his father was no exception. However, morally and artistically, he had to admit he regretted the day he'd decided to make (and star in) *Couch Boy*, even if most people loved the story and its long, steamy sex scenes. True, the money it made had saved him from the brink of financial ruin and had financed a significant portion of his expensive production of *Drowning Mr. Rat*. So for that he was grateful.

Drowning Mr. Rat was a serious short film that went deep inside the soul of a Mafia boss. When the audience first meets him, he's deciding whether or not to kill a human "rat" as the traitorous informer pleads for his life. Flashbacks fill in the blanks about how these men came to this sorry crossroads. Ultimately, the boss lets the "rat" go, even though he's risking his own survival by doing so.

The audience ended up walking away sobered, reflecting on their own moral codes. The film had garnered great reviews and was given major play in domestic and international film festivals. But it hadn't shown a profit because it was a short.

Still, it was Brahim's first major showpiece, and it had increased his access to bigger players in the film biz.

His second-biggest showpiece (and big spicy secret) was *Couch Boy*. It hadn't exactly been his life's dream to parade around naked and fuck like crazy on film, but now he was free of the financial problems that had initially pushed him into porn.

Like most regrettable experiences in life, Brahim had moved on, telling himself it'd all been for the best. He'd had a strange taste of filmmaking success with it, it had "stroked" his ego forever by memorializing his sexual prowess in celluloid, and it gave his father something to razz him about for the rest of his life.

Brahim looked at Bernie now as he hungrily eyed the small group of obviously wealthy women he now wanted Brahim to chat up, offering promises of great returns on their investments.

He nodded their way. "Seduce and destroy, son. Seduce and destroy..." Bernie goaded.

Oy.

CHAPTER 42

Pumping the Fund

Later, as the party got into full swing, Brahim and Bernie were in the Knickerbocker Club, spying on the party guests from behind a fake ficus tree decorated with tiny lights. Brahim looked over at his father, who surveyed the room like a hungry shark ready to tear into the flesh of the impossibly rich. They were all here in this room, eager to get in on a good thing before Fund II closed out.

That was one of Bernie's stealth fund-raising strategies: give people the impression that an investment in one of his funds was a limited-time-only offer open only to the clever few who stepped up, money in hand, early in the game. Of course, in reality, it was open to anyone and everyone who had at least two hundred thousand dollars to burn, and was willing to sign the "informed or accredited investor" document familiar to most high-net-worth individuals.

The fund "close" and "maturation" dates were, however, unclear. And as to the "prospectus" (the document outlining the fund's strategies, allocations, and risks), very few had been printed out, and only when requested. Most investors never read them, as they were filled with complicated financial jargon—a clever pastiche of terms and conditions stolen from other, legitimate hedge fund documents.

In other words, the fund's documentation could have qualified for use as toilet paper for these rich folks' asses, but nobody was reading it that closely. Those closest to Bernie (and part of the great lie) assured potential buyers that even under close scrutiny, the fund appeared beyond reproach.

Brahim himself was unaware of the very shaky ground these documents stood on; his father certainly wouldn't tell him, and all Brahim was focused on today was getting a big slice of the Big Apple investors' pie. He'd just arrived on a wing and a prayer, hoping for a better relationship with his father. He'd hoped that he'd get off on the right foot by supporting him with his fund-raising gig.

Too bad good old Dad hadn't changed a bit, despite his near brush with death. He still tossed off the same criticisms, condemning innuendos, and foul-mouthed insults that would distance his son from him, despite Brahim's long-held prayer that his father would undergo a miraculous personality change.

Thank God for Mom, he thought, as he felt all the sharp angles of working with Bernie closing in on him. Well, at least he could work on a new documentary while he was in New York. The city always had a "person of interest" or lifestyle to probe.

Suddenly, Bernie groaned aloud, "Oh, shit...*him*..."

Brahim looked up and recognized someone standing in the corner of the party room. It was Nicolos Copolos, a fifty something, hulking, silver-haired Greek with a prominent gut and a large zodiac necklace nestled in his hairy chest.

Bernie sneered. "That sewer rat, Nicolos Copolos, is here, sniffing around for movie money. He's always at my fund openings looking for new investors for his piece-of-shit films. Oh well, what can I say? He's already subscribed in the funds..."

Brahim, too, saw someone he knew and sighed. "Oh, no. I can't get away from *her*, either."

"Who?"

"Nic's *daughter*, Puffy."

Puffy Copolos was a voluptuous torpedo of a young woman, crusted over with significant jewelry and stuffed into a short bandage dress that pushed up her big boobies and hugged every roll of fat around her midriff. Her derriere, well contained by the signature Alaïa elasticized fabric, appeared to contain two soccer balls bouncing in unison.

Down below, hidden by the fabric, Puffy had meaty, strong thighs mottled with cottage cheese cellulite that only a wrestler could love.

And further below that, her calves had a certain quality that a heartless Beverly Hills cosmetic surgeon, in the privacy of his office, had once referred to as "piano legs."

Bernie, on the other hand, looked pleased at Puffy's presence as she greedily surveyed the options at the buffet table, holding an already loaded plate.

"What, son? Does she scare you with those *gigantoid* titties?"

"Dad, you're out of line. Please. Try to see the whole picture," Brahim cautioned calmly. "Women are more than the sum of their parts. In Puffy's case, well, she's much more than her big, bad bazookas."

"And don't forget that big Sherman tank of an ass. So what's your beef with Copolos? He's one of our biggest individual investors, you know. He's made all kinds of money with that *Gang Green Ganja Beast* franchise."

"Yeah, sure," his son chuckled. "And don't forget *Potty Monsters: The Toilet Trilogy*. Horror films for kids—that's a first."

"He's an innovator! A goddamn genius, if you ask me. Why didn't you think of something like that? So what happened with Nic?"

"Copolos rejected me for a lead role in his last film, *Up Crack Creek*."

"From *Up Crack Creek* to up shit creek, huh, son? What's the bugaboo? How'd you mess it up?"

"Copolos rejected me because I refused to marry his daughter. Your girl, *Puffy*."

"*Her?*" Bernie eyed Puffy more closely and a bit salaciously. "What's not to like about a girl built like a brick shithouse with more jewels than the Taj Mahal?"

"For one thing, she's not my type."

"Type? You mean, the Miss Piggy type? Someone should go over and tell her what that famous pig used to say about buffets..." Bernie winked at Brahim.

"What?"

"Never eat more than you can lift!" he laughed, making two snorting sounds.

"Oh, God..."

Bernie suddenly pushed Brahim out from behind the lit-up ficus tree. "Enough talk. Push, push in the bush, son. Get out there and pump the Ripcore! Now!"

Brahim suddenly felt like a pimply, lonely teen from a dysfunctional family all over again. But he pushed back his shoulders and reminded himself that he was now grown up and a very accomplished man. This was just a crazy little stop on his way to even bigger and better things. Call it "research for a story." And let's face it, he was here, as a good son, to help his ailing father. End of story.

Meanwhile, en route to the party, Melisse was nervously confiding to Harold Quint, "These cocktail parties always make me so uncomfortable, but thank you for inviting me, Harold. I always enjoy our time together, wherever it is!"

They sat together holding hands in the back of his chauffeured limo on their way to the Knickerbocker Club. Harry looked at her, waiting for more. "Why the hesitation to attend cocktail parties, honey?"

"I don't know....I guess it's like putting on a performance. You have to make small talk with people you don't know or care about. Do I *have* to talk to anybody, Harry?" she asked plaintively.

She squeezed his hand and leaned her head on his shoulder, which she knew he loved. "I really only want to talk to *you*," she said sweetly.

> **Spicy Secret: Men in high places like to have their hands held and be leaned on in secret places. And they like to feel that they, alone, are privy to your most private confessions.**

"No, honey. You don't have to talk to any of those nasty old men," Harry chuckled.

She giggled. "Sometimes when people ask me what I do for a living, I just want to say something like, 'Ohhh...I'm just a sexual athlete. I won a gold at Lillehammer, but I still train!' or, 'Oh, I do topless euthanasia... Can I give you my card in case you ever have a pet or a loved one you want to put down?'"

Harry snorted. "Now you behave yourself tonight, Melisse. Just be my arm candy for a few hours, and nobody will suspect that I'm there getting information for this sting." Quint showed her the tiny recording device running along the inside of his jacket.

Melisse smiled and shook her head. "Amazing. What did you tell your wife that you're doing tonight, in case one of her friends is here and sees you with me?"

> **Spicy Secret: Don't ever bring up a client's wife unless absolutely necessary to manage or avoid a potentially bad situation.**

"Oh, that. You're my real estate consultant, married to one of the lawyers in the firm, just in from Nice, and we're here to fit in some time to talk about the property in the South of France I may purchase for a small luxury hotel project. You know, the one for the La Fantasia project..."

"Ah, yes! I imagine I could drum up quite a bit of interest in my La Fantasia project at a party like this. All those frustrated, high-level female executives who need to de-stress, and the neglected wives, the rich cougars on the hunt..." She giggled again, knowing that she could never do such a thing in Harry's company.

"Well, my dear, when La Fantasia becomes a reality, I'm sure you'll have no trouble getting it booked up years in advance, with *very little marketing*," he said, squeezing her hand. "These days they're calling it 'hush marketing.' Basically, that's the same as word of mouth."

"Hush marketing? Hmmmm..."

"You look gorgeous, by the way," he told her. "I love that new dress on you."

Melisse smiled, thinking, *You mean, the one I found in the back of my closet?*

As Brahim and Bernie moved through the crowd toward Nic Copolos, women looked over their shoulders at Brahim, now being deposited by his father before Nic, who sported a superior grin.

Bernie said, "Nic, I think you two have already met in L.A. Brahim's back in the city to help us out at the firm. I'm putting him on your account, effective immediately." He then walked off, leaving Brahim to shake Copolos's hand vigorously, then take Puffy's hand, which he shook and kissed gently as he looked up at her.

"Mr. Copolos, Puffy. It's always a pleasure. How are you two enjoying the party?" This was an awkward moment, considering that the last time Brahim had seen them "up close and personal" had been two years ago at a dinner in L.A.

It was at the Diaghilev Restaurant in West Hollywood, where "stars eat like czars." The place had been the backdrop of many marriage proposals, and in their case, this was another marriage proposal, except that Copolos had proposed that Brahim marry his daughter.

His rationale? "We could be one big, happy family in the movie-making business."

Nic had implied that, in exchange for Brahim's hand in marriage, they would likely give the new member of the family a lead role in both directing and starring in *Up Crack Creek*.

The proposal was neither subtle nor romantic. Brahim, in addition to being offended by the offer, also recognized that it went against every deep belief of his in the magic of the Universe to bring two soul mates together—regardless of any advantages in the film biz.

Physically, the thought of *living* with Puffy forever made his stomach churn; in fact, he felt ill right now just thinking about it.

"No…no, no, no…" Brahim had said, rising from his seat to make a dash for the lavatory, his gorge rising. "My love is not for sale or exchange, contrary to what it might seem… Sorry, Puffy. I'm sure you're a great girl, but I'm not the one for you, and fuck you, Copolos. You should know better."

He'd managed to overcome his nausea and pushed his way out of the posh restaurant, using the other diners' chairs as supports on his way to the front door. He'd barely made it outside before puking into the gutter on Sunset Boulevard.

And that was the last time he'd seen Puffy and Nic Copolos. Until now.

CHAPTER 43

Thunder Down Under

As Harry Quint and Melisse entered the party room, all eyes turned for a moment to "New York's Best-Dressed" gentleman and his diminutive date. Melisse had all the presence of a small Marilyn Monroe, and her elegant royal blue dress with its flirty full skirt knocked it out of the field.

"Wow! Who's the little hottie?" Copolos asked Brahim.

Turning to look, Brahim saw Melisse, blinked and then felt as if he'd been kicked in the head. My God! This woman was the Universe's gift to him, delivered to him at this party, of all places!

In a moment of complete egotistical male-ness, he thought, *And she'll soon find out I'm God's gift to her.* It wasn't her physical appeal that melted him; it was something else. He saw right through the pretty dress clinging to the curvy little body and sensed something so soft and sweet and innocent and untouched within her, he wanted to curl up against it every night of his life!

She was also like a little jungle cat. He sensed a wildness swirling around her sweet, sensitive little soul, and he rose to the challenge of taming that cat (to some extent, anyway). He had always been intrigued by unpredictable women, finding them worthy of special respect and reverence. His mother was unpredictable, and he adored her. She certainly set a standard for all women: loving, unconventional, charming, spiritual, practical, and outspoken. Who could ask for more?

Brahim kept staring at Melisse, whom he immediately thought of as "fun-size." She was about five feet tall, much shorter than he, but he knew he could give her a giant-size helping of pleasure. He imagined what it would be like to have her surrender to his large cock, a happy surprise for every woman he'd ever bedded.

"Built like a jockey, hung like a horse," they had teased on the set of *Couch Boy*. Now, Brahim felt a hard tap on his shoulder and saw Puffy looking a little hurt as she gave him an up-and-down inspection.

"Excuse me! We're over here," she said bitterly.

"Oh, sorry, Puffy!" he said politely. Caught!

"Yeah, so…back to business…" Copolos looked at Melisse out of the corner of his eye while continuing to talk to Brahim.

A bit later, Copolos bit into a now-crispy Pig in Blanket while Brahim glanced over to observe Melisse leaving Harry Quint's side, easing into one of the club chairs near the bar. She was now within touching and hearing distance of where he, Nic, and Puffy were having their conversation.

Melisse had actually positioned herself to hear every word. She was more than curious about the adorable short bald guy in a white T-shirt with perfectly muscled arms. She had sent him another glance on the way to the bar and, sure enough, saw that the rest of him was in perfect form, particularly the buns.

But like a cat that desperately wants to be petted, yet is waiting to be approached first, she sat aloofly, supposedly surveying the room. The resonance of his voice immediately made her think of liquid testosterone mixed with chocolate liqueur, equaling pure sexual energy. Now, she listened carefully, hoping to learn more about him.

She heard Nic Copolos ask Brahim, "So this is a switch for you, from documentaries to hawking *this stuff*? Well, whatever. I'm sure you'll make it a go. Listen, kid, things are heatin' up at Copolos Productions. I need you…"

"Yeah, Brahim. It's wonderful!" Puffy cooed.

"What's up?" Brahim asked.

"So Jazzy, this friend of mine, a rich oil sheik from the Middle East, saw *Crack Creek*, liked our highbrow approach, and now he wants to invest in more of our productions."

"Is that so?" Brahim asked.

Melisse raised her eyebrows at this news. *That's interesting*, she thought. *Are they talking about the man who just proposed marriage to me with a huge, heart-shaped canary diamond? Are these the L.A. people Jazzy was talking about in Dubai…the people he wants to make films with, starting with the story of his charmed life?*

She couldn't believe her ears, but in her strange world, anything was possible.

"Yeah, Sheik Jazzy. The Emir al ibn Jazzizi, whatever—right, Puffy?"

Copolos popped another Pig in Blanket into his mouth while Puffy expounded on Jazzy's charms. "Everyone just calls him Jazzy. Filthy. Filthy. Filthy rich. Oil rich, just swimming in it. A little nuts, but a great backer for Daddy and me. He's very hands off."

Copolos continued with his mouth full. "Yeah, but really twisted. A horny desperado with three wives and about a hundred live-in girlfriends."

"He has a huge palace," Puffy continued.

"Got himself a harem of girls over there, out in the middle of nowhere. I think he recruits them out of the Miss World pageant. Anyway, I've never seen anything like his setup."

"Daddy, tell him about the pigs!"

"So Jazzy collects these rare albino potbellied pigs. They eat up all the palace garbage, the scraps, whatever. Then they have this contraption that uses the pig shit to create combustible energy that runs his generators and the swamp coolers that cool off all his women. It also heats his pool for those bare-assed naked night swims. He keeps his costs really low like that."

"Everyone knows potbellied pigs make great pets!" Puffy added. "And his pigs don't need to fear for their lives because it's forbidden for the sheik to eat bacon. And in a hot climate like that, why would you slaughter and eat the source of energy for your air conditioners?"

Brahim tilted his head, crossed his arms over his chest, and pondered all this for a moment. "OK. So let me see if I understand this correctly. Some oil-rich guy who owns a pipeline is using pig shit to power his own home. Doesn't that tell you something about what he thinks about the future of our oil reserves?"

"Yeah, "Copolos said, struggling for the right words after his fifth martini. "It tells *me* that one day the CIA is going to go blow up some more of our own Twin Towers so we can go over there and start a war over potbellied pigs, that's what that's telling me!"

"Wow!" Brahim grabbed his temples. "You're a genius, Nic. That's a brilliant observation!"

He heard a snort and then a giggle from somewhere behind him. He looked around and saw Melisse trying to suppress a big smile. She was shaking her head and apologized, "Sorry, that made me laugh." Then, she stood and shot him a sweet look as she walked away.

Puffy, who missed nothing, sent her a stabbing look as Melisse turned and walked back towards her date.

> **Spicy Secret: "The two women exchanged the kind of glance women use when no knife is handy." —Ellery Queen**

If there was one thing Melisse couldn't understand, it was the "dirty looks" and "mean glares" she often got from other women when she was all dressed up and looking particularly good. Were these looks supposed to discourage her or stop her from looking great and being nice? And what did other women gain by behaving this way?

> **Spicy Secret: "We ask ourselves, 'Who am I to be brilliant, gorgeous, talented, fabulous?' Actually, who are you not to be? You are a child of God. Your playing small does not serve the world. There is nothing enlightened about shrinking so that other people won't feel insecure around you. We are all meant to shine, as children do. We were born to make manifest the glory of God that is within us. It's not just in some of us; it's in everyone. And as we let our own light shine, we unconsciously give other people permission to do the same." —Marianne Williamson,** *A Return to Love*

Melisse went over to the bar and asked for a glass of Evian with fresh lime to get some distance from the situation.

Daddy Copolos followed her every slinky move with his bloodshot eyes, then nodded to Puffy, a signal for her to leave. "Hey, get yourself another spritzer and bring me another 'tini, toots."

Puffy wandered off, giving Brahim a long, significant stare as she moved away. But *his* eyes were on Melisse standing at the bar, squeezing her lime.

"She's a firecracker," Brahim told Nic, speaking of the recently departed Puffy, but imagining lighting Melisse's fuse with one hot kiss.

"She's a fire*bomb*," Nic countered. "So, back to *The Big Baksheesh*. That's the one this Emir, Sheik Jazzy, is financing. It's gonna be the story of his charmed life. Not a darn thing happened, actually, but we have a screenwriter working on that. There are big bucks for the lead role, Brahim, and you've got the right look for it."

Brahim kept watching Melisse, barely listening as Nic continued.

"I'd be cool with letting you do the final polish on the script as long as the sheik character is engaging in gratuitous violence and bedding beautiful women every five minutes of script. I think you'd make a great sheik, Rosencrantz."

"Really?" Brahim shot him a quizzical look. "Why?"

"You got that Arab look and it sure beats the hell out of being a porn star." Nic coughed and gave Brahim a significant raise of his eyebrows.

"Thanks for the offer," Brahim countered, brushing off the veiled reference to Ronny Cockmeister. "But I've got stuff to do here in the city, including research for a new documentary."

"Brahim, I'm puttin' it out there. It's a chance to star in a big-budget production that you've got a lot of control over. Most actors would kill for a shot at this. and I'm just handing it to you on a…"

"Yeah, I'll mull."

"You do that. Mull it over. You'll never get another offer like that in your lifetime," Nic nodded, looking over the guy that his daughter coveted more than anything in her life. And what Puffy wanted, Puffy was given.

Nicolos surveyed the babes in the room while Brahim pretended to contemplate Nic's offer. When Brahim looked over at Melisse, having seen her smile and heard her delightful giggle, he'd already decided. The stirring in his pants never lied. Only the few greatest loves of his life were ever able to do that from all the way across a room.

For all their promise, Nic's next words now sounded like gobbledygook as Brahim's head filled with images of Melisse in the throes of pleasure only he could give. And together, maybe their chemistry would be so strong, he wouldn't want to slip out unseen the next morning.

"Why don't you go have a drink with Puffy and she'll tell you more about the project? She looks lonely," Nic suggested.

"That's a tempting offer, Nic. But a nice girl like Puffy won't be lonely for long in a place like this. Listen. My dad needs me to work the room tonight. I'm on his clock now. So maybe some other time," Brahim declined politely.

"OK. I'll just stand here alone. You know what a babe magnet I am. I'll just let them drape themselves all over me. Let them slither their wet bodies all over my…"

"OK, Nic." Brahim feigned an officious tone with a twinkle. "This is a corporate event for a white-shoe investment house. Try to keep your dick in your pants tonight. The research librarian and our senior analyst are the only ladies here desperate enough to fuck a bonehead like you."

"Are they drunk yet?" Copolos asked with a smile. "Can you point them out to me?"

CHAPTER 44

Arm Candy

Brahim left Nic Copolos and saw Melisse head for another club chair, then sit down with her drink. There was an empty chair facing hers, and if ever the Universe was offering him a chance to speak to her, this was it! Brahim took the Universe very seriously; he'd learned that he could suffer miserably if he didn't tune in to its messages. Now, he actually felt a slight tremor run through him as he took the chair across from Melisse.

"Hi," he said. "I'm Brahim. I've been watching you; I've wanted to talk to you, but I have a feeling this party isn't really your thing. Am I right?"

She looked up at him, surprised by his honesty—and his quick take on her. "Hello," she replied demurely, "I'm…Melisse." She looked up at him, and as their eyes met, an unfamiliar feeling rose up inside her. She'd been right! This man was definitely interesting; his vibe was so different, so warm, so vital—all of which made him *so hot*. And he'd had the balls to come over and talk to her.

Butterflies, of all things, took off in her tummy.

Her eyes lightly touched on the button on his jeans, which bulged pleasantly, and she twitched a bit under her white lace La Perla panties. She felt her crotch become damp and warm as she looked at his molded forearms, always a major turn-on. *This is ridiculous*, she told herself. *He's only said hello, for God's sake.*

"So what were you laughing about back there?" he asked, startling her with his candor. *Oh, he's dangerous: a point-blank question right out of the box.*

"Oh, it was nothing," she said, smiling. "Just nervous laughter. And you're right—I'm not comfortable at these things, especially the small talk."

"I'm with you there," he agreed. "Nobody should have to define themselves by what they do for a living. I prefer questions like, 'What do you do for fun?' or 'Did you leave any pets at home?'"

This one got her going.

Spicy Secret: Average men are scared away by cat lovers, but the right guy can handle all that pussy.

"Yes! I have a big orange tabby cat! I left Butterball to come over here." She felt herself grin at the thought of her adorable puss.

"Really? I love cats!" he said slyly, knowing this was a line that made every crazy cat lady get juicy. But in this case, it was true. He did love cats, and was already willing to adopt Butterball as his new furry child and run off with its beautiful mother.

He noticed that Melisse was shivering next to a breezy open window. "You're shivering!" He came over, leaned down from behind her, and put both arms around Melisse's shoulders, rubbing her arms for warmth.

Melisse, against her better judgment, let herself cuddle into the feelings it brought up. It was like a slice of heaven, and when she felt herself sinking deep into him, she pulled back slightly.

Brahim immediately felt her withdraw and backed off.

And this impressed Melisse even more! This good-looking little guy was bold enough to come over and talk to her, cared about her comfort enough to try to warm her, and then hugged her like an old friend, while most men hung back from her, completely intimidated by her looks and her seemingly aloof manner.

Spicy Secret: "Someone with courage is the kind of man you want to live with," GG had once told Melisse.

> "And the very first sign of that courage is their ability to risk rejection."

"I don't like to see a girl shivering," Brahim said, closing the offending window. "I'd give you the shirt off my back if I had a warmer one on me!"

Melisse looked at his T-shirt and read it. "'I like it. A lot.'" She grinned. "Well, I'll take that one if that's all you have to offer."

Spicy Secret: "If all a man has to give is one penny, take that one penny from him and let him feel the pleasure of sacrificing for you. This increases his sense of power as a man." —GG

He looked delighted, stood up slowly, pulled the shirt up over his stomach, and made a show of "almost" giving her the shirt off his back, but he didn't go all the way. She felt herself near hysteria at the possibility of getting a peek at his beautiful brown skin and six-pack abs. He pulled the shirt down suddenly; it was just a tease. Under different circumstances and in a less stiff environment, she knew for certain that he'd do it.

He smiled down at her. "I can't do that," he chuckled. "Not here." He smiled and looked around sheepishly. "This T-shirt is not right for you anyway. You're not a T-shirt kind of girl. I'll buy you a cashmere sweater at my earliest convenience."

"*Oui*, OK, *chef*." She nodded with a bit of sarcasm, using one of her colloquial Frenchy terms.

He lit up. "OK, mademoiselle." He winked.

For Melisse, this was more fun than she could remember having at a party like this. What a character this guy was!

And then, Bernie Rosencrantz arrived on the scene. "Brahim! Goddamn it, get your tushy the hell out on the floor. Now!" he said before skulking off.

Brahim smoothed the T-shirt back over his body as his smile disappeared into his dimples. "That's my *boss*, Bernie."

"Tushy?" Melisse repeated, a gleam in her eye.

"He also favors the word *tookus*. Did I mention I'm Brahim Rosencrantz, by the way, at your service?" he said, extending a hand to her. They held their handshake a moment and watched Bernie running around like a wild man.

"And I must confess, that was actually my dad. He's the founder and chief investment strategist of the Ripcore Fund I, II, and all the other ones. And…" Brahim sighed as he watched Bernie. "He's a living example that money can't buy class."

Money can buy ass, but it can't buy class was one of Shisha's favorite sayings whenever she saw someone acting pretentious and rude in the Living Room of GG's bordello.

Melisse let out a small giggle, just thinking of Shisha saying it. Shisha would be getting an earful soon enough about this guy.

"Are you laughing at me again?" Brahim asked as Melisse tried not to melt into his questioning eyes.

"You? No, of course not," she said, acting as if he were insignificant, when really, in that moment, he was everything. "You're not funny in the least!" she teased.

She looked over at the buffet table and saw Bernie and Harry Quint deep in conversation. Harry was leaning in unusually close to Bernie, and she realized that this was the one conversation that Harry wanted to record tonight.

It then hit Melisse hard when she made the connection that this darling guy, Brahim, was *Bernie Rosencrantz's son, and Bernie was the guy being investigated by the Feds for financial fraud.*

"Are you OK?" Brahim asked, picking up on her change of mood. It was as if a great sadness had washed over her in one big wave.

"Oh, yes. So…so that's your dad?" Melisse asked, trying to seem nonchalant.

"Yup. I'm his prodigal son, coming back to consult for him as an ambassador to promote his hedge fund."

"Ah. I see. So what are you selling, exactly?"

"Good question, Melisse. Yesterday I was living the good life in L.A. And the next thing I know, I'm over here helping my dad sell something called the Ripcore Fund. Make that, Ripcore Fund II."

Melisse smiled nervously. "You *just* moved to New York?"

"Well, I knew I was coming back beforehand. In the story of the prodigal son, the father kills a fatted calf and has a party upon his son's return. In my case, I got an investor's shindig and pigs in blankets! But they *are* damn crispy. My dad made sure of that." He laughed as they looked at Harry Quint and Bernie, apparently bonding nicely.

Brahim changed the subject. "Is that titan of finance you came in here with your date?" he asked, nodding toward Mr. Quint.

"Um, he's an old friend. He likes arm candy, but he doesn't need to eat it."

Melisse got up from the chair when she saw that Harry was finished with Bernie.

Following her, Brahim linked his arm in hers and leaned in. "Let me walk you over, real slow, because I hate to give you back to him. And just so you know, unlike *your* date, I actually eat *my* arm candy."

"Oh, really?"

"Yes. Did I happen to mention that my grandfather owned Willy Wonka's chocolate factory?"

She laughed easily now; it had been a long time since anyone this handsome and charismatic could also make her laugh. *Charlie and the Chocolate Factory* was her favorite book as a child.

"I have the winning gold wrapper in my wallet to prove it. I can show it to you later *in your bedroom* if you want to confirm it."

She felt a pink blush spread across her chest. *Finally, a man with a smart, spicy sense of humor who isn't afraid to use it (instead of money) to get me into bed.*

Melisse released her arm from his as they approached the buffet and her date. The book (and her secret bible) *The Rules: Time-Tested Secrets for Capturing the Heart of Mr. Right* had advised her on how to leave a man wanting more. And since Harry was a treasured client, she mustn't make him jealous by talking too long with someone else.

"See you later, Brahim. It's been fun getting to know you," she cooed as she walked away, smiling over her shoulder.

As Melisse joined Harry, they began to circle the sumptuous buffet. She was starving by now, her voracious appetite fueled by her stimulating conversation with a cute, creative, obviously accomplished and disciplined guy with chutzpah in spades. And he was obviously fascinated with her, too!

Harry whispered, "Don't worry, Melisse, I turned my wire off. The young man I saw you with—who is he?"

"He's a character, that's for sure," she replied, trying to hide her fascination.

Harry squinted through his glasses as he regarded Brahim, now chatting up a mature woman dripping in jewels. An amused expression came over him as Melisse loaded her plate with goodies, dreaming of the picnics in bed she and Brahim could have after some hot slamming sex in her love pad.

"Oh, my Lord," Harry suddenly muttered.

"What?"

"You know very well who that is. You've only watched his film with me *at least seventeen times.*"

Melisse looked over at Brahim as Harry squinted even harder through his glasses.

"No…*Couch Boy*? Devin Wannabe? I mean, Ronny Cockmeister?"

"Yes. I'm sure of it, aren't you?"

Melisse took a much closer look with "new eyes" at her mark. There *was* a striking resemblance.

Both Melisse and Harry tried to contain their glee. "You're right! It's absolutely *him*," she gushed, thinking of the scenes of Devin Wannabe and his perfect dream cock, the best one she'd ever seen in a porno flick—it was the one she'd prayed to God to send her.

"He's been living in L.A. for a while, too. I'm pretty sure it's him," she mused.

"Ronny Cockmeister," Harry reflected as they headed toward a small, beautifully set table for two and sat down. "My God," Harry continued, "that young man has the world by the balls. What's he doing here?"

"Apparently he's here researching his next role in life as Hedge Fund Man. It's his first day on the job and he doesn't know what he's doing, but it gets even worse, Harry…"

"What?"

"His dad is Bernie, the one running the funds, the guy you're investigating!"

Harry stopped chewing. "No way! Oh, no. The poor guy! Oh God. Here he is, doing a favor for the dad, and the man's going to send him up the river. The kid's life will be ruined! Do you think he knows what's going on with Bernie?"

"No, absolutely not. He said he's been away from New York for a long time. He feels like a prodigal son coming back, and his first night selling is tonight."

Melisse saw Brahim approach them, and tapped Harry under the table. "Here he comes!"

Harry whispered, "Introduce me!"

Melisse motioned for Brahim to join them as Harry pulled over a third chair from another table.

"Sit!" he invited Brahim jovially, extending his hand.

Melisse said, "Brahim, I'd like you to meet Harry Quint of Quint Holdings. Meet Brahim, of the...?"

"Illustra Funds. I'm Bernie Rosencrantz's son."

"So what do you have to sell me tonight, Rosencrantz?" Harry challenged him.

Brahim sounded a bit nervous. "Well, uh, there's a closed-end fund called Ripcore II. It'll rocket profits into your pensioners' pockets in about three years."

Harry contemplated the absolutely worthless propaganda that Brahim was unknowingly promoting for his criminal father.

"Uh-huh. And what's your background in selling hedge funds?" he asked.

"Well, I've made a good living myself in the Forex markets, so I know the technology and science of what I'm selling. I was educated in economics and investment finance at Yale. I also interned at all the best Wall Street money management firms as a kid. And I can build a hell of a financial model when I have to. I own a substantial property portfolio *and* I'm great at selling. But I'm great at selling because I'm great at scripting and acting—and my dad needs me here selling, for the moment."

"Way to toot your own horn," Harry chuckled. "I'd hire you on that pitch alone!"

"Hey, if I don't toot, who will? If life's an orchestra, then I'm the maestro *and* the first horn." Brahim laughed.

"Ha! Sounds like you're a good son. Almost too good for him. I'm wondering how you can stand to work for your father when he's such a prick?"

Melisse interrupted, "Harry! That's not very nice!"

Brahim shook his head. "No, no, Melisse, he's right. Everyone knows it. My father is a bona fide ass. But I've got to love him in all his faded glory…because *he's my dad*! I was brought into this world to learn something from my time with him. It was part of my sacred contract when I was born into his family."

"Sacred contract?" Harry looked confused. Brahim explained as Melisse enjoyed the sound of his deep voice washing over her.

Well, that was a new one! Melisse hadn't given much thought to the concept of loving her own dad as he was, rather than as she wished he could be. And she'd never dreamed she'd meet another person who believed in sacred pre-birth contracts dictating that she was fulfilling a special destiny, as seemingly "weird" as her life was turning out.

Maybe this man could teach her something and help remind her that she was a spiritual being having a human experience—between sweet shaggings in her sheets, of course.

Brahim robustly dipped into some cheese on his plate with a cracker and tasted it thoughtfully. "Mmmm…Burrata…*delicioso*," he said, pronouncing it perfectly in Italian.

Melisse paused. "Wait. You speak Italian?" she asked, after which they began a friendly conversation in Italian that sensuously covered the topic of Italy's delicious foods, but could have been a metaphorical conversation for the pleasures they would both like to indulge in later in bed, preferably in a suite on the Amalfi Coast or Tuscany.

Harry smiled knowingly at the two of them and arose, seeing someone that he absolutely had to talk to. "I thought you didn't want to talk to anyone tonight, Melisse," he teased as he scooted past her chair. "Watch her, Brahim, she's dangerous! I'll be back, and then I want to have a talk with you. In *English*."

As he moved on, both Brahim and Melisse instinctively looked over at his father, now busily "working" a woman in a Chanel suit. Brahim used the moment to drape his arm around the back of Melisse's chair and lightly touch her arm as he talked. She tried not to react, but her skin tingled at his touch.

"Your *date*—a nice guy, by the way—made me talk all about myself tonight, but what about you, Melisse? What is Melisse dreaming about?" He leaned in close, pulling back a strand of her hair to reveal her ear, into which he then whispered, "Besides making love with me?"

She sighed. This man was pure sex, obviously a seasoned player but highly educated, intelligent, and tender, too. Wow! What a breath of fresh air that was!

And, she noted with glee, he had super-nice Continental manners and hadn't picked his teeth absentmindedly, wolfed down his food like a hungry one-eyed German shepherd, *or* talked with his mouth full. *And* he hadn't interrupted her while she was talking—one of the major annoyances she had with many of her dates while she was working.

"Let's not talk about that tonight," she chided gently, remembering a rule from her Bible of handling men—especially ones like him. "Excuse me a moment…" she said, pushing her seat out from behind her dramatically with a little pump of her ass, then turning on her heel and looking down into his eyes.

"I hear the call of the wild," she said mysteriously, smiling slyly as if she were a tigress who needs to return to the jungle. Really, she just needed the powder room so she could make sure all this excitement hadn't made her nose too shiny.

"I'll be waiting, tigress."

She slunk away, leaving him with nothing but his plate of food and his sexual longings.

CHAPTER 45

In the Shadows

Melisse needed a breather, and walked up the stairs to another area of the Knickerbocker Club. She hoped it had a ladies' room that led to an open roof garden, but instead there was just a long corridor.

She heard a noise and turned to see Nicolos Copolos emerge from the shadows, stinking drunk.

"Oh! You scared me!" she said, startled.

He fiddled with a spoon and a small container of cocaine. "It's a rush, getting scared." He grinned, slurring his words. "Isn't that the same rush you get from entertaining strangers for money, honey?" He extended the loaded spoon, and Melisse felt the old dread return to her body after the heights of the flirtation downstairs.

"Want some blow?" he asked.

"No. Put that away. And what makes you think I get paid, anyway?"

"You're famous—everybody knows about 'Miss Melisse.' The best in New York, I'm told. I've seen your websites, your videos… I love the one with the trains, planes, and automobiles…"

"Really?" She wasn't excited about spending time with a cokehead. They were always so much work, especially if they got too high and rambunctious and there was no Valium on hand to help them come down. And besides, she was booked.

"Yes, and I'd love to experience the best before I go back to L.A. tomorrow morning."

"Sorry, but I don't know you. You would need to go through my screening process, and that takes time."

"Yeah, OK. Well, here's my profile for your 'process.' I'm Nicolos Copolos: Hollywood movie producer. You've probably seen my movies in the theaters: *Pot Monsters, Up Crack Creek, Machete Runner.* Then again, you look like you don't get out much to see big trashy, gory, or violent movies. But anyway, they quickly go to DVD, sometimes straight to DVD."

Copolos chuckled at his false modesty and took a snort off the spoon. "But the millions I make off them always goes straight to the bank."

"Ah, yes. I know who you are now. I had the fortune of seeing *Up Crack Creek*," she said, remembering how badly it sucked. "I'm so sorry, Mr. Copolos, but Miss Melisse is not available this evening."

"Do you act, honey?"

"Why are you asking?"

"Listen. I'm producing a new movie, *The Big Baksheesh*. I'll let you audition for it in my room over at the St. Regis tonight. It's an epic film about sluts and sheiks rutting in the sand. It's *Eyes Wide Shut* meets *Lawrence of Arabia* meets *I Dream of Genie*." He eyed her up and down. "I'm really jacked up about it."

"I'm sure you are. I'm sorry, but I have a very full schedule already."

"What if I give you a piece of the action? You'll get points, honey, if you give me a piece of *your* action."

Melisse handed him a business card from her purse. "I don't work for points, Mr. Copolos. I work for cash. Or I take American Express. Call me when you're clean and sober again and we might be able to make a date."

"Aw, honey. I'm harmless. You know that. My cock is useless when I'm like this. I just wanna have a sweet girl like you watch TV with me, and then sleep next to me tonight and have room service with me at breakfast. I have an early flight. I don't bite. I have a beautiful daughter your age and I wouldn't hurt a fly. I just want your company. I don't want to be alone tonight. Don't make me be alone," he whined.

A statement like that was usually screening enough for Melisse, who heard the sincerity and the loneliness come through in a heartbeat.

She knew that loneliness all too well herself. She wished she could help, but she was busy tonight with Mr. Quint.

"Right. I'm sorry. I just can't make it. I'd like to meet with you another time, though. Just remind me of this conversation when you call, okay? Good night, Mr. Copolos," she said, coming over and giving him a little hug.

The hug blew him away. She was truly a high-class, caring lady. Exactly the kind of woman he needed in his life.

> **Spicy Secret: Even the wealthiest, most successful men in the world, with every appearance of outer wealth, may be experiencing a shortage or recession of hugs in their life.**

She walked away and felt a bit regretful leaving him in the dark like that, alone with his coke and a spoon, but it was time to focus on Mr. Quint, her date for the night.

CHAPTER 46

Sweet Adieu

When Melisse returned to the party room, she found Harry and Brahim engrossed in a serious conversation back at their table. Harry gave her a wave and walked over to her, taking Melisse aside and out of Brahim's earshot.

"Go ahead and take the limo home," he told her. "I need to talk to Brahim a bit longer." He confided that he wanted to find a way to lure him away from Bernie without telling him about his dad and ruining the investigation.

Brahim would not only be an asset to his firm, but it would also save *Couch Boy* from a possible arrest and prison time for aiding his father in fraud.

Although Melisse appreciated his motives, she was still a bit miffed. "I thought we were booked for all night. You could have told me earlier so I could have made…other arrangements. Now I've lost…well, you know…I gave up my whole schedule to come to the party…"

> **Spicy Secret: Never remind a major client that you're with him for the money. You're with him for the enjoyment of his fabulous company, which you can't possibly live without, even if cash were not involved.**

"I can't believe you're acting like this," Harry said, surprised and disappointed. "Can't you give me a break? Does *everything* have to be a transaction? I think I've been a very *supportive* friend to you." He was truly offended.

She immediately realized how wrong she'd been to speak to him that way. "Sorry, Harry, you're so right." She gave him a big hug. "I don't know what got into me. Let's do dinner on Saturday at the hotel if your wife throws you out again, so I can have you all to myself. And the night is on me."

"No harm, hon. But that was so unlike you. I'm just going to let it go. Because *I* know what got into you," he said, not letting her off so easily. "You're pouting because you don't have a boyfriend to go home with tonight. And I'm not being a very good client, either. So you're not getting love *or* money—just another empty night that you'll have to fill with some last-minute, late-night guy. And I know how much you hate the late-night callers."

> **Spicy Secret: For escorts "on call," know that little good happens after 11:00 p.m. or midnight. Late night clients are like the creatures (that turn into monsters) from the movie *Gremlins*. Remember the famous instructions? "No matter how much it cries or begs, don't feed it after midnight!" As evening turns to the wee hours, the calls and clients will just get more and more low quality. Best to avoid the late night calls from people you don't already know.**

"Please, Harry, that's ridiculous," she replied, though she knew he was right. "Where do you get these ideas? The client part is true, but the other thing, about a boyfriend..."

"I know you, Lisse. And I know how it is. Go home and take a nice hot bath."

"You're the best," she said, hugging Harry good-bye and looking over again at Brahim. She wanted to stay and ease into his arms again by the chilly window.

He was so difficult to categorize—not a client and decidedly *not* a Category B...so what was he? Probably just a guy who was cute on the surface but would later mess up her life and her dreams. It was probably better to stay away from someone who defied categorization.

She suddenly thought of Nicolos Copolos, who might still be upstairs. Looking over at Brahim, she could see that, while darling, he was already hampering her ability to do business. This was the classic "boyfriend/lover" dilemma for professional ladies, and it was now rearing its ugly head.

Brahim had innocently prevented her from getting an overnight fee from Harry, which he traditionally gave her on nights like this. And emotionally, she was on such a high that spending the night with Nic would feel like torture and she might not be able to perform as well as he would expect.

"Do you think *Couch Boy* knows anything about what his father is up to?" she asked suddenly.

"Him? No, he's totally innocent. I could use a guy like that on our team. He's got the smarts, the education, the honesty, the chutzpah, the intuition, the charm. He just needs a little polishing and training about how we operate."

"Ah," she said, nodding. "I think he's deep into other things, other interests, and he's just helping out his dad, but good luck."

"He seems very smitten *with you*. I'd take a second look if I were you."

"Please…that little guy is *not* the man of my dreams," Melisse lied, knowing that to keep a client happy she could never appear attracted to another man in the client's presence.

Spicy Secret: Clients (and men in general) are always much more sensitive and insecure than people ever suspect. Whatever you do in your dealings with men, know this, and treat them (with kid gloves) accordingly.

Melisse and Harry rejoined Brahim.

"Well, Brahim, you've stolen Harry Quint right out from under me tonight. I'm leaving now, and he's all yours!" Melisse said, only half pretending to be annoyed.

Brahim looked at her closely. "If you don't mind my asking, what do you do for a living, Melisse?"

"I'm a...a..." she stammered.

"She's a real estate consultant. South of France Properties," Harry interjected, wanting to steer his friend on the road to true love. They both knew it was way too soon for her to tell Brahim her true profession.

"Yes. Fantasy properties on the Côte d'Azur. In fact, Harry might want to buy one, isn't that so?" Melisse smiled at both men, the picture of charm and self-assurance.

"Definitely. I'm just deciding now if I want to buy in Mougins or in Cannes Californie..."

"So you speak French then, Melisse?" Brahim asked, in French, suddenly marveling at his mother's words long ago: "*You'll be glad you speak fluent French someday, when you meet a beautiful woman who also speaks French!*"

"Yes. And you?" she answered in French. "How long have you...?"

Harry quickly interrupted, "Oh, no, no. Please don't start speaking languages again, you two polyglots. I've got serious stuff to discuss with Brahim. In English. Now, just go on your merry way, pretty lady."

Harry gave Melisse a hug good-bye and whispered in her ear, "Let's talk tomorrow, honey. I'll book La Grenouille for our 'long lunch' next Friday. Same booth?"

"OK!" she whispered back.

"Don't roast too many weenies tonight." She shook her finger at them. "You two Eagle Scouts."

"Take the car, honey!" Harry ordered. "Brahim, will you see her out? She's dangerous when she's alone. One fall in her high heels alone could kill her." Brahim joined her, slipping his arm back into hers.

He went to the coat-check girl and got Melisse's coat, generously tipped the girl, and then gently helped Melisse into it. Melisse suddenly remembered GG's explicit instructions: "Go for the gusto with the one who gives you great sex and treats you right. Everything else is negotiable."

Well, so far he's treating me right, she admitted to herself. Could this be too good to be true? Or might her luck with men finally be changing?

When they stepped outside, Brahim surprised her by saying, "Come here for a minute. I need to ask you something." He led her by the hand to a more secluded part of the building's facade and then stopped and looked deeply into her eyes.

"What's your question?" she asked a bit nervously.

"May I call you Lisse? Because I'd really like to kiss you, Lisse." and without waiting for an answer, he took both sides of her face firmly into his hands, pulled her to him, and slowly kissed her mouth. Unable to resist, she kissed him back passionately, and gave him her lips, her tongue (rare for her) and when it was over, buried her face in his neck and breathed in his gorgeous scent. They both sighed deeply, their hearts pounding.

Then, Brahim folded her into another long hug and she realized that something very unusual was happening. *This feels like love. My God, I feel as if I've finally come home.* She allowed herself a moment to fall into what felt like the most delicious soft cushion ever created, where nothing could ever hurt her again.

Then she came to and was immediately filled with shyness and fear. How would this affect her as the consummate call girl? How would she take care of herself if she had a boyfriend? How would she ever buy the villa and start La Fantasia?

Turning away, she whispered, "I need to go, Brahim." Then, almost running, she took off down the street, trying to escape the consequences of a kiss that promised more than she had ever possessed.

"Lisse!" he yelled behind her. "Please don't go! I don't have your number!"

"Get it from Harry!" she yelled back, wondering if she would regret those instructions.

Then, as Brahim faded into the background, she walked by the long line of double-parked limos waiting for their clients. She heard Sade's "Smooth Operator" playing from the open window of one of them. And accompanying the music was Nicolos Copolos, singing off-key, leaning out the window and howling at the moon.

Melisse glared at him, but when he saw her he shut off the music and opened the door of the limo. "Get inside, Miss Melisse. We're going to the St. Regis Hotel for the night. I've got thousands in cash burning a hole in my pocket. And you know you want it. All of it."

Melisse looked around her. Nobody was watching.

Then she slid in beside him, and he slammed the door shut.

Spicy Secret: Don't think that Melisse is a coldhearted, money-grubbing bitch. Consummate call girls hellbent on taking care of themselves learn to emotionally separate their money-making activities from their lovemaking activities, even if they occur within the same day (or the same hour). This is what Dale Carnegie called "living in day-tight compartments."

CHAPTER 47

Movie Night

Melisse's night with Nicolos Copolos was fairly routine, yet she felt like a changed woman. They sat on a plush couch at the St. Regis for half the night. As she listened to his coked-up drunk talk, he clicked through the TV channels and talked nonstop about himself and his projects.

She watched the shows, but her mind was replaying every detail of her interaction with Brahim.

She hated the fact that here she was sitting with yet another john she clearly didn't love (but was servicing for the money), when her heart was soaring from a real-life romantic meeting that had suddenly put the drawbacks of her "love for sale" lifestyle into sharp relief.

While Brahim had spent his youth building his "golden goose," Melisse felt that she'd spent her best years tying up a "golden noose," and often enough she'd felt that her soul was hanging from it, finally dead to true love. But tonight had shown her otherwise, and how she longed to be anywhere but here.

Pull it together and perform. You're getting paid to show this guy the time of his life and make him feel like a worthwhile human being. It's a privilege to make this much money and work with "gentlemen" in the nicest places in the world. Think of the poor women in every dark and dirty corner of the world who work just to eat. And to do so, they've got to service fifteen men in a day who treat them like a piece of exercise equipment.

During the course of the night, as Nic snorted from his mound of stash, he and Melisse watched three of Nic's movies on the pay-per-view system. It was actually less a viewing system and more a money machine that had earned Nic enough to lead an unbelievable lifestyle in L.A. Unfortunately, it had also made him the butt of every joke there, too.

Nic turned to *The Sin Slicer,* a horror movie about a priest who tortured and killed people after they made incriminating confessions in his booth. The movie poster apparently read (in a blood-stained scrawl), "Hate the sin, and kill the sinner," and was a hugely popular slasher film in non-Catholic countries.

"This one got me in trouble with the Vatican," Nic explained, rubbing his nose.

"I'm sure many people converted out of Catholicism after watching it," Melisse said with a straight face.

The next film they watched that night was *Tweedies,* which made Melisse laugh quite a bit, and this pleased Nic. The synopsis read, "Teenage nymphomaniacs in a posh female boarding school get out of control when they take over the neighboring boys' school for one wild weekend."

"You're so smart!" Melisse said, putting her arm around Nic as they sat on the couch after raiding the hotel's minibar for snacks in the middle of the night.

> **Spicy Secret: "You need not be well educated or highly intelligent to follow a clever man's discourse. In his pleasure at having himself admired, he seldom notices that his conversation is not fully understood." —Helen B. Andelin in *Fascinating Womanhood***

"Damn right!" Nic said, cuddling her. "I've never won an Oscar, but I'm sitting here with *you*. How much of a dumbass can I be? It was worth it all if I ended up here with *you*."

"Ah, that's sweet!" Melisse gushed. Maybe he wasn't so bad after all. He did say the right things…

The grand finale of Nic Copolos's personal film festival was *Hockum's Poke 'Em,* another reason Melisse wouldn't be able to sleep: the movie would induce nightmares in anyone who watched it.

As Nic explained, "See, Hockum is a sick motherfucker who runs a carnival fun house that's secretly rigged to kill and dispose of people. You go in, but you don't ever come out. His favorite things to use are small sharp 'pokers' that suddenly come out of the walls. It's some scary, sick shit."

"Scary stuff," Melisse laughed.

"But I'm just a pussycat," Nic said in his gravelly voice, pulling her into a hug. "Just misunderstood. I think up lots of sick shit, but in real life…"

"Just a big softy, I know," Melisse said, snuggling into his embrace. "But you're a *smart* softy who knows his business and what people want."

Spicy Secret: "Women have served all these centuries as looking glasses possessing the magic and delicious power of reflecting the figure of man at twice its natural size." —Virginia Woolf

She absently fondled the diamond-studded zodiac necklace nestled in his copious gray chest hairs.

"What is this necklace all about?" she asked.

"I know it's obnoxious, but it reminds this poor kid from Brooklyn of the first time he tasted success. The first film I ever wrote *and* made money on was called *Geminis Must Die,* and the character wore this in the film when he was out cruising bars, looking for victims. There wasn't that much actual killing in the film. It was more of a psychological thriller. You know, the guy is asking around about people's birth signs, starting conversations with people, and you don't know who he's gonna kill next."

"Sounds pretty scary," she said, snuggling into him for emphasis.

"Yeah. So don't let anyone ask your astrological sign because you never know where that shit's gonna lead…"

Melisse laughed. "I don't think men use that line anymore in the bars. That's something from the seventies."

Nic was silent a moment and frowned slightly. Melisse realized her faux pas, but Nic let it go.

Spicy Secret: When entertaining a mature friend, don't make references to the (advanced) age of your client or the seemingly (ancient) aspects of the era he grew up in. You're there to help him feel young, vital, and important.

"Anyway, once I got the dough, I replaced the fake stuff with real diamonds and I've never taken this off since. It's my lucky charm," he said, gently pushing her back "below" to indicate she should try going down on him again.

She'd had to occasionally go down on his limp, unresponsive cock all night, which he was convinced would get hard if she just tried again. He wanted his balls licked, too, even though she sensed he couldn't feel anything down there, either.

He had finally shut off the early morning TV crap, which she felt was poisoning her mind as she watched the force-fed infomercials and star-fuckers on the "entertainment news" reruns from the evening before.

Nic knew everyone in Hollywood and had the inside scoop on all the gossip, and Melisse was amused by his unedited insights. But she decided to ask him about someone much more intriguing to her than a celebrity.

Spicy Secret: Do recon and get third-party verification whenever possible on important or mysterious matters, especially where potential partners are concerned.

"So…" she ventured, "How do you know that guy, Brahim? The one I saw you talking to last night at the party, with the T-shirt on?"

"Ha! Him? My daughter wants to keep him for a pet. And what Puffy wants, Puffy gets. I've had some *dealings* with him. He's a pretty nice guy, actually. A little googly-eyed about getting into the movies as an actor, but he's a talent on the documentary side, and he's produced and directed a new short film that's getting a lot of buzz. He's dabbled a little in some soft-porn stuff and thinks nobody knows about it, but it's all over town. But it was well done, you know? The guy has a good heart and that's rare. On the other hand, his father is a total shit, but he makes me money from his funds, and that's what counts for me in the end."

"Ah, I see. So what kinds of subjects does he document?"

"Well, honey, you can just Google him. He likes to attack the areas of life most people think are cut-and-dried, you know, either right or wrong, black or white. He takes us into the gray areas and shows us where we've been making mistaken assumptions, and you come out of there rethinking your blacks and whites, and you're a little more tolerant of the grays."

"Really? What are his subjects?"

"Enough talk, babe. Let's go to bed," Nic said, rubbing his eyes and yawning.

I'll have to find out on my own, Melisse decided.

Finally, Nic crashed in the king-size bed with barely a "good night" to Melisse, just a touch on her arm as she joined him. Soon, he fell into what sounded like one long snore, punctuated by a few gasping breaths.

She stayed as far to one side of the bed as possible, barely sleeping. Usually the "power men" in her life were light sleepers: any little move she'd make would wake them up. She'd feel that a) either they would hold it against her for "waking them up all night" or b) moving would cause them to keep touching her all night. Drunks and addicts usually had no idea how creepy their touches felt when they were out of it.

Melisse lay stiffly in bed with Nic, not moving, and let her mind wander. This "not moving" during overnights always reminded her of what it must feel like to be buried alive, enshrouded in dirt. Or like a prisoner lying in a prison bed, reflecting on every detail of every experience from the past, or making up new dreams to keep her sane during her imprisonment.

She would surely be wrecked the next day and have to sleep off this all-nighter, but it was a small price to pay for making this much moolah in one swoop.

Pivot to the pleasant thoughts! was her mantra, borrowed from the Abraham-Hicks spiritual audiotapes she listened to when she felt herself descending into depression. It popped up every once in awhile, born of a life with no true love, passion, or "real" fun.

On the horizon was a seemingly endless parade of more "theatrical" performances and more sweet little tricks. And that meant more smoke and mirrors about the high-maintenance, "mutually satisfying" relationships carried out in the dark of the night, or in secret afternoon interludes.

She rationalized that *I'm in it for the money and for my time and for the travel*, which to her was more precious than money. And, of course, she was stashing most of it away so she could start up La Fantasia.

She could imagine actually managing her small, discreet, luxurious retreat where women could get away from stress and indulge in spa pleasures and sensuality of all kinds. It would be her unique contribution to the world of women, and provide her with a comfortable retirement and a way out of The Life.

And then her thoughts turned to Brahim, and she found herself replaying his passionate, yet loving, kiss good-bye. She could still feel his gentle palms on her face, and knew that whatever she needed to know about him was in that kiss.

Of all the goodnight kisses she could ever remember, Brahim's had flooded her with a loving vibration and (as boring as it usually sounded to her) the potential for a "passionate companionship." He seemed to be someone who could be a true friend.

Simo the Excellent's goodbye kiss, on the other hand, had electrified her with pure love and affection—even now, it held her in a constant state of pleasurable suspense. She could still feel the warmth of his lips on her forehead and the sincerity behind his kisses—and his lovemaking—in the bedroom.

Simo's bedroom....

The thought of it made her body heat up.

Some way, somehow, she wanted to feel that good again. But would she ever see either of them again?

Spicy Secret: "If you can't get someone out of your head, maybe they're supposed to be there." — **Unknown**

THE END

EPILOGUE

As Melisse lay in bed with Nic Copolos at the St. Regis... on the far other side of the world, Simo the Excellent was working in a large, elegant, cedar-paneled office. It was here where he was expected to make decisions that often affected large numbers of people, not the least of whom were a large temporary immigrant population who relied on his business decisions for their welfare. Final decisions for the financing of construction projects in the region he "ruled" came down to him, and he always felt the pressure of this responsibility.

In fact, the pressure to please everyone in every deal was unrelenting.

Then, at home, he felt the pressure of having to look at all the expensive things his wife bought that day while a team of servers and assistants attended to the family.

As if he cared. He cared for his children, of course. He adored them. But the woman who'd borne them? He barely knew her. And what he knew of her (or found out after their practically arranged marriage) was that she was a good mother and a good shopper, but she was *not* the love of his life.

One of the things that he worked on daily was de-centralizing and streamlining his life so that he could eventually be free to manage things and people from anywhere, simply with the tap of a keyboard or via a mobile phone.

All his life he'd dreamed of traveling and seeing the world. Not just seeing, but tasting, experiencing, and savoring.

As he'd done for the few delicious moments stolen with Melissa. God, how he wanted to *get away*.

With her.

His fingers nervously dialed the number she'd written on the hotel stationery. He had butterflies in his stomach. What a wonderful feeling.

Melissa…Melissa.

Jazzy is a fool and a liar. He is not marrying this girl, as he boasted. There's no way she'd want him.

"This number is no longer in service," the computer lady's voice confirmed.

His heart dropped like a stone. He dialed again. Same message.

Before his heart sank lower, there was a knock at the office door.

Something urgent to attend to. Yet again.

What could be more urgent than this?

"Just a moment," he said, tucking the piece of paper into a drawer and locking it. He composed himself.

"Yes, enter," he commanded.

He breathed in deeply. His hopes of seeing her again had buoyed his spirits, but now his hope seemed dim.

Never mind. He would find a way.

Please continue to

The Spicy Secrets of a Jet $et Temptress
Part 2: Love in The Life

*Please visit www.TheSpicySecrets.com
for information on purchasing books in this series.*

ACKNOWLEDGEMENTS

I would like to thank my editor, Claire Gerus, for holding me to her exacting standards matched only by her enthusiasm, inspired ideas, and friendship. Much gratitude also to my proofreader, Michael Mandarano, for his work on refining this manuscript.

Thank you also to those who have either personally taught, consulted, or inspired me on the long path of becoming an author, starting from the very beginning: Pat Atkins, Linda Elliot, and Shelli Cline. Robyn Bell, Michael Delp, Terry Caszatt, and Jack Driscoll. André Aciman, Robert Dunn, Susan Minot. Karl Iglesias, Richard Walter, and Eric Edson.

I especially wish to thank my friend and mentor, Marilyn Horowitz, who helped me bring this basic tale to life first as a screenplay and who, in the process, taught me the classic steps of telling a good story.

ABOUT THE AUTHOR

Lantana Bleu was educated in classical literature and creative writing at the Interlochen Arts Academy in Michigan, the University of California at Santa Barbara, and The New School in New York City. She has also trained privately with master teachers in the art and craft of screenwriting.

She enjoys world travels, slow walks and sensual adventures.

Please learn more about Lantana Bleu at
www.TheSpicySecrets.com

Dear Reader,

Thank you so much for taking the time to read my book!

If this part of The Spicy Secrets of a Jet $et Temptress was a book you truly enjoyed and would recommend to others, won't you please consider posting a review of it to Amazon or another book review site of your choosing?

If you do so, please drop me a line with a link to your review, via the "Contact" area of my website, at www.TheSpicySecrets.com.

I would be very grateful and also it would help me to know what you loved, liked, (or even hated) in this book.

I would also welcome further story ideas of the characters or situations you'd like me to follow in next books.

Once again, a big thank you with spice on top!

All my best,

Lantana Bleu
- Author

Made in the USA
Charleston, SC
06 April 2016